COME SPRING

Jove titles by Jill Marie Landis

COME SPRING

JILL MARIE LANDIS

J

JOVE BOOKS, NEW YORK

A Jove Book / published by arrangement with
the author

ISBN: 0-515-10861-8

Jove Books are published by The Berkley Publishing Group,
200 Madison Avenue, New York, New York 10016.
The name "JOVE" and the "J" logo
are trademarks belonging to Jove Publications, Inc.

PRINTED IN THE UNITED STATES OF AMERICA

To my brothers, Jeff and John Davis;

To the real *Annika and her sisters,*
Marieke and Adriana;

To "Old" Ted Kitzmiller and his dog,
Minnie Mouse;

To Pat Teal, agent, friend, mentor.

❦ 1 ❦

I T was the perfect day for a wedding.

Not two days before, a strong storm had blown in off the Atlantic, battered Boston with freezing blasts, and held the bay-side town in its relentless grip. But today the temperature rose steadily as golden sunlight shimmered on the snow-cloaked landscape and glanced off the black-lacquered carriages that lined Beacon Street in front of the Storm town house. Matched pairs of horses standing in their traces flicked their tails and stamped impatiently as they stared at nothing in particular and waited to carry their owners home again.

The grand house had been the central focus of the Storm family's life for nearly twenty years. As solid and staid as its counterparts that lined the Back Bay streets, the mansion reflected the seemingly well-ordered lives of its occupants. A monument of brick and stone, it had been embellished inside with satin-textured woods of ash and walnut. Mantels, mirrors, and bookcases were adorned with cartouches, scrolls, and gracefully curved brackets. Plaster cornices and medallions lent a touch of elegance to the ceilings.

Inside the imposing structure, a girl with honey-blond hair piled high in a neo-Greek coiffure stood before a bay window in her room in the second story and stared with Delft-blue eyes at the carriages below. In a white *peau de soie* gown that had been created especially for her by Jean-

1

Philippe Worth, she was a vision of both innocence and love-liness. Orange blossoms held her tulle veil in place; a match-ing corsage was artfully pinned at her shoulder. The gown's full sleeves puffed at the shoulders but fit close from elbow to wrist. The bodice tapered to accentuate her narrow waist and created the hourglass figure that fashion demanded. Barely a glimpse of white silk stockings showed beneath the skirt that neatly cleared the floor. Satin bows adorned the low-cut slippers that matched her white kid gloves.

As if she had all the time in the world, Annika Marieke Storm pushed aside the Belgian lace panel and watched crystal water droplets form and fall from the ends of the ici-cles draped over the eaves. They dropped with a steady beat like passing minutes marked by a ticking clock. Annika turned away from the sight, and the curtain fell back into place with a hushed sigh.

Her wedding was the talk of Boston's Back Bay. Her groom, Richard Thexton—handsome, wealthy, and truly de-voted to her—was from an old Bostonian family. Her par-ents approved of the match. Friends and family had assembled in the reception room downstairs to await the cer-emony. The dining room had been readied for a gala celebra-tion following the wedding. The flower-bedecked cake stood three feet high. Gifts of fancy dresser sets, bride bowls, silver, crystal, and china were on display in her fa-ther's library. No detail had been left to chance.

Everything was perfect.

Everything except for the fact that Annika Storm was not at all certain she wanted to be wed.

The idea had not come upon her suddenly. In fact, she had been harboring doubt for more than a month, but whenever she decided to talk things over with Richard, he would do or say something so charming and endearing that she wondered how she could entertain any questions at all.

Annika looked about her room and felt like she was seeing it through the eyes of a stranger. The usual clutter that she seemed to cultivate without really trying had been removed, her clothing—an overabundant assortment of fur-trimmed tailored suits; silk day dresses; evening gowns of exquisite fabrics; petticoats of glacé silk, satin, and brocade that were meant to rustle intriguingly from beneath her skirts; hats to match them all—everything had been packed into the various trunks and traveling cases, hatboxes and valises that she had planned to take along on their honeymoon tour of Europe. Now, instead of littering the bed, hanging from drawers or over the dressing screen, her clothes were all out of sight. As she looked around, she realized that it had been years since she had seen the chintz upholstery on the chaise in the corner.

"Annika?" The soft sound of her mother's voice was followed by swift tapping against the locked door.

Annika quickly glanced at her reflection in the ornately decorated mirror above the fireplace and bit her lower lip. They were so close that she knew once Analisa Storm took one look at her face, she would know something was amiss. Her mother and father heartily approved of Richard and somehow seemed relieved to have her soon permanently settled with an adoring husband who was able to provide for her in the manner in which she had been raised. Her parents and older half brother, Kase, had always been highly protective of her; so much so that she had cause to wonder if she were marrying Richard because she loved him or because her new status as wife would afford her a chance at independence she had never had before.

"What is it, Mama?" Annika called through the door. She tried to bring some color to her cheeks by pinching them.

Her mother answered in her familiar, heavily accented English. "A wonderful surprise. Just in time, Aunt Ruth is home from her holiday."

As a genuine smile of excitement replaced her expression of worry, Annika opened the door. As her mother walked in, Annika ushered her across the room. "Oh, Mama, I'm so glad she's here! The day just wouldn't seem complete without Aunt Ruth." Not only that, she thought, more relieved by the news than her mother would ever know, but her "aunt" Ruth Storm was the only person who might lay to rest the niggling doubt she had about going through with her wedding. "Where is she?"

"Getting dressed." Analisa smiled with a shake of her head. "As soon as she came in, I told her about the dress you chose for her to wear. I think it is good that it is ready for her, Annemeke, because she arrived in something not so suitable for the wedding." Analisa finished by rolling her gaze heavenward.

Annika laughed. "You know Auntie Ruth, Mama. She has a style all her own when it comes to fashion."

"*Ja.* That she does. And today it was bloomers." Analisa took a step back and looked her daughter over, then shook her head as her eyes filled with a mist of tears. "So beautiful," she said, then she reached out and put her arms about Annika. They shared the moment in silence before Analisa drew back and smiled as she brushed away her tears. "Today is not a day for crying. It is a day of joy that I have always wished for you."

Annika felt her stomach toss. "Mama, I—"

"You will never know how much it means to me to see you happy. To see you safe."

"Safe, Mama?"

Her mother quickly shook her head and frowned. "Maybe I use the wrong word."

"Secure?" Annika offered. After twenty-four years in America, her mother was still murdering the language.

Analisa frowned, then agreed. "*Ja.* Secure."

A quick knock on the door drew their attention before Annika could broach the subject of Richard Thexton and her qualms about marrying him. Ruth Storm partially opened the door and peered in. "Where's my little girl?"

Annika crossed the room and hugged her aunt as the woman stepped through the door. Although Ruth was really her father's widowed stepmother, she had always been an integral part of the family. Nearly seventy and more than a bit scatterbrained, Ruth was a self-taught astrologer who did nothing without consulting the stars. When their quick but hearty embrace ended, Ruth set a stack of pages on Annika's bureau.

After she took a deep breath, Annika turned to Analisa and requested, "Mama, would you mind if I have a word with Auntie Ruth alone?"

Analisa smiled. "Of course not. I have left your papa too

long alone to greet the guests. Welcome home again, Ruth."
She gave the older woman's hand a squeeze as she left them.
Her heartbeat accelerated with trepidation as Annika
looked at her aunt and smiled. Ruth's choice of clothing was
usually as exotic as her hobby, but for today, Annika and her
mother had made certain Ruth had a stylish gown to wear.
Instead of the mismatched, Gypsylike garb she usually
donned, Ruth wore a bright lavender creation, the silk bodice sporting a jabot of cascading lace. Annika—who was tall
like her mother—towered over the diminutive, white-haired
lady whose hazel eyes usually winked with mischief. Today
she appeared far too thoughtful.

"I was afraid I wasn't going to get here in time to tell
you," Ruth said before Annika could express her doubt.

"Tell me what?"

"Maybe I'm being a bit premature. Why don't you just explain what you wanted to talk to me about?"

"Well"—Annika took a deep breath and then blurted
out—"I'm not certain I want to marry Richard. But look at
me"—she indicated her wedding finery with a downward
wave of her hand—"Mama and Papa have a house full of
people downstairs, Richard and his family are waiting, and
I'm still up here debating with myself. I'm due to be wed in
ten minutes, but I stalled, praying you'd get here before the
ceremony. Everyone else is so convinced I'm doing the right
thing—"

"Everyone but you?"

"I can't help it, Auntie, it's this feeling I have that there
should be more. And it's not just that. I want to be free for a
while before I marry. I've just received my degree so my education is behind me. Now I want to see some of the world
on my own without Mama and Papa or Richard telling me
where to go and what to do. But they are so excited, so happy
that I'm to be married." She paced over to the window again
and back. "I've wrestled with this over and over for the last
few weeks and I even convinced myself that if I don't love
Richard enough right now, that my love will grow. But I've
always trusted your judgment, Auntie Ruth, and the predictions you read in the stars. Now I want to know what you
think. Did you get Richard's birth date in my last letter?"

Taking care not to trip over the train of her gown, Annika let Ruth take her hands and pull her over to the bed, where they both sat down.

"And I'm glad you did," Ruth said, studying her carefully. "I must admit I was surprised when I received the wedding invitation. You've barely known Richard six months."

"He can be quite persuasive, and both Mama and Papa have been so excited and pleased. They were expectant from the moment they met him."

"They are not the ones marrying him, Annemeke," Ruth reminded her.

"I know that"—Annika twisted her hands together in her lap—"but they've always been so careful where I was concerned, so supportive and protective, that I convinced myself that they are right about this, too."

Ruth frowned. She had often disagreed with the cloak of protection Caleb and Analisa wove about their only daughter. Smothering, she called it. Annika had overheard discussions between the three on more than one occasion. "But it sounds as if you haven't entirely convinced yourself you are doing the right thing," Ruth said.

"I haven't," Annika admitted.

Ruth patted the top of her own head in a futile search for her glasses. Then, she tapped her hips, feeling for the deep pockets she usually required of her dressmaker, but found them missing from the formal gown. Finally, she slipped her hand inside her bodice and withdrew the thick spectacles she had shoved inside for safekeeping. "Why aren't you sure?" Ruth slipped on her glasses.

"It's probably a silly reason." Annika fought down her embarrassment.

"Not if you don't think it is. Come now, this is your Aunt Ruth you're talking to. Have I ever said *anything* was silly?"

Annika shook her head and blurted out, "I just think there should be more fire when he touches me, some inner need, some . . . some passion!"

They both jumped up at the sound of a knock at the door. Ruth called out, "Who is it?"

"Susan," the downstairs maid answered. "Your mother said to tell you it's time to come down, Miss Annika, and meet them in the library so that your father can escort you into the reception room."

"Tell them she's not ready yet," Ruth snapped. She walked to the door and pressed her ear against it until the sound of footsteps retreated. Her usually smiling face was serious as she looked at Annika squarely. "Recently I've seen some trouble coming in your life, Annika, something the stars are not clear on, but it has to do with love. Your letters reached me all over Europe, but always weeks late. First the engagement news, then the wedding announcement, and I wanted to be happy for you. I waited to see if things would clear up, but they didn't. There is this shadow of doubt as Saturn, the great teacher, moves through your sign. And finally"—she looked away as if drawing upon her own courage to tell Annika some ominous news—"when you sent me Richard's birth date, I knew."

"Knew what?"

"That your marriage to Richard Thexton would be a mistake—at least right now."

Annika hit her fist against her open palm. "I knew there was more to this than just a case of nerves!" Even though Ruth's statement might upset and confuse her mother and father, not to mention Richard Thexton, Annika felt relieved for the first time in days. Then she turned to Ruth again, one question still on her mind. "If you knew that, Auntie, how could you let things go this far?"

"As I said, your letters always arrived late. The last one reached me in London and I immediately packed up and left, meaning to send a telegram to you first, but . . ." Ruth looked sheepish as she shrugged. "I'm not infallible. I wanted to see how things stood between you and Richard. I had hoped that by now, everything might have worked itself out. You can't imagine how I felt when I arrived just now to a house full of wedding guests."

"If I hadn't said anything, would you have let this wedding go on?"

"At this point, if you had not voiced your own doubt, I would have let the wedding proceed. It's not my place to interfere in people's lives, Annika. I just read the stars, I don't like to direct the outcome."

Suddenly, another knock, this one more determined, rang out. They both turned toward the door at once.

From the other side of the door, Analisa called out, using the familiar nickname reserved for family. "Annemeke? *Wat is er aan de hand?* What is going on? Everyone is waiting for you downstairs. Are you sick?"

Annika shook her head. "No, Mama. Not sick. I just had to talk to Auntie Ruth for a minute."

Analisa came into the room and looked at both of them carefully. Analisa's unlined forehead wrinkled when she frowned. "What is it, Annika? Are you afraid of what is to come tonight? Are you afraid of Richard?" Analisa's voice held such a note of tension and concern that Annika could no longer ignore her. She put an arm about her mother's shoulders, glanced quickly at Ruth and then back to Analisa.

"No, Mama. I'm not afraid. It's just that . . . I still have so many questions about life. There is so much I have not done yet. So many places I wanted to see before I married, so many things I wanted to do. I'm twenty, Mama, and all I know of life is what you and Papa have shown me." Annika was surprised by the look of fear that shadowed her mother's blue eyes.

"What is there to do that you cannot do it with Richard?" Analisa asked her.

"That's not what I meant," Annika protested, but somehow knew that her mother would not understand.

Analisa reminded her daughter, "You have your education. If you still want to be a teacher, Richard will let you."

Annika hated the thought that she would have to worry about any man *letting* her do something. "I know, but it's not that, either."

Annika steeled herself for the coming scene and then sighed. "Sit down, Mama." She indicated the tufted chair near the window. Annika carefully lifted her train, walked over to the bed, and gingerly sat down.

"I think I'll just leave you two alone," Ruth said, and tiptoed toward the door.

"Please stay, Aunt Ruth," Annika begged, then stared back at Analisa for a moment. Her Dutch mother was always a vision of beauty and composure, even when she was working with Cook in the kitchen and managed to wind up with flour on her nose and wisps of hair escaping the neat bun atop her head. Today was no exception. Like Annika, Analisa's dress was another Worth original, this one of sky blue silk taffeta. Ruffles gently graced the stylish crisscross bodice. Analisa had golden hair of a far lighter shade than Annika's own. Today it was styled in an elegant twist. Their eyes were the same rich, cornflower blue. Annika had inherited her mother's features and stature, but from her half-Sioux father, Caleb, had come the dark honey-gold skin tones that enhanced her light hair and eyes by giving her an exotic, earthy glow.

Nervous, Annika toyed with her gloves until she worked them off and tossed them aside. "Mama, you still love Papa passionately, don't you?" It was really more of a statement than a question.

Analisa was visibly taken aback for a moment. Her feelings were clearly evident in her startled expression. Her cheeks flamed. "Passion? Why do you speak of such things, Annemeke?"

Again, Annika sighed and hesitated as if she had all the time in the world, as if there were not a crowd and a fiancé waiting for her downstairs. "It's important to me. I can tell that you and Papa are still as wildly in love as you were when you first met."

"It was not passion that brought us together; it was the measles."

Annika laughed. "You're always so literal. I think the way you met Papa was the most romantic tale I've ever heard."

Analisa smiled a faraway smile as if she were looking back over the past twenty years. "It was always your favorite story."

"And still is," Annika added. "Papa rode into the yard of your sod house and got off his big black horse."

"A horse as black as midnight. His name was Scorpio."

"And then Papa walked up to the door . . ." Annika prodded.

"I was so scared," Analisa went on, "I had taken *opa*'s gun from the wall and pointed it at the stranger's heart."

"Thank heavens you didn't use great-grandfather's gun to kill Papa."

"Only because Caleb passed out before I could decide to do so." Analisa laughed.

"Then you dragged him inside the house . . ."

Analisa nodded. "*Ja*. And then I saw that he had the measles. Many had been sick with it that winter, but not so sick as the Indians on the reservation to the north. Your Papa might have died."

"But you nursed him back to health and he married you, adopted Kase, you two had me, and we all lived happily ever after."

Analisa smiled wistfully and straightened the corsage at her daughter's shoulder. "Which I wish for you, Annemeke, this happy ending, but this will never be if you do not soon go downstairs. Papa is trying to entertain the guests, but he will not be able to do so much longer. And poor Richard looks so worried. Will you come down now?"

Annika shook her head. "No, Mama. Not now that I've talked to Aunt Ruth and she told me what's in the charts."

For the first time her mother looked truly worried. "Charts?"

"Yes."

"Annika, God is in charge of your life, not the stars."

Ruth cleared her throat, bustled over to the bed, and quickly spread the pages she'd carried in with her around Annika, who bent to study them curiously even though the symbols were indecipherable to her.

"Now where are my glasses?" Ruth asked, patting her bosom.

"You have them on, Auntie," Annika informed her gently.

"So I do." Ruth lifted a page and wagged it beneath Annika's nose. "*This* is what I was talking about earlier. Your stars are in the wrong positions for this marriage to work. The planet Jupiter is rising and Pluto—well, since you don't understand I won't go into Pluto. And then there's Saturn. My goodness, let's just say that getting married today would be one of the biggest mistakes of your life."

"A moment please, Ruth." Analisa stood up without try-

ing to make sense out of the circles with their neat pie
wedges drawn on the various pages.

"She asked my advice, Anja," Ruth said.

"That's true, Mama. I told Ruth I didn't want to marry
Richard before she told me the stars were all wrong."

"Don't want to marry him? But, Annika—"

A swift knock interrupted the women's argument. The
door swung open and Caleb Storm stuck head and shoulders
around it and asked, "What's going on? Are we having a
wedding today or not?"

"Come in, Papa." Annika smiled weakly. Her father had
always treated her like a princess, so much so that ever since
she could remember she had had everything her heart de-
sired. She knew she had no need to fear his reaction to her
decision, but she did wish she could have saved him the expense of the aborted wedding.

"So, what's going on?" Caleb shoved his hands into his
pockets.

She couldn't help but feel proud each time she looked at
him. Not only was he well educated, a lawyer and a former
undercover agent for the Bureau of Indian Affairs, but also
he was well connected in Washington, still fighting for Indian rights. Now, as she looked at her father, she smiled. At
fifty, he looked ten years younger. A tall, striking man with
waving coal black hair sprinkled with gray and startling blue
eyes, his complexion, like her half brother Kase's, was of a
rich cinnamon hue. Today Caleb appeared quite dashing in
his swallow-tailed coat and formal white shirt adorned with
ruffles. An orange blossom *boutonnière* similar to the corsage on Annika's shoulder, graced his lapel.

"Papa, what would you say if I told you I don't want to
marry Richard?"

Caleb exchanged a quick glance with Analisa before he
asked, "What did your mother say?"

"Nothing yet. I've just now made up my mind for certain."

Analisa, her face grave with worry, gave her husband a
perplexed half smile. "She asks if we have still the passion
for each other."

Caleb's cheeks colored with embarrassment. He bit back a smile and cleared his throat.

"You don't even have to answer, Papa. I can see it with my own eyes whenever you look at Mama or she looks at you." Annika stood up and began to pace the room, no easy task with her six-foot train trailing behind.

"Why is this passion so important now?" Analisa asked.

Forgetting the train, Annika spun around and nearly tripped. She righted herself and said, "Don't you see?"

"No." Analisa shook her head.

"Not a bit," her father said.

"You'd best explain it, dear," Ruth advised as she picked up Annika's train and began to follow her around the room.

Annika attempted to put her feelings into words. "I want to share that same kind of passion with the man I marry and it's just not there."

"I thought you loved him," Caleb said.

"I do. But it feels more like the way I love Kase and you and Mama and Auntie Ruth. Richard is more like a brother or a good friend. I don't come alive when I see him, I don't feel sparks fly when he kisses me, my heart doesn't beat itself to ribbons when he walks into a room. After all, I've only known him six months."

"He kisses you?" Analisa wanted to know.

"Anja," Caleb said softly, "of course he kisses her."

"And that is all, I hope," Analisa said, looking Annika over carefully.

"Of course, Mama," Annika assured her. "It's just that Richard seems like a comfortable old shoe."

"More like an expensive boot," Ruth mumbled.

"Auntie Ruth's arrival is a sign, Papa. I was uncertain, and now here she is telling me the stars are all wrong for this. That only confirms the way I have been feeling; it explains my doubt," Annika told him.

Caleb paused, at a loss for words. He looked at his wife, who was waiting for him to utter sage words of advice. He glanced at Ruth, a hopeless romantic, who was watching Annika carefully, nodding agreement with her every word. Finally he turned to his daughter. "So you want to call off the wedding?"

Annika felt overwhelming relief just being able to admit as much to him. "I do. At least for now. I'd like to go to Wyoming and visit Kase and Rosa. By myself," she added quickly when her mother started to speak. "I've never been any place by myself. Why, look at Aunt Ruth, she's traveled the world alone."

"Now, Annemeke—" Her mother looked truly frightened but Annika had no time to wonder why as she argued her case.

"Rosa invited me to visit when they were last here for Christmas. Maybe if I put some distance and time between Richard and me, then I might miss him so much that I'll be dying to see him again. Maybe in a few months I'll want to marry him so badly that I'll be about to burst."

"Maybe you'll feel that missing passion," Ruth added, her expression hopeful. "Six months from now your stars will align correctly for love and marriage, but until then, there's only trial and tribulation in store."

Annika was most concerned about Analisa. Her mother, whose face had drained of all color, had not said much at all. "Mama? What are you thinking?"

As if struggling to find her voice, Analisa swallowed and said softly, "It is your decision. Of course, you must not marry if you are not ready, but Annika, I think that perhaps you are acting a little bit crazy." She cast a frustrated glance at Ruth. "You know nothing of life except what you have lived here in Boston. You have been sheltered, spoiled by all of us."

"Then don't you think it's time I experienced life on my own? Goodness, Mama, it's almost the twentieth century, not the Dark Ages! I want to see something of the world and form a few opinions of my own before I give myself over to a man."

"You aren't exactly selling yourself down the river," Caleb reminded her. "Richard Thexton is the kind of man any woman would be proud to marry. He comes from a fine family—"

"Papa—"

He held up his hands and quickly added, "But it's up to you." He turned to his wife and took her hand in his. Indeed, the passion they shared still lived. It was a silent, vibrant thing that was almost tangible as they exchanged a smile. "Let's go downstairs, Anja, and start the party. There is no need to let all that food and champagne go to waste." Caleb then turned back to Annika and Ruth, who waited expectantly. "We'll make excuses to the guests, Annika, but it's up to you to break the news to Richard."

Annika felt as if a great weight had been lifted from her. She ran across the room with Ruth in tow and hugged her parents each in turn. As she did, she felt truly lighthearted for the first time in days.

Head high, in a voice filled with determination, Annika said, "Send Richard up, Papa, and I'll tell him the wedding is off."

❦ 2 ❦

February 1892, Rocky Mountains

A brilliant full moon hung over the mountain peaks, casting the valleys into dark shadows while it bathed the open, snow-covered hillsides with silver blue light. The air was still and cold, the forests that covered the base of the hills and lined the valleys silent. Moonlight illumined the high scattered clouds that floated like lost spirits across the night sky.

Near one particular valley floor, tucked amid the lodgepole pines and stands of leafless aspen, an old cabin stood beside a rambling creek. Its weathered split-rail walls looked as ancient as the mountains that surrounded it. Golden lamplight spilled out of the small, uneven windows that flanked the door, above which hung an enormous pair of elk horns. Hides were tacked to the outer walls of the cabin, lush fur pelts of wolf, bighorn sheep, and beaver. The snowy ground around the place was littered with wood chips scattered from the woodpile, a chopping block for splitting kindling, various bits of animal hooves and horns, and much-trampled earth. There was a small lean-to shed behind the cabin; and even more than the main dwelling itself, it appeared ready to fall over. A footpath through the snow had been cleared from the door to the edge of the nearby woods.

Inside the sparsely furnished dwelling, two men sat in hushed conversation before a fire that popped and crackled in a stone fireplace that covered one entire wall of the cabin.

15

One of the men was a visitor. He was old. His grizzled white hair and full beard attested to his age as much as the deep creases etched across his full features. Faded hazel eyes that had seen more in one lifetime than ten men could remember paused for a moment to watch in silent contemplation while the flames licked at the logs in the fireplace. Seated on a straight-backed hand-hewn chair, the old man leaned forward with both elbows resting on the crude table that separated him from his host. His clothing, an assortment of tanned hides and nearly threadbare wool, was as rugged as the life he led. His coat was made broad at the shoulders, for he was a big man, and it hung open to allow for his wide girth. He was known simply as Ted, Old Ted to be exact, his surname long since forgotten. Like most mountain men, Ted traveled alone, except for a scroungy, balding, long-haired Chihuahua he called The Mouse and carried inside his jacket. He'd had the dog ever since the day he had traded a Mexican a mule for it, and most folks agreed the Mexican had made the better end of the deal. The Mouse, who had a great aversion for anyone but its master, lay snuggled against Ted's chest beneath his beard, snoring.

The younger man, Buck Scott, stared not at the fire but at Old Ted. Buck fidgeted in his chair, his gaze often roving to the big bed in the far, shadowed corner of the cabin's only room. He alternately tapped his thumbs against the edge of the table while he leaned against the wall, balancing the chair on its two back legs. As he chewed on his lower lip, he frowned, but his worried expression was barely visible in the dim firelight. Buck took stock of his home and possessions, trying to see them the way a stranger might. More to the point, the way the woman he would bring home with him in a few days' time might view them.

Brown was the color that first came to mind when he thought of having to describe the place to his new bride. Brown and dingy. The wooden walls were bare, except for the patch above the mantel that had been papered with newspaper and in the spots where they were chinked with mud. The floor was as brown as dirt, because it *was* dirt. He'd meant to save enough grain sacks to stitch together to form a makeshift floor covering, but by the time the idea came to him he'd used the sacks for other things. A bag of potatoes slumped tiredly against a side wall. Shelves lined the space above and beside the bag. Tins of staples—dried beans, cornmeal, honey, molasses, yeast, soda, and baking powder—stood in a row like culinary soldiers. Buck hoped the woman would find everything to her liking.

He knew for certain that he wouldn't miss doing his own cooking and cleaning; and as his thoughts turned to the tasks, he hoped he had everything she might need. He'd never seen a fancy kitchen nor did he know what a city woman might think she ought to have in one. Since his sisters had been gone, he hadn't paid much attention to such details and had lived on a diet of meat, biscuits, canned vegetables, and dried fruit. There was a turnspit for meat in the fireplace, heavy iron kettles, a Dutch oven, and a skillet for frying. He'd made a new broom by tying dried brush to a smooth pole with a strip of rawhide.

Besides the table of split logs and the two real chairs, there were two stools fashioned from nail kegs that had been padded with moss and covered with canvas.

The huge bed took up nearly one side of the room. Buck had made it for himself because he figured a big man deserved a big bed. There was plenty of room in it for him and the woman both to sleep comfortably—even if she didn't take to him right off.

When his thoughts drifted in that direction, Buck quickly drew his gaze away from the bed and looked across the table at Ted. As he watched the old man take a sip of whiskey, Buck hoped he'd done the right thing when he asked Ted to look after the place while he went down to Cheyenne to meet the train. Dropping the front legs of the chair back to the ground, Buck straightened and ran a hand across his chin. His half-grown beard felt rough against his palm. He reckoned he should shave it, then decided to wait until he got to Cheyenne where he could have a real barber attend to it for him. He'd have his hair cut too, since it had grown thick and so far past his shoulders that he wore it tied behind him with a rawhide thong. He had the same wild blond mane that had made his father stand out from the other trappers. Even now, whenever Buck ran into some of the old buffalo hunters they knew who he was because of his great height and his abundance of wild blond hair.

Ted belched. "You leavin' at first light?"

"Soon as I can see my hand in front of my face."

"Thought about it a long time, have ya?"

His impending marriage was all Buck had thought about for weeks. If he had any choice he wouldn't be getting married at all. But he didn't, so he shrugged and said, "Nothing else I can do. It will all work out."

"You don't look as sure as you sound, but I 'spect it will. What'd you say her name is?" Ted leaned forward and rested his stubbled chin in his hand.

"Alice Soams." Buck tried to conjure up the image of the woman he'd been writing to for six months, but even though she'd told him she was blond, thin, and taller than most women, nothing came to mind. He guessed fear clouded his mind's eye.

"How'd you find her?"

"Remember that paper you carried up last year? The one Jonesey gave you from Boston?"

"No."

"Well, you did. Anyway, I saw an advertisement in it and answered it. A lady from Boston wanted to move west, was looking for a husband. Said all she required was a home of her own and someone who could provide for her. She picked my letter."

"Seen a pitcher of her? Hear tell most men that gets a bride by mail has seen a pitcher," Ted said knowledgeably.

Buck shook his head. "No. No picture. She said she's blond. Said some might say she's attractive."

Old Ted looked skeptical. "'Spect it's too late now, anyway."

"I guess it is, since she'll be in Cheyenne day after tomorrow. Coming in on the noon train." Buck tapped the shirt pocket where he kept his last letter from Alice Soams that gave the date and time of her arrival. "It'll take me four days there and back."

"You ain't stayin' over in Cheyenne?"

"No time." Buck glanced across the room and back at

Ted. "We'll be married soon as she gets off the train and then pack up. I hope she doesn't have a passel of trunks with her."

"I hear women don't often go anyplace without such. Need 'em for their geegaws." Ted took another sip of whiskey and smacked his lips. "It's been a mild winter, but what if the pass gets snowed in and you can't get back in the valley?"

Buck set his jaw. "It won't."

"Hell, it's only February. It might."

"I'll get through. I'll be back in four days."

"Draggin' a woman behind you? Why didn't you tell her to wait till the spring thaw? Why's she comin' out here in the dead of winter?"

"Because I sent her the money and told her to decide when she wanted to leave Boston."

"Well, I hope to Christ for your sake you don't let her make too many more decisions, then," Ted said.

Buck ignored the old man's comment and stood up. "I guess we better be turnin' in."

"I'll sleep on the floor," Ted volunteered. "You don't need to wake me when you go, just stir up the fire. I 'spect I'll be up soon enough after you leave."

"Yeah, you will." Buck stood in the middle of the room and stared down at Ted, who hadn't moved yet. "You sure you'll be all right looking after things here?"

"Don't you worry about a thing. The Mouse and I will do all right. You jest hurry on back, though, and do your sparkin' here. My achin' joints tell me there's a storm a comin'. I can't guarantee how long I'll be able to keep things runnin' aright if you're gone too long."

Buck didn't want to think about the consequences of getting snowed out of the valley, so he turned away from the sight of Ted, who had reached down to scratch his poor excuse for a dog behind the ears. He wondered what it would be like to have a woman around the place again. Three years ago there had been two women underfoot and he'd been more than happy to let them take care of the chores. Then Sissy, his youngest sister, had died of typhoid and Patsy—who'd been crazy ever since her common-law husband died—got so bad he couldn't trust what she would do next.

He'd had to take her down the mountain and trust her care to an old Scotswoman Ted knew who lived outside Cheyenne.

Now that he'd asked Alice Soams to marry him, there would be a woman in his life again.

And things were bound to be different.

ANNIKA Storm touched the frosted glass of the windowpane beside her seat on the Union Pacific train bound for Cheyenne and parts west. She traced an ever-widening circle with her index finger until she created a peephole large enough to see through, but all it revealed was a vast stretch of snow-covered land.

She took one look outside and sighed with boredom. The bleak landscape had not changed for the last five hundred miles. She glanced down at the journal lying open in her lap and fingered the well-worn pages. Today's entry would read much like the past few days. *Still traveling westward. Open plains and snow all around.*

Before she could open her slant-lidded, hand-carved writing box, take out pen and ink, and add the entry (no little feat with the ceaseless rocking motion of the train) Annika felt a sudden jolt and the train ground to a halt. The other passengers around her began to stir, shaken from the lethargy brought on by the earlier, hypnotic motion of the train.

She set her journal beside her on the plush, tufted upholstery of her first-class seat, put her hands on her waist at the small of her back, then arched and stretched. She had no idea when she left Boston that the journey ahead of her would be so long and tedious. As the train halted with a dramatic hiss of steam and screech of brakes, Annika braced herself by putting her hand against the seat in front of her, then reached down for the perky hat that she had set atop the valise that contained her overnight necessities: comb and brush, a nightgown, buttonhook, a fresh shirtwaist, a book, and the tin that held her precious button collection. The hat itself was of her own creation, a low-crowned man's felt hat with a narrow brim to which she had added a satin hatband of pale blue on navy. The fabric was the same as that of the shirtwaist she wore with the heavy chocolate wool skirt topped by a fitted, single breasted, three-quarter-length jacket. Her "mountain dress," as she called the ensemble, had served her well during the long trip, but now she was thoroughly tired of wearing it. She could hardly wait to reach Cheyenne and the comforts of her brother Kase's home where she could unpack her various trunks and boxes and change into something else.

Annika pinned on her hat and stood up so that she could draw her cloak over her shoulders. The black satin *merveilleux* cape enveloped her clothing. She'd brought it along, not only for added warmth, but to repel dust and soot, unwanted additions to any train ride. She fluffed the wide ruffle that covered the shoulders of the cape and tied the ribbons that held it closed beneath her chin. She was especially fond of the scrolled initials, *AS*, worked in heavy gold thread on the edge of the collar above her right breast.

A few moments later, the harried conductor, portly and balding beneath a stiff black cap, entered the Pullman and hurried down the aisle. He paused when Annika glanced worriedly up at him. He leaned toward her. In a voice loud enough to carry to the other curious travelers who had paid dearly to ride in the well-appointed sleeper where the seats were converted into upper and lower berths at night, he explained their sudden stop in the middle of nowhere.

"We dropped a crown sheet," he said matter-of-factly.

"A what?" she asked.

"Crown sheet. Dropped down on the hot coals of the engine and the thing exploded. Blew the windows right out of the cab when the firebox door flew open."

"Was anyone injured?"

"All three men in the cab were scalded. Brakeman's the worst of the lot. Things would have been worse if they hadn't had on so many heavy clothes. We'll have to send someone down the line to wire Cheyenne for a new crew. If we're lucky, we'll be on the way within a few hours." He pushed his cap onto the back of his head with his thumb. "Never forget the story of the train that stalled in 'seventy-five. Bound for Denver out of Kansas, trapped by a storm for eleven days. I heard the passengers ended up eating oysters that were part of a shipment to California." He straightened, faced the rear of the car, and announced, "You may as well get out and stretch your legs for a while, but don't wander too far away. Hopefully we'll be leaving before too long."

He hurried on to spread word of the accident through the rest of the passenger cars. The ladies and gentlemen aboard began to stretch and talk among themselves. Annika joined the more adventuresome travelers who began to leave the car.

It was not until she reached the metal stairs and grabbed the freezing handrails on either side that she realized she had left her gloves in her valise. Anxious to feel more of the clear, crisp air on her face she decided not to go after them, but to continue on and return to the car if her hands became too cold. She stepped out of the train carefully and then, when she was standing on the uneven ground near the tracks, paused to look around.

The land was as wide and endlessly barren as it had appeared from the window of the train. Here and there patches of snow had melted, giving the impression of open tears in the fabric of the landscape. The earth was mud brown against the snowy whiteness surrounding it. Tufts of thick, winter-brown buffalo grass and scattered stones added texture to the ground. The air was cold, the wind sharp and stinging, but she found it a relief from the dry, close heat generated by the stove inside the train.

As she began to walk away from the small crowd milling alongside the train, Annika looked toward the west and noticed the gradual, almost imperceptible slope of the land. She realized that since they were still east of Cheyenne the train must be stalled somewhere near her brother's ranch, which was located on land that backed up to the Laramie Range not far from the small town of Busted Heel, Wyoming. She thought it ironic that Kase had arranged to meet her, not in Busted Heel, but in Cheyenne. He had written that he wanted to combine meeting her at the station with a trip into town for supplies. Instead of being but a few miles away, he was waiting for her down the line.

As she raised her face to the sun and let its warmth vie with the chilly air that touched her skin, she tried to remember what she could of the years her family had lived on the Dakota plains. From the time she was two years old until she was seven, Caleb had been stationed at the Sioux reservation at Pine Ridge. She knew they had a small wooden house, that she had been jealous of Kase because he had been allowed to learn to ride and later to shoot a revolver, and that her mother had kept her close to her side. She thought she remembered the same endless stretch of sky that she saw now, and the wind that never seemed to rest, but that was all.

She rubbed her hands together, cupped one around the other, and blew on them to bring some warmth to her numb fingers. Then she folded her arms, hoping to keep the cold at bay a little while longer as she enjoyed the fresh air and sunshine. When she heard footsteps behind her, Annika slowed her pace, hoping to strike up a conversation with one of the other passengers. A young couple walked past her, nodded, and moved on. She heard them speaking a language that sounded Germanic, but it was not Dutch, which she had learned from her mother. She watched as they moved on down the tracks together.

For a moment she felt a fleeting loneliness as she watched the young lovers walk away hand in hand. If she had not called off her wedding, she and Richard would have been married for two months now. They would have shared their first Christmas together and perhaps, she thought with a shiver, she might even be carrying his child. Her loneliness gradually ebbed when she silently admitted to herself that she did not think she was ready to face motherhood and all of its inherent restrictions yet.

Richard had been shocked, but kind and understanding when she broke their engagement. During the holidays and all of January while she corresponded with Rose and Kase and prepared to go to Wyoming, Richard had continued to call on her. He had even accompanied Caleb, Analisa, and Ruth to the station to see her off. Willing to give her time to find herself, he told her to see some of the world on her own, to take as long as she needed. On that last day in Boston as the train was about to pull out of the station, he held her hands and promised to be waiting for her in six months when she returned. When she tried to return his ring, he refused to accept it. She left it in her mother's care.

His acceptance of her decision was smoothly acknowledged without shouting or tears. But then, Richard had always done the right thing, the acceptable thing, throughout their courtship. Following the strict rules set down by society, he had never offered her his arm in the daytime until they were engaged, nor did he give her gifts until she had agreed to marry him. He refused to stand outside her door to bid her good night longer than the proper five minutes, and on those occasions when she asked him in, Richard politely left after the respectable time limit of a half hour had passed.

He had been as predictable in his agreement to give her time to think things through as she had expected, and now that she could look back over their brief relationship, it was that very predictability that she was running from. Life with Richard would always be sane and safe, predictable and proper. Those were the qualities her parents had seen in him and admired. It was not necessarily the life she wanted.

The wind whipped the edges of her cloak open, so she tugged them closed and held them, but her hands were freezing. When she stumbled, nearly turning her ankle on a loose rock, Annika decided that her brief sojourn outdoors should reach its end. She took a last, deep breath of the winter air and turned around. Farther down the line, passengers were huddled in small groups, talking idly, staring at the landscape around them as if, like Rip van Winkle, they had slept for years.

As she approached the sleeper, she was forced to step aside to allow a passenger to descend the stairs. The woman was thin, almost to the point of emaciation. Her hair was lank and long, not really blond, nor was it brown, but a faded, indiscriminate color. Her eyes were blue, her skin sallow. The pinched lips, held tight beneath her narrow nose, made the woman appear older than she really was. Although Annika nodded in greeting, the woman ignored her and moved on. With a shrug, Annika stepped aboard and quickly put the incident behind her. She took her seat again, left on her cloak because the car had become drafty with both doors open, and opened her journal.

AT ten minutes past twelve, Buck Scott cursed himself as he rode down Capitol Avenue toward the Union Pacific passenger station in Cheyenne. He had lost track of time when he made one last stop at Myers and Foster's shoe store on Sixteenth, and now feared he had missed meeting Alice Soams when the noon train arrived. As it was he was so far behind that he had not had time to get a haircut or a shave. He had taken longer than necessary when he stopped at Tivoli Hall to partake of some St. Louis beer, went into Zehner and Buechner and Company to buy a simple gold wedding band, then there had been those last few moments he'd spent standing in front of the window at the Wyoming Hardware Company staring at an ornately decorated Aladdin ventilating stove, wondering how he could get one up the mountain.

If not for all the delays he would have been at the station well before noon, for he had made it to Cheyenne in record time—a day and a half—but it had been a day and a half of hard riding leading an extra mare and two pack mules. He could only hope the trip back into the mountains would go as smoothly, especially with an inexperienced rider and all her possessions in tow. As he urged his horse on, careful to avoid the buggies and wagons vying for space in the crowded, muddy street, he tried to quell the roiling nervousness that had plagued him since he neared Cheyenne. What would Alice Soams be like? How would she take to him and life in the Rockies? Why in the hell had he ever decided that marriage was the only way he could cope with his present predicament?

He was used to his life of isolation. Hunting and trapping filled his days, sporadic trips into Cheyenne took care of any need he ever had for companionship. Whenever he wanted a woman to ease his loneliness, he'd bought and paid for one for a night. Until now, that had always been enough. But now, matters were such that he couldn't even leave the cabin unless there was someone there to watch over the place, so after endless hours of careful deliberation, Buck took the only option he felt was open to him—he had answered the advertisement in a Boston newspaper and found himself a wife.

There was a crowd milling about on the platform. Even though he was a good head taller than almost everyone there, by the time he had tied up his animals and mingled among them, he still had not spotted anyone who might have been Alice Soams. There was only one unaccompanied female in the group. She was standing off to the side of the platform alone, but she was nearly seventy years old. He hoped to God she wasn't Alice.

Buck took off his hat and ran his hand over his hair. He'd tied it back into a thick queue with a strip of leather, but the stuff was so naturally wavy that some of it was always working its way out of the tie. He slammed his hat back on and pushed his way through the crowd to the ticket window.

When he had the clerk's attention he asked, "There been a lady here askin' after Buck Scott? She was due in on the noon train."

"She couldn't have asked," the clerk said shortly, "because the noon train's late."

Buck looked around at the crowd, passengers waiting to depart, folks there to meet new arrivals, and asked, "How late's it going to be?"

"No tellin'. When I hear anything from down the line, I'll announce it." With that the man motioned forward an impatient couple standing behind Buck.

Buck shoved his hands into his pockets and tried to move closer to the edge of the platform. He looked down the tracks, willed the noon train to appear, and when it didn't, he glanced up at the sky. When the wind had picked up, blowing in from the northwest as it usually did, he remembered Old Ted's prediction of a storm. Buck concentrated on the train again as he stepped from one foot to the other. *Damn!* he thought. His impending marriage hadn't even taken place and already things had started to go sour.

He looked around at the crowd again, uncomfortable among so many people in one place. He'd never liked being surrounded by milling bodies; it reminded him too much of being part of a herd. He'd seen one too many animals die because they let the lead bull do their thinking for them. Buffalo would run right off a cliff because they followed the lead bull. Working alone was the way he liked things; living alone had been his way, too. But now all that was about to change.

Buck glanced over his shoulder and couldn't help but notice the only other exceptionally tall man on the platform. The man was well dressed, outfitted like a prosperous rancher in a fleece-lined leather jacket, black wool pants, and a new hat with a ring of silver conchos for a headband. His boots caught and held Buck's attention, for they were glossy black, polished to a high shine and as clean as humanly possible to keep them with all the mud in the streets. Like Buck, the man wore his hair long, past his shoulders, and tied back out of the way, but this man—well over six foot three—was a half-breed. Sioux, Buck guessed. Sioux and white.

And the man was staring back at him with a cold, hard look in his deep blue eyes.

Buck turned away. He'd seen that look before. It seemed even 'breeds thought they were better now than buffalo hunters.

The wind whipped across the platform, a chilling, cutting wind that shook Buck out of his dark thoughts. The sky was still raw blue and clear, but he knew now, as sure as Ted had, that a storm was on the way. He had to get back through the pass before it hit. He turned and pressed his way back through the crowd toward the ticket window. Just before he reached it, the clerk opened a small door in the side of the building and stepped out. He cupped his hands and shouted, "Train's blown a crown sheet down the line outside of Busted Heel. Don't know how long it'll be before we can get another engine down to bring 'er in. Maybe you folks ought to get in out of the cold until she pulls in. We'll blast the whistle loud and long to let everyone know when it's here."

Buck listened to the grumbling around him and ignored it as he stepped up to the window where the clerk had safely ensconced himself inside once again. He grabbed the bars that separated him from the clerk and said, "Where'd you say that train's stalled?"

Annoyed, the man stared at Buck's rough hands. "Down the line. Near Busted Heel."

"Which is?"

"'Bout an hour's ride east of here."

Buck Scott mumbled the one word he should have never

uttered in mixed company and shouldered his way off the platform.

KASE Storm listened to the station clerk's announcement and shook his head in frustration. It was just like his half sister to board a train that was meant to break down.

He loved Annika, loved to spoil and pamper her just as his mother and stepfather did, and any other time he would be glad to have her visit, but when her last letter came informing him that she would arrive in less than two weeks' time, Kase had wanted to wire her and tell her to wait until spring. But Rose, his Italian wife, had stopped him.

"How come you say this, Kase?" she had asked. "Your sister, she can help me, and this way I can know her better, like a real sister, before the baby comes."

Kase didn't have the heart to tell Rose that Annika would be little help. His sister had never done a day's work in her life. Unlike Rose, who had come to Wyoming alone, started her own restaurant, sold it for a tidy profit, and still insisted she do all the cooking for the hands at their ranch, Annika had never had to lift a finger to do anything for herself. Their parents had seen to it that Annika was educated so that she would be able to support herself if the need ever arose, but both he and Annika had been endowed with ample trust funds, a legacy from Caleb's father's fortune, that would provide for them for a lifetime.

Two ranchers on the platform smiled a greeting before they moved on, and Kase nodded in acknowledgment. He'd made a name for himself as marshal of Busted Heel before he gave up his badge and went into ranching. More often than not, men he didn't even recognize called him by name. He wondered how different his life might have been if he hadn't taken the job of marshal six years ago and helped rid the area of the Dawson gang. And where would he be now if he hadn't married the one woman in the world who could have helped him forget his heritage and see himself as a whole man?

Kase felt his anxiety build as he thought of Rose. She was pregnant again, due the first of May. It was the fourth time in five years they'd waited for a baby and now he was even afraid to hope that nothing would go wrong. His wife had miscarried once, then given birth to a stillborn boy. On the last try, their daughter had not lived more than a few hours. So this time, although he wished it could be otherwise, he had received the news of her pregnancy without joy, but with overwhelming fear. He couldn't face the thought of building another small wooden coffin, didn't want to bury another child any more than he wanted to risk losing his Rose, but motherhood was her one burning desire, so all he could do was see that Rose had the best of care, and wait. And pray.

Right now all he wanted was to collect his sister and get back out to the ranch as soon as he could so that he would be there if Rose needed him. He knew all the hands were at her beck and call—there was no one who could resist the petite Italian's charm—but Kase still preferred to be within shouting distance of her most of the time. But Rose had insisted he go into Cheyenne to greet his sister properly, said that they should have dinner at one of the finest restaurants and attend the opera, then spend the night at the Interocean Hotel before he drove Annika out to the isolated ranch. After much argument—and although he would never admit as much to anyone, he was proud of the way his Rose could argue—he decided to give in to her and go all the way into town.

But now the train was late with no word of how much longer it would be before it arrived.

Kase watched in silence as a huge man dressed in the trappings of a buffalo hunter shoved through the crowd and jumped off the platform. The giant, bearded blond had to be a good six feet four if he was an inch, his hair was long and wild, pulled back in an attempt to tame it into a more civilized style. He was dressed in buckskins well greased to keep out wind and water, in clothes that appeared to be handmade. Long fringe swayed from the sleeves and yoke of the man's hooded jacket. Knee-high moccasins adorned his feet. Kase frowned when he glimpsed the long sheath hooked to his belt and tied to the hunter's thigh. It held a skinning knife.

He'd seen the rough-looking giant earlier, studied him as they stood near each other on the platform, wondered if such a young man could have indeed taken part in the last of the

buffalo hunts. It had been years now since a herd of any size
had been spotted anywhere outside of the Yellowstone area.
Twenty years ago millions of head of buffalo had thundered
across the prairies. Now, except for a few lone stragglers and
small, privately owned herds like the nineteen head Kase
had rounded up, there were no buffalo to be found. Hunters
like the man who had just left the platform had slaughtered
them one by one, selling off boxcars full of hides and leaving
the carcasses to decay on the open plains.

With the killing of the buffalo came the near annihilation
of the Plains Indians, and although Kase had not been able to
fully accept that part of him that was Sioux until a few years
ago, he had always respected the Indians as a people, just as
he respected all life. Caleb had taught him as much, and so
too had his mother.

Before his anger could block out reason, Kase turned
away from the sight of the hunter and left a message for
Annika with the station clerk. He decided to go to the
Interocean Hotel and reserve a room for each of them, do
some of the shopping as he had promised Rose, and then return to check on the progress down the line. If the delay was
to last much longer, it would be wiser for him to ride on
back to Busted Heel and collect Annika there before he went
back to the ranch.

As he stepped off the platform and began to make his way
up Capitol toward the Interocean, he saw the buffalo hunter
leading a mare and two pack mules and riding flat out down
Fifteenth Street.

◈ 3 ◈

ALICE Soams disliked just about everything she had seen
so far on this hateful trip, and now that the train had
stopped dead in the middle of nowhere, she even hated the
Union Pacific Railroad. It was bad enough that she'd been
cooped up in the confines of the first-class sleeper with the
stove drying up what little moisture there was left in the air,
but now that she'd decided to step outside and stretch, even
the weather had turned against her. She tried to hold on to the
lapels of her thick woolen coat as she bent forward into the
wind and struggled up the gentle incline toward the tracks.

For the past day and a half she had spent her time mulling
over her decision to marry Buck Scott, the man who answered the advertisement she had put in the paper on a
whim. She certainly didn't regret accepting the first-class
fare he had promptly mailed her when she accepted his pro-
posal, nor did she look back with any sorrow at leaving her
sister's home. She was tired of playing the part of the spin-
ster sister, tired of living off Muriel and her husband, sick of
wearing her sister's old clothes and feeling beholden for every scrap of food she ate from their table merely because she
had never found a man willing to marry her.

As she stalked down the snowy patch already trampled by
the other passengers, Alice did not look right or left but at
the ground. She couldn't abide talking to strangers, never
saw the good in it. Waste of time, if anyone ever asked her,
but they never did. She looked down the right of way and
watched a couple ahead of her swinging their clasped hands
between them. "Immoral and indecent," she grumbled to

31

herself, still unable to avert her gaze. They were as bad as the flashy blond girl riding three seats ahead of her in first class.

Alice had seen her type before, knew the girl for what she was—a society debutante decked out in her finery, all too willing to lord it over the rest of the world. The girl had the conductor eating out of her hand from the moment she had boarded the train. Alice thought it was disgusting.

She had hated the girl on sight. It was almost too much to bear, watching her flash her big blue eyes at every man on board, having to witness the open, friendly way she greeted everyone. Anyone with a lick of sense knew that a body shouldn't go around speaking to strangers, but the tall blonde didn't seem to know it, even if Alice did. Probably never had a care in the world, that girl. It was all too clear she had more money than sense. Her clothes were new—cut fashionably and showy. She had an ornate, hinge-lidded lap desk she kept her writing things in and to top if off, a new valise. As if all that weren't bad enough, she flaunted a shining black satin cloak with AS, the same initials as Alice's own, emblazoned on the bodice in gold.

Alice thought of her own worn coat and protectively clutched it tighter with her long, thin fingers. As soon as she reached Cheyenne and married Buck Scott her worries would be over. She'd have money enough then, and she'd show them all. After all, she thought, he'd sent her first-class fare without question, and his last two letters had been filled with descriptions of Blue Creek Valley. His letters had never been long, but they were neatly penned. He told of the riches to be had in the valley, of how the place was all his, about the home he'd built that they wouldn't have to share with anyone.

Alice looked up, braving the wind long enough to turn and stare down the tracks. She had walked farther than she realized, so she quickly turned around and began to make her way back. The last letter she had received from Buck Scott was tucked safely in the pocket of her coat. She might need it to prove her identity if she had to—if he didn't recognize her right off. Not that he shouldn't, but when she faced the truth, she knew that she had taken a bit of license when she'd described herself to him. But how could she have written to the only prospective husband she had ever had and tell him that she was painfully thin, had lanky, light brown hair, sharp features, and faded blue eyes? She couldn't. And she hadn't. But she figured she could clear all that up when she met him face-to-face.

She wondered what she would do if Buck Scott had lied to her about his appearance the way she had. He said he was taller than most men, blond headed, and promised he'd be easy to please. She had imagined him more than once, envisioned a successful land-owning man in a dapper, houndstooth check suit and bowler hat, bouquet in hand, anxiously awaiting her in a new carriage ready to whisk her off to their mountain home.

There seemed to be a crowd gathering up ahead, so she hurried toward them, planning to stand on the outskirts and watch whatever uneventful happening was about to unfold. As she drew near, she noticed that everyone was watching a rider approach from the west. He rode alongside the tracks across the slight ditch that ran parallel to the rail line. Alice sniffed in disgust as the man neared. He was huge, his clothing dark and greasy, his white-blond hair curling wildly, showing well past his shoulders beneath his hat. She was as speechless as the rest of the crowd as he thundered to a halt, followed by the string of animals he led behind him.

Alice leaned forward to listen as the man strode over to the black-uniformed conductor. The wind, luckily, was blowing in the right direction. It carried his words to her ears.

"I'm Buck Scott, and I'm lookin' for a blond woman from Boston that's supposed to be on this train."

Alice nearly reeled into the young German couple who was standing beside her. Instead, she tried to catch her breath, grabbed the handrail behind her, and scrambled aboard the train without another moment's hesitation. Inside the door, she paused long enough to let her racing heart slow a bit and, with her face averted from the scene outside, continued to listen.

The conductor was rocking back and forth from the balls of his feet to his heels. His head didn't quite reach the bigger man's collarbone. "Boston?" The conductor looked him up and down. "I just can't say. Can you describe her any better? Besides," he said, suddenly possessive of his passenger, "what is it you want with this woman anyway?"

The man reached inside his dirty buckskin jacket and then, much to Alice Soams's dismay, withdrew a well-worn envelope. She knew without seeing it clearly that it was one of her letters to him.

"I have a letter here that says she'll be my wife. I paid for her fare, first class," he added, "and this is the train she said she'd be on. I went into Cheyenne to meet her, but when they told me you were stalled out here, I came straightaway to collect her because a big storm's comin' in," the big man explained carefully.

The crowd seemed to inch closer to him with every word. The men were watching him warily, while the women stared in awe. Some of them watched with tears glistening in their eyes when they heard his gallant reason for finding the stalled train before a snow storm kept him and his fiancée apart.

"Her name's Alice Soams," Buck Scott added to reassure the conductor.

Straightening, the portly conductor finally smiled. "Never wanted to be one to stand in the way of cupid's arrows," he said. "Right this way." With a grand flourish, he waved Buck toward the first-class car. "I believe the blond lady you're looking for is waiting for you right in here."

Alice did not wait to hear more, because one look at Buck Scott told her all she needed to know—she could no more marry the crudely outfitted, wild-haired mountain man than she could fly. Without hesitation she thanked her lucky stars that she had told Buck Scott that she was an attractive, statuesque blonde. As she hurried down the aisle, she discreetly drew the man's letter from her pocket. Then, when she passed the young blonde whose attention was centered on her writing, Alice stealthily dropped Buck Scott's last letter to her on the seat beside the other girl's valise.

Before the conductor led Buck Scott up the stairs and over the threshold of the sleeper, Alice Soams had disappeared into the next car.

February 3, 1892. Although a stalled train isn't much to celebrate, at least I have finally encountered some sort of adventure during this otherwise uneventful journey west. The unscheduled stop has afforded me time to walk around outside. The scenery is breathtaking, the sky seems to stretch endlessly in every direction. The wind is freezing. It carries with it a particularly lonely moaning sound, but the sun is shining. It sets all the snow-covered land asparkle. I can hardly wait to reach Cheye—

A loud noise in the doorway caused Annika to pause and look up. The conductor was heading down the aisle toward her, his face wreathed in smiles. He looked very much like a man who could not wait to shout "Surprise!" A large man moved up the aisle behind him, a man Annika had not seen previously on board the train. Although the conductor blocked some of her view of the stranger, she could still see his head and shoulders. He embodied everything she had ever read about the "Wild West" in the periodicals, from his untamed hair and beard to his buckskin clothing. He was even taller than Kase, and there weren't many men larger than her brother. Annika watched with undisguised curiosity as the giant followed the conductor down the aisle.

A line of passengers walked in behind the two, some of the braver ones managing to squeeze past the conductor and his companion and slide into the seats they had previously occupied. Everyone was quiet; a hush of expectation hovered in the air. She wondered what was going on.

Annika was speechless when the conductor stopped beside her seat and motioned the huge man forward. "Here she is, safe and sound," the conductor said. "Your blonde from Boston."

Annika blinked once, looked from the conductor to the other man, and said, "What?"

"Your fiancé heard we were stalled and rode all the way out here to get you, miss."

"My what?"

"Fiancé." The conductor nodded.

The big man stepped as far forward as the small space in the aisle would allow. "I'm Buck Scott, ma'am." He smiled and pulled off his hat, then nodded as if the name should mean something to her.

Annika watched him warily, but still wasn't too concerned about the mistake. He was obviously nervous. If he squeezed his hat any tighter in his big hands, she thought it would disintegrate. His tanned cheeks pinkened above his beard.

She opened her mouth to speak, closed it, then shook her head. Finally, she said to the conductor, "I don't know what either of you are talking about."

"It's me, ma'am, Buck Scott. The man who sent you the money for the ticket?" He reached into his coat pocket and pulled out a ragged envelope and held it up in front of her face. "This is your letter to me, Miss Soams. Your promise to marry me."

"That's right, Miss Soams," the conductor added.

Annika looked down, slowly and carefully blotted her pen, corked the ink bottle, and then set them inside her writing box along with her journal. She closed the hinged lid and set the box down beside her on the seat. She smoothed out her skirt and pulled her cloak tightly about her. Then, as regally as a queen, she drew herself up and said directly to the obviously insane person named Buck Scott, "I am not Alice Soams and I have no idea who you are, sir."

The low murmur of whispers ran through the car.

The conductor frowned. "Are you sure, miss?" he asked.

"What do you mean *am I sure*? Of course I'm sure. I've never seen this man before in my life and furthermore, my name is not Alice Soams."

The conductor looked confused.

Buck Scott looked angry. He reached past the conductor and picked up an envelope that lay on the seat beside Annika's valise.

"Then what's this?" Buck demanded in a tone laced with sarcasm.

"How should I know?" Annika fired back.

"It's a letter from me, addressed to you, and it just happens to be lying here next to your bag."

The murmurs of the other passengers were no longer hushed, but excited. Annika tried to ignore them as she concentrated on what this man was trying to tell her.

"Let me see if I understand you correctly. You supposedly wrote me that letter, my name is Alice Soams, and you are harboring some delusion that I am going to marry you?"

"That's right. But it's not a delusion."

She stared at him for a moment longer, then she burst out laughing.

Buck's fist closed around the letter.

The conductor turned beet red.

Everyone around them stopped whispering.

Annika noticed the deadly silence and stopped laughing. She wiped the tears from her eyes and smiled up at the two men. "Very entertaining, gentlemen. I can't wait to write home about this."

The conductor turned to Buck for help.

Buck nodded toward the door. "Leave."

The conductor left.

Buck hunkered down in the aisle alongside the blonde. His heart was pounding like a buffalo stampede. She was more beautiful than he could have ever hoped. Her eyes were round as a full moon and as blue as the clearest mountain lake he'd ever seen. The sight of her buttercup-yellow hair, thick and waving, made his hand itch to touch it. Still, as exquisite as she was, she did not give the appearance of a pale hothouse flower. Her skin was sun-kissed gold, the color of clover honey. Her eyes, surrounded by a thick circlet of dark lashes, had a slight tilt to their outer corners. High cheekbones gave her an exotic, aristocratic air.

Afraid he'd embarrass himself by reaching out to touch her just to see if she was real, Buck kept his hands balled into fists around both letters, his to Alice and hers to him, and his hat brim. Aware that all eyes were on them, he lowered his voice and leaned closer so that only she could hear him. Once he was face-to-face with her, he immediately regretted his move. He was assailed by the mingled scents of heady soap and rose water.

"Miss Soams, I know damn well why you claim you don't know me." His blue eyes darkened as he struggled to find the right words. "I know that I'm not what you expected." He ran a hand through his tangled hair. "I meant to clean up a bit before we met, but I ran out of time."

He hated having to apologize for his appearance in front of the others, but if he was going to hurry her up and get her out of her seat and off the train so that they could head back to Blue Creek in time, he knew he had to do some fast talking. He glanced out of the window behind her. Thankfully there was not a cloud in sight.

"A bargain is a bargain and I kept my end of it. I mailed you money for your ticket and here you are. Now"—he looked at her valise and writing box—"if this is all you have, I'll carry them for you so we can get on our way."

When he reached for her valise, Annika grabbed it and hugged it close as if protecting it from his touch. "I'll thank you *not* to touch my things, Mr. Scott."

She stared at him now, openly experiencing fear for the first time since this whole nightmare had begun. On close inspection he was not as wild as he appeared, but he was obviously sincere in his intent to force this Alice Soams to keep her end of the bargain. From the desperate way he was watching her, Annika knew that this impending marriage meant a lot to this man. She tried to see beyond the curling, shoulder-length hair, past the dirty buckskins and callused hands. He was still clutching his hat and the two letters, leaning forward so that the entire carload of passengers could not overhear what he had to say.

He was not as old as his stubbled beard and sun-creased skin made him seem. She guessed he wasn't quite thirty. His eyes were clear and blue, but they were the eyes of a much older man. Old eyes in a young face. Suddenly, Annika felt compelled to explain, without hurting him, that she was not Alice Soams.

"I'm really sorry, Mr. Scott, but I'm afraid there's been a terrible mistake. I don't know where that letter came from, I really don't. I'm not Alice Soams, although I am from Boston . . ."

He leaned toward her.

Buck reached out and gingerly traced the gold letters embroidered on her cape. "A S." He arched a brow and shook his head. "Even your cloak gives you away. Am I that repulsive?"

Annika stared down at the long finger pressing against the

spot above her heart before she looked him square in the eye. "My name is Annika Storm," she said slowly.

He stared back, then his gaze moved over her face, her hair, her clothing. Annika could almost see the wheels of his mind at work. When he came to a decision, he abruptly stood. Then, without hesitation, he put the letters in his pocket, shoved on his hat, and then reached down. He grabbed her valise.

"Are you coming, Miss Soams, or do I carry you off this train?"

"If you so much as touch me, I'll have you arrested."

"A bargain's a bargain, Miss Soams."

"Will you *stop* saying that?"

A man three rows back called out, "A bargain's a bargain, just like the man says."

Suddenly everyone else felt compelled to chime in and offer their opinions.

"Stick to your guns, mister!" a drummer in a bowler hat called out.

A young cowhand shouted, "Come on, lady, go with him!"

"Haul her out of here!" advised an old gent.

"She shouldn't ough'ta have to go if'n she don't wanna," a woman yelled from the back.

Annika looked around and spied the conductor hovering near the door. She tried to appeal to him by shouting over the ruckus, "This is ridiculous! If you'll just wait until we reach Cheyenne, I'm sure my brother can clear up this whole situation. Wait"—she reached for her writing box—"I know I must have something in here with my name on it."

Before she could open it, Buck leaned down and grabbed the box and shoved it under his arm. "We'll take this, too." He grasped Annika by the wrist and jerked her out of the seat.

She tried to pull away, but he was so much bigger that she might just as well have been a dust mote fighting against a tornado. Before she could do more than struggle against his relentless grip, Annika found herself standing before the open doorway of the railroad car. The conductor stood outside watching them with a worried frown of indecision on his round face.

"You can't just stand there and let him do this!" she called to him.

The conductor looked hopeless as he measured Buck Scott's stature.

Buck Scott stepped down onto the uneven ground beside the track and then pulled Annika down the steps behind him. "He doesn't have a thing to say about it, Alice. A deal's a deal. Everybody knows that. Besides, if you don't intend to carry out your end of the bargain, then I'll have you arrested for stealing my money."

"What money?" she yelled.

He leaned close and said very slowly and distinctly, as if she were an idiot, "The money I sent you for train fare."

With that, Buck abruptly turned around and began dragging Annika down the line toward his horses. She dug in her heels. He jerked her off them. The conductor, followed by a crowd of passengers, some that had disembarked again just to watch, hurried after them.

When Buck reached his horses and mules, he started to release Annika, then thought better of it. He glanced up at the sky, tried to ignore the harsh wind that had begun to whip around them, and wondered how he was going to tie her valise and writing box to the mules with one hand.

"If I let you go are you going to run off?"

She couldn't believe he was stupid enough to even ask. "What do you think?"

He shouted over his shoulder to the conductor. "Come over here and strap these things onto that front pack mule."

"Mister, listen," the conductor said with sudden reservation, "maybe we should wait until we get to Cheyenne. You can come aboard, we'll haul your animals back in the stock car and—"

"No. I don't have time."

"Listen," the man tried again, "I don't see that it would make much difference one way or the other. Whether she's your fiancée or not, this lady doesn't want to go with you. I think it would be better all around if you waited so we can clear this up in Cheyenne."

Buck stared at the crowd around them. Ladies and gentlemen from the East, farmers, traveling salesmen, a cowhand
or two, some wide-eyed immigrants. They were all watching
him intently. Watching and sizing him up. It had been that
way since he was fourteen years old and taller than most
grown men. Even back then people took him to be much
older, far rougher than he really was, and for that reason he'd
been challenged time and time again by men who had to
prove they were better than the overgrown son of a wandering buffalo hunter.

He recognized the expressions in the eyes of the women.
Some of them watched him with undisguised fear, while others merely stared at him with disdain. He was big and rough,
crudely dressed and he knew it, but his appearance reflected
all that he had experienced during his lifetime. Changing the
outside wasn't going to change all he carried around inside.

He could feel the emotion of the crowd as it slowly shifted
from support to one of suspicion. Sensing his hesitation, the
girl began to struggle harder against his grip. He squeezed
her wrist, was immediately contrite when he saw her wince,
but didn't ease up. As he jerked her to his side, he thrust the
valise and writing box toward the conductor, who had no
choice but to grab them before they hit the ground.

With a lightning swift move, Buck drew his skinning
knife from the sheath anchored to his thigh and pulled
Annika into his arms. He pressed the tip of the knife against
her throat.

She stopped struggling and stiffened immediately. He
glared at the conductor. "Now tie those things on the mule."

The crowd standing nearby was silent. Buck kept his gaze
roving over them, carefully watching the men for any sign of
movement, any indication that one of them was reaching for
a gun.

"I didn't want to have to do this to you, ma'am," he
growled low in her ear, "but you didn't leave me any choice.
You'll see that when we get to the cabin."

Annika was afraid to move. The warm breath that crept
along her ear and neck did nothing to calm the fear that
spurred the uneven beat of her heart. For a moment she
feared she might faint, but never one to be a shrinking violet,

Annika didn't intend to start now. Besides, she thought, she had to keep her wits about her so that she could escape this madman at the first opportunity.

The drummer in the crowd slipped his hand inside his coat and pulled out a handgun. Buck Scott froze and held Annika tighter. He threatened to use his knife, pushed it closer against her tender skin. "Don't do it," he warned the man. "Drop the gun."

The drummer dropped his gun.

When Buck started to walk backward, holding her tight against him with the wicked blade of the long knife pressed against her throat, she did not struggle, but moved with him instead. It was like walking with a solid wall at her back. She knew when they reached his horse, for he paused and lowered the knife long enough to grab her around the waist. Before she expected it, he tossed her up onto the saddle. Ever conscious of the weapon that threatened her rib cage, Annika made no move to escape. Instead, she met the eyes of the conductor and said slowly and carefully, "My brother will be waiting on the platform in Cheyenne. His name is Storm, Kase Storm. Please, please tell him what happened, and tell him I'll be all right until he can find me."

The conductor nodded, afraid to make a move that might anger the man who had vaulted onto the back of the horse behind her and grabbed the reins. The knife was at her throat again.

With the slightest movement of his knees, Buck controlled his prancing horse. The rich brown bay backed away from the crowd. The extra mount and the mules were forced to follow. Buck stared down the crowd until he was far enough out of gunshot range to feel safe, then he spun the bay toward the west, sheathed his knife, and kicked the horse into a gallop.

BUCK Scott couldn't believe his bad luck.

It was one thing to finally come to the decision that he had to marry, but it was altogether another one to learn that the woman who had promised to do so was refusing so adamantly. He wished like hell that he had taken the time to clean himself up, bought a new shirt, and tried to impress Alice Soams. Maybe then she would have come along with him willingly. Maybe.

But as soon as he thought it, he knew that even a new shirt probably would not have helped. She was far too beautiful, too finely dressed, too citified for a man like him. He could tell just by looking at her that she would never fit into his life, never adjust to the cramped quarters of his cabin or the loneliness of life at Blue Creek. So why in the hell didn't he just turn around and take her back?

He'd been asking himself that question for the last few miles, but the answer was not swift in coming. He tried to tell himself it was because she had promised to marry him and a deal was a deal. He'd always stood by his own promises. But deep down when he wasn't trying to fool himself, Buck knew that the real reason he'd carried her off the train in the first place was because she was the most beautiful thing he had ever seen or could ever hope to call his own. From the moment he'd laid eyes on her, it had been impossible to stop himself from wanting to keep her. Time would be on his side, he decided. In time he'd convince her to accept him.

Annika had been too scared to speak for the first few minutes as they thundered across the landscape and he held his knife tight in his fist, close enough to her side to scare her, but expertly enough so that it would not cause her any harm at all. As soon as he had sheathed the weapon she had started arguing with him, adding to the incessant rattling sound from her satchel. Whatever was inside it kept banging and clanging against the side of the pack mule. She had hollered at him for a good quarter of an hour and although he'd tried to drown her out, he couldn't.

"When my brother hears about this, he'll kill you!" She squirmed in his arms, trying to get a better look at him.

Buck didn't let her twist an inch in his embrace. He jerked her up against him and she reacted immediately by trying to pull away. She continued to babble about her brother. He was determined to ignore it.

"My brother's twice the man you are. It won't take him long to find you, even if you plan on riding to the ends of the earth."

Thinking of the secluded cabin in Blue Creek Valley hidden beyond the pass in the Laramies, Buck nearly told her that the end of the earth was exactly where they were headed.

". . . Kase Storm's no coward," she was saying. "No, sir."

The ground beneath them flew past as the big bay horse thundered northwestward. Somehow her words finally registered. Finally he concentrated on the name she threatened him with. Buck eased his hold a bit. "*What* did you just say?" he asked.

"I said you had better release me this minute, or—"

He shook her. "Not that. Who'd you say your brother was?"

He felt her gloating even though he could not see her face.

"Kase Storm!" she shouted over the pounding hoofbeats.

"*The* Kase Storm, the one who used to be the marshal of Busted Heel?"

"Exactly. The Kase Storm who is a crack shot, the man who wiped out the Dawson gang six years ago."

Even Buck had heard of Kase Storm. If this woman's claim was true, Buck knew he was in worse trouble than he could ever imagine.

He nearly believed her. He almost stopped dead in his tracks and turned around, but then he recalled one pertinent fact—Kase Storm was a half-breed.

This striking blonde with the wide blue eyes could not possibly be the man's sister.

Buck smiled smugly to himself and urged his horse on. "My guess is that you heard stories about Kase Storm on the train and now you're using his name to get me to let you go."

"That's not true. He is my brother and when he finds you he's going to beat you to death and shoot you between the eyes, skin you alive, and slowly roast you over hot coals!"

She was really worked up now.

"Jesus, lady. Just pick one, will you?"

She pounded on his thigh with her balled fist. "I'm not joking. If you know what's good for you, you'll turn around and take me back."

"Not a chance, Alice."

"I'm not Alice!" she screamed.

He detected a hoarseness in her voice and was pleased. Anything that might give him some relief from her constant protestations would be welcome.

"You had better shut your mouth, Alice. This cold wind will give you a sore throat if you get it down your windpipe."

She groaned in frustration and then pouted in silence for a while before she said, "I have to relieve myself."

"Sure you do."

"Damn you!"

"Shut up, Alice."

Buck stared up at the base of the mountains looming before them. Even riding double they had made good time, but he knew he would wear his mount into the ground if he didn't put Alice on the mare soon. He glanced over his shoulder. There was no sign of anyone following; nothing but open plain stretched behind them for miles. He decided he had better ride a mile farther before he stopped and tied her to the other horse.

🕉 4 🕉

Annika clung to the pommel of the saddle, her hands numb with cold, and wondered how she would ever escape from this wild man. She ached all over. Her shoulders screamed with pain. He had tied her wrists together and then anchored the rope to the saddle. They raced over the uneven, barren ground against the biting cold wind, heading for the mountain range that lay to the north and west, judging by the position of the late afternoon sun.

Fingers of clouds reached over the ragged mountaintops. Barely streaking the sky, the gathering wisps did not appear to pose a threat to them yet, but Annika knew by the harsh pace the man had set for himself and the way he kept glancing up at the sky that he was certain his earlier prediction of a storm would come to pass.

She was freezing, her satin opera cape little comfort against the sharp wind. Thankful that she had worn her woolen traveling suit, she still chided herself for being foolish enough to bring such an impractical cloak, but she'd never intended to be out riding in it in the first place. She had chosen the satin creation only because it would keep the dust off the suit and if she were totally honest with herself, because it was her favorite new piece of clothing. Before she had called off her wedding, she had envisioned wearing the cape to the opera in Paris while she and Richard toured the Continent on their honeymoon. As she glared at the broad back and shoulders of the man who had abducted her, she wondered if she would ever live to see Richard Thexton again or anyone else, for that matter.

46

Staring straight ahead, she had become mesmerized by the rhythmic pounding of horses' hooves mingled with the rattle and clank of her button collection in the tin inside her valise. The satchel had beat against the pack mule every step of the way. When they suddenly halted, the absence of sound startled her out of her lethargic state.

Buck Scott leapt from his horse in a surprisingly fluid movement and stomped back to where Annika sat imprisoned on the mare. He glared at her long and hard, then started toward the lead mule.

"I've had just about all I can take of that godforsaken rattling," he mumbled aloud as he began to untie her valise. "I don't know what the hell is makin' that noise, but whatever it is, I'm throwing it out."

She nudged the horse with her heels until it turned enough to permit her to watch with growing horror as Buck took her valise off the mule.

"You can't do that!" she yelled. "Don't touch my things."

"Watch me." He started to rifle through her most intimate belongings. When he found the gold embossed tin that was the cause of his annoyance, he shook it and then shook his head.

Annika knew she had to talk fast to dissuade him from pitching the thing away and moving on. "Please, Mr. Scott, I beg of you, don't throw that away. Stuff something into it, if you will, and it won't rattle. That's my button collection. I've had it for years."

"If you've had it for years then it's high time to get rid of it," he said coolly.

"Wait!" She hated the frantic sound in her voice, but he had already raised his arm as if to hurl it away. Annika tried again. "You can't possibly be this cruel. What will it hurt for you to stuff my nightgown in the can so that buttons won't rattle?"

"You won't need them where we're going."

That's exactly what she was afraid of, but she tried not to show her fear. "I might. Besides, they aren't really meant to be used anymore. Most of them are antiques." She ignored the ache in her hands, as she tried to shout over the wind.

"Some of them are very, very old, Mr. Scott. Some of them are from the Revolutionary War."

He dropped his arm and stared at the tin and then back at Annika.

She tried to bargain with him. "If you don't throw them out, I promise not to complain any more until we get to wherever it is we're going."

He cocked a brow and stared up at her for a long moment as if weighing the worth of her promise. Then he reached into the valise and pulled out her delicate white batiste nightgown.

She watched as he wadded the fine material between his huge, rough hands, opened the tin, and stuffed the fabric atop the buttons. A shiver ran down Annika's spine. She was still too scared to feel triumphant over her small success.

After making the silent decision, he shoved the tin back into the valise and then retied it to the mule. Buck walked back toward Annika. She stiffened when he stopped beside the mare and reached up to check the rope that bound her wrists. The skin under the rough hemp was raw and angry looking, her fingers numb. She watched him frown as he stared at her hands. When he glanced up at her, she almost thought she saw concern reflected in the deep blue of his eyes, but she immediately convinced herself she was wrong. A man who would treat a woman so callously would never show concern.

She bit her lower lip and suppressed a shiver of fear when he began to untie the rope. He rewrapped it about the pommel and then took her hands between his own gloved ones. Without a word, without another glance at her face, he began to rub life back into her fingers.

The surprising gesture so unnerved her that she looked away from the sight of his hands on hers. She looked instead at the odd hooded buckskin jacket that had obviously been hand sewn and wondered who had taken the time to carefully fashion the garment for him. It appeared to be lined with fur of some kind, a soft, rich gray pelt that kept him as warm as she wished she were. With the hood up, the fur framed his tanned face. His cheeks were reddened by the wind and cold, his eyes a far brighter blue than she had noticed before. At such close range she could see the fine, curling gold lashes that rimmed his eyes and was astonished to note that such a rugged, uncivilized man possessed eyelashes any woman would envy.

He startled her by glancing up just then to meet her gaze. She found herself staring into his clear blue eyes and then, suddenly aware that he had let go of her, she clasped her hands together.

He cleared his throat. "I'm sorry about your wrists." He began to strip off his gloves.

The apology surprised her, but didn't soften her feelings toward him. She wanted to snap at him, wanted to say that if he hadn't wanted to hurt her he would have never taken her off the train, but, afraid of pushing him too far, she bit her tongue and merely nodded. He reached up and took her right hand and slipped his own glove over it, gently fitting her fingers into the proper places. He did the same with her left.

"Why didn't you bring any heavy clothes, Alice? Don't you own a proper coat?"

Without bothering to again protest the use of the name Alice, Annika shook her head in frustration. "Own a coat? Ha! I own *four* coats, all of them perfectly good, and all of them in my trunks in the baggage car. If you had *listened* back there, if you had only ridden on to Cheyenne and found out who I *really* am, you'd realize I have *four* trunks and *three* crates of clothes I was taking with me to my brother's. But no, you had to act like a barbarian and drag me off the train . . ."

She stopped when his expression darkened. His brows drew close over hooded eyes and he crossed his arms over his massive chest. In a low, barely perceptible tone he said, "You said you'd quit complaining if I didn't throw out the buttons."

Annika clamped her mouth shut.

Buck stared hard at her for another few seconds, then turned away. She watched, wondering if he would really be cruel enough to throw out the tin after all. He walked to the second mule, quickly untied a rolled bundle, and shook out a thick wool blanket. He carried the blanket back to Annika and handed it up to her.

"Put this around you. We've got a long way to go before we camp for the night." With that he stalked back to his own horse and mounted, took up the reins to Annika's horse, and without even a backward glance to see if she had a grip on her mount, started off again at the same breakneck pace.

She struggled to pull the blanket tight around her without losing her seat, and managed to finally tuck it under her. Then she grabbed the pommel and held on for dear life. She had ridden since she was twelve, but never like this, never without control of her own mount. Annika realized it was this lack of control that made her so furious now. This man, this Buck Scott, was now in total command of her life.

She hated that fact as much as she hated him.

As he pushed the horses on, Annika realized that he knew the land well. He followed invisible guideposts as they moved higher, leaving the broad, open plain behind as they entered the foothills. Trees became abundant, changing shape as they climbed. Soon they were surrounded by lodge-pole pines and aspen. The air was colder, dryer. She was glad Buck Scott had seen fit to give her the blanket, and although she tried to convince herself it was the least he could have done, she wondered how he could stand the cold now that he had given her his own gloves.

The mare beneath her was so hot that its sweating hide steamed around her. The horse snorted and blew as it struggled ever upward. She thought to call out to Scott, to beg him to spare the animals, but since her teeth rattled, her bones jarred, and she ached all over, she knew she wouldn't really care if the mare did collapse beneath her. At least then this insane journey would halt.

Annika did not know exactly when they slowed down, for she had dozed in the saddle, but she woke with a start when Buck Scott shouted, "Wake up, Alice, before you fall off."

She had long since stopped protesting that she was not Alice, but at the mention of the other woman's name she wished she could put her hands around Alice Soams's throat and squeeze the life out of her. Or perhaps, she thought, Sioux torture would be more fitting. She had never paid particular attention to her father's vast collection of Indian weapons, but she wished she had some of them right now.

It had grown increasingly dark and gloomy. While she'd dozed the sun had dropped behind the mountains and darkness had gathered in the hollows and ravines that creased the mountainside. She thought they were still traveling northwest, but could not be certain without the sun. She realized, too, that she had lost the urge to escape her captor, at least for now. There was no way she could survive alone in the darkness, no way she could find her way down the mountain. She was in the middle of nowhere, as far as she was concerned, and she did not intend to endanger herself further.

Ignoring the man riding beside her, she straightened, refusing to let him see her exhaustion. She tried to think of a story to take her mind off her mounting trepidation, but unfortunately, the novel in her satchel was Hugo's *Hunchback of Notre Dame*. Since she was at the point in the story where Esmeralda had just been carried to the bell tower by Quasimodo, she couldn't help but liken the poor Gypsy's experience with her own. Between the haunting questions that plagued her, between asking herself where Buck Scott was taking her and what he was planning, she could only relate to the darkness and terror of the tale. Annika surreptitiously glanced over at Buck and then away. There was nothing comforting in thinking about the hunchback. Nothing whatsoever.

So she thought about her family. Had the train pulled into Cheyenne yet? If so, what must Kase be thinking? She hoped that her brother would have the presence of mind not to wire their parents until he attempted to find her himself. She hoped to spare her mother worry, for she knew how frantic Analisa would become. Although her mother had tried to hide her worry behind a brave facade, Annika knew Analisa had been very concerned about her traveling alone. When her mother learned of this abduction, there was no telling how upset she would get.

Annika had no inkling where Buck Scott was headed, nor did she even want to guess what he planned to do to her when they got there. If she had not insisted on experiencing life on her own, if she had not sought adventure, she would not be in this predicament. Silently she cursed a niggling, perverse sense inside her that secretly thrilled to the idea that she was, indeed, having an adventure the likes of which she had never dreamed. And as was her way, she would not let herself accept anything but a hopeful outcome: Kase would find her before anything happened.

He had to.

Except for the short time they paused for a hasty meal of shoe-leather-tough jerky and dry cornbread washed down with a swig of water from his canteen, they did not stop. Reneging on her promise, Annika complained loud and long that she had to relieve herself. Buck finally walked her into a thick stand of trees, intricately tied one end of a rope to her waist and one to his wrist. He told her she had fifteen seconds.

She was too cold and tired, too scared of the black forest around her to even think of escape. She hurried through her task and returned to his side. Determined to fight him every step of the way, she refused when he offered her water to wash her hands and face.

She could tell by his reaction that he didn't take kindly to her stubbornness. When he turned his back on her and led her toward the horses, she tried to smooth her hair, but found it hopelessly tangled. Her hat, or what was left of it, was tilted rakishly to the side of her head. The once-jaunty feather was missing, the hatband loose and trailing over one ear. She ripped the band off and tossed it aside, hoping anyone who might be following their trail would find it. Farther along, she thought about unpinning her hat and dropping it too, but it had become a talisman, a symbol of the civilization she had left behind. No matter how badly battered it had become, she refused to throw her hat away.

It was late afternoon the next day when they reached a pass high in the mountains. The snow had begun hours earlier and continued to drift down in silent, silver dollar–sized flakes. Annika had long since drawn the blanket up over her head, her hat included, and huddled under it. Snow mounded in the hills and valleys of the folds of the blanket. She stared down at her lap, too tired to care where they were going, and watched the wet snow deepen on her lap.

As they started down the pass into a small valley divided by a twisted creek, she could no longer hold up her head.

Maybe I'll fall off. Her thoughts drifted lazily as she dozed. *Maybe then he'll be sorry.*

BUCK glanced over his shoulder and tried to see through the thick curtain of falling snow. Alice was weaving dangerously in the saddle, her head bowed over her hands. He stopped his own horse and pulled her mare up beside him. They had made it over the pass in good time. He could afford to stop.

When Alice's mount came alongside him, Buck dismounted. Without disturbing her, he climbed up behind. He wrapped his arms around her, gently pulled her back into his embrace, and kicked the horse on at an easy walking gait. The longer Alice slept the better she would feel when she woke up. At least that was what he hoped, anyway. Maybe a little sleep would improve her disposition.

As they rode down the trail into the valley, he thought about the consequences of his actions if she happened to be telling the truth. If the girl in his arms was not Alice Soams, then he most likely would be forced to pay for his actions when the truth came out. But deep down he still believed she was Alice, and deep down inside where it hurt, he knew why she was denying it. Who'd want to marry a no-account trapper anyway?

He was angry for having had such a stupid idea as marriage in the first place, but then, his hopes and dreams had never been very realistic. When he was a young boy he had dreamed of becoming a doctor. At twelve, he saw that hope disappear. Not too many years back he had used his untrained skill and prayed he'd be able to save Sissy's life when she took sick. But he'd lost her. He thought he could take care of Patsy, too, thought he could keep her safe until she got so bad he couldn't reason with her or break through the shell of insanity that held her in its grip. Finally, he'd been forced to take her away. It was one of the worst things he'd ever had to do, and he'd had to do some pretty horrible things in his life.

Alice swayed. He pulled her closer. She was a sight. Not quite the polished lady he had first laid eyes on. Covered with trail dust, her hair was soaked and dripping with melted snow. The little hat she'd been wearing so proudly was battered and useless, squashed flat beneath the blanket she'd pulled up over her head. Her many-buttoned, low-heeled dainty boots were scuffed beyond repair. The only decent piece of clothing she had on was his pair of gloves. He hoped that some of Sissy's things would fit her, but he could tell just by looking that she was nearly a head taller than his little sister had been.

He looked past Alice when they rounded a bend and saw the cabin nestled safe in the valley. Blue Creek was not frozen yet; it curved and twisted along the valley floor like a shimmering silver snake as it reflected the leaden sky.

Smoke spiraled up from the chimney. The welcome sight of it set his mind at ease. Old Ted seemed to have been able to manage. He smiled to himself with relief, the problem of Alice and her reluctance suddenly insignificant when he thought of what he stood to lose if Ted had been slack about his responsibilities.

ANNIKA realized that they had stopped and groggily fought to wake up. When she was fully conscious she became all too aware of the fact that Buck Scott was mounted behind her, holding her gently in his arms. She was warmer than she'd been for two days.

She looked around. They were standing before a small cabin, so small that she thought of it as a shack. The entire dwelling would fit in the reception room at home. Thick white smoke escaped from the chimney, and she found herself looking forward to warming herself by the fire. The windows were shuttered on the outside, so she had no idea how many others of Buck's ilk might be waiting inside. How many more barbarians might be waiting to pounce on her?

She forced herself to think of the fire burning inside, of being warm, of having something to eat.

He drew away from her, and when he did she missed his warmth. Buck dismounted and paused long enough to stare up at her with a threat in his eye. "Don't think about going anywhere," he warned.

"Why should I, now that we've arrived at such elegant accommodations?"

Oddly enough, her comment hurt him. She could see it in the tensing of his jaw and the way he glanced at the ramshackle cabin and then back at her before he stared at the ground. She never thought that he might be concerned about her opinion of the place. Was this his home? Was this all he had to offer Alice Soams? With sudden clarity Annika knew why the woman had duped him. The real Alice Soams probably took one look at him and changed her mind.

Wordlessly, he turned away and began to pull the trappings off the mules and pile them in the snow-covered yard. He slapped each animal in turn on the rump and watched as they moseyed over to a trough full of grain that was partially covered by a crude lean-to.

He walked back to the mare and reached up for Annika. Before she could protest that she could dismount alone, he grabbed her around the waist, pulled her down, and stood her on the ground.

Her knees buckled and she nearly fell over.

Buck caught her around the waist and held her until she steadied herself. Weakly she attempted to brush his hands away.

"Let me go," she demanded.

"You going to fall over?"

"No."

"You sure?"

"Let me go or I'll scream."

He cocked his head to the side. "What for?"

"For help, that's what for. Is everyone around here as insane as you are?"

The change in him was immediate. His face flamed crimson and then went white. He stared at her, his eyes cutting blue shards of ice as forbidding as the glacier-topped peaks that surrounded them. For a moment she thought he was going to reach out and backhand her. Instead, he turned away and stalked off toward the cabin. He did not look back to see if she was following him or not.

After what he had put her through for the past thirty-six hours, she did not think anything else could surprise her. She was convinced the door of the cabin would swing wide to reveal a scene out of hell.

As Annika stepped over the unpacked snow, as she felt the cold white stuff spill over into the tops of her once-shining boots and melt around her ankles, she thought of Esmeralda again. She was about to enter the bell tower. Her imagination ran wild. And for the first time ever, she wished she hadn't been such a voracious reader.

Buck Scott had disappeared inside with her valise and writing box. The door was standing wide open. She could just glimpse the edge of a crude table beyond it. The floor appeared to be hard-packed dirt. She heard low voices inside and didn't know whether to be thankful or not that she wouldn't be alone with Buck Scott.

Curious and frightened, she folded back the bright blanket, now soaked from the falling snow. It weighed as heavily on her shoulders as her fate. Annika uncovered her head and drew the blanket around her shoulders. Beneath it her beautiful satin cape was ruined. It was limp—water stained and wrinkled as a steamed spinach leaf. Trying not to dwell on her loss, she made herself move forward, trepidation more than exhaustion slowing her steps. When she reached the threshold she could not force herself to step inside. Instead, she stood gazing in disbelief as one might study a painting in a museum. She had envisioned myriad scenes being played out inside the log cabin, but none could compare to reality itself.

Buck was speaking to an old bearded man who lounged in a straight-back chair pulled up before the fire. The men were oblivious of her as they exchanged greetings. The old man's face was covered by more than a few days' growth of stubble—a few years' growth would be a more accurate description. The beard was gray and long, trailing halfway down his chest. It came to rest just above his protruding abdomen. Above the beard, his cheeks were ruddy, but from heat, cold, or too much liquor, she could not guess.

The old man was dressed much the same as Buck Scott. His clothing was made of hand-sewn leather and wool. He wore worn brown boots instead of moccasins.

"How did everything go, Ted?" Buck asked.

"I don't know how you do it." The old man sighed. "Ain't no wonder you had to get yourself a wife. No way could I do this night and day. I ain't had a good stretch of sleep since you rode off."

"Things were quiet when I left," Buck said.

"That didn't last long," Ted informed him with a grunt.

Annika followed their gaze and nearly gasped aloud when she saw the object of their quiet discussion.

A little girl, a child who looked no older than three and dressed in a creation fashioned from gunnysacks, sat tied to a chair, happily ignoring the men as she proceeded to smash boiled beans on the surface of the table. Her face was covered with beans and her hair, which Annika assumed was blond, was matted with the same substance. Food was everywhere: on the child, the tabletop, the chair, the dirt floor beneath her. Oblivious of the grown-ups, the child played happily, occasionally stuffing a handful of beans into her mouth.

It was the most disgusting thing Annika had ever seen.

Before Annika could react, Buck looked up and noticed her in the doorway.

"Come in and shut the door. You're letting out the heat."

At the sound of his voice, Annika started. At the same time, the child looked up from the enamel plate before her. She swept the plate aside and it thudded to the floor. "Buck! Buck!" She started to squeal as she waved her hands about, wildly seeking his attention.

Annika turned to see what Buck would do and found him studying her intently.

"Mama! Mama!" The little girl turned her wide blue eyes on Annika.

Annika glanced around the room waiting for the child's mother to materialize but no one appeared. Then she noticed the baby was still staring at her with eyes exactly like Buck Scott's.

"Why is she calling me mama?" Annika whispered to Buck.

"Why *is* she doing that?" Buck asked Old Ted.

Unconcerned, Ted shrugged. "Baby's been pesterin' me since she woke up and found you gone. I had to tell her where you went, so I told her you went to fetch her a mama."

"Oh my god," Annika whispered. "So that's why you

asked Alice Soams to marry you? So you could bring her here to raise your child? When were you planning to tell me—her—about this?"

"That's *not* my child," Buck said.

"Ain't this Alice Soams?" Ted asked, indicating Annika with a wave of his hand.

Buck shook his head. "She says not, but that's just because she doesn't want to keep her end of the bargain."

Annika glared at Buck and then at Ted. "I'm not Alice Soams. This man abducted me from the train and dragged me here against my will—" Her blanket had slipped down around her shoulders. She hiked it up again.

"You agreed to marry me," Buck interrupted, but he suddenly sounded as tired as Annika felt.

Ignoring him, Annika appealed to Old Ted. "If you'll take me back to Cheyenne I'll see that you get paid anything you want. My family has money. Lots of it. They won't care how much you ask."

"Would you please come in and shut the door?" Buck's impatience was evident as he issued the sharp command. He walked over to the table and carefully untied the messy child and miraculously, without getting beans on his hands, set her on the ground. The baby then scuttled under the table where she sat contentedly collecting stray beans and piling them in her lap.

Annika ignored them both and concentrated on Ted. "Will you do it?" She hiked the blanket up from where it had slipped down past her shoulders. Her once-festive hat sat askew, barely clinging to the side of her head.

He shook his head. "No, ma'am. I'm gonna leave you two to argue it out. I ain't one to take sides in marital disputes." He dismissed her as he began to gather up his things, a jacket much like Buck's, a rifle he'd laid on the wide wooden mantel, a hat made of a small, furry animal.

Annika felt hope drain away as exhaustion returned to replace it. She leaned against the doorjamb. Taking a deep, resigned breath, she stepped over the threshold. No sooner did she do so than a small, half-balding rodent ran out from behind a barrel near the hearth. Before she could react with more than a scream, it began hopping toward her on spindly

legs and shaking uncontrollably. She thought she was losing her mind when she heard it bark. She didn't think rats
could bark, but then, she'd never been attacked by a rat before.

Its protruding eyes bulged as it sank its teeth into the toe
of her boot. Fortunately for Annika, the animal did little
damage before she shook her foot and sent it scuttling away.
Annika ran across the room and stopped only when she
bumped into the bed, the most substantial piece of furniture
in the room. "That thing just bit my boot!" she protested.

Old Ted stomped across the room and scooped the yap-
ping dog up in his arms, kissed it on the lips, let it kiss him,
and then tucked it into the front of his buckskin jacket.
"What do you expect after you attacked poor little Mouse
like that?"

"It attacked me! Besides, that not a mouse, it's a rat."
Annika shook with anger as she pointed at the offending animal.

Ted looked grievously offended. "Come on, Mouse. We
know when we're not wanted."

Annika turned to Buck. Her appeal fell on deaf ears. "It
bit me," she whined.

"You set on leaving, Ted?" Buck chose not to deal with either the attack or Annika's discomfort.

"I'm not staying here. If I get snowed in, no telling how
long I'll be stuck with all of you.'

"Thanks for taking care of Baby for me," Buck called out
as Ted slammed the door behind him.

Buck and Annika stared at each other in uneasy silence
until the little girl crawled out from under the table. She toddled over to Annika and stopped a foot away. One sniff told
Annika that there was more that needed to be cleaned off the
child than beans.

The baby stared at her, one finger in her mouth. With the
other hand she patted the mashed beans clinging to her hair.

"Mama?"

Annika sighed, dropped to the edge of the bed, and covered her face with her hands.

"How about making us something to eat?" Buck said.

At the sound of his voice, Annika slowly lowered her

hands. She stared down at the dirt floor. Here and there, small bits of grass and pine needles were imbedded in the well-packed earth. She knew he was waiting for her to answer, that he was standing there staring at her as he had done since the moment she stepped inside. Dragging her across the country at a breakneck pace had not been enough. Now, when she was so tired that she thought she might close her eyes and sleep sitting up, he wanted her to make them something to eat.

When she finally looked over at Buck, Annika was glaring. "Are you talking to me?"

"Who do you think I'm talking to?"

Annika glared at the messy baby who had just taken another step toward her. She made no gesture that might encourage the child to come any closer.

Buck glanced at the baby and then at Annika. "You can cook, can't you? I'm hungry enough to eat a bear."

When he turned away, dismissing her as he lifted one of the packs that he had just carried in, Annika stood up. The blanket fell away from her and dropped to the bed. She reached out and grabbed the first object she could lay her hands on—a brass candle holder that rested on a rough crate upended beside the bed.

Taking careful aim, Annika drew her arm back and let the candle holder fly.

❧ 5 ❧

T HE candlestick hit him square on the shoulder.

Instinctively, he ducked and swung around, ready for another attack. "What the—" Buck crouched behind the table when a whiskey crock flew past his left temple, hit the wall, and shattered behind him. The odor of white lightning permeated the room.

The woman was in a rage. He watched in fascination as she reached up and tried to jerk her hat off her head. She winced when the huge hat pin yanked her hair before she could untangle it. Tossing the ruined hat aside, Alice marched toward him, brandishing the long, lethal-looking pin.

"Come out from behind there, you coward." She shoved aside one of the barrels he had fashioned into a chair and started around the corner of the table. Buck held his hands out in front of him.

"Listen here, Alice."

"Stop it!" she screamed. "I can't take any more. *I'm not Alice.* Do you understand?" She leaned close, her face scrunched with anger, her tone threatening as she pointed to herself. "I'm Annika Marieke Storm. I was born in Boston on October seventh, eighteen seventy-one. I don't know you, I don't even *care* to know you, and if you don't take me back to Cheyenne right now, I'm going to kill you!"

"With a hat pin?" He couldn't help himself. He started laughing. His reaction obviously did not seem to sit well with her, for she drew back her arm, intent on stabbing him.

Buck reached out and grabbed her wrist. With very little

pressure at all, he squeezed until she opened her hand and dropped the pin. He let her go, then stooped to retrieve the silly weapon before Baby found it and hurt herself.

He stared down at the ornate object in his hand, amazed at how something as simple as a hat pin could tell so much about a person. It was five inches long, topped by a perfectly formed gold butterfly poised in flight. Tiny pearls and small, colorful jewels ornamented the filigree wings. He twirled the pin between his fingers and studied the butterfly a moment longer, as resignation began to replace what had only been a nagging suspicion until now.

He had indeed abducted the wrong woman.

Why else would someone who was apparently so wealthy, not to mention beautiful, have accepted his offer of marriage in the first place? This woman would not have needed train fare, not by the looks of her possessions. He looked up and found her still fuming. She watched him closely, her breasts rising and falling rapidly with every breath. She looked like a wilted hothouse flower with her black cape sodden and limp, the hem swirling about her ankles as it brushed against the dirt floor. The once-rich satin, as dark as midnight, was out of place against the natural furs, wood, and fibers of the crude contents of the cabin.

When he failed to respond to her outburst, as he alternately stared at her and then the hat pin, she lowered her voice, shook her head, and said, "I think you're a stark raving lunatic."

He reacted before he could think. The hat pin was forgotten. It fell to the floor as he reached out for her, grasped the edges of her cape in his two brawny hands, and jerked her off her feet. Nose to nose, he glared down into her startled eyes and rasped out in a voice even he did not recognize, "Don't you ever, *ever* say that again." He gave her a vicious shake. "Do you understand?"

Speechless, the woman nodded. Tears quickly flooded her eyes. He reacted to them as if she had slapped him. Then Buck suddenly realized that he was holding her off the ground by a handful of material bunched at her throat. He let her go instantly and stepped back as if touching her had scalded him.

He thought she would react with her usual cutting anger and berate him with her tongue. Instead, she backed away. He was breathing as if he'd tried to run up the face of the mountain. When she quickly put the table between them and scurried away to sit perched on the edge of the bed, he knew he must have scared the hell out of her.

Buck opened his mouth to apologize, then snapped it shut. He'd be damned if he apologized to her. She'd goaded him into his outburst when she voiced his one great fear aloud. Besides, this was the most quiet she'd afforded him in nearly two days and he didn't want to do anything to set her off again.

I'll just let her stew awhile, he thought as he bent to re- trieve the hat pin and then walked over to set it out of Baby's reach on the wide mantel above the fireplace.

He glanced over his shoulder and found Baby sitting con- tentedly in the middle of the floor before the fire, happily playing with the sorry hat Alice had thrown down during her tirade. He couldn't think of her as anyone but Alice yet, no matter who she might be. A glance in her direction told him he'd scared her into submission, at least for a time, but he didn't think the respite would last long.

Feeling an intense need to get away from her and her downtrodden expression, Buck pulled up the hood of his coat and crossed the room. He tossed a command over his shoulder, "Keep Baby out of trouble," and slammed the door behind him.

HANDS clasped together in her lap, Annika stared at the door. Never, not once in her entire life, had any man ever laid a hand on her in anger. Her father and brother were big men, both capable of violence when called upon to fight injustice, but gentle as lambs around her and her mother, or any other woman for that matter. Richard had never even raised his voice to her. Annika sat immobilized on the edge of the huge, hand-hewn log bed and wondered exactly what had set Buck Scott off like a powder keg. After all, she'd been in- sisting that she was not Alice Soams ever since they first laid eyes on each other. Why had calling him a lunatic suddenly turned him into one?

She stared at the child sitting nearby and watched her repeatedly put the ruined hat on and take it off again. Then the little girl looked up and smiled through bean smears and said, "Mama?"

"I'm not your mama."

"Pretty?" The baby looked up at her, a mischievous smile on her dimpled face.

Annika tried to ignore her but found it impossible. "Gorgeous." When she heard the thick sarcasm in her tone, she immediately felt contrite. It was not, after all, the child's fault her father was a madman. "It's really pretty, honey. You can have it."

"Keep it?" The child stood up and slowly toddled over to her, seeking approval again. "Pretty?"

Annika stared down at the little girl with the unevenly cut hair that was still adorned here and there with mashed beans, the dirty mouth, and spotted, sackcloth gown. Annika shrugged, but could not help but smile in return. "Real pretty. Pretty as a picture."

"Got a pitcher!" The child ran to a wooden box that sat against a far wall. She bent far over to the side of the box until her head and shoulders disappeared, her back end up like a duck diving for dinner. A round, tin-backed mirror hit the floor, then a string of glass beads. Finally, Baby pulled out a crumpled piece of paper from a *Harper's Bazaar* and ran back to Annika with it.

"Pretty ladies," the baby said.

Annika held out her hand and accepted the tattered page. She glanced down at an illustration of women's fashions that had to be a good six years old, older than the child herself.

"That's very pretty." She handed it back to the little girl and asked, "What's your name?"

"Baby."

Annika frowned. "That's your name? Baby? Do you have another name?"

Baby shook her head.

Annika persisted. "Is your name Ann? Or Susie?"

Obviously, the child thought her daft, for she laughed with glee. "Baby!"

"My name is Annika." It felt good to say it aloud. Good to know she had not completely lost her own mind.

"Ankah."

"Sort of. Try Ah-nee-kah. Can you say that?"

Baby nodded. "Ankah."

"At least she won't call me Alice," Annika whispered to herself.

The door swung open and Baby's attention was quickly diverted. "Buck! Buck!" she yelled, and ran to hug him about the knees.

Buck Scott, loaded with more goods from the pack mules, looked over at Annika the minute he entered the room.

Just as quickly, she looked away.

She heard him moving about, stacking things here and there, but refused to look at him. Not only was she furious at the way he had treated her, but also she was afraid that he might lose his temper again. If he hit her, there was no way she could protect herself, no way she could stand up to his strength. For once her instinct for self-preservation took precedence over her anger. It was suddenly all too clear that she was alone and helpless, confined to a small cabin where almost anything could happen to her while he held her prisoner.

He wasn't an easy man to ignore. She heard him ask, "Old Ted give you a bath, Baby?"

As he shrugged out of his coat and hung it on a peg near the door, Annika noticed that the flannel shirt beneath it fit him like a second skin. Without the thick coat he didn't seem as imposing, but the outline of muscles that bunched beneath the tight shirt did little to calm her nerves.

Baby shook her head no in answer to his query.

"Then you need one, don't you?" he asked.

"Uh uh." Baby shook her head.

"Oh, I think you do."

Annika wondered how he could sound so nonchalant after the intensity of their confrontation. How could he simply refuse to acknowledge her presence? She glanced over at Buck again and found him busy setting a half barrel on the floor before the fireplace. Then he proceeded to fill it from a kettle that was hanging above the fire.

Baby was trying to pull her dress over her head. Annika saw the pitifully tattered underwear the little girl wore, her bare but perfectly shaped little legs, her dancing feet. She watched the two as they chatted. Baby told Buck how she had chased "the Mouse," which Annika assumed was Ted's repulsive little dog. Buck told the child he had bought her a surprise in Cheyenne. That nearly put off the bath when Baby demanded he give her the gift immediately. Buck turned it into a bribe by promising to show her only after the bath.

He threw another log on the fire and stirred the embers beneath the burning wood. The room was already warm, the air close and dry. Exhaustion had quickly replaced her fear as Annika watched Buck and the child he simply called Baby. She stood up slowly, moving quietly to avoid calling attention to herself, and drew off her cape. She draped it over the back of a chair.

Her traveling suit was wrinkled beyond hope, but the cape had kept it relatively dry. She finger combed her hair, which helped very little, and then walked back to the bed. She longed to stretch out and lose herself in sleep, but did not dare, not with Buck Scott so close and her fate as yet undetermined. Instead, she propped herself up with the pillows leaned against the wall and stretched her legs out before her, careful to dangle her feet over the side so that she did not rest her boots on the faded quilt.

She folded her arms beneath her breasts and sighed, wondering briefly if absentminded Aunt Ruth had foreseen any trouble of this sort brewing in the stars and had forgotten to warn her.

Buck continued to ignore her. The splashing and giggling had increased as Baby enjoyed her bath before the fire. Half asleep already, Annika watched as Buck hunkered down on his haunches beside the tub and scrubbed the little girl until her pink cheeks shone like a sunset sky. He convinced her that he would not get soap in her eyes if she let him wash her hair, and amazingly enough he did not. Soon the once-dingy-looking hair had been transformed into ringlets of gold. Watching the two of them together, Annika marveled at the incongruity of the big, rough man with the tenderness he displayed toward the little girl.

Annika thought of her own matted hair, her aching muscles, and wished she was the one in the half barrel soaking in the warm, soapy water having her hair washed for her. She could almost imagine what it would be like to feel clean again, to wrap up in one of the thick woolen blankets or furry pelts piled near the end of the bed and sleep until she was no longer tired.

She yawned and felt herself slouch lower, sinking into the pillows behind her.

BUCK lifted Baby out of the makeshift tub, set the soap on the hearth, and wrapped the little girl in a thick blanket. He used an end to towel her hair dry, then carried her over to the table where he sorted through the packages. Finally, he located a small pair of black leather shoes and pulled them out. He'd measured her little foot with a string and carried it into Cheyenne where he bought the shoes at Myers and Foster's after reading the advertisement in the store window. The Little Red Schoolhouse shoes had cost him ninety cents, but they were guaranteed not to rip.

He pulled them out of the pack and handed them to her. Baby hugged them close, cradling her first pair of real shoes as if they were the greatest treasure in the world. "Shoes and hat," she announced.

"A hat?"

"Ankah's."

Buck glanced over his shoulder at the woman asleep on his bed. She'd been so quiet for so long that he had suspected as much, but ashamed of his earlier outburst, he had been able to avoid looking at her. He was relieved to see that she had not been too scared to fall asleep. He needed time to think without her staring holes in his back.

"You're a lucky girl," he told Baby softly.

She agreed with a nod. Her curls bobbed up and down.

"A sleepy one, too."

"Nope." She shook her head.

"Yep." He nodded. "How about if I lay you on the bed by

. . . the pretty lady and you go to sleep. You have to be still, though."

"Shoes?"

"You can't wear them to bed, but you can hold them."

After a moment she agreed, and Buck carefully laid Baby far enough from Annika so that the child would not disturb her. The bed was wide enough to accommodate all three of them comfortably, but tired as he was, Buck turned away from the tempting sight.

He tucked the blanket around Baby and motioned for her to stay silent. Baby put her own finger to her lips and said, "Shh," in response. When Buck turned away from her, she was playing quietly with her new shoes. Annika did not budge.

Buck returned to the table and studied the woman's slant-topped writing box that was sitting beside his things. It was bordered with gilt scroll work, the writing surface padded with rich, brown leather. He reached out to touch it, glanced over to see that Annika still slept, then lifted the lid. The contents were in a jumble from the ride to the cabin. He imagined she usually kept them all neatly arranged. He took out the inkwell, which in itself was like none he'd ever seen, but he had heard of the spill-proof sort. He studied it intently, then set it aside. There were various sheets of plain paper, matching envelopes, a small case that contained pens and nibs. There was a odd, rectangular book decorated with hearts, flowers, and cherubs, all mingled in wild disarray on the cover.

Buck picked it up and opened the cover. The flyleaf read, Forget Me Not . . . A Collection of Thoughts and Observances. And beneath that, in the same beautiful handwriting was the name Annika Marieke Storm, 1892.

Buck carefully returned the book to the box without reading more.

"My brother is Kase Storm."

He had not believed her.

"When my brother hears about this, he'll kill you."

The Kase Storm he'd heard about would probably do just that.

What would happen to Baby then?

Buck dragged a chair over to the fire and sat down heavily. He crossed his long legs at the ankles and his arms over his chest and stared into the flames. There was no getting around it now. He'd done a stupid thing when he had not listened to her. Wanting to convince this beautiful woman he thought was Alice Soams that she should indeed follow through with their bargain and marry him was one of the biggest mistakes he'd ever made. He'd have to apologize to Annika Storm tomorrow and then take her back down the mountain to her brother. There was no getting around it.

He wondered how his letter to Alice Soams had ended up beside Annika Storm on the train, then realized all too clearly that the real Alice must have seen him long before he'd seen her and left the letter beside Annika just to throw him off her trail. Her rejection was all too clear.

"I think you're a stark raving lunatic."

He was mad to have forced Annika Storm off the train. It was a stupid thing to have done even if she had been Alice Soams. He should never have decided to marry. Never. It was a ridiculous idea. What woman in her right mind would want to marry a potential madman?

Buck turned around to look over at Baby and found her curled up asleep beside Annika Storm. The child looked like an innocent cherub with her pink cheeks and thick blond ringlets. When he took the woman back down the mountain, he ought to find a decent home for Baby, too.

No one would fault him for giving her up, no one but himself. He had tried to keep her for three years now, even gone so far as to carry her along hunting and trapping in a pack on his back once she grew too old to leave her behind asleep in the cabin in the big box crib he'd made her.

Now she was getting far too old and rambunctious to carry on his back papoose-style, and Baby was much too active to sit by quietly while he stalked the game that provided the furs for their livelihood. Leaving her home alone was impossible. He had thought that marriage would solve his dilemma, hoped that Alice Soams would accept the responsibility of raising his niece along with her other duties as his wife, but now his well-laid plans had gone awry. Alice

Soams had rejected him outright and he had kidnapped the sister of the man who had wiped out the Dawson gang.

Things couldn't get any worse.

Buck stood and ran his hand through his hair. Baby's dirty dress lay on the floor near the tub, so he picked it up and rinsed it out in the tepid bathwater. Wringing it out, he hung it near the fire where it would dry. He realized the voracious appetite he'd possessed earlier had flown, but he ambled to the table and opened one of the packs anyway and took out a strip of leftover jerky. He opened the door and glanced out at the still-falling snow. The large flakes drifted soundlessly to earth, a thick curtain of white that prevented him from see-ing farther than a few inches. He hoped it stopped before the pass was closed. Buck reckoned Old Ted had made it through or he would have been back, pounding on the door by now.

If the old man stuck to his usual habits, Buck wouldn't see Ted until spring. It was a stroke of luck that the old man had happened by when he did and was able to care for Baby, or Buck would have been forced to take the child with him to Cheyenne.

The fire had burned low. Buck threw on another log and sat back down. Maybe he was already crazy and didn't know it. Crazy as Pa and Patsy. Pa hadn't even known him at the end. *Why should I be any different?* he wondered.

No, things couldn't get any worse. Of course, he'd been thinking that most of his life now, and fate had tended to make him a liar. Things always got worse. He could hardly remember the good years anymore because they hadn't lasted long at all.

He'd been born in Kentucky in 1860, and then his father, Silas, went off to fight for the Confederacy a year later. They lived in the hill country then, and Buck grew up running the hills and hollows barefoot and carefree. His mother, Irene, a midwife for the surrounding hamlets, let him roam as far as he cared to go as long as he promised to follow the creek bed so he wouldn't lose his way. She took him with her when-ever she went to deliver babies.

Silas returned from the war defeated in spirit and took to moping about their log cabin, unwilling to do little more than swill whiskey, stare at the wall, or make love to his wife. When Buck was six, his sister Patsy was born. Two years later, his mother had Sissy. Irene kept them together by selling her home-brewed elixirs and midwifing. From the time he was old enough to learn about the herbs and potions she mixed as curatives, Buck had dreamed of becoming a real doctor, a healer.

When Buck was twelve, Irene Scott ran off with a handsome drummer who'd come to the door trying to sell them a new frying pan. Two things came of her betrayal: Silas Scott was forced to get up and care for his children, and Buck's dream of becoming a real doctor died.

A drifter passing through told Silas there was money to be had hunting buffalo out West and one man's word was all it took to convince the elder Scott to pack up Buck and the girls, who were then six and four years old, box a few staples, and leave Kentucky behind. They set out for Dodge City in a rickety wagon pulled by two old mules. Buck had charge of the girls from then on. He was to see that they were fed and "made to mind," as his pa put it.

Just as his mother had taught him to read from the only books they owned—*Doctor Jayne's Medical Almanac and Guide to Good Health*, a frayed-edged Bible, and a tattered copy of *Antony and Cleopatra*, one volume of a set another drummer had left behind as a sample—Buck taught Patsy and Sissy to read. Patsy took to reading like a duck to water, but Sissy had been another matter. Whenever she had tried to concentrate, a passing butterfly, a sudden noise, or a mere daydream would cause her to stare off into space. Her lack of attention was more than Buck's patience could stand and he soon gave up on her. Patsy read until she had memorized the story of the Egyptian queen and made Buck and Sissy act out the drama with her.

The winter of 'seventy-two was the first that the Atchison, Topeka, and Santa Fe operated out of Dodge City. The coming of the railroad helped to further eradicate the wild buffalo herds around Dodge, for the hunters could then ride along and shoot the animals from the windows of the train. Hides were loaded on box cars that sat waiting on spur lines, cars piled from floor to ceiling with buffalo skins. So many

of the beasts had already been destroyed that by the time
Silas Scott arrived in Dodge with his children, the herd had
almost been totally annihilated.

They lived like nomads. Buck tried to control the girls, but
they ran wild most of the time, blond, dirty-faced urchins
who had only each other for friends. They never stayed in
one place long enough to plant the seeds of friendship, nor
did any of the town's children extend their friendship. Like
Gypsies, his family traveled from place to place, always living on the outskirts of towns in ramshackle cabins or cheap
boardinghouses.

When the Kansas plain was played out, word spread that
there were buffalo to be had in Texas, so Pa moved them
south. By 1876 the Texas and Pacific Railway had completed a line to Fort Worth and another massacre began in
earnest. Buck was sixteen by then and had been skinning
alongside his pa for two years, ever since the day he became
fed up with trying to care for his sisters. He thought of those
years as a skinner as the bloody years, because all he saw
from morning until night was blood, until it seemed the
world was awash with it.

A good buffalo hunter could skin from one hundred and
fifty to two hundred buffalo a day, and Buck was one of the
best. Down in Texas he worked with one hand on the knife
and another ready to grab his rifle in case of an Indian attack
whenever the local tribes did not take kindly to the slaughter
of the mainstay of their diet.

Not only did he learn to skin, but he alternated with the
others in his crew in stretching and baling hides. The odor of
death was always about him, death mingled with blood and
grease. He spent every waking hour killing and stripping
buffalo of their hides.

When it looked like the Texas herd was nearly gone, Silas
Scott wanted to be ahead of the rest, so they moved north in
'seventy-nine. They'd been working the north for two years
when the Northern Pacific laid track across the Montana
plains. They and others like them had become so proficient
at their work that in two years there wasn't a buffalo to be
seen. Silas Scott found himself out of work for the first time
in ten years.

Buck asked his father if he ever thought about farming when homestead land was up for sale in the north, but Silas would have none of it. Why should they break their backs sweating over the soil when they had made a small fortune hunting? Silas ignored the fact that he had spent most of their fortune on fancier rifles, whiskey, ivory-handled knives, women, and gambling.

They became wolfers then, joining the many who poisoned the buffalo carcasses and took the hides off the wolves, badgers, kit foxes, and coyotes that came to feed on the carrion. When the carcasses were stripped clean, money could still be had by scavaging the hooves, horns, and bones that had been left behind. The same railroads that had once hauled hides now transported tons of buffalo bones to the East. Sugar refineries used fresh bone char to purge raw sugar liquid. Phosphorous fertilizer was made from weathered bones.

Sissy grew more and more vacant over time. Still, she helped them during the wolfing and bone scavaging. She was never one to want to leave and go off on her own like Patsy, who often disappeared for weeks at a time and then would show up back in the camp with one of the hunters. The men in camp took advantage of Sissy as often as they could get away with it. For a bauble or a new ribbon she would sleep with them, until Buck spent as much time fighting to protect her as he did skinning.

Buck had finally insisted they needed a real home. Over the years his father had become more and more forgetful and irresponsible, so much so that Buck finally decided it was time to make the decisions for all of them. He rounded up Patsy and her common-law husband along with Sissy and Silas and moved them all to Blue Creek Valley high in the Laramies where they could survive doing what they had done for the past ten years away from the condemnation of polite society in the small towns and growing cities of the West.

Thus the "bloody years" ended, almost as quickly as they had begun. Although he was still hunting, trapping, and skinning, his work was secondary to the way things had fast deteriorated among the occupants of the mountain cabin. He called the ensuing years the "crazy years," and for good reason. By then, his pa had gone completely insane, former forgetfulness deteriorating into sheer madness.

It tore at Buck's insides whenever he thought about the way he'd had to keep his father tied to his bed when he was not around to control him. But it was that final day, the last day he saw his father alive, that would burn forever in Buck's memory.

He hadn't been far from home when the screaming had started. As was his usual habit, he was up the mountainside checking his traps when he heard it, high and piercing, like banshees from hell. He'd never forget how he had prayed that the haunting screams would stop as he pounded down the mountainside toward the cabin. But the hideous screaming went on and on, intensifying as he burst in the door and found his father standing over the blood-soaked body of Patsy's common-law husband. Patsy clutched Sissy in the corner. Their eyes were wide and wild, both of them screaming incessantly as they watched Silas methodically slice the skin off the other man with the same skill and dexterity he'd once used on buffalo.

Buck hadn't hesitated. He'd shouldered his rifle and killed his father then and there.

Suddenly, the slightest sound behind Buck startled him out of his dark thoughts. He sat up straight in the chair, glanced over his shoulder, and saw Annika Storm sitting on the edge of the bed, looking disheveled and disoriented.

He stood up and shoved his hands into the waistband at the back of his pants. The way she was staring at him made him want to shake her again, but that was exactly why she was looking at him as if he were some sort of monster. A log on the fire behind him popped and shattered, sending sparks up the chimney. He knew he should put her mind at ease, tell her he knew who she was and that he'd take her back as soon as they could travel, but damned if he didn't hate to admit he had acted like the crazy man she'd accused him of being. The crazy man he was sure to become.

He watched her stand and steady herself with a hand on the edge of the bed. Her wool skirt and matching jacket were a mass of wrinkles, her hair had fallen down around her shoulders. It was longer than he had suspected, fine as spun golden threads. Her eyes were deep, dark pools of worry, smudged with purple shadows beneath them.

"I know who you are," he said slowly.

"Here we go again," she mumbled.

He heard her clearly and shook his head. "No, really. I know you're who you claim to be. I read your name in your book."

"My book?"

"The one in your writing box."

She nodded. She didn't like him touching her things. "It's too bad you didn't think to do that before you dragged me off the train." Then she glanced at her valise and the writing box on the table. She looked at Buck again. "When will you take me back?"

He wished she would stop staring at him with such accusation in her eyes. It was beginning to wear on his nerves. She was holding her hands together in front of her, clutching her fingers against her waist as if to keep them from trembling.

He was no good at this and he knew it.

"We'll head back to Cheyenne as soon as the snow lets up," he said.

"Good."

"Your brother really is *the* Kase Storm?"

A look of smug satisfaction lit her face the minute his words were out. Vastly relieved, she said, "Yes, indeed he is, Mr. Scott, and I'm sure you'll live to regret what you've done."

"Ma'am, I already do, believe me."

She took a step forward, her fear forgotten for the moment. He was glad of that at least, but he was certain, too, that it meant she was about to return to her outspoken ways.

"Don't think you can just apologize and I'll be willing to forget what you have put me through."

"Don't think I'm going to apologize," he warned, " 'cause I'm not."

She took another step in his direction. "No?"

"Nope."

"Perhaps you'll apologize when you are looking down the barrel of my brother's gun."

"Don't hold your breath."

She turned red. "Just wait and see."

"You always go running to your brother to fight your battles for you?"

"I've never had to before, but then I've never been abducted before."

"That what you call it?" He stepped closer to her until they were nearly toe to toe.

"What do you call it?"

"Mistaken identity."

"Ha!" She practically shouted the word. "*I* was never mistaken. I knew exactly who I was. You wouldn't listen."

Compelled to touch her shining hair, he reached out to lift a lock of it off her shoulder.

She swatted his hand away.

"How can Storm really be your brother when he's a half-breed?"

She stiffened as soon as the word was out. "He's half Sioux. And he's my half brother. I look like my mother. She's Dutch."

Buck sighed. There was no reason for her to lie when there was her name in her journal to back her up. It wouldn't do any good to take her to Cheyenne and dump her there. By now Storm had his description from the other passengers and would ride him down. He suddenly remembered the well-dressed half-breed he'd seen waiting on the platform for the noon train. A sinking feeling in his gut told him that man must have been Kase Storm.

Baby mumbled in her sleep and both of them immediately looked in her direction. Then Annika looked at Buck.

"Ted's gone. What will you do with her when you take me back?"

He shrugged. "I'll take her along. She's used to riding with me."

He watched her frown. "But it's freezing outside," she said.

"She's used to it."

They were silent for a moment. He waited while Annika

looked around. She was certainly a beauty. Tall, too. Tall enough not to make him feel like an awkward giant the way most women did. Her stubbornness he could do without, but he liked her courage. The only time she'd lost it was when he'd grabbed her, and Buck had to admit to himself there weren't many men who wouldn't have backed down under the circumstances. He couldn't help but admire the way her body filled out the unflattering suit she was wearing. He wondered what she'd look like in a real dress, a soft one that clung to her like a second skin.

"You married?" He wanted to bite off his tongue the minute the words were out.

She looked startled, then masked her surprise with a haughty glare. "That's none of your concern."

He reached out and grabbed her left hand before she could react, took a look at it, then let her go. "No ring."

"Don't even think about it, Mr. Scott. I wouldn't marry you if you were the last man on earth."

"No, I expect not. Not that I'd even ask you." He turned away from her and strode over to a big half barrel in the middle of the floor. Straining, he picked it up and carried it as far as the door, set it down, and then opened the portal. Without looking back at Annika, he hefted the barrel, stepped out into the cold, and heaved the dirty bathwater out into the snow.

When he turned around she was standing right behind him.

"I didn't mean that the way it sounded," she said, wondering why she was even half apologizing.

He paused and let the cold air wash over him as he stared down at her, wondering what she was getting at. "I think it was pretty clear."

"I mean, there's someone out there who's perfectly suited to you, I'm sure." She twisted her hands again, not really able to imagine anyone who would marry such an intimidating hulk of a man.

He closed the door behind him and set the makeshift tub aside. The smell of liquor still rode so heavily on the air that he could almost taste it. Wishing he had a swig right now, he contented himself with picking up the remains of the whiskey jug and wiping up the mess with a dishrag.

"Did this woman, this . . . Alice, mean a lot to you?"

Buck looked up from where he knelt on one knee, carefully stacking pottery shards in his hand. "I never even met her. Only wrote her a few times," he admitted. "I answered an advertisement she put in a Boston newspaper."

She pulled out a barrel stool and sat down, then leaned her elbows on the table. "Yet you wanted to marry her."

"I needed someone to watch over Baby while I'm out hunting."

"Your child needs a mother, you mean?"

He stood up and stacked the shards on the workbench. "She's not mine."

"There's no point denying it, Mr. Scott. She looks exactly like you."

He thought Annika Storm looked far too smug as she sat waiting for him to deny it again. "She's my sister's," he informed her.

"Where is your sister?"

He put both hands on the table and leaned down so that he could look her right in the eye when he told her. "She's insane."

He almost smiled. Annika Storm was finally speechless. But not for long.

"Insane?" She eyed him warily.

"That's right. She's living with an old Scotswoman on a ranch outside Cheyenne."

⚅ 6 ⚅

Annika glanced up at Buck Scott and realized he was not the type of man who would tease. She doubted he even knew how. She rested her head in her hands and began to rub her temples with her fingertips.

"Let's see if I have this straight," she said, thinking out loud as she stared down at the worn surface of the table. "I've been abducted by a man who claims he mistook me for his mail-order bride—a woman he only wanted to marry so that she could care for his sister's child. His sister can't care for the child herself because she's insane." Lifting her head, she stared up at Buck and asked, "Have I forgotten anything?"

"Ted's dog bit your shoe."

"Ah, yes. How silly of me." She fought back a smile. So, he had a sense of humor after all. She studied him carefully, wondering what to say next.

It was suddenly all too clear why he had become so furious earlier. In her anger and frustration she had called *him* insane and now that he had quietly admitted that his sister was indeed mad, Annika realized what her unthinking words had meant to him. Her first reaction was to apologize, but again pride stopped her. It was not her way to apologize when she didn't really feel she was at fault. How was she to know that someone in his family was insane? Thank goodness that Buck, like Mr. Rochester in *Jane Eyre*, did not have his sister locked up somewhere in the house.

He turned away to light another lamp and set it in the center of the table, then proceeded to clear away his packs. She

79

watched him as he worked in silence, ignoring her. Somehow learning about his sister made the big man seem more vulnerable. Until now she had thought of him only as an unthinking brute who had kidnapped her and hauled her across country. Suddenly he had become a man with a tragic secret, a man who had proposed to a stranger so that he would have someone to care for his niece. Now it was easy to understand the necessity behind their breakneck journey before the storm hit. He had to get back to the child.

"Are you hungry?"

His soft-spoken question startled her. She started to say no, then realized that she was famished. But would he ask her to cook again?

"A little," she admitted.

Buck wasn't sure when his own appetite had returned, but now he was ravenous. Annika Storm looked far too tired to do anything more than sit, so he proceeded to put together some simple fare on his own.

She watched him as he moved about the room. It gave her a chance to study Buck Scott in his home. He reached up to take a stone crock off a wide shelf lined with similar containers near the table. He set it down and then lifted the lid of a barrel on the floor beneath the shelf. A long, low bench made up the rest of the makeshift kitchen area he had set aside directly behind the table.

Reaching for the knife sheathed at his thigh, he opened the lid of the barrel and then cut off two hunks of the meat that was soaking in brine. He threw them in a frying pan and covered them with water, then set a grate over the coals.

From a dishpan on the low bench, he took a rag and moistened it with water from a bucket nearby. Then, with painstaking care, he wiped off the table. He took two plates from a set of chipped dishes on the bench and set one before her. The utensils stood in a small pitcher on the shelf where Baby could not get to them. Buck gave Annika a knife and fork.

Finally, he spoke. "It won't be much. Probably not what you're used to at all."

Annika tried to smile. "I'm really hungry." When he didn't meet her eyes she knew he was embarrassed, ashamed of his home, his meager possessions. She looked around the place, wanting to say something, anything to make him feel better. Someone had partially papered the wall above the fireplace with illustrated newspaper advertisements in a crude attempt to decorate the dismal surroundings. The futility of the effort was heart wrenching. The pictures had been arranged in a wild collage, the edges ragged and uneven, one overlapping the other. There were advertisements for stoves, shoes, ready-made clothes, and fabric. The lamplight barely illuminated them all.

Had her mother's sod house been so crudely furnished and designed? All these years Annika had glorified the image of her mother living alone in her soddie in Iowa, but somehow in her flights of fancy she never pictured the place with such stark reality. How had her mother survived? Suddenly she realized how very little she knew about her mother's life during those years.

Annika realized that if she were left to fend for herself here in Buck Scott's rustic cabin she would have no idea how to see to even her most basic needs.

She was staring up at the newspaper on the wall when he said, "What were you doing on the train?"

Annika shrugged. It all seemed so long ago now. "I was on my way to visit Kase and his wife." She was thankful for the opportunity to say something, anything, to try to ease the situation, but she decided against mentioning her broken engagement. It was none of his business.

Hunkering down before the fire, he turned the simmering meat with his long, deadly-looking knife. It was a lethal thing; she wouldn't soon forget the feel of it against her throat. She glanced over at the bed where Baby slept peacefully and wondered where Buck Scott intended her to sleep.

"Does Baby have a real name?" She blurted out the question, then fidgeted with her hair.

"That is her real name."

"That's it? Baby?"

"What's wrong with it?"

Unwilling to anger him now that things seemed to be going more smoothly she said, "I just wondered how she'll like being called Baby when she grows up."

"I never thought about it. We just kept calling her Baby and the name stuck."

He pulled up a chair across the table from her while they waited for the meat to finish cooking. Buck was staring at her again. He knew it wasn't proper, but he couldn't help it. She kept looking away from him, and he could almost see her mind working as she tried to come up with something else to say. It surprised him that she had not asked about Patsy again, and he guessed she was dying to know more but avoided questioning him.

Annika wished he would stop staring. She stood up just to escape his eyes. She crossed the room and paused beside her valise, which he had moved earlier. She opened it and took out her hairbrush and then sat down on the edge of the bed. She had no idea how long he intended to cook the meat, so she began to work the brush through her tangled hair while she waited. As she became intent on the task, she nearly forgot about Buck's presence. The feel of the boar bristles working through her hair was soothing, so much so that she expressed her relief with a sigh.

Glancing up, she saw that Buck had not moved. Indeed, he seemed frozen in time as he stared at her in the flickering firelight. His gaze was so bold, so heated, that Annika had to force herself to look down. She wanted to be certain her clothing hadn't just fallen off.

She jumped up abruptly, put her hairbrush back into her valise, and began to pace the small area between the bed and the table. "How old are you, Mr. Scott?" It seemed a safe enough topic.

"Thirty-two."

She stopped her pacing momentarily. "I thought you were younger."

"How old are you?" He found her presence irritated him more than he wanted to admit. He was thankful she had not turned out to be Alice Soams, because the last few hours made him glad his plan had not worked out. He'd lived alone too long to adjust to having someone underfoot. Baby was one thing—she was easy to handle. A talkative woman was another matter altogether.

She drew herself up proudly. "I'm twenty."

"That old."

Annika immediately turned on him. "How old is Alice Soams?"

"She said she was twenty-five."

Annika sniffed.

Buck was hard-pressed to hide a smile.

"Do you think that meat's done yet?" She folded her arms beneath her breasts, saw his eyes follow the movement, and suddenly dropped them to her sides.

"I expect it is." He made no move to get up. If he was stuck with her until tomorrow he decided he might as well keep her on her toes.

She arched a brow and took on an icy tone. "Do you think we might eat before morning?"

"I thought maybe since I cooked it that you could dish it up."

"Think again."

"You used to servants waiting on you, Miss Storm?"

She wanted to snap that, as a matter of fact, she was, but the humble cabin was an all too real reminder of the differences between them. She said nothing.

Buck picked up a cloth and wrapped it around the handle of the frying pan. "If you plan on eating you'd best sit." He stabbed a slab of meat with his knife and dropped it on the plate on her side of the table. "Dig in."

THE lights of Busted Heel shone like yellow beacons through the swirling snow. Kase Storm would rather they had been the lights of his home, but he was thankful enough to reach the outskirts of town before thickening darkness and the dense snowfall caused him to lose his way. He rode straight to the local livery, used the side door that he knew the blacksmith always left open for just such emergencies, and led his black stallion, Sinbad, inside. The warmth in the huge barn was comforting after the ride from Cheyenne, the sounds of the animals bedded down for the night familiar, soothing ones. He saw to his mount, hung the saddle over the side of an empty stall, and let himself out of the barn.

The snow crunched beneath his boot heels as he made his

way down Main Street toward the jail, surprised at the amount of snow that had fallen in so few hours. Disappointment lay heavy on his mind because he knew he would have to spend another night away from his own ranch and Rose, but with the storm as bad as it was turning out to be, there was no way he could go on and chance getting lost in the dark.

He stepped up onto the wooden walk and scraped his boots against the planks before he crossed to the door of the jail and knocked. A lamp was shining in the darkness; he could see it just beyond the window, sitting in the middle of the desk that he once called his own. His short term as marshal of Busted Heel seemed to have been a lifetime ago, but in reality it had only been five years.

No one responded to his knock, so he tried again, louder this time. He heard a muffled curse and smiled to himself. Zach Elliot, his old friend, had taken on the position of marshal when Kase left the job to start his ranch. The only problem was that Zach was past seventy now, just how far past no one knew, and although everyone in town thought he was long past retirement, no one had the nerve to tell the cantankerous old man to quit. They compensated for his slight loss of hearing and occasional forgetfulness by covering up for his mistakes and extricating him from awkward situations.

Not long ago, Zach had misplaced the key to the jail cell—not that there was ever anyone occupying it—but when a drifter decided to shoot out the lights in Paddie O'Hallohan's Ruffled Garter Saloon, everyone had to help look for the missing key before the prisoner could be locked up.

The saloon owner, Paddie, and Slick Knox, the local gambler-turned-barber, acted as deputies when and if they were needed, which was beginning to be more often ever since Wyoming had become a state.

The door opened a crack and Kase found himself staring down at Zach, who was still half asleep. The old man was as colorful in appearance as the life he had led. The former army scout had lived in Texas where he had married a Comanche woman, fathered a son, and then left the area when his loved ones were killed. He was missing one eye, but that never slowed him down. A long thin scar ran down the side of his face. Scar tissue had formed over the sunken hollow where his eye had once been.

Kase never saw the man clean shaven, but the lower half of his face was perpetually covered with stubble. Never a full beard, never smooth shaven. Always stubble.

Zach had taught him to ride, and along with Caleb, taught him to shoot. Zach had been there during the lowest ebb of his life, had helped him patch things up with Rose back when Kase had been too stubborn to admit he loved her. Zach Elliot was as much a part of their family as Auntie Ruth.

"You comin' in out of the cold or you just intend to stand there starin' at me?" Zach barked.

"Open the door a little wider, old man, and I will."

"Shit," Zach grumbled. But he stepped aside, careful to keep all but his head and shoulders well hidden by the door. When Kase stepped inside the reason became clear. Zach was outfitted in his long red drawers.

A black cast-iron stove in the corner of the room kept the building toasting. Kase welcomed the close heat as he stripped off his gloves and hat and laid them on the cluttered desk nearby. Then he began to brush the snow off his coat. He shook his long hair until the snow that still clung to the ends fell away. "I see you haven't cleaned this place since I left it," he said.

Zach countered, "I figured since this mess was here when you were that it was part of the desk." He walked into the open jail cell where he slept, stripped a blanket off the bed, and wrapped it around his shoulders, then trudged back into the main room.

"I know now why you never arrest anyone." Kase nodded toward the empty cell. "Where would you sleep if you did?" He rested his foot against the nickel-plated footrail on the stove and held his hands over the top.

Zach scratched his crotch and yawned. "What are you doin' here anyway? I thought you was pickin' up your sister in Cheyenne yesterday."

Kase's features darkened. "I went to get her, but she never got off the train."

"She miss it on her end or somewhere in between?"

Shaking his head, Kase said, "Neither. You have any coffee? It's a long story."

Zach took a battered coffeepot off the stove and stared down into it for a moment before he shuffled over to a water barrel near the door. Dipping the pot in, he filled it, then set it on top of the small stove. While Kase watched in silence, the old man pulled open the desk drawer, took out a small sack of coffee beans, and spread a handful on top of the desk.

"Pull up a chair and start the tellin'. This'll take a while." Zach then walked back into the jail cell, slipped his gun out of the holster, walked back to the desk, and proceeded to smash the coffee beans with the butt of his gun handle. Except for those few that flew off and hit the floor, there was a sizable pile of smashed and broken coffee beans left, enough for Zach to brush them over the edge of the desk into his hand and carry them over to the pot. "It'll be boiled in a minute."

"I can hardly wait," Kase said as he slipped off his coat and hung it over the back of a chair near the stove. "Ever think of buying a bean grinder?"

Zach ignored his question. "So what happened to your sister?" His concern showed in his face if not his manner as he pulled up a chair next to the stove and sat down opposite Kase. Leaning forward, he listened intently.

"When she didn't get off the train, I found the conductor was already looking for me." Kase stared down at the toe of his boot. "Actually, he was looking for 'the brother of Alice Soams, the blond woman from Boston.' Finally, we realized we were talking about the same woman when I described Annika, but for a while he didn't believe I was her brother."

"Well, you don't look a good goddamn thing like her."

"It took some convincing. Finally, I had the station master tell him who I was. He told me that Annika had been taken off the train when it broke down not far from here by a man who claimed she was this Alice Soams who'd agreed to marry him."

"Sounds like a tall tale to me. Wouldn't the man know his own intended?" Zach rubbed his eyes and shook his head.

"The man didn't know what his fiancée looked like be-

cause he'd never met her face-to-face. He was convinced
Annika was lying."

"Why didn't Annika tell him who she was?"

"She tried. The man took her at knife point. There was a
letter lying on the seat beside her, a letter from this man to
his intended. When Annika tried to deny it, no one believed
her. They thought she was just trying to get out of her promise to the man."

"Well, hell, it's still a free country from what I hear. Why
couldn't he accept the fact that the woman changed her
mind—even if she wasn't the right one?"

"He paid her train fare. I guess he felt that sealed the bargain."

"You say he paid Annika's train fare?"

Kase shook his head, exasperated. "No," he said, raising
his voice, "I said he paid this Alice Soams's fare. And he
thought Annika was Alice. When the conductor described
the man that took her, I remembered I'd seen him on the platform in Cheyenne waiting for the train."

"How could the man be in two places at once?"

Kase sighed in frustration. He was nearly yelling when he
said, "We were all there waiting for the noon train, but it
broke down just outside of Busted Heel. This big trapper
took off riding like a bat out of hell when the announcement
was made. By the time the train finally came in three hours
late, he already had Annika."

"At least you got a look at him."

Kase wished he hadn't seen the man at all. He might have
been able to stem his hatred and worry.

"That coffee smells ready," he told Zach.

The old man got up and picked up two cups from the side
table. "I forgot all about it." He crossed the room, put a
spoonful of cold water into one of the cups, went back to the
stove, and lifted the pot. He set it on the edge of the desk,
trickled cold water down the spout to settle the coffee
grounds to the bottom, and then, a moment later, poured
them each a cup.

It was a moment or two after he had his first sip before
Kase spoke again. Zach respected his silence. Finally Kase

said, "He was a big man, taller than me. Had to be six foot three if he was an inch. Long hair down to his shoulders."

"Indian?"

Kase shook his head and tried the steaming brew. "Buffalo hunter. Long blond hair, beard, blue eyes."

"Buffalo man, huh?"

Without saying so, both men knew that neither respected the men who had participated in the buffalo slaughter. There had been nothing gallant about the work that had been glorified by the periodicals. The poor-sighted animals had been easy pickings for even the least skilled marksman.

A man was now hard-pressed to find one buffalo where countless multitudes had once thundered across the open prairie. It had been men like the one who had carried off his sister that had helped kill them off. Kase had spent five years searching for any stray he could round up until he had a growing herd of twenty head. He'd felt compelled to save the animals that had been the life source of his ancestors.

"Yeah, a buffalo man," Kase said again, "and if he hurts her, I'll kill him."

"What if your sister ain't harmed?" Zach asked.

"What if she's not harmed? What do you think he took her for? To play chess when the nights are long and cold?" Kase slammed the cup down on the top of the stove and stood up. He raked his hands through his hair and walked over to stare out the window. All he saw was his own reflection and turned away. "I'll find her," he promised himself and Zach. "I'll find her and bring her home."

"You gonna tell your folks?"

"Not yet. I went to the police in Cheyenne and offered a ten thousand dollar reward for her return."

"For ten thousand dollars I might just get off my butt and go lookin' for her myself."

"I'm hoping everyone in Wyoming, Montana, and Colorado will be out looking for her."

"Anybody know the man?"

Kase nodded. "Everyone on the train heard his name. Buck Scott. The sheriff called in another trapper who works the southern range who thought Scott lived in the Laramie Mountains just northwest of here."

"I can't imagine a Storm not standin' up for herself."

"She's never really had to, Zach." Kase felt his heart sink. His half sister had followed him around from the time she could walk. She was the one person in his life besides Rose who made him feel strong and wise and good. If anything happened to her, he knew he couldn't live with himself until he saw the score settled.

"You aren't thinkin' on headin' to the ranch tonight, are you?" Zach stood up and stretched. Outside the window, the snow was still falling like thick cotton. "It's too dark for you to see, let alone battle the snow."

"I'll stay at Flossie's tonight." He pulled his watch out of his pocket and flipped it open to check the time. "Things ought to be slow over there with this storm blowing in."

"She's probably still got your old room ready." Zach smiled. "I hear her gals ain't been happy since you married Rose and moved out of the whorehouse."

Kase smiled. "Don't let 'em kid you. I wasn't that good a customer. Only reason I ever lived there was because that old biddy that ran the boardinghouse didn't want a 'breed' living under her roof."

"Well"—Zach scratched himself again—"I can't blame you for that." He stood up and drew the blanket high around his shoulders and neck, pinching it closed with his trail-worn hand.

Kase stood too, picked up his coat, and shrugged into it, then put on his hat. "There'll be reward posters arriving on the train from Cheyenne, so have John Tuttle at the depot hold them for me, will you? I'll be heading out at first light."

The old man walked him to the door and they both looked out into the night and watched the snow fall. "You goin' home in the morning?" Zach asked.

"Yep. I have to tell Rose what happened." Kase stepped out onto the covered walkway. He looked at the sky, wondered where his sister was and how she fared, and said, "I hope the snow stops soon, Zach, 'cause I've got some hunting to do."

SHE couldn't exactly call it a meal. He'd cooked the salt pork, but served no vegetables, fruit, or bread. They ate in uneasy silence, Annika alternately staring down at the plate and then at Buck Scott. He'd been preoccupied with his meal. Whenever she glanced up at him, she found him intent on stabbing a knife into his meat, slicing off far too big a chunk to chew carefully, and ignoring her completely.

When they had both finished, he stood up, took her plate without asking if she was finished, and tossed both plates into the dishpan on the bench against the wall. As the cutlery rattled in the pan, Annika glanced over at Baby. The child slept on undisturbed.

An ever-increasing sense of unease began to unfurl itself inside her when she realized that the time had come for them to bed down for the night. With the big man moving about the room, she was unable to sit any longer, so she stood and shook out her skirt. The wool mountain suit was hopelessly travel-stained and crumpled. Her boots—of a once-dapper, above-the-ankle cut with a row of jet buttons adorning the suede inset—were water stained and mud caked. She rocked forward on her toes and back on her heels as she held the hem of her skirt back and stared down at her ruined boots.

"The storm's picking up. I'm going out to see to the animals. You can get ready for bed." Buck drew on his fur-lined buckskin coat and raised the hood.

Annika stiffened immediately. She turned on him. "I don't think so, sir."

Snow swirled in on the cold draft of air that swept into the room as he paused in the open doorway. He crossed his arms and leaned against the doorjamb. "If you're going to sit up all night, fine, but I intend to get some sleep."

"Just exactly where will you sleep?"

He glanced at her, the bed, and then back to her again. "On the bed."

Thinking that perhaps she had been too hasty, Annika contemplated a night spent on the dirt floor. "And if I choose the bed?"

Buck shrugged. "It's big enough for all three of us."

She felt her face burn with embarrassment. Hating the way he continually ignored her genteel sensibilities, Annika turned away.

"If you're going to change clothes, do it before I get back. It's too cold for me to be waiting around outside very long."

She did not turn around until she heard the door close. If it was not for the fact that she was so tired of wearing the filthy traveling outfit she would have slept in it. Anxious to at least feel a bit cleaner, Annika hurried over to her satchel and took out her button can. She opened it, careful not to send stray buttons flying, and slowly pulled out her batiste nightgown. It was a mass of wrinkles. She held it over the table and shook it in case any of her precious buttons were still caught in its folds.

One slipped out, an English button with a pastoral scene of a couple hunting on horseback engraved on enamel. Scooping it up, Annika stared down at the idyllic scene that was worlds away from the breakneck ride she had experienced with Buck Scott. Carefully replacing the button, she remembered his warning that she should hurry.

Despite the fire crackling in the huge stone fireplace, the room had grown steadily colder. She shivered when she undid the tabs at her waist and slipped out of her skirt. With one eye on the door, she quickly unfastened the long row of buttons down the fitted suit jacket and slipped it off, then hurriedly did the same with the blouse beneath. Deciding to work her underclothing off after she had donned the nightgown, she hastily drew the voluminous gown over her head and shoved her arms into the sleeves.

The wind was beginning to howl around the cabin. She glanced at the ceiling and hoped that the crude dwelling would hold together should the storm worsen. Just as she finished wriggling out of her underclothes and petticoats and was tugging them out from beneath the hem of her nightgown, the door opened and Buck stepped in.

Snow had already built up on the hood and shoulders of his jacket. He looked like a shaggy, hulking bear as he stood in the doorway shaking himself off. He shoved back the hood. His gold and white hair picked up the weak light of the oil lamps. The sky blue of his eyes had deepened to sapphire when he paused to stare at Annika. She stood stock still, clutching the modest, high-necked collar of her nightgown.

☙ 7 ❧

SECONDS passed without a sound as they stared at each other.

Buck wasn't quite sure what to do next. Although neither Patsy nor Sissy had ever thought anything of undressing in front of him, he had found it awkward and always left them alone. He thought he'd given Annika Storm enough time to change. Not only had he gotten damn cold outside waiting for her to slip into her gown, but he thought he'd given her ample time to get into bed.

Instead, he found her rooted to the floor with a stranglehold on the neck of her nightgown. He couldn't help but notice her hands. Her fingers were long and exquisitely tapered, the skin creamy white and unmarred by work or weather. As his eyes swept her from neck to toe, he saw that she still had her shoes on.

"Sleep in your shoes, do you?"

"For your information I haven't had time to take them off."

Buck shrugged out of his coat and hung it on the peg near the door. When he turned around, she still hadn't moved.

"You going to stand there all night?"

"Since you dragged me away with nothing but the clothes on my back, you wouldn't happen to have a dressing gown I might borrow, would you?"

He ran a hand through his hair. "Something in silk, I guess?"

"You don't have to be sarcastic, Mr. Scott. This situation is intolerable enough as it is."

"I'm not exactly thrilled about it either."

He walked over to a lopsided wooden chest that stood at the end of the bed and hunkered down on one knee. Lifting the lid, he reached in and stirred the contents until he came up with a long nightshirt made of thick plaid flannel. Without ceremony, he tossed it at Annika. She caught it and clutched it to her.

"Thank you." Her tone was as chilly as the air in the cabin. Despite the fire, the room was growing colder by the minute.

He watched out of the corner of his eye as she shook out the shirt and carefully inspected it before she pulled it over her head and gown. While she was struggling to get the full sleeves of the nightgown into the sleeves of the shirt, Buck turned around and added more wood to the fire. He checked the stack of wood beside the hearth and decided there was enough to see them through the night. As cold as he expected it to become, all the wood in the world wasn't going to help keep them warm.

He drew a bucket of water out of the barrel by the door and sloshed it into the same basin he'd used to wash the dishes. The woman was sitting on a chair undoing the numerous buttons that fastened her once elegant shoes. In a quick glance he took in her feminine symmetry, her long slender neck, the gentle curve of her shoulders, the indentation of her waist as she bent sideways to reach her foot. Her figure was lush without being full, gently curved in all the places where a woman should be soft and alluring.

Buck bent over and splashed the freezing water on his face and neck. He screwed up his eyes and rubbed handfuls up to his hairline and down over his beard. When he was thoroughly wet, he reached for a bar of soap on the kitchen bench and lathered up, paying no mind to the mess that splattered around him.

Eyes closed, he felt for the scrap of cotton towel, grabbed it, and wiped himself dry. He felt her eyes on his before he turned around, and when he finally faced her, Annika Storm was staring at him again. Wrapped in her nightdress, she was perched on the chair, her feet propped on the rungs. The bright plaid nightshirt almost reached the hem of the snowy white gown beneath it.

A heavy gust of wind hit the north side of the cabin so hard that the place shook. Fine powdered snow hissed through the chinks in the split-rail walls. The oil lights fluttered. The lamp on the mantel sputtered and died.

Buck walked over to the side of the bed and carefully drew the covers over Baby, who had curled into a tight ball. He then moved to a stack of folded pelts on the floor and chose two that were thick, lush gray wolf fur. He spread them atop the bed and folded one side down so that he could slip in. It was too cold to sleep in his underwear as he usually did.

He glanced over his shoulder at Annika seated in silence at the table. She was watching the ceiling as if she expected it to blow away at any moment.

"You plan to sit up all night, that's your doing. I'm turning in."

He watched her stiffen. She glanced at the bed, then at him. "Thank you so much for the grand hospitality."

"I offered you the bed. If you'd wanted it, you'd be in it by now."

Her gaze took in Baby, the wide expanse of empty space, and then darted away. He sat on the edge of the bed and unlaced the rawhide thongs that held his knee-high moccasins closed. "You can make yourself a pallet in front of the fire." He indicated the pile of furs with a nod and said, "Use some of them. When you're done, blow out the light."

SHE couldn't believe the sheer audacity of the man. Annika shivered and rubbed her arms, watching in disbelief as Buck climbed into bed and buried himself beneath the pelts, rolled over with his back to her, and proceeded to go to sleep. She found herself envying the comfort and warmth the bed offered as she went after her own pile of pelts and hides. She spread one on the floor as close to the hearth as she dared, then piled the others atop it.

When she reached for a log to add to the fire, she heard Buck mumble from his lair, "I wouldn't do that if I were you.

Fire gets too hot you won't be able to sleep close to it. Sparks might fly out and set your bed afire."

She dropped the log back on the stack and huffed over to the table to blow out the lamp. The firelight flickered and played over the walls, highlighting the area in front of the hearth, throwing the rest of the room into shadow. Buck Scott was nothing more than a hulking mound in the bed.

Annika crept into the pallet, pulled the thick pelts over her, and tried to ignore the aches and pains she had acquired on the rough overland ride. She rolled from one shoulder to the other, but the hard-packed floor offered little relief. Finally she decided to try sleeping on her stomach. It was better, but not comfortable. Closing her eyes only intensified the sound of the wind as it rattled the shutters and eddied about the outer walls, so she lay awake and watched the flames lick at the logs in the fire.

She tried to imagine what Kase might have done when she didn't get off the train in Cheyenne. Had he wired her parents? She hoped not—not yet anyway—for if all went well and Buck Scott kept his word and delivered her safely to Cheyenne, there was no need to upset them. If the conductor told her brother what had happened, perhaps Kase had started out after her already. She hoped so. She prayed that he ran into them on the trail tomorrow and scared Buck Scott within an inch of his life.

The front door rattled, giving her a start, but it was only the wind trying to get in. The snow was more successful. It continued to force itself through the cracks and chinks in the walls. Mud daubing used to seal the many openings had frozen solid, cracked, and fallen out. She wondered if there would be anything left standing by morning.

The fire burned low; the room grew chill. Still, she could not sleep. When she heard the bed ropes creak and the rustle of blankets, Annika squeezed her eyes shut and feigned sleep. She gripped the covers tightly beneath her chin and waited, afraid to twitch or even breathe while Buck Scott was up prowling around. He padded across the small space, and although she dared not look, she could feel him standing over her.

She didn't move a muscle. He just stood there.

Finally, she peered out from beneath her lashes, but he was still somewhere behind her where she couldn't see him. Just as her taut muscles began to ache unbearably, Buck moved. Carefully stepping over her, he bent and picked up a length of wood.

Annika waited in horrified silence while he raised it from the pile.

This is it. He's going to bash my brains in.

She was ready to scream, set to roll away to try to escape the killing blow when he carefully set the wood on the fire. He hefted a poker, stirred up the embers, and put the poker down. Finally, cupping his hands, he blew on them, stepped over her again, and padded away.

Annika breathed an audible sigh of relief.

She closed her eyes again, then realized he was still moving about the room. Once more he approached her pallet. Again he stopped just behind her. This time he dropped another cured pelt over her and pulled it up to her chin.

The back of his weather-roughened hand accidentally brushed her cheek as he pulled the cover tight around her. "Better get some sleep."

His voice, far gentler than she'd ever heard it, was close to her ear. She was afraid to turn and look over her shoulder, knowing his arresting blue eyes would be very near. Refusing to acknowledge his kindness, she kept her eyes shut tight.

It was a little late in the day for Buck Scott to try to make up for everything he had already put her through.

BUCK woke with the first light that oozed through the cracks in the lopsided shutters. The weak morning light outlined the frost in the freezing room. Snow had built up on the floor in miniature drifts beneath the largest chinks in the wall. Fully clothed, he was loath to get out of bed, unwilling to face the shock of cold beyond the thick fur covers, but someone had to build up the fire and set the water boiling for the morning meal.

He lay on his back and stared up at the weathered boards that formed the ceiling, for a time doing little more than conjuring imaginary faces and figures formed by the knotholes and scars in the wood. He heard Annika Storm stir restlessly on her pallet and wondered if she had slept at all. It had been hours before he lost himself in sleep, hours spent listening to the soft rustle of her bedclothes and Annika's frustrated sighs. Each sound only served to set him thinking about the fool he had been for taking her off the train. He rolled to his side and stared across the room at the legs of the table and the barrel stools beneath it.

Last night he had convinced himself he was crazy. He'd acted exactly the way a madman would have when he'd forced Annika to go with him and refused to believe she was not Alice Soams.

The wind rattled the door as it had for hours. He didn't need to open the shutters to see that the snow had piled itself in high drifts against the outer walls, not to mention the pass into the valley. He threw back the covers and braced himself to meet the cold that attacked his joints just as he knew it would. He stifled a groan. Too many winters spent wading through frozen streams to set traps had stiffened his joints until he felt far older than his years.

He trod softly across the room, careful to avoid stepping on Annika as he reached across her to add more wood to the fire. She seemed to be truly asleep, not merely feigning it this time. She had given up tossing and turning sometime before dawn. He stood for a moment and contemplated her as she slept unaware. The covers were pulled up to her hairline until all that was visible was the top of her golden head. Her thick hair shone brightly against the rich wolf pelts. As he turned away from the tempting sight, Buck raked both hands through his own shoulder-length hair and shook it back, then set out to fill the kettle and hang it over the fire.

A layer of ice had formed atop the water in the tall barrel beside the door. The frost shattered and bobbed as he dipped a ladle in and filled the blackened copper kettle. He filled a pot with cornmeal and set it aside until it was time to make the mush, the usual morning fare.

Across the room, Baby sat up abruptly and smiled. "Me get up," she announced as she started to crawl out from beneath the covers.

Buck kept his voice low so as not to awaken Annika. "You stay put until I get you dressed. It's freezing today."

He took her little dress off the chair where he had hung it the night before. The material was dry but cold, so he held it close to the fire to warm it, then carried it across the room. Once the dress was on, Baby dove beneath the covers to retrieve her new shoes and insisted Buck put them on her feet.

He started to slip the hard leather shoes on her when he realized that unlike her soft, martin-lined moccasins, the stiff leather shoes would require stockings to warm her feet and prevent blisters—but he hadn't thought to buy socks.

"No new shoes today, Baby. Why don't you wear your old ones until it gets warmer?"

Baby tossed her mussed blond ringlets and said emphatically, "No!"

"Please." He tried cajoling her, his voice low but firm, "You can't wear these without socks. You'll get blisters."

"Me want me shoes."

"You want your feet to bleed and hurt?" Trying to discourage her, he scowled and shook his head.

"Me want me shoes!"

"No." He tried to take the shoes from her. Out of sight, out of mind. "You can't wear them yet."

"Would you just put those shoes on that child?" The muffled grumbling came from the pallet at the foot of the bed.

Buck hefted the struggling Baby and walked over to stare down at Annika. She had pulled the pelts down far enough to stare over the edge at him. Her eyes were bloodshot from lack of sleep and the dry air. His guest was none too happy with either him, Baby, or the circumstances.

"Well?" she said.

"Well what?" he said.

"Will you put those shoes on that child so she'll quit whining? And when are we leaving?"

"Leaving?"

Her brow furrowed as her eyes narrowed suspiciously. "You said you'd take me to Cheyenne today."

He turned away and carried the now kicking, squirming child to the nearest chair where he plopped her down and reached for the tiny moccasins on the floor.

"No! No! Me want shoes! Shooooose!" Baby worked herself up to a full roar.

Buck concentrated on shoeing the flailing feet as he applied gentle pressure to keep the child on the chair.

"You said you'd take me home!" Panicked now, Annika pulled herself to a sitting position and shoved her hair back off her face with both hands. "You have to. You promised. If my brother finds you first you may as well—"

Baby's small foot connected with Buck's jaw. He stumbled back, nearly upsetting the table as a colorful expletive escaped him.

He straightened, pinned Annika with a stare, then jerked his gaze away and glanced down at Baby, who was howling with fear and frustration. The tiny moccasins in his hands crumpled into wads as his fists balled at his sides. Without another word to either angry female, he threw the moccasins on the table and turned his back on them both.

He grabbed his coat off the peg and jerked the door open.

The drift outside the door fell inward, showering the floor with snow as the wind did its utmost to blow more in behind it.

Buck kicked enough snow out of the way to get the door closed and then stepped out into the blinding white world beyond.

As the door slammed closed behind him, Baby abruptly stopped howling and Annika crossed her arms. New shoes in hand, Baby climbed down off the chair and toddled over to Annika, marched across the wolf pelts, and plopped down on her lap.

"Shoes?" Trustingly, she offered her prized possessions to Annika and waited for the woman to put them on her feet.

Annika closed her eyes and wished away the whole scene, opened them and tried to smile at the moon-faced child gazing up at her with such hope in her eyes. She could count on one hand the firsthand experience she'd had with children. Speaking slowly, she tried to sound sure of herself and as logical as possible, but it was hard to think clearly and fight off the mounting fear that Buck Scott no longer intended to take her back to Cheyenne.

"Listen, Baby. You let me get up and get dressed and then

I'll find something you can use for socks and we'll get those shoes on. All right?"

Baby sniffed, shuddered with dramatic gasps, and then nodded. She held her shoes to her chest and stood up, trampled back across Annika's makeshift bed, and then sat on the hearth beside the fire.

Annika felt a surge of success and decided that dealing with children might not be as hard as she thought. She noticed Baby was shivering, whether from emotion or cold she couldn't tell, but as soon as she crawled out from beneath the covers and stood up, she knew. Despite the fire, the cabin was freezing. She threw another log on the already good-sized blaze and then hurried to put on her clothes. She took up her rumpled, water-stained suit and decided not to take off her nightclothes. Instead she pulled her petticoat over the two nightgowns, then donned her wool skirt. The fitted jacket barely closed across the bodice with so many layers beneath, but she soon succeeded in buttoning most of the buttons.

Once she was dressed to her satisfaction, she put on her own shoes, thankful that she had left her stockings on all night, and as she did, she wondered what she might use to line Baby's shoes. With efficient motions, she stuffed her shirtwaist in her bag, pulled out her comb and brush, and worked them through her hair. She twisted her hair into a thick knot atop her head and smoothed the fabric of her shirt with her palms.

Baby was still sniffling and shivering by the fire.

"Where's your coat?" Annika asked.

The child pointed to a peg on the far wall above the box of pitiful items she called toys. Annika took down the coat, a smaller, fully-lined version of Buck's own fringed buckskin jacket, then helped Baby pull it on before she went to look through her bag for something to cut up and fashion into stockings.

She fingered her blue shirtwaist and shook her head. She would need the blouse. Her eyes lit on the pelts at her feet and she wondered if she could somehow cram pieces of fur into the shoes, much like the lining of the moccasins. "May I see your new shoes?" She stood over Baby and reached out her hand.

Baby hugged the shoes tighter, shook her head no, and sucked on her thumb.

"I need to see them if I'm going to make you some socks that will fit."

Another shake.

Annika sat on the hearth beside Baby, cupped her numb hands, and blew on them. The water in the kettle had started to hiss. She longed for a cup of hot tea, but ignored the sound and concentrated on Baby instead. There was a pitiful hopelessness in the child's slumped shoulders and the way she kept glancing at the door, waiting for Buck to return.

"Don't you want to put the shoes on anymore?"

A lone tear trickled down Baby's cheek. She nodded yes.

"Then you have to let me see them so that I can make you a pair of socks." Suddenly Annika had an idea. "I only need one. You keep one and I'll take one."

Baby stared down at the shoes and then up at Annika. With slow uncertainty, she handed her one shoe.

Annika stood up and thanked the child.

"W'come," Baby said softly.

At least Buck Scott had taught her some manners, Annika thought. She picked up a wolf pelt and wrapped it around the child's bare feet. "Now, don't move and I'll fix you right up."

Instead of using anything of her own, Annika opened the lid of the chest from which Buck had procured the nightshirt. She rustled through a pile of well-worn clothes—mismatched stockings, shirts that were frayed and faded, some gingham and calico gowns in equally poor condition. She set aside a cigar box and pulled out a pair of rough woolen ladies' stockings with holes in the heels and smiled in triumph. Then, she rummaged through her own valise until she found a small pair of scissors, then cut the feet off the stockings.

With the tubular legs of the stockings in her hands, she went back to Baby and slipped them on her feet. They were bulky but snug, and except for the fact that the toes were open, Annika thought they fit considerably well. Baby studied her feet and legs, then silently watched Annika, who was chewing on her lower lip, trying to decide how best to proceed.

Her valise contained a small sewing kit with only enough thread and a needle to sew on a few buttons. Now, as she faced the challenge of the socks, Annika pulled the kit out and set to work. In no time the toes were closed and Baby was shod. The black stockings reached well up to the child's thighs.

"There," Annika said, her own gaze shifting to the door, "that was simple. Now, let's see about some tea."

It took a few moments to convince Baby that even though she must wear her coat, they were not going outside with Buck. "If we're lucky, he'll freeze to death," Annika whispered to herself as Baby climbed onto a chair and demanded mush.

"I don't know how to make mush," Annika said sternly. "And I don't intend to learn, so sit quietly and I'll let you have a sip of tea. Your uncle will see to your mush when he gets back."

Baby amused herself with staring at her new shoes and alternately climbing off and on the chair and walking around the room while Annika searched through the tins lining the mantel. "There has to be some tea here someplace," she mumbled to herself. She rearranged the crocks, tins, and bottles in her search. Opening a wide-mouthed jar, she reeled back when an odious smell from a greasy substance nearly knocked her over. Quickly screwing the lid down tight, she shoved the jar aside. Dried herbs and stinking tonics filled most of the containers. Finally in the back row she discovered a small, octagonal tin with the faded, gold embossed letters T-E-A. She was on tiptoe, stretching to reach the battered tin when the door opened and Buck Scott strode in.

"Dammit!" He was across the room like a gunshot. Grabbing Annika, he pulled her back and threw her down on the floor.

She screamed and tried to roll away. He lifted his foot and started to stomp on the hem of her skirt. The faster he stomped, the louder she screamed. Buck stopped as sud-

denly as he started. Annika quit screaming. He reached
down and jerked her to her feet.

Eyes wide and wild, she shoved him away. His shoulders
heaved as he fought for a breath. "Don't ever touch me
again," she finally managed.

"Fine." Still breathing hard, he turned away and picked up
Baby, who had begun to whimper again. "Next time I'll just
let you burn." Ignoring Annika, he took the kettle off the fire
with his free hand while he held Baby against his hip.

"Me shoes, Buck." Baby smiled happily and lifted her
foot for his perusal.

"I see." He inspected the improvised socks.

A scorched smell permeated the cabin. Slow realization
dawned and Annika looked down at her many hems. A sooty
black line of charred fabric outlined the edge of her wool
shirt like unevenly sewn piping. She glanced up at Buck and
caught him watching her, but when their eyes met, he looked
away and busied himself with his task.

She opened her mouth to speak, then shut it again.

If he had not returned when he had and acted instinctively
to stomp out the fire, she might indeed have burned to death.

Annika swallowed.

Buck poured boiling water over the cornmeal in the pot.

"I'm sorry," she said, hoping she spoke loud enough for
him to hear. "I guess I owe you my thanks."

"I guess you owe me your life," he grumbled, half to himself. "Watch yourself in front of the fire from now on."

She couldn't resist snapping. "There won't be from now
on. We're leaving soon, aren't we?" When he was silent, she
repeated, "Aren't we?"

"You that anxious to leave all of this?"

Annika spread her arms wide. "Anxious? Yes, I'm anxious! I've been carried halfway across the country against
my will, I spent the night trying to sleep on this cold, hard
floor. I don't know if my parents are beside themselves with
worry. I'm stuck here with you and a child with no name. My
clothes are ruined, I'm freezing, and I just nearly burned to
death! Anxious to leave? Yes, Mr. Scott. I can hardly wait!"

He stirred the mush and reached for a crock of honey.
Bowls clattered as he set them on the table. Annika stood,

catching her breath, glowering at him from across the room. Finally Buck looked up.

"Well, at least you're not complaining."

She started toward him with murder in her eyes, tripped over the pallet on the floor, and nearly fell on her face. Quick footwork saved her but did little to cool her temper. She bent over in a fury, scooped up the pelts, and flung them on his unmade bed.

"Want some mush?" Buck plopped some into a bowl in front of Baby, who sat waiting expectantly.

"No!"

He spooned up some of his own and set the pot near the fire to keep it warm. While Annika watched, silently fuming, he poured warm honey over both helpings and then hunkered down to eat.

When his bowl was half empty he paused, looked again at Annika, and sadly shook his head. "You better have some. It's gonna be a long day."

"I don't think—"

"In fact," he interrupted what he knew was bound to be another tirade, "it's going to be longer than a long day before I can take you back."

"What do you mean by that?" Her hand was at her throat again, her blue eyes wide and questioning.

"I mean we're snowed in."

❦ 8 ❦

"SNOWED in?"

Annika narrowed the space between them until she reached the table. Palms down on the scarred wood, she leaned toward Buck. "*How* snowed in?"

"Pass is bound to be closed after a storm like this one." He made her wait while he swallowed two huge spoonfuls of mush. "Could be days, could be months. Depends on when this storm stops." He shrugged. "Get one good chinook wind though, and it'll melt in a few hours." He bent over the bowl of steaming gruel. "Hard to tell."

Unable to face him, unwilling to let the odious man see the stinging tears that welled in her eyes, Annika turned away. The wind was still beating against the north side of the cabin. Snow hissed in through every sizable crack. She paced over to the window. The glass was covered with frost; the shutters blocked out all but muted daylight. The lack of sunlight cast the interior of the cabin into a dreary netherworld of firelight, weak lamplight, and shadows. Feeling despondent, Annika wrapped her arms tightly about herself and whispered, "What am I going to do?"

"Have some mush."

She whirled on him. If it had not been for Buck Scott and his stupidity she would not have to endure his constant presence nor her captivity in his dismal excuse for a home.

Although he didn't appear to be laughing at her, she took two steps forward with murder in her eyes. "You can take your mush and—"

He cut her off. "Remember the child."

105

"Don't try to hide behind that baby. This is unthinkable. Unspeakable! I can't stay here for months. I'll go crazy."

"Why? After all, I'm the one that has to live with *you*."

She thought of the possibility of days and weeks of living in the same small space with him. Months of lying on the pallet before the fire fighting off sleep, knowing he lay but a few feet away. She could feel her fear and anxiety steadily building but was unable to stop them. Glancing toward the window again she said, "Couldn't you at least go out and open the shutters? It's so gloomy in here."

Still staring at her intently, he shook his head. "Drifts snowed them shut. Sometimes I can't dig them out until spring."

She clasped her fingers together and walked back to the table. With slow, forlorn motions she pulled out one of the chairs and sat down. Propping her head in her hands, she groaned, "I really can't stand it here."

"There's no need to starve to death." He leaned back in the chair, stretched toward the bench behind him, and grabbed another bowl. As he ladled up her mush, Buck stared at Annika's bent shoulders, certain she was about to cry. He didn't know what he would do if she did.

"Look"—he set the bowl of steaming cornmeal mush in front of her and then got her a spoon—"if it's any consolation, I apologize for this whole sorry mess, but there's nothing I can do about it now. Nothing at all."

She batted away tears before she looked up at him again. He shoved the bowl closer. "Are you sure we can't get out?" There was a catch in her voice.

"When it stops snowing I'll go out and scout around. We'll need fresh meat anyway." Annika looked so sad he tried to reassure her. "If there's any chance at all of getting through the pass, I'll take you out."

She looked up and found him standing over her. She didn't know which frightened her more, his size or the fact that he was always watching her as if he were waiting to catch her unaware so that he could—could what? Perhaps what frightened her most was that she couldn't quite fathom his intentions. "And until then?"

"Until then—we'll just have to do the best we can to get along with each other."

Baby's spoon clattered against the empty bowl. "Down!" she shouted.

Buck lifted Baby off the chair, an indulgence since she had been climbing up and down on her own all morning. The child beamed when he lifted her high over his head before he set her on the floor again. "Go play," he whispered softly, then paused to watch her toddle to the makeshift toy box filled with the cast-off objects she called playthings.

Annika studied Buck as he watched Baby cross the room and was reminded of the tender way the big man had dealt with the child the night before. She found herself wondering exactly what manner of man Buck Scott really was.

He collected the empty bowls and set them in the wash-tub, then walked to the fireplace and picked up the kettle of simmering water. When he passed by the table, all he saw was Annika Storm staring despondently at her bowl of rapidly cooling mush.

OUTSIDE, the storm continued to rage through Blue Creek Valley. Inside, Buck and Annika held to a tenuous truce while the hours slowly passed. With uneasy moves they avoided each other as they walked about the small cabin like dancers performing an unfamiliar reel. While he washed up the breakfast dishes, Annika straightened the pelts she'd tossed onto the bed and then crawled beneath them for warmth. He studiously avoided her and began to shave off his three months' growth of beard.

While Baby crawled beneath the pelts beside her and pestered Annika to play with a wooden doll that was as poorly dressed as Baby herself, Annika couldn't help but sneak sidelong glances at Buck Scott, curious what he would look like when he finished his shave.

Unwilling to let him catch her staring curiously, Annika turned her attention to the child at her side. The little girl did look enough like Buck Scott to be his own child. Their compelling blue eyes continually demanded attention. Evenly drawn golden brows emphasized Baby's thoughtful expression, one that was very much like Buck's.

Annika reached down for the sorry little doll that the child
offered to let her hold. As if it were made of the finest porcelain, she cradled the wooden baby in her arms and smoothed
the frayed piece of red flannel that served as its blanket.

"Me baby," Baby said.

"It's very pretty," Annika told her, thinking of her own
collection of dolls back in Boston. Her father used to bring
her one every time he traveled on business. He still surprised
her with one on occasion. As she handed the crude doll back
to Baby, she wished she had one to give her—or all of them,
for that matter.

Minutes passed as she and Baby spoke softly, trading the
doll back and forth, and when Annika glanced at Buck, she
noticed with disappointment that he was once again seated at
the table at such an angle that she could not see his face. His
long curly hair hid his clean-shaven face while he repaired a
pair of snowshoes by weaving thin branches of white ash
onto a bear paw–shaped frame and tying them off with strips
of rawhide. Although he must have noticed, he had made no
mention of her sitting on his bed. Since she hesitated to call
attention to herself, she continued to ignore him by keeping
Baby amused.

Lack of a good night's sleep coupled with the thick mattress and warmth of the pelts that formed a soft cocoon
around her made Annika drowsy. She fought to keep her
eyes open as Baby spoke gibberish to her doll, wrapped and
unwrapped it, and then inspected her new shoes and socks.
Finally, too sleepy to care what Buck Scott thought, Annika
gave up and fell sound asleep.

Even with the low moan of the wind and the soft crackle
of the fire, Buck soon became aware of the woman's slow,
rhythmic breathing. Since she had slept little the night before, he did not begrudge her a few moments of peaceful
slumber. As he turned around to watch her, he was thankful
that he could finally do so without her furious blue eyes bor-
ing into him.

She was half sitting, half reclining, propped against the
pillow that rested against the log headboard. A silken skein
of her glorious blond hair had worked itself loose from the
bun she had knotted atop her head. It unfurled over one

shoulder and lay shining with the glow of firelight caught in its strands. He was half tempted to cross the room just so he could reach out and lift the curl, measure its texture and worth much as he would a prime pelt. Then he looked down at his callused hand and balled it into a fist against his thigh.

He had no right to touch her. No right at all.

But he wanted to.

Lord, how he wanted to. Finally admitting it to himself didn't make matters any easier.

Buck stood up and paced over to the fire. Trying not to disturb her, he silently added another split log to the blaze. When the task was complete, he turned around and leaned one arm against the mantel and continued to contemplate the woman in his bed.

Her skin was flawless, her cheeks made pink by cold and wind. Thick crescents of honey blond lashes lay against her golden cheeks, and even in sleep, her lips pouted, ripe and tempting. He wondered if it were a sin to take advantage of the chance to study her while she was so vulnerably unaware. He knew for sure that if she were awake, Annika Storm would be mad as hell at him for staring.

But she was still sleeping, after all, and a man ought to be able to do what he wanted to in his own house—within reason.

He let his gaze roam over her face again, then down the satin length of her neck to the securely buttoned collar of the chocolate wool traveling suit she wore atop her nightclothes. Buck bit back a smile when he thought of all the layers she had on, then quickly frowned when he remembered the way she had set herself alight by standing too close to the fire. He wondered if she really was as helpless as she seemed. If he were to get her back to her brother in Busted Heel unharmed, he would have to look out for her every minute.

One of her hands rested open on the pillow beside her. Her fingers were long, much like her limbs. Again he noted her beautiful hands, smooth and unmarred by drudgery. He thought of his mother's and sisters' hands and how they were rough and lined long before they should have been from the use of harsh lye soap and demanding chores. He wondered if Annika Storm had ever had a blister in her life.

With a shake of his head, Buck remembered the quirk of
fate that had brought Annika to him and then thought of Alice Soams. Wherever she was now, she was far better off
than she would have been married to him. Now that he saw
Annika against the backdrop of his life, he knew it would be
too much to ask someone he loved to give up civilization and
live in such isolation. It wasn't any more fair to demand it of
a virtual stranger.

His gaze drifted to Baby and his heart constricted with the
bleak realization that he had no choice but to give her up.
There was no way he could continue to raise her as his own,
not while he had to be free to leave the cabin for hours—if
not days—while he checked on his traps and did the dressing
and skinning that was required before he could start home.
She was too precious to him to endanger her by taking her
out any longer. She was too old to carry everywhere, too curious to keep entertained while he worked, still too young to
leave alone.

There was nothing he could do but give Baby up, at least
until she was full grown.

As he watched Annika roll to her side, he knew she could
never be the wife he needed, but he wondered if she still
might not be the answer to his dilemma.

ANNIKA rubbed her eyes and stretched, then abruptly pulled
herself to a sitting position when she found Buck Scott towering over her at the side of the bed.

Though they offered scant protection, she clutched the
wolf pelts to her and tried to assume an expression of command. "What do you want?"

"I'm going out."

The thought struck her that he was arrestingly handsome
without his beard. His jawline was strong and even, his lips
full but far too stern. There were lines about his eyes, creases
she figured were carved by the sun rather than smiling over-
much, but they did not detract from his good looks. Without
the beard he looked much younger, more vulnerable, but still
as strong and commanding. He had tied his hair back with a
rawhide thong, and she could see now that it was not a pure
gold color, but bleached nearly white in places by the ele-

ments. Instead of his heavy hooded jacket he was wearing an
ankle-length buffalo hide coat. She doubted that she could
even lift it. A rifle rested casually against his shoulder, while
his long knife was strapped to his thigh.

She swung her feet over the edge of the bed and pushed
the pelts away. Baby was sound asleep beside her. "What do
you mean you're going out? I thought we were snowed in?"

He sighed, as if explaining were a chore. "The pass is
closed. We're snowed in in the valley, not the cabin. I just
spent the past half hour digging out around the door. The
storm's nearly spent—it's just snowing lightly now—so I
thought I'd go have a look-see and find out how bad it really
is out there."

"And what am I supposed to do?"

"Stay with Baby."

Groggy with sleep, she followed him to the door. He already wore a heavy fur hat on his head, tied tight beneath his
chin. His face was curiously pale where the beard had been,
his cheeks tanned from long exposure to the sun and reddened by the cold. Annika was tempted to lay her warm
palms against them, but immediately thought better of it.

She took a step back. "I'm not a nursemaid, Mr. Scott."

"I'm sure you're not." He looked as if he wanted to say
more.

"Well?"

"I don't exactly know what you're good for, ma'am, but I
think if you try hard enough, you can watch over a three-
year-old for a few minutes' time."

With that he opened the door, stepped outside, and then
closed it in her face.

Speechless, Annika stared at the wooden planks of the
door, wishing he would step back inside so that she could
give him a piece of her mind.

The wind had indeed stopped and the snow that had
sneaked in through the cracks was beginning to melt, turning
the floor to mud in various spots about the room. In the silence that pervaded the cabin, Annika realized that for the
first time in three days she was no longer in the company of
her captor. Immediately she readied herself for escape.

She glanced over at the sleeping child, grabbed her satchel

from the floor, then looked for her opera cape and found it hanging on a peg near the door beneath his buckskin jacket. Pulling both of them off the hook, she donned the cape, then Buck's long coat and found herself nearly too bundled in clothing to move. It took but a few seconds to locate the gloves in her satchel and work the cold, stiff leather over her fingers, but once she had accomplished that, she was ready to leave.

Carefully, quietly, she pulled open the door. Snow swirled in on a current of cold air as she stepped outside. The world was blinding white; the only other color she was immediately aware of was the deep forest green of the undersides of the pine boughs.

The door was nearly closed behind her when she heard the child inside cry out, "Ankah? Me go too!"

It was a mistake to go back in.

Baby scrambled off the bed and rushed across the room toward her. Annika stepped back inside and shut out the cold. She set her satchel down and frowned at Baby. "You can't go, Baby. You have to wait for Buck."

"No."

"Yes. He said you have to wait here. He'll be right back. Do you want him to be sad if you aren't here?"

"Ankah go with Buck?"

"No. I'm going home now. You have to stay here and wait for Buck. Can you do that?" She watched the child's eyes widen as the little girl looked around the deserted cabin. "You won't get into any trouble, will you?"

Baby began to pout. "Me go too."

"No. You have to stay here."

"Me go with Buck."

Annika crossed her arms. She tapped her foot against the frozen floor. The log in the fireplace popped; sparks fell amid the ashes. She glanced down at the charred hem of her skirt.

Then she looked at Baby again.

What if the child strayed too close to the fire? What if she tried to imitate Buck and put on another log? What if she fell headlong into the fireplace?

Annika looked around. The cabin that provided shelter

and a home for the child was as dangerous as a pit of vipers. There were knives on the cook bench that Baby could easily reach by standing on a chair. A heavy Dutch oven or kettle might topple down on her. She could climb on a chair and fall off, or worse yet, open one of the many tins or jars of foodstuffs and eat something that might make her deathly ill.

Annika closed her eyes and counted to ten. There had to be a way she could escape without endangering the child, for as much as she hated Buck Scott, there was no way on earth she would wish any harm to come to his niece. Suddenly she remembered the way the old hunter, Ted, had tied the baby to the chair. In seconds Annika had crossed the room and plundered the chest at the foot of Buck's bed. She found a worn petticoat of muslin so thin she could nearly see clear through it. Annika tore a long, wide strip while Baby stood and watched with her thumb in her mouth.

Ready at last, Annika grabbed Baby's hand and pulled her across the room, lifted her onto a straight-backed chair, and then quickly tied the muslin binding around the child before she could begin to struggle for freedom.

"Now," Annika said as she stood, hands on hips and surveying her handiwork, "you just sit tight until Buck comes back. He said a few minutes." She silently prayed he meant it.

Alligator tears began to roll down Baby's cheeks.

"I have to go," Annika began. "Don't you see? Your uncle might be lying. Maybe I can get out of here on foot. Why, who knows? I might walk to the top of the first ridge and find that we're right next to a town." She hunkered down in front of the child and wiped the tears away. "You'll be fine. You're a big girl."

When she stood again, Annika crossed the room and found the wooden doll amid the bedclothes. She carried it back to Baby and put it in her arms. "Here. You take care of your baby and don't cry."

With that, she refused to look at the forlorn little girl again and headed for the door. She stepped outside and blinked against the intense light. As she closed the door behind her, she wished she could shut out the pitiful sound of Baby's sobs as easily.

She saw the deep snowshoe tracks that led away from the cabin and decided to try to go in the opposite direction. One step off the small patch of snow Buck had managed to shovel away from the door and she was knee deep in powder. Within seconds her boots and stockings were soaked, so too were her skirts and petticoats. Annika felt as if she were trying to walk through thick glue, and although it was still cold and snowflakes were drifting down from the slightly swaying trees around her, she was perspiring from her effort.

If it was hard going trying to lift her feet and legs out of the drifts far enough to take a step, it was nearly impossible to carry her satchel. She thought of leaving it behind, then remembered her buttons and the silver-backed comb and brush and knew that she had to keep the mementos no matter what the effort cost. The silver dresser set had been a gift from Richard. And the buttons, well, the buttons had survived Buck Scott on the trail. She would keep them just to spite him.

Baby was crying louder now—her wails drifted easily through the cabin door. Moved by feelings of guilt, Annika glanced back at the cabin and lost her footing. Falling headfirst into the snow, she struggled to push herself up and out of the deep, cold stuff without success. Finally, she was able to roll over. Forced to admit she was now soaking wet from head to toe, she brushed off as much of the fine powder as she could and then pulled her satchel out after her.

Suddenly two things were all too apparent: she would get nowhere without a pair of snowshoes like Buck's, and he had not lied about the amount of snow that had fallen during the night. Annika knew that there was no hope of climbing out of the valley if she could not even manage to make her way out of the yard.

With a heavy heart and even heavier steps, she extricated herself from the snow and carefully picked her way back the few feet she had come until she reached the cleared path and finally the front door. Angry at herself for failing, at the snow for falling, and at the child inside for her incessant howling, Annika jerked the door open and stalked back inside. She slammed the door, startled Baby into silence, and

began to strip off the wet coat, cape, and then her wool suit
jacket and skirt.

She pulled the barrel stools before the fire and spread the
clothing over them. In her nightgown and the flannel nightshirt Buck had given her, she marched back to where Baby
sat sniffling and inhaling ragged, sobbing breaths. She untied the mournful child, hefted her to her hip, and then one-
handedly picked up her satchel and slammed it on the table.
Annika found the tin of buttons, set it on the table, pulled up
a chair, and with Baby on her lap proceeded to calm the little
girl by showing her the precious cache inside the tin.

AN hour later, the door opened without warning and Buck
Scott stepped over the threshold and closed the door with a
bang. Defiantly, Annika met his stony glare. He didn't have
to say a word. She knew that he knew she had tried to leave
when he took in all the clothes drying before the fire. His
gaze swung back to hers. His cheeks were red from the cold,
his lips nearly blue. They were pursed in a taut line. His
gloved hands were tightly clinging to a cord slung over one
shoulder. His rifle rested on the other. His long, wicked knife
rode in the beaded sheath on his thigh.

She held her silence. So did he.

For a long while he merely stood there and stared at her
while she continued to hold Baby on her lap. The child
scooped buttons by the handfuls and let them sift through her
fingers. Baby pushed them into a pile, then spread them out
again, all the while ignoring the adults engaged in a silent
war of wills.

Finally, Buck moved. He took one step toward the table
and halted. Annika could tell just by looking at him that his
temper was leashed on a very tenuous thread.

"I thought I told you to stay with Baby." He ground the
words out.

"And I told you I'm no nursemaid."

His scathing glance raked over her and the child. Without words he labeled her a liar. "Looks like you do well
enough."

"You can't keep me here against my will."

"I'm not, but you can't leave this valley until the snow

melts, so you might as well face it. And as long as you're here, you'd better do as I say."

"Or what, Mr. Scott?"

"Or you might end up hurt."

"Are you threatening me?"

He stepped up to the table. She saw his fingers tighten on the rope in his hands. "No. I'm warning you. There are a thousand ways to die just outside that door, ma'am. Maybe a million. I don't want to be blamed for your death if it happens because of your own stupidity."

Knowing full well how crazy she had been to even try to escape through the impassable drifts of snow, she had nothing to say in her own defense. She shifted the child on her lap and refused to meet his stare.

"Worse yet"—his voice was low now, threatening—"if anything happens to Baby because you decide to pull one of your stupid stunts, you won't have to worry about your health, because I'll take it out of your hide. Do you understand me?"

She flashed him a brittle smile, then dropped her eyes to the buttons again. She wished she could control the blaze of embarrassment that stained her cheeks. "I understand you all too well, Mr. Scott."

"Good. Then as long as we are both of a mind to weather out the snow together, we ought to be of a mind to be civil."

"Fine."

"Fine. They why don't you start being agreeable by cooking dinner for all of us?"

She smiled, but no warmth reached her eyes. "I have no idea how to begin."

Buck smiled a cool smile of his own. "Then I guess now is as good a time as any to start learning." He lifted the cord from his shoulder and swung it around. Without warning, he dropped two lifeless rabbits dead center on the table.

Baby clapped her hands. The buttons rattled and rolled. Annika immediately blanched and closed her eyes.

Buck Scott smiled with satisfaction.

❧ 9 ❧

"**Y**ou don't intend me to actually touch those, do you?"
Annika didn't try to hide her chagrin as she stared openly at the dead rabbits on the table. The occasions when she had accompanied her mother or Ruth to the butcher shop had been rare. There was no way to compare the skinned rabbits she had seen then to the two lifeless, pitiful creatures that lay in front of her now. She tried not to imagine the white snowshoe rabbits playful and full of life, foraging about in the snow protected by their thick white pelts.

She looked down at Baby's curly blond head to avoid the gruesome sight.

"Come on." His voice startled her so that she flinched. "I'll teach you how to clean and cook them."

Annika's stomach turned over. She remembered once when her father had gone fishing and had later asked her mother to prepare his catch for supper. Analisa had said, "If you clean them I will cook them," and Caleb readily agreed. Annika looked up at Buck and tried to smile halfheartedly. "If you clean them, then I'll try to cook them," she offered.

But she was not dealing with Caleb Storm.

"You're going to cook them anyway. You still need to learn to skin them yourself." So saying, he picked up the rabbits and turned toward the door. "Put your wool clothes back on and bring Baby outside. It won't hurt her to go out for a bit to ward off cabin fever."

It angered her to think he was worried about Baby getting cabin fever when he had been so furious at her own attempt

117

to get out. But then again, she thought, there was no need to worry that Baby might try to escape.

"I don't want to watch," she argued.

Buck turned around with a sigh. He set the rabbits down, walked around the table, and took Baby from Annika's lap. The child clung to him and hid her face against his neck. Buck eased the hood of Baby's coat up over her head.

"Outside?" Baby asked.

"Outside," he affirmed as he lifted the rabbits again. "You too," he said over his shoulder.

Annika said, "I'm not going. I don't want to."

He paused before the door. "I don't care what you want. Your life might depend on your being able to survive alone up here." For the first time that day his eyes met hers without a hint of anger. Instead, his expression was sober and painfully honest. "Anything could happen to me out there. I could get caught in one of my own traps or someone else's; a bear or mountain lion could happen along at the wrong time. I could fall or be buried by an avalanche. You'd find yourself alone here, having to fend for yourself and Baby."

She watched him as he looked down at the rope in his hands and the rabbits dangling from it as if he were weighing his next words carefully, deciding just how much to tell her. "That's the reason I answered Alice Soams's advertisement in the first place. I don't need anybody, but Baby does. I have to know she'll be cared for—" He cut himself off abruptly, unwilling to express the depths of his worry.

For a fleeting moment, Annika understood his concern, but then she made the mistake of glancing down at the rabbits twirling from the rope. "Couldn't you just start by teaching me to make mush?"

As suddenly as it had appeared, his vulnerability was gone and he was the Buck Scott she had known for the past few days—hardened, stubborn, unapproachable. He turned toward the door and threw a sharp command over his shoulder. "Meet me at the shed out back in two minutes or I'm coming back to get you. And I won't be happy about it."

WRAPPED in her traveling suit and cape again, Annika stumbled through the snow banked about the outer cabin walls until she found the shed. When she saw what Buck had accomplished before she got there, she wished she had lost her way.

The rabbits had been strung upside down and were hanging headless from a support beam of the lean-to, their crimson blood staining the snow in ever widening circles. She stopped eight feet from the sight and choked down a gag, unwilling to show any weakness in front of the man who was watching her. She took a deep breath and fought to control her nausea, then crossed the snowy ground until she was as near the shed as she intended to get. When Baby saw Annika, she pulled herself up from where she was rolling in a low snowbank and scrambled toward her. She toppled onto her backside at Annika's feet.

"How can you do this in front of a child?" Annika lifted Baby to her hip and tried to brush off the snow that all but covered the little coat.

He watched her as she held Baby close. "Nothing wrong with learning about life early."

"Life? This isn't part of life; this is butchery, this is inhumane, this is—"

"This is only a rabbit. This is what people do to survive. You mean to tell me you don't eat meat?"

"Of course I do, but—"

"Where do you think it comes from? The butcher shop?"

She'd never tell him that was exactly where she preferred to think it came from—already dressed, cut, and ready to cook. The closest she had ever come to a dead rabbit before was accepting a neatly trimmed and roasted portion from a platter. For the hundredth time she wished she were safe at home in Boston where she didn't have to think about curly-topped waifs or bloody rabbits.

He wouldn't leave the argument alone. "If you'd been exposed to this at Baby's age you wouldn't think anything of it now."

"It's not fair to the child. She has no choice."

"As far as I can see, she's paying no attention."

Annika looked down at Baby and noticed he was right. She happily ignored the slowly dripping rabbits and was intrigued by the satin frogs that held Annika's cape closed.

Turning away from her, Buck cut the rabbits down and carried them to a combination workbench and chopping block against the back wall of the shed. From the looks of the many pelts and antlers tacked to the wall, it was apparent he had a knack for hunting. He brushed the snow off the block and motioned Annika forward. She raised her chin defiantly, but did as he asked rather than stand and argue in the freezing cold. She willed the contents of her stomach to stay put as she moved close enough to watch, horrified, while he skinned the first rabbit.

As long as she stopped thinking of the mass of fur and flesh as a fluffy little bunny whose family was no doubt pining away in a hidden warren, she was able to keep from retching. Baby had lost interest in the cape and wanted to be put down on the snow. Annika lowered her to the ground and moved up behind Buck when he motioned her closer. She stood off to one side, trying to detach herself from the scene by staying partially behind Buck so that she didn't have a clear view of the headless carcasses on the table.

As Buck slid the deadly looking ivory-inlaid handled knife from the sheath at his thigh, he glanced over his shoulder to be certain Annika was close enough to hear and see what he was doing. "Rabbits are probably the most important animal in the wild." He swiftly cut off the rabbit's feet and set them aside. Annika failed to respond, but he continued talking anyway. "You might say this animal was put on the earth just to be eaten. Nearly every fur-bearing animal feeds on rabbits, not to mention some of your bigger birds."

The blade of the knife flashed as he cut a slit in the skin along each of the back legs and then up the center of the rabbit's belly. Setting the knife aside, he began rolling the skin down toward the front legs. Annika was surprised to see him pull all the fur off in one piece, much the way a man might pull a shirt off over his head.

With the ivory inlay of the handle again hidden by his hand, only the wicked, sharply honed blade was visible. As much as she hated what he was doing, Annika could not help but admire Buck's skill. His large tanned hands moved with the speed of familiarity with the task and expertise that might be envied by an accomplished surgeon.

He talked the whole while he worked on the first and then the second rabbit, carefully explaining each and every step as if he believed that someday she actually would carry out the gruesome task herself. At some point in the process, Annika realized she was listening with interest as he pointed out the gall bladder. "Don't ever cut into it," he warned as he carefully removed it with the other innards. "It'll ruin the meat." He set aside the liver, heart, and kidneys, pointing each out in turn and explaining that they were all edible.

The still-warm organs steamed in the frosty air. Buck wrapped the dressed meat in a piece of thick muslin and turned to hand it to Annika. When he saw the gray pallor of her complexion and the way she held one hand pressed against her midsection and the other over her mouth, he decided it would be best if he carried the meat indoors himself.

"Get Baby," he said over his shoulder as he headed for the cabin, knowing she had no choice but to follow.

The sky darkened again, as the brief respite from the shroud of gray clouds passed. He tried to fathom Annika's reaction to a task so vital to survival, tried to conjure up visions of what her world was like. As he walked through the snow heading for the door, he could hear Baby chatting to an unresponsive Annika. Buck watched his moccasins appear and disappear as he worked his way through the snow and thought of how excited he had been the first time he'd been allowed to dress his first kill.

Squirrel hunting in the hickory timber in Kentucky had been a chore most boys looked forward to with a passion. He became a crack shot at picking squirrel off swaying limbs—sport that required a steady hand and a good eye. But those carefree days ended all too soon, and at a time when most boys his age were still targeting squirrel, Buck was a full-fledged buffalo hunter and highly skilled skinner.

He reached the door and waited for her to catch up as she struggled through the snow with the child on her hip. Buck stepped back to let her open the door, his hands still somewhat bloody and occupied with the bundle of meat.

"Go ahead." He nodded toward the door. He half expected her to comment on his sudden show of manners. Her silence warned him how upset she truly was.

Annika preceded him into the cabin and set Baby down on the closest chair. The child immediately scrambled down and tried to pull off her coat, now damp from the melting snow clinging to it.

As Annika took off her cape and then helped Baby remove her coat, he began to anchor the rabbits to the turnspit in the fireplace.

Without removing his own coat, Buck watched Annika as she held Baby's small coat forgotten in her hands and stared at the floor. He could tell she was fighting back the urge to vomit as she swallowed repeatedly and concentrated on a spot on the ground between her shoes.

He quickly washed his hands and toweled them dry. Thinking it might be better to say nothing than to say the wrong thing, he silently took Baby's jacket from Annika and set it on the bed. Then he pulled out a chair for her, gently lay a hand on her shoulder, and guided her to the seat.

When his hand touched her shoulder, her eyes flashed upward and met his for a brief moment, then she looked away. She held her hands clenched together in her lap.

He started to turn away.

"I suppose your sister cleaned rabbits," she said.

He wondered what she was getting at. "She did."

"Oh."

"What about it?"

"Is that why she went crazy?"

He couldn't see her face, but he had the distinct feeling she was dead serious. The vision of his father flaying Jim's corpse flashed through his mind. "No. That wasn't it at all."

"I'm surprised." Her tone was as cold as the air outside.

He hunkered down before her so that she was forced to look at him. "Listen, I didn't do that to punish or torture you, no matter what you might think. I did it because there is a very real possibility that anything could happen to me while I'm out hunting. I'd like to think that you could take care of yourself until the thaw. Old Ted's bound to come back by then and he could get you out. If Ted or someone else doesn't happen by, then you'll have to pack up the mules and leave on your own with Baby. Follow the trail up out of the valley, go through the pass, and then head toward the rising sun—remember, away from the setting sun—and you're bound to hit Cheyenne, or come close enough to find a ranch or a smaller settlement."

For the first time since he'd laid eyes on her, she looked at him with something less than disgust. "What about Baby?"

"When you get to Cheyenne, see that she gets a good home. Maybe there's a preacher who can take her or at least find someone who will. Maybe your brother knows somebody who wants a child."

"You'd trust me to do that?"

"Do I have a choice?"

"What about her mother?"

"Don't even look for her. Patsy can't be trusted with her."

"But—"

He turned on her before she could say another word. "Not Patsy. Do you understand?"

"Nothing's going to happen to you." She sounded fearful rather than positive as a host of possibilities occurred to her now.

"Just do the best you can. You don't owe me, I know, not after what's happened, but you seem to like Baby well enough."

Annika was silent. Her mind raced as she thought of Kase and Rose and the babies they had lost. And here Buck Scott had one to give away.

Buck stood up again and walked back to the fire. He bent down and turned the spit. The rabbits were beginning to roast, the outer skin that had been seared by the fire was now dripping juice that hissed on the glowing logs below.

"I'm going back out for a while," he told her. "I have to clean up the shed and dispose of the entrails and parts of the rabbit we don't need."

She turned to him, her blue eyes shadowed with question. "Are you going hunting again?"

"No. Just out to clean up."

"How long will you be?"

"Planning another escape now that you know which way to go?" He shook his head. "I wouldn't advise it. The storm's not played out yet. It's going to snow again."

She straightened, the concern in her eyes turning to impatience. "I'm not that stupid, Mr. Scott. I was just wondering how long you plan on being out so that I might know at what point I should begin worrying that one of the many dire predictions you've made might have occurred."

"I should be back within a quarter of an hour."

"Fine."

He had his hand on the door handle when she said, "Exactly how am I to procure the game that is to keep us alive in the untimely event of your demise?"

He gave her a half smile as he said, "Don't worry. As soon as it stops snowing, I'm going to teach you to hunt."

ROSE Storm brushed aside the lace curtain and rubbed a peephole in the frosted oval window set in the back door. She stretched on tiptoe and stared out into the thickening gloom of the late winter's afternoon, watching for her husband. The stable yard behind the house was empty; squares of lamplight shone in the bunkhouse windows across the way, marking the only sign of life in the snow-draped surroundings. She sighed and let the curtain drop. Smoothing a hand over the swollen mound beneath her burgundy serge gown, Rose walked out of the kitchen and into the parlor. She left the lamp burning in the center of the kitchen table so that Kase would not have to walk into a dark room.

She roamed through the house, which seemed so very silent with Kase gone, and wondered when he would return from Cheyenne. She had guessed that the storm would hold him back, but she had half hoped that somehow he would get through despite the snow.

Rose lit the lamps in the downstairs parlor. The golden glow highlighted the home in which she took so much pride. Every nook and cranny, every piece that decorated every room of the two-story house had been lovingly selected by her and Kase together. Rose had opted for simplicity and comfort rather than the fashion of the times when she chose a simple house over the more ornate Queen Anne Kase had wanted to have built for her. She had preferred something typically American, something the likes of which she had never seen in her native Italy. Although she was able to dissuade Kase from building her a mansion, their home was far from a cabin.

"We may live on the plains," he told her, "but that doesn't mean we shouldn't have all the modern conveniences." So saying, he had installed front and back stairs, a huge pantry, gleaming brass chandeliers, and even linen roller window shades beneath the Belgian lace curtains. A wide veranda encircled the house and from every angle the view was magnificent, whether it was of wide-open, rolling plains or the widespread skirts of the mountains that seemed to extend almost to the back door.

Rose sat on the deep cushioned sofa near the fire and smoothed the pristine collar and the white lace cuffs of her gown. It was simple but stylish, and again, Kase had a hand in choosing it for her. Her dark hair was piled on her head, twisted into a simple knot at the crown. She felt the child inside her move, the flutter as soft and hesitant as a captive fairy's wings. She placed her hand protectively on the swelling mound where her child grew.

She closed her eyes and said a silent prayer, asking God to deliver this child to them safely, not so much for her as for Kase, for she knew he could not stand to lose another baby. Some innate instinct had seen her through each of her previous tragedies, some inner voice that told her once the mourning and tears had subsided that this was a land where a less than healthy child could never survive. Nature took care of her own. Rose believed that the weak infants that had died before reaching full term would never have survived the harsh Wyoming winters or the dry dust of a windblown summer.

Already she had carried this child far longer than the first two, but their third loss had been a little girl born just last year. Little Katerina had lived but a few hours, and when she suddenly died it had been Kase who had grieved the longest. He had been so withdrawn for a time that Rose had been afraid he would refuse her more children, but in the end she had convinced him that she needed to try again.

She smiled to herself when she thought of the way he treated her like a queen. "My Roman goddess," he teased even now that she was swollen with his child. Kase had been insisting of late that she hire someone to help her with the cooking, for she prepared all the meals for the ranch hands herself, but she had refused any outside help. When word arrived that his sister was coming to stay for an extended visit, Rose had pleaded with him not to hire anyone because Annika could help him with the cooking. She remembered how he had laughed, his blue eyes bright with merriment, as he shook his head. "Annika, dear Rose, probably couldn't pick out the stove if you showed her around the kitchen."

"Good, then I will have someone to teach. Maybe she will help a little."

Kase had smiled. "It'll be good for her. She's never really had to do anything for herself."

"And that is her fault?" Rose had asked.

With a shake of his head he had answered, "No. We were all more than willing to spoil her to death."

"As you do me," Rose whispered aloud in the empty room.

The sound of the back door brought her to her feet. She hurried through the house, her heartbeat accelerating the way it always did whenever Kase walked in. For that moment there were only the two of them in the world; all else was forgotten. She greeted him without words and stepped straight into his arms. He enfolded her gently and held her as their heartbeats commingled, then pulled away far enough to lower his head and kiss her tenderly.

"I missed you," he whispered afterward.

"And I you."

He kissed her again, deeply, passionately, until she suddenly remembered the reason he had left and and pulled back, resting against the circle of his arms. "Where is your sister?"

She looked up into the dark, handsome face, brushing back the stray strands of hair that had escaped the beaded ornament that held it in a shoulder-length queue. His expression hardened.

"Come sit down first." He began to usher her back toward the parlor.

She refused to budge. "No. Tell me now."

"Rose . . ."

"Kase, tell me."

He sighed and pulled a chair away from the kitchen table.
"Then sit here."

"Is she all right?"

"Sit," he said, knowing full well she would do as she
pleased unless he held his silence.

Rose sat, knowing he would not say anything until she did
as he demanded.

He pulled a chair up close beside her and took her hands.
"Annika was abducted from the train."

"You are joking with me, yes?"

"I wish I was."

"But why? Someone knows your family is rich? They ask
for money?"

Kase shrugged. "The conductor told me that man who
took her thought that Annika was his mail-order bride."

"She is mailing what?"

Kase sighed. "A mail-order bride is a woman who is engaged to a man she has never met. They correspond first and
then agree to marry."

"But why did—"

He cut her off before she could ask more questions. "I
don't know why, Rose, all I know is that this man has kidnapped my sister and has ridden off with her.

"What about your mother and Caleb? You sent the telegram to them?"

He shook his head. "I'm hoping to put it off as long as
possible. I don't want to worry then unnecessarily. I've offered a big reward and had flyers printed up while I was in
Cheyenne. In a few days I'll have to let them know because
the paper already interviewed me and the story is sure to
spread. I'd hate to have them read about it in the news."

"What can I do?" She watched him carefully and prayed
silently that his sister's abduction didn't force him to pin on
a lawman's badge again.

"You can fix me a cup of coffee. It's cold enough to make
a polar bear hunt for cover."

❧ 10 ❧

F EBRUARY 7th. Somewhere in the Rockies.
    As I look back upon the last few entries in this journal, I realize that until now I did not know how kind life has been to me. This morning I am writing hunched over a scarred and battered table, hoping that my ink will not freeze again. I have been kidnapped by a man the likes of which I have never seen, a mountain man of sorts, but not the romantic stock the dime periodicals would have one believe the West is made of.

    I won't even sully the pages of this journal by adding his name. Suffice it to say that he is unkempt, ill-mannered, unsmiling, and uncivilized, just to list a few of his better traits. He is a hulking bear of a man clothed in hides and fur who lives with an endearing child with the face of an angel. I have tried to ignore her but I cannot. I am here because he believed me to be the woman he was to marry, but the only reason he wanted a wife at all was to fill the position of drudge, scullery maid, and nanny. So far he has tried to enlist my services, but is finding me none too malleable.

    I am both tired and filthy, not to mention frightened, although my fear has lessened now that I have been in this man's company for four days and he has yet to physically harm me. Not that I don't think him capable of it, but I believe that somehow he has his own set of rules, a moral

*code which does not allow for cruelty to females. At least
I pray I am correct.*

*I am certain my family is frantic to ascertain my where-
abouts. And, although I don't wish them any undue suffer-
ing, I do pray that Kase will hurry and find me. All I know
is that we are living in a miserable excuse for a cabin,
somewhere in the mountains northwest of Cheyenne, Wyoming.*

*If only I had a change of clothing, I feel I might better
handle this situation.*

*As I look around I can't help but think of my mother and
wonder how she was able to survive the years she existed
in a sod house on the Iowa prairie. I try to imagine what it
must have been like for her, an immigrant, virtually alone
and lonely in her crude surroundings. How easy it was for
me to picture her former life as a romantic adventure! I
am now certain the reality of the situation was quite the
opposite.*

"How long have you been up?"

When Buck Scott's voice cut into her reverie, Annika
jumped, leaving a blob of ink at the end of her last sentence.
She swung her long braid over her shoulder and glared at
him. He was lying propped against the pillow of his huge
bed, his arms crossed over the chest of the red overalls which
he had stripped down to the night before. The rest of his
length remained hidden beneath the covers.

"Unlike you, Mr. Scott, I don't intend to sleep the day
away like a hibernating bear. I've been up for some time."
She curled her stockinged feet up beneath the hems of her
gowns.

"Did you start the coffee?"

"No."

"Last night I said the first one up should start the coffee,"
he reminded her.

"I have a feeling that's exactly why you chose to sleep
in." She capped her traveling inkwell and, in lieu of a rag,
tried to blot her stained fingers on the edge of the table.

He scratched his head. "You're staining my table."

"How can you tell? It's already a mess."

He pushed the covers back and swung his legs over the edge of the bed. Annika averted her eyes and kept them on the journal lying open in front of her. Her face flamed.

"It's the only table I have, Miss Storm, even if it isn't what you're used to. Now, what about that coffee?"

She heard the swish of his pants when he picked them up off the floor. He was standing not two feet from her as he pulled them on.

"Well?"

She answered without looking in his direction. "I couldn't remember if you said to boil the water before adding the coffee or after."

His voice was muffled as he knelt down and fished around beneath the bed for his moccasins. "I said to fill the pot with water and bring it to a boil. While it's boiling you grind the coffee beans. Then you add the coffee and one of those broken eggshells in the can beside the grinder."

"How much coffee?"

"One spoonful per cup and one for the pot. I put in nine, ten if I want it stronger. After the coffee is the color you want it, you have to trickle in some cold water to settle the grounds to the bottom."

"I couldn't remember all that."

"I don't think you wanted to. Didn't you say you were trained as a teacher, Miss Storm?"

"In a weak moment I might have admitted it, yes."

"Then I think you can probably remember something as easy as how to make coffee. Shoot, Baby could do it in a year or two."

"But can you wait that long for a cup, Mr. Scott?"

"I don't intend to. You're going to do it."

"Or what?"

"Or we'll go without today."

Annika almost agreed, but the thought of giving up the heady smell of the rich brew and the chance to hold the steaming cup between hands that had been impossible to warm was something she hated to miss, even if it meant giving in to him.

She stood up and began to fill the coffeepot with freezing

water from the barrel by the door. "You need a decent stove."

Buck ignored her and shrugged into his flannel shirt. As he worked the buttons closed, he thought about the peace and quiet he had enjoyed before he brought Annika Storm home. As sorry as he was that he had mistaken her for Alice Soams, he was still glad that he had not ended up with a wife. He could just imagine the complaints she would have about the cabin, the lack of amenities, the isolation. He saw as much in Annika's eyes every time she looked around. A wife's every sentence would start with "Do you know what you need?" He would have to put up with the complaining or make endless trips to Cheyenne to cart the items she demanded up the mountain.

By the time he was completely dressed he was certain he would never marry. A wife would want things he couldn't give, and yet, as he watched Annika filling the pot with water, he realized that even her nightgown and the borrowed nightshirt could not disguise her all-too-feminine curves. There was no denying his physical attraction to her; even though he was trying like hell not to show it, he found himself watching her far too often and much too closely. Everything about her intrigued him, from the way she brushed her hair to the way she walked across the room. There was one thing a wife could give him that he hadn't had in a very long time.

Unaware of his scrutiny as she ground the coffee, Annika spoke to him over her shoulder. "Why do you have to hunt anyway? I would think that in the winter there's nothing out there to catch."

"Trap." He walked to the workbench and picked up the enamelware mugs and two spoons. "Beaver, wolf, rabbit, whatever wanders into my traps are welcome because the pelts are prime in winter. They're best when there's an *r* in the name of the month. September, October, November, De—"

"I know the names of the months," she snapped. Annika folded her arms across her midsection while she waited for the water to boil. "Why don't you move to Cheyenne? Then you wouldn't have to worry about Baby or about stealing a wife. You could simply hire a housekeeper."

Buck paused in the midst of measuring out cornmeal for the morning mush. It was the first time she had asked him anything remotely personal in days. He watched her curiously as she bent to peer into the coffeepot she'd positioned as near the fire as she could.

"And do what?" he asked.

She shrugged. "Anything."

"Store work? Clean out stables? Smithing?" He shook his head. "That's not for me. Why should I work for anyone when I can live free and be my own boss?"

She was studying him intently now, watching him as he added boiling water from the blackened kettle to the pot of meal. "Why do you think that's all you're capable of?"

He set the pot down with more force than he intended and frowned. When he met her gaze he could see that she was not chiding him but seriously asking for an explanation. "Look at me, Miss Storm. I'm a buffalo man, a skinner. That's all I know; it's what I do well. I make enough money to live off it. The problem is that there aren't any buffalo anymore—so I do what I can and I still take in a good wage for the pelts I cure and deliver. Besides, I'm not educated for fancy work. And I hate towns."

She looked about her—at the humble interior of his cabin, at the crude furnishings and the dirt floor—and wondered what he considered enough to live on. "My brother's a rancher now. I'm sure he hires extra hands, and he's trying to raise buffalo. Knowing them as you do—"

"I know how to kill them, Miss Storm. Besides, can you really see Kase Storm welcoming me with open arms?" He laughed aloud at the thought. "I'll be lucky if he doesn't put a bullet through me before I can explain that this whole thing was a mistake."

Crumbling an eggshell, she mixed it with the coffee grounds and measured them into the pot. He was right, she thought. No matter what she might suggest, she couldn't quite imagine Kase offering Buck Scott a job, not after the worry the man had put him through. She knew her brother's temper wouldn't allow it and could almost hear the two of them snarling at each other. Nor could she imagine Buck Scott living in the confines of a city the size of Cheyenne, or having to limit himself to the rigid rules and regulations of Society. The idea of the big man dressed in a nappy tweed suit nearly made her laugh aloud. But she was a firm believer that a man could become anything he wanted. She decided then and there to start thinking about what Buck Scott might do in Cheyenne.

She glanced up and found him staring at her again. "What are you looking at?"

He started stirring the mush. "I was wondering why you were even wasting time figuring out how I could provide for Baby in town. Seems to me after what I've done you wouldn't care what happens to us."

Annika wondered the same thing but searched for an answer that would appease him without admitting the truth. "Baby ought to have a decent home."

"And this isn't?" His blue eyes challenged hers.

"If you could provide for all her needs, why did you write to Alice Soams?"

Unwilling to admit that he was regretting his plan to marry Alice Soams, or anyone else for that matter, he tried to divert her attention to another topic. "Why don't you check the coffee?"

When Annika turned away, Buck thought about what she said and hated to admit that she was probably right. The only way he could keep Baby if he didn't find a woman to live with him would be to move closer to town and find someone who could care for her. But what about him? What could he do in Cheyenne or anyplace else? He thought of a line from an old rhyme, "Butcher, baker, candlestick maker." What talent did he have besides hunting, skinning, and butchering? It was all he'd known since he was fourteen, that and mixing up the home cures and remedies he'd learned from his mother.

As he spooned out two bowls of mush he thought that perhaps he'd make someone a better wife than a woman as ill-equipped to take care of herself as Annika Storm. He watched as she carefully poured cold water into the coffee-pot spout to settle the grounds. When she straightened and found him staring, her face flamed, then her brows dipped into a frown. "If you'll turn around, I'll dress."

"You've got two nightshirts on as it is. What's to see?"

"It's not my fault that I haven't anything decent to wear. If I had the contents of just one of my trunks I might be able to keep warm, but as it is, I'm just trying to make do."

When she planted her hands on her hips, he knew he'd riled her again.

"Don't you think I'd like something clean to change into? I can't believe I have to wear these same clothes until you get me out of here. They're already filthy, I'm filthy, and I—"

"I know, I know. You hate it here."

She crossed her arms and nodded. "Exactly."

"Why don't you take a bath?"

Stunned, she eyed him suspiciously, not daring to hope for such a luxury. "Where?"

"Right here in front of the fire. I'll bring the washtub in after breakfast."

"And what will you do while I'm bathing?"

"I'll ignore you. What's the fuss? I had two sisters."

"And I have a brother, but you're not him."

"No. I'm not."

"So where will you go while I bathe?"

He was about to say no place, then reneged. "I'll go check on my traps. The storm's passed by now."

"Good. I'll lock the door while you're gone."

"The door doesn't have a lock. Anyone who wants in is welcome. Nothing here worth taking," he said low.

Annika couldn't help but look over at Baby still asleep in the big bed.

Guessing the train of her thoughts he added, "A cabin door's always open in an out-of-the-way place."

"Not when I bathe," she assured him.

BUCK pulled the hood of his coat close about his head and cursed loud and long since there was no one within earshot except the horse that stood beside him and the pack mule tied behind it. It was the fourth morning that he'd been ousted from his home so that Annika Storm could bathe and he regretted ever having given in to her demand the first time. Daily she reminded him to stay away as long as possible, and he usually had no problem obliging her while he used the time to check on the beaver traps he set along Blue Creek. But today it was colder than an eskimo's grave and he'd never set traps so many mornings in a row.

He unpacked his mule and started walking, encumbered like a beast of burden with his rifle slung over his shoulder and a packboard on his back in case he had to transport a heavy load. He hefted the trap chain, swung it over his shoulder, and wished he hadn't taken to shaving every morning. His face was cold, damn cold. Why should it matter to him in the least what Annika Storm thought of him anyway? She'd never even mentioned his having shaved at all, so he didn't see why he'd taken to doing it every day. But he had.

As he slogged through the snow beside Blue Creek, hunting for signs of a beaver slide along the bank, he mentally went over the provisions he had stored away in and around the cabin. Yesterday he had shown them to Annika, had carefully pointed out the barrel of apples layered in dry sand, the bucket full of eggs packed in salt, the canned fruits and vegetables that lined the shelves beneath the workbench. She had refused to eat any meat since the rabbit skinning, but he showed her the small smokehouse behind the cabin anyway. Today he hoped to come across some game that he could add to the larder.

Even as uncomfortably cold as he was, Buck couldn't help but smile when he thought of the exchange the barrel of apples had inspired. He'd shown them to Annika and had added, "I was kind of hoping you'd volunteer to make an apple pie."

"I was kind of hoping I would be at my brother's home by now."

Unable to resist baiting her he added, "I should have guessed by the way you make coffee that pie is out of the question."

"You should know by now that even if I did know how to bake pies I wouldn't do it for you."

Ducking beneath a low branch, he shook his head and smiled to himself. She was a stubborn cuss, he'd grant her that. He recalled how he'd almost laughed during the exchange, but he didn't want to let her know he was enjoying her company. The woman would no doubt use the knowledge to get him to do something else he didn't really want to do. Hell, he was already stranded outside every morning and shaving every day, even though a good growth of beard would keep him warmer.

She'd be gone come the first thaw, so there was no sense in letting himself enjoy anything about her, not her quick wit nor her beauty.

A flicker of movement in the thick aspen across the stream caught his eye and he slowly, quietly lowered the trap to the ground. He shouldered the rifle and took aim at an elk that had paused, ears alert and nose in the air, not fifty feet away. If he could bring the big bull down, there would be more than enough meat to last for weeks.

He raised the gun and took aim, knowing that in the aspen and the heavy timber behind it one shot was all he was likely to get. To kill the bull outright, he would have to break the spine where the neck joined the shoulders or hit him at the point of the elbow right behind the shoulder.

When he pulled the trigger, the sound of the rifle reverberated in his ears. The big wapiti fell, its legs giving way beneath it as it crumpled to the ground.

Buck shouldered his rifle again and jogged through the shallow water of the stream until he reached the dead bull elk. It was as big an elk as he'd ever seen and he figured it would take hours to butcher and would dress out at over four hundred pounds.

He set down the packboard, glad to have it along because he would need it to haul the meat back to the pack mule he'd left downwind. Loosening the ax that he'd tied to his waist, he set it on the ground beside the animal and then unsheathed his knife. He slit the inside of the legs much the way he'd done the rabbits' and then found the break joint just below the knee, cut into it, and snapped the leg bone over his knee so that he could easily disjoint the elk.

He glanced up at the sky, thankful that the sun was once again shining brightly above the mountain peaks that fenced the eastern side of the valley. The sky was crystal clear and as blue—he noticed with much irritation—as Annika Storm's eyes. As he began to skin out the elk, he hoped she'd be able to manage Baby all day. Not that she would be very happy about it. Although Annika had begrudgingly taken to caring for the child whenever he went out, he could not help but notice the gentle way she always treated Baby.

Working as quickly as he dared, Buck slit open the belly and began to cut the paunch and the entrails away from the backbone. The viscera steamed as he rolled them out onto the snow. As he pulled out the heart that had been alive and beating only moments before, he paused, reminded of how fragile a thing life is and how quickly it can be extinguished.

The sobering thought forced him to hurry, unwilling to leave Annika and the child alone any longer than necessary.

"AND then, believing they should be free like men, Tonweya painted the tips of the eagles' wings bright red and took them to the mountaintop. They spread their wings and flew away as he bid them good-bye. And that is why some eagles still have red-tipped wings."

Annika smoothed back the wayward curls from Baby's forehead and covered her with a wolf pelt. The child had fallen asleep long before the end of the Sioux legend, but the telling of it had reminded Annika of her father and home, and missing both, she had finished it for her own sake.

She pulled herself out of the all-too-comfortable bed and walked across the room to collect her cape. Drawing it across her shoulders, she stepped outside and wrapped her hands up in the folds of the rich satin. She paced the length of the yard, packing the snow that had already become trampled by their footsteps during the past few days.

Able to walk to the gentle rise a few yards away, Annika pulled her cape tighter and stared out across the valley floor. She could see the silver blue of the shallow stream as it meandered like a twisted snake past the cabin. Leafless aspen stood like gaunt skeletons on the lower slopes with the dark, rich pines crowded nearly one atop the other higher up. The place was so silent compared to the city that she paused to listen. The wind whispered through the treetops, here and there snow dropped off overburdened branches to plop heavily onto the drifts below. Annika took a step and heard the snow crunch beneath her feet. She saw no signs of forest life nor did she see anything that remotely resembled Buck Scott.

There had been no sign of him since morning and now that the sun was just about to disappear over the western slope of the mountains, Annika was beginning to fear the worst.

"Damn the man," she whispered aloud, remembering the multitude of catastrophes that he claimed might befall him. Then, immediately contrite, she prayed nothing had happened.

There had been little unusual about the morning, although now she tried to remember if he had told her he was going to be gone all day or not. Their days had settled into a routine of sorts as both of them tried to stay out of each other's way as much as possible in the confining space of the cabin. Every morning he would leave so that she could bathe in private, and afterward, as a thank-you, she would bathe Baby for him. The morning ritual had become a godsend, for although she was forced to wear the same clothes day in and day out, now at least she felt clean underneath.

He was usually good enough to give her an hour or two alone before he returned, and then they would pass the daylight hours functioning under a truce. Buck had taken it upon himself to teach her all she would ever need to know and more about surviving alone until spring, and she had taken it upon herself to act as if she didn't care to learn any of it.

Until today she never fully believed anything could possibly happen to a man as big, as stubborn, or as vitally alive as Buck Scott. But now, as she stared out over the valley searching for any sign of him, worry chilled her more than the frigid, dry air lifting the hem of her cape.

She strained to hear some sound that might indicate where he might be, but although the breeze whispered to her from the tops of the pines and the stream lapped gaily against its rocky bed, they held no answer. Soon it would be dark and she would be alone with the child. That was a reality she did not relish facing, but it was too late to go off in search of Buck on her own. His horse's trail was still clear in the snow, but whether it veered off farther up the valley or not was anyone's guess. She did not want to have to carry Baby out into the cold on a dangerous, perhaps fruitless mission.

Taking a deep breath of the clear mountain air, Annika turned away from the sweeping view of the wide-bottomed valley floor. The air inside the dimly lit cabin was close and warm. She didn't relish going back inside, but she had begun to shiver. As she carefully worked her way across the icy yard, she told herself she was being foolish, that Buck's expertise and survival instincts would see him safely home.

A week ago if anyone had told her she'd be praying for a chance to set eyes on Buck Scott again she would have called him mad, but just now all she wanted was to see Buck ride down the mountainside sitting tall in the saddle, leading his pack mule.

And when he did arrive, she intended to give him a generous piece of her mind.

IT had been dark a good hour before the cabin came into view. As Buck nudged his horse forward, he let the animal take its time and pick out a patch across the frozen ground. The thin streams of light that shone through the shutters of the cabin slowly grew from pinpoints to ribbons of light that spilled across the snow.

He wondered if Annika was still awake or if she had fallen asleep with the lamp burning. He hoped she had already bedded down, for as much as he wanted her to think that he was unaffected by her presence, it was becoming nearly impossible. Night seemed to intensify the intimacy of their situation, for it was then that she unplaited her long braid and combed her sunlit hair until it shone like spun honey. At night she let down her guard and became vulnerable, starting at every howl of coyote or wolf, watching the door. Watching him more closely.

For the past few nights when she made up her pallet he had been tempted to trade places so that she might sleep more comfortably. It was becoming nearly impossible for him to sleep with her so near anyway, especially when the firelight cast her shadow on the wall as she sat near the fire reading her book or writing in her journal. When she finally fell asleep her soft breathing was so magnified that he counted every breath and imagined the way it would feel playing against his ear. It was during those times that he would lie in bed fighting the hard quickening of his desire beneath the covers as he willed his mind to go blank.

There was no moon to light his way tonight, but he kept his horse moving, knowing the animal could find its way home even in the dark. Both animals were weighted down with elk meat—he'd even tied the wide rack of antlers on top of the mule's burden. A good half hour's work still lay ahead of him; he had to unload the meat in the smokehouse where he could string it up. He would then have to unpack his equipment and feed the weary animals.

The elk had provided him with a meal that evening when the task of dressing the huge animal was over. Bone tired from skinning and butchering, packing and hauling, he had feasted on fresh liver roasted on a stick. Now he was tired, but well fed, and knew that tonight even Annika Storm's presence would not prevent him from sleeping.

INSIDE the cabin, Annika sat at the table with her chin in her hands and stared at the door. Her worry had become anger and then turned to worry again. What if Buck Scott were trapped under an avalanche or maimed by a wild animal? What if he had fallen off the side of a mountain? What if he never returned and she were left to care for Baby until the snow melted or another trapper happened by? How would she know who to trust?

She covered her face and sat there, elbows on the table, trying to remember everything Buck had tried to teach her over the last few days. Her stomach churned between nervous flutters. He *had* to come home. He *had* to be all right.

He just had to.

All day she had tried to deny the fact that she missed him sorely. Instead of relishing the time alone, she found the cabin far too silent and foreboding. The isolation of the wilderness had intensified with every hour he had been gone. Each time she paced the yard to stare across the ever-darkening landscape watching for some sign of him, she realized how very alone she was without him.

Baby offered slim consolation. The child had been happy enough during the morning hours and seemed content to sort the buttons and play with her makeshift toys, but as the day wore on and Buck did not appear she grew fussy, whining that she wanted Buck, until nothing Annika did for her was enough to stop her tears. The ceaseless whimpering heightened Annika's own anxiety until she swore that if and when Buck Scott walked back in the door she would murder him herself. Finally she managed to cook Baby a fried egg and then made the child go to bed. Baby finally cried herself to sleep.

Straightening, Annika pushed the loose strands of hair back off her face and decided it would do no good to sit and stare at the door. She decided to ready herself for bed as if it were any other night and hope that Buck returned at first light. She took off her wool suit and folded it as neatly as she could and hung it over the back of a chair. Then, she washed her face in the basin of cold water on the bench. This time of night Buck was usually settling Baby down, telling her a story as he sat beside her until she fell asleep on her side of the wide bed.

Annika recalled the evening she asked him why the child didn't have a bed of her own.

"I tried it once," he had explained, "but she wouldn't stay in it, so to save room I took it down. Why?"

"I don't know." She shrugged. "It's just that some people, well . . . some people might not think it proper for a man to be sleeping with a little girl."

She had regretted the words as soon as they were uttered. She knew him well enough by now to know that he would never harm the child. Buck had turned red, then his embarrassment changed to a slow, simmering rage. It was hours into the next day before he even spoke to her again.

As she strained for any sound outside that would signal his homecoming, she made her bed on the floor and then sat beneath the fur covers while she brushed out her hair. The fire had burned low, but the cabin was warmer than it had been in days. The temperature outside had risen, which boded well for Buck if he were spending the night outside. It was not the first time that she wondered if he had been lying to her, hiding the fact that they were not really trapped in the valley, but were still close enough to civilization that he could ride in and out at will.

Perhaps, she thought, with a furious stroke of the hairbrush, he was in a warm saloon in some frontier town right now. Maybe—she threw the brush back in her satchel and snapped it shut—he was visiting with some of his cronies, laughing at her at this very moment. She could almost see him, his wild mane of hair picking up the glow of lamplight, his full lips parted into a rare smile, his blue eyes shining with laughter.

Maybe he was with a woman.

Annika threw the covers aside and stood up. She grabbed a piece of wood and tossed it on the fire, then regretted her unthinking move as sparks showered dangerously close to her bed. She picked up the twig broom in the corner of the room and swept the hearth clean, making certain she had not left any ash or cinders glowing outside the fireplace.

She didn't intend to be made a fool of by anyone, especially Buck Scott, and she was determined to tell him so the minute he walked in the door.

If he walked in the door.

❦ 11 ❦

Weary to the bone, Buck led his mule past the cabin and dismounted beside the smokehouse. Piece by piece he unloaded the meat, strung it, and hung it from the low beams in the small wooden structure. It was cold enough to let it hang overnight, but come morning he would start the fire in the pit outside to begin the process that would cure the meat and preserve it for months.

He hoped Annika was asleep. If she was, he planned to heat enough water for a bath, soak for a while, and then crawl into bed. If she wasn't asleep— He decided he would wait to see what kind of mood she was in.

His hands were cold inside his gloves, his fingers stiff from working unprotected from the weather all day. It took him longer than usual to unsaddle his horse and untie the mule, then pour grain into the feed trough.

He could smell the wood smoke escaping from the chimney, and felt a bit warmer just knowing the fire was still burning inside. Before Annika arrived, he and Baby would often return home to a fire that had grown cold with no one to feed it. Before Annika he could never have taken so long to butcher an elk, not with Baby in tow. Most of the spoils would have gone to the wolves.

Before Annika . . .

Try as he might, he couldn't deny his growing anticipation at the thought of seeing her again. She had been on his mind through the long, tedious hours of the day. He found, much to his surprise, that he even missed their sparring, and as the

143

hours passed, he realized just how much her presence had helped to ease the loneliness that was part of his days.

By the time he slapped his horse on its broad rump and started for the cabin, he was even debating about finding another mail-order bride. He hated having lost the train fare to Alice Soams, but maybe companionship was worth taking another chance on.

But now he could only imagine someone the image of Annika Storm answering his letter.

She had tried to pull the table across the room to barricade the door as soon as she heard the sound of someone moving around behind the cabin, but the heavy wooden table with its lodgepole pine legs would not budge. Her heart was still beating wildly, even though the muffled noises had subsided. She sat straight as a poker on the edge of the bed, clutching the butcher knife in her hands, and she took little solace from the fact that Baby slept on. She wondered why the sound of her pounding heart hadn't disturbed the child.

At first she thought it might be Buck, but it was his habit to walk in, see that all was well, and then go out to care for his horse and clean whatever game he'd have caught. Alert to every sound outside, straining to hear footsteps on the snowy ground, Annika wondered who or what had been moving around outside. She imagined a bear, at the very least, for it had to be something big enough to make the thumping, pawing sounds she had heard.

It had been a while since she had heard anything at all, so she allowed herself a deep breath and a sigh of relief; but just as she did, she heard someone, or something, fumbling with the door handle.

Before she could change her mind she was off like a shot out of a cannon. She clung to the knife handle, more willing than able to use it to defend herself and the child if the need arose. Unable to stand the suspense any longer, she reached out to pull the door open and catch the intruder off guard.

On the other side of the door, the handle was ripped from Buck's grip. The door swung inward and he found himself face-to-face with Annika Storm brandishing a knife in his face. Her hair hung unbound, brushed to a high shine. Her eyes were wide with fright. He was so close he could see her moist lips all too well and the way her lashes outlined her eyes. Her cheeks were alive with color. The plaid flannel nightshirt covered her once-white batiste gown, her stockinged feet peeped out from beneath the swaying hems.

She was staring up at him, too stunned to speak, the knife still raised threateningly.

"Well," he said slowly, not quite sure what to make of the situation, "kill me if you're going to or let me in."

Relief flooded through her. She dropped the hand that held the knife and tried to blink back the tears that suddenly filled her eyes. Annika had never seen a more beautiful sight than Buck Scott as he filled the doorway. Darkened by the shadows, his usually light eyes were watching her warily. She looked him up and down to be certain, but there did not appear to be a scratch on him. He was still wearing his familiar buckskin jacket, the hood pulled tight to frame his face with the thick wolf fur. His face was sunburned to a deep bronze that emphasized the creases around his eyes. Every breath he took frosted on the night air. He looked cold, exhausted, and surprised by her odd greeting.

But at least he was home.

"Where have you been?" she yelled.

"Why are you shouting?" He pushed her aside and stepped over the threshold, intent on getting warm. Walking straight to the bed, he stood for a moment and gazed down on Baby as she slept, then turned to survey the room. The fire was burning brightly, there was a stack of clean dishes on the kitchen bench. He was relieved to note that everything looked fine.

Everything but Annika. She was still glaring at him.

"Close the door," he said softly, so as not to wake the child.

She slammed it shut. Baby stirred and rolled to her stomach.

"Are you going to tell me where you've been or not?"

"I was until you started ranting. What are you so upset about?"

"Upset? Upset? I'm not upset! I'm furious. How dare you leave me here all day to watch over this place and that child while you go traipsing off, God knows where. I won't do it again, do you hear?"

Buck sighed and shrugged out of his coat. Annika moved forward, set the knife on the table, grabbed his jacket from him, and then hung it on the peg beside the door. He watched her perform the small service for him with wonder.

"And I suppose you're hungry?" she snapped.

He knew whenever she planted her hands on her hips it was a sign of open defiance. "Not really, but I could use a cup of coffee." He smelled it simmering by the fire.

"You're just lucky I kept it warm." She marched to the workbench and picked up his chipped cup, crossed to the fire, grabbed a wadded towel that served as pot holder, and poured him a cupful of brew that looked strong enough to lift the table.

Amazed, Buck pulled out a chair and sat down while Annika bustled back and forth, handing him a plate, then lifting a towel off a dish of biscuits he'd made the day before. "Biscuits and coffee is all you get this late."

He wondered if a full-cooked meal might have been an option if he'd have arrived an hour earlier.

"If I thought I would have gotten this much kindness out of you I'd have stayed away all day long before now," he said around a mouthful of biscuit.

She gasped aloud and turned on him. "You are an outrageous imbecile, Buck Scott."

"Anyone ever taught you any manners, Miss Storm?"

"What's that supposed to mean?"

"I mean real manners, like not shouting in the house, not making too many demands on a person, like giving out a bit of the milk of human kindness?"

She lifted her hands and appealed to the ceiling, "And this from a man who dragged me here against my will."

"A mistake you're not ever likely to let me forget."

"Not while I live and breathe."

Buck threw back his head and laughed. It wasn't a mere chuckle, nor was it a quick bark. It was loud and long and came from the depths of his soul.

And it stunned Annika speechless.

It was the first time she'd seen him really laugh with enjoyment, and for the life of her she didn't know why he was doing it.

"Why are you laughing?"

Buck paused to wipe the tears from his eyes. "You want to hear something really funny?"

She watched him suspiciously. "What?"

"I actually missed this today."

"Missed what?"

"This"—he waved his hand back and forth between them—"this bickering, this arguing." He ducked his head and took a sip of coffee. "It gets mighty quiet out here, Miss Storm, but I'm still surprised to find I even missed you."

She sat down hard in a chair across from his and stared at him as if he'd lost his mind.

Then she started to smile. It was slow at first, but as realization dawned, her smile grew until she found herself shaking her head at her own reaction to his admission.

"It was pretty quiet around here today," she admitted softly, but she could not bring herself to admit she actually missed him. At least not to his face. "Except for Baby. She started crying this afternoon and wouldn't stop until I put her to bed and made her stay there."

"I never left her this long before, except when I went to Cheyenne to get Alice."

"I can't imagine how your friend Ted stood it for two days. She put up a real fuss."

He looked over his shoulder at the sleeping child and then back at Annika. "I guess there's one person alive that likes me."

She looked at her hands, then back at him. "So where were you?"

"Killed an elk and decided to take the meat. I think there's near four hundred and fifty pounds of it that'll last all winter. I won't have to worry about you bein' left here without. After the rabbits I knew there was no way you could skin anything yourself."

"It was talk like that which put me into such a state. All I could think of was you lying dead someplace, or hurt and freezing to death in the snow."

"And did you care, Miss Storm?"

148   JILL MARIE LANDIS

She tried to look away but something in his eyes held hers. "I was worried." She cleared her throat.

He ate another biscuit and sipped the coffee in silence, enjoying the warmth of the place and the fact that Annika was still seated across from him. When he was nearly through he decided to see just how worried she had been.

"Would you mind filling the kettle and setting it to boil?"

She was up and moving before he had finished his request. Buck smiled to himself. She'd been worried all right. He made a silent promise not to put her through such misery again.

"Are you going to wash up?" she asked.

"I'm going to take a bath."

"Here?"

"Where would you suggest?"

She twisted her fingers together. "But it's dark."

"Yes, it is."

"And cold," she added.

"I know."

"I can't very well go outside and wait until you finish," she said.

He stood up and went to take the tub out of the corner. "I didn't ask you to."

"But . . ."

He smiled again. "I think I can trust you not to look."

Buck had another cup of coffee and half filled the tub with freezing water from the barrel while he waited for the water to boil. Annika took her journal out of her satchel and told him she'd sit on the bed, facing the wall, and that he was to let her know when he was completely dressed again.

He watched her arrange herself with her back to him, her journal open in her lap. She seemed intent on reading it, not entering anything, as she pored over the pages covered with her neat, curling letters. Surely she'd seen a naked man. Hadn't she? Long before they were Annika's age Sissy and Patsy both knew firsthand what a man hid beneath his trousers. But he had no knowledge of cities at all, nor what went on there, and he realized with sudden clarity that Annika Storm might not have ever seen a naked man.

The longer he splashed and spluttered, soaped and soaked, the more he hoped she hadn't.

ANNIKA shifted as the cramp in her back grew worse. It wasn't easy to sit upright in the bed trying to face the wall without anything to lean on. She swung her legs over the side, careful to keep her face averted from the big washtub before the fire. She'd read her journal over from the beginning of the year to date and closed the cover. Tired of staring at the back wall, she wondered when Buck's bath would end.

At first he had entered into the event with so much splashing and sloshing that she almost turned around to see exactly what kind of a mess he was making. For the last few minutes he had been so absolutely still that she thought he might be watching her, waiting for her to turn around; but in the past few days, some inner voice told her when he was staring at her. She did not feel his eyes on her now, but he was so still that she could hear him breathing.

After a few more silent moments passed, Annika slowly, barely perceptibly, turned her head and tried to see what he was doing through lowered lashes.

As far as she could tell, he was slouched down in the tub, with his head resting on the high back rim. His arms hung over the sides, his fingers relaxed. Even though the fire had burned low, she could see him well enough to know that his eyes were closed.

Annika stood in a huff. While she had been straining to act as good manners and breeding dictated, he had been thoughtless enough to fall sound asleep and keep her waiting.

She marched across the room and stood, hands on hips, staring down at him. There was something so vulnerable about the way moisture still clung to his spiked lashes that she did not wake him immediately, but realized how tired he must have been to fall asleep sitting in a tub full of slowly chilling water. His hair was still damp, but already springing to life with curl. Tighter golden curls covered his chest and tapered to a trail of down that disappeared below the surface of the soapy water. His knees thrust up through the water like islands in a murky sea.

As she reached out to touch him on his naked shoulder, she quickly drew her hand back, unable to explain the reason why. She only knew that she feared touching his flesh, not because of the way he might react, but because of the way her hand began to tingle even before she made contact with him. How would it feel to touch him, to feel his skin and the soft muscle beneath the surface? What would it be like to have his strong arms about her, not as they had been when he carried her off, but if he held her with affection? How would his kiss compare to Richard's?

The direction her thoughts were headed frightened her. A quick glance around the room and her eye caught sight of the water barrel near the door. She tiptoed around the tub and lifted the hook-handled ladle off the rim of the oak barrel. Balancing a dipperful of water, Annika tiptoed back to the side of the tub and then poured the whole thing over Buck Scott's head.

He wasn't a man given to waking up happy. Nor did he react with a shake of his head. Instead, when the freezing water hit him, he roared and leapt to his feet. A tidal wave of water sloshed over the edges of the tub. Annika was paralyzed at the sight, opened her mouth in amazement, shut it when no sound issued forth, and continued to stare with her eyes as big as saucers as any questions she had about male anatomy were answered.

"What in the hell did you do that for?"

She blinked rapidly and tried to blot out the sight of him looking like a well-muscled Poseidon rising from the sea. His hair dripped water down his massive chest and shoulders. It ran in rivulets along his corded thighs. There was no denying his hardened, aroused state or the fact that he did nothing to hide it as he stood with his hands on his hips, demanding an answer.

Annika closed her eyes tight, but stayed her ground. "I wanted to go to bed and I can't do so as long as the tub is right where I sleep." She opened her eyes and stared at the sloppy, wet floor at her feet. "Now, thanks to your outburst, it looks as if I'll have to sleep in mud."

"Thanks to my outburst?" He reached around her to grab a towel off a chair.

She peeked through her lashes. He was seesawing the towel across his back and down around his waist. She turned around while he was still occupied and walked back to the bed where she noticed that Baby had kicked off her covers. Annika pulled them up as Buck stepped out of the tub. She heard him open the chest at the foot of the bed and pull out more clothes, but she refused to look back at him.

Finally he said, "I'm decent."

"Ha!"

"Well, I'm dressed anyway."

She turned around and found him sporting baggy long johns, much the same as the ones that lay in a heap with his dirty clothes on the floor. His moccasins completed the outfit. She almost laughed, but thought better of it and held her mirth as he shook his damp hair like a shaggy dog and then dipped a bucket of water out of the tub and went to throw it outside.

When the tub was finally empty, Buck came back inside and pulled it back into the corner. "You want the bed?" he asked her gruffly.

"What?" Annika turned to stare at him in amazement.

"Do you want to sleep with Baby? I'll take the floor tonight."

She wondered what initiated this sudden act of kindness. With a longing glance at the huge, inviting bed, she shook her head. "No, the floor's fine."

"There's a dry spot near the table."

She picked up the makeshift bedding. He blew out the lamps and banked the fire the way he did every evening.

Annika crawled wearily beneath the thick wolf pelts and pulled them up high beneath her chin. She rubbed the luxurious gray fur against her cheek as she closed her eyes.

Buck smiled to himself in the darkness. He'd give all the money he had saved in the empty succotash can buried under the table to have a photograph of Annika's face when he shot up out of the water right in front of her. Serves her right, he thought as he stifled a chuckle. The cold water had been a shock, but not enough to diminish the throbbing hardness that had come on him in his sleep.

He rolled over on his side and crooked his arm to use it as

a pillow. Now her bed was even closer to his and he could see her quite clearly as she snuggled down in the furs. Her eyes were closed. He could see her slowly fingering the gray wolf fur.

He wondered again if he were the first naked man she had ever seen. Even if he weren't, he hoped he'd given her something to think about.

A lacy coating of pine needles lay scattered over the snow as the three occupants of the cabin made their way along the bank of the stream during their early morning outing. When the sun came up and the day offered them another brilliant blue, cloudless sky, Buck insisted Annika and Baby don their coats and follow him outside—"to ward off cabin fever."

As they walked along the swiftly moving stream, Annika paused now and again to take in the still but awesome power expressed through nature. Pines so dark they were almost black massed below the gray-blue of the stone peaks towering above the valley. The Blue Creek, a tributary of a small lake farther up the valley, had remained unfrozen. It rushed along the valley floor, bubbling over rocks and fighting to escape the sandy boundaries of its banks. In some places it pooled into deep eddies, swirled, and then moved on.

The snow had crusted and settled; the tips of sagebrush showed through in a few places, but not enough to give Annika any hope of freedom through the snowbound pass. They walked single file, Buck in the lead carring a heavy beaver trap and wearing a backpack he had fashioned to tote Baby should she become too tired to slog through the snow. For now she insisted she could walk, and because he was in no hurry, Buck let her. The child toddled along between him and Annika, who righted her whenever she slipped.

In her first real venture outside the cabin, Annika decided to forget the circumstances under which she'd arrived and enjoy the surroundings. She glanced down to be sure Baby was progressing without help and then paused long enough to stare across the stream. At first she sensed a movement among the trees, then straining to see, she recognized the shape of a beautiful deer standing amid the aspen grove on the far bank. Afraid that Buck would shoot the stunningly handsome creature, Annika watched in silence as the deer stripped bark off the trees.

She glanced up and found Buck watching the doe and held her breath. She couldn't stand the thought of him shooting the deer and shattering the peace and serenity of the indescribable morning. She knew full well that if he killed the deer he would not be content until he taught her how to skin it.

Annika quickly tugged off her gloves, put her fingers between her teeth and whistled—loud and shrill—the way Kase had taught her to when they were children.

The deer bounded away.

Buck stood in the middle of the trail, his arms crossed over his chest, shaking his head at her.

"I didn't want you to kill her."

"I wasn't going to."

"How was I to know that?"

"You might have asked," he said matter-of-factly.

They continued to stare at each other until Baby toddled up to Buck and grabbed him about the knees, laughing. He bent to pick her up, but she started kicking, demanding to be set down again.

"Me walk!" she shouted.

"Be my guest," he said, turning away from both of them.

They walked a few minutes more before Buck knelt in the snow and began pulling on a length of chain attached to a trap submerged in the creek. With mounting unease, Annika watched as he pulled, hand over hand, until the end of the trap was visible. She already envisioned a dead animal brutally smashed between the jaws of the iron trap and let out a pent-up sigh of relief when the thing came up empty.

"This area's about played out," Buck said over his shoulder as he carefully opened the jaws of the trap and set the trigger again. He tied a thong to one of the links of the long chain and then tied a stick to the other end of the thong, explaining, "With this bobber, when I put the trap back in the water, I'll be able to find it even if a beaver might happen to drag it along the streambed."

Annika couldn't help but picture a beaver helplessly trying to escape the trap by dragging it downstream. "How long can they breathe underwater?"

"About ten minutes. They have oversized lungs. There's been sign of beaver along the banks near here, so I thought I'd give this area a try; but I don't hope for much, they're nearly gone around here."

"Ankah?" Baby distracted her for a moment as she pulled at her hem and then toppled backward into the snow. Annika continued to watch Buck as she righted the child and dusted the snow off her heavy coat.

"Is it worth it?" She watched him wade into the icy water, his feet and calves protected by the moccasins waterproofed with beargrease. He gently lowered the trap.

"Beaver fur is some of the best you can buy. The coat is waterproofed with a natural oil and it mats until it's like felt. I can get more for beaver than 'most anything else, but as I said, it's been played out around here."

He waded out and they walked on a few more feet. Suddenly he paused on the path and wordlessly pointed to a spot just to the left of the trail.

A small field mouse had stopped long enough to stare at them. Annika couldn't help but laugh as it gathered its courage and then scuttled away over the snow. She met Buck's eyes across the space that separated them and continued to smile. It seemed incongruous that the big man would stop to point out such a small creature to her, but then there was really nothing about him that had not surprised her over the past few days. He appeared to be as wild and hardened a man as any she might have imagined, and yet he had proved gentle and loving to the child left in his care.

When she'd first laid eyes on him she'd thought him frightening, a hulk of a creature clothed in garments pieced together from his environment. But more often now whenever she looked at Buck she found him handsome, almost stunning, with his clear blue eyes and bountiful mane of sunlit hair.

And when he smiled, well, when he smiled she thought him almost beautiful.

He was the first to break the spell as they gazed at each other across the snow. Continuing along the bank, Buck straightened his shoulders and picked up his pace, almost as if he wanted to widen the space between them.

Annika tried to find the field mouse again, but the little creature had disappeared. She gazed up at the mountaintops and wondered at their grandeur. The Rockies were like nothing she had ever seen, nor did she think she did them justice when she described them in her journal.

When she heard a low splash that seemed out of place against the reverberating rush of the stream, Annika turned to see what had caused it. Expecting to see a hapless beaver thrashing in a trap, she was too shocked to call out when she realized the small, silent form she saw bobbing away along on the current was Baby. She allowed her instincts to take over and plunged into the stream after the child. The place where they had halted along the bank was a good three feet deeper than the spot where Buck had waded in to set the trap. When she hit the icy water, the shock drove the breath from her lungs. Annika tried to stand up, but found the forceful current swiftly pushing her along downstream. She could still see Baby's buckskin jacket bobbing ahead of her as she thrashed at the water, damning all the heavy layers of clothing that slowed her down.

The child had not made a sound when she slipped into the water and now Buck, too far ahead to hear them struggling against the current, walked on unaware of the drama unfolding a few feet behind him. As she quickly grew numb from the frigid water, Annika began to panic. What if she couldn't reach Baby in time? She fought her way downstream until she was able to stand, then waded on, aided by the force of the tumbling water.

As soon as she gained her footing, she paused long enough to scream Buck's name. Her terror ripped the cry from her throat, but she could not afford to turn around and lose sight of the child just to see if he had heard. She screamed for him again and plunged on.

The child's coat dipped out of sight just as Annika had almost closed the space between them. They had reached a deep pool where the water swirled and carried the child down beneath the surface. Without thinking of the danger to herself, Annika dove, keeping her eyes open and her hands outstretched as she felt for the child.

Water swirled before her eyes; bubbles and reeds, mossy rocks along the bank flashed by. She stayed down until her lungs were about to burst and just as she needed to surface, something slammed into the side of her head. Instinctively her hands closed around the soft, pliable object. She forced her numb fingers to tighten their hold as she pulled the bundle close and surfaced.

Buck shouted and ran back along the bank, having already passed by in his search for them. Annika found her footing and struggled toward the sandy shoreline. As Buck slid down the side of the bank and splashed into the water toward her, she crumpled to her knees and lifted Baby aloft.

He grabbed the lifeless form of the child and climbed up the bank. Annika shoved her fist against her trembling lips, unable to bear the sight of Baby's small body lying limp across Buck's arms or her little feet, still shod in the precious leather shoes she had insisted on wearing, dangling ominously.

Somehow Annika managed to stand and began to drag herself up the bank, finally gained a toehold in the snow. She heard Buck imploring the child to wake up, to breathe. Panting, trying to gulp air into her own lungs, Annika made it to the top of the bank and then dropped down beside him.

She gasped out, "Is she breathing?"

❦ 12 ❦

"**D**AMN it! She's not breathing."
Annika cringed inside when she saw the big man's hands shake as he held the lifeless child. Baby's usually radiant skin was so pale it was nearly ashen. Her lips were blue. Buck shook the child fiercely, as if he could shake life back into her. Her head rolled to the side and water rushed out of her mouth.

"Give her to me!" Annika reached out, begging for a chance to help.

Kneeling in the snow, he pushed her away and held Baby in his arms, rocking back and forth.

"You have to get her to breathe. Oh, Buck, try!"

"She's dead."

Annika pounded on his shoulder, grabbed the hood of his jacket, and forced him to look at her. Frantic, pleading, she said, "Please, please try! Breathe for her."

As if her words finally penetrated his pain, Buck laid Baby in the snow and bent over her. He forced the child's head back and took a deep breath. His lips were numb as he gently placed them over the little girl's nose and mouth. He slowly blew a shallow breath into Baby and then lifted his own head for another breath.

Buck stared down at the child, his eyes ghostlike and vacant.

Annika watched, her hand clutching the hem of his jacket.

"It's no good," Buck whispered between breaths.

"Again. Try again," she shouted.

157

He lowered his head and tried once more, then leaned back, his eyes closed, his face as white as the snow.

Baby coughed and sputtered, then begin to gasp air into her lungs. Buck looked down in awe, then grabbed Baby again and cradled her in his arms. He spoke softly to her all the while. "That's it, little girl. Come on, honey. Come on."

The relief coupled with hope in his eyes was almost too much to bear. Annika watched as Baby took one breath after another until her struggling gasps turned into weak cries. Finally, the child's eyes opened. She focused on her uncle, then reached up and tried to put her arms about his neck.

Buck lifted the baby to his shoulder and hugged her tight as he dipped his head and buried his face in the fur lining of her sodden coat. Tears poured unheeded down Annika's face as she watched him kneel there in the snow with the child in his arms. His shoulders shook as he shed tears of his own.

Seconds later, Buck raised his head. Holding Baby in one arm, he reached out to take Annika's hand in his and squeeze it. Overcome with relief, shivering with cold and the lingering residue of fear, Annika pulled her hand from his grasp, threw her arms around both of them and sobbed with relief.

When the tears subsided she let go, embarrassed at her own forwardness, certain he would forgive her for being carried away by the moment. She was shivering uncontrollably, as was Baby. Thankfully, Buck was finally able to think clearly enough to get them all moving.

"We have to strip her out of these wet clothes." He appealed to Annika for help as he set the whimpering Baby in the snow. She helped him take the sodden mass of clothes off the little girl and then wadded them inside the jacket. Careful not to lose Baby's precious shoes, Annika put one in each of her pockets.

Buck took the pack off his back and opened it, then had Annika hold it while he lowered Baby into it. It was a wide pouch made of hide with holes cut in it for her legs to dangle through.

"Hold her." In an effort to hurry, Buck was curt, handing the child in the pack to Annika. He stripped off his own coat, then slipped the pack straps over his shoulders backward, so that Baby would ride in front of him. He put his jacket back on and pulled it close around them both. He had to hold it closed with his hands.

Giving Annika a quick once-over he said, "You'll have to keep your wet clothes on but we'll go as fast as we can. If I get too far ahead of you, just follow the stream to the cabin. I'll put Baby in bed and come right back for you."

Her teeth were chattering together so fiercely that she couldn't even answer him. She nodded.

His eyes were bright with tears again as he put his hand on her shoulder. "I don't know how to thank you."

Annika shuddered, holding Baby's wet things against her. "J-j-j . . . just . . . g-g-get . . . g-g-g-go-ing."

She tried to keep up with him, but her legs were shaking so that he was soon far ahead of her. Fear that he would not return never entered her mind, but she did wonder how long it took a person to freeze to death. From the way she felt, she guessed not long. Her wet hair was plastered to her head and neck; her sodden clothing was wet through to her skin. She struggled on through the snow, attempting to stay in the tracks they had made earlier, but her feet were so cold encased in the wet leather boots that she found herself slipping and sliding.

It was impossible to move any faster. Annika tried to pick up the pace of her steps, but soon found herself gasping in the thin mountain air. Her lungs ached. Every muscle felt stretched as tight as a bow string. Shivering fiercely now, she could hardly stand.

There was no sign of Buck on the trail. She tried to take her mind off the intense cold, tried not to notice that her clothes were starting to stiffen. Her kid gloves were so hard now that she could barely bend her fingers. She forced herself to think of Buck, of how he would be chafing Baby's fingers and toes, tucking her safely beneath the bedcovers, drowning her in thick furs.

Annika stopped to shield her eyes against the intensity of the sun reflecting off the snow. She closed her eyes and lifted her face to the sun. Its brilliance burned through her shuttered lids—gold, then red, then a blaze of white—but even the fiery orb could not warm her.

From the direction of the cabin, a shrill whistle sounded. Annika opened her eyes. Buck was on the way.

She struggled forward for a few more steps, paused to look for him, and then tried to go on. An intense ringing in her ears frightened her so that she stopped and closed her eyes. Her head began to spin. Fighting for balance, she took a single step forward.

Her foot hit a rock hidden beneath the snow and she slipped, the force of her own weight pitching her forward. Just before she hit the ground she saw a large rock that jutted out of the snow. Before the world went black, Annika heard the sound of her skull as it hit the stone and saw a brilliant flash of red.

BUCK stepped over the threshold of the cabin and kicked the door closed behind him. A trail of blood spatters followed his footsteps across the floor. Annika lay unconscious in his arms, her blond hair matted with crimson. From what he could tell, the wound did not appear to be life threatening, but it would have to be stitched closed. He stretched her out on the bed beside Baby, who had cried herself to sleep. He put his hand on the child's forehead—it was warm and dry—then turned his attention to Annika. Her wound was seeping slowly now, but still bleeding; he left her long enough to find a dish towel. He tore a strip from it, wadded the rest, and temporarily bound her wound.

That done, he began to strip off her wet clothes. He tossed her cape aside. When his fingers fumbled with the minute round buttons down the front of her fitted wool jacket, he cursed in frustration, grasped the edges of the fabric, and sent the buttons flying. It would give her something to do when she had to sew them all back on.

He lifted her by the shoulders, pulled the jacket off her arms, and threw it on the floor atop the cape. Her skirt was easier to remove. The pile grew until all of her clothing was heaped beside the bed. He stripped her of her underclothes and then quickly drew the blankets and furs over her.

Her tightly fitted gloves were impossible to work off her hands. He pulled his skinning knife from its sheath and carefully slipped it up inside the palm of one glove and then the next, then peeled them back and off her fingers.

Buck trapped her cold hands between his own, trying to bring warmth to them. There was no frostbite on her fingers or toes, which in itself was a miracle.

But he was not surprised. It was a day for miracles.

Her body was still quaking with cold. He left her long enough to brew some snakeroot tea to drive away the chills. While the tea was steeping he went to the clothes chest at the foot of the bed and found the wooden cigar box that contained his sewing supplies. The spool of black silk thread was on top of everything else. He took it out and set it aside. Then he picked up the swatch of cloth that held the needles and chose the one with the finest point.

He wondered if she would wake up while he stitched her wound closed and hoped not, but just in case, he poured a glass of whiskey and set it down beside the bed. Before he started, Buck washed his hands and then carried the basin of soapy water to the bedside so that he could wash the blood out of Annika's hair.

Before too long, everything was ready. He cut a length of thread and dipped it in the whiskey, hoping the fiery liquid would numb the skin as he pulled the thread through. Then he doused the needle, too.

His hands were steady as he threaded the silk through the tiny eye of the needle.

Buck took a deep breath, rolled Annika's head to one side, and then reached out to close the angry slash near the corner of her eye.

ROSE Storm's dining room was the heart of her home. The former owner of Rosa's Ristorante never poured a cup of tea or served as much as a cookie without ceremony. Heavily starched, elegantly embroidered white-on-white cloths always adorned the oval table in the center of the room. Bowls of fruit and dried flowers added color from nature's pallet to the table settings. An etched glass spoon holder provided extra silver spoons, although she had taken great care to see that their guest for the midday meal had a proper place setting.

Rose was such an adept hostess that Zach Elliot was as comfortable at her table as he would have been eating a can of beans behind his desk at the Busted Heel jail. He never hesitated to ask for second, third, and sometimes fourth helpings, his excuse always being that he might not get another home-cooked meal for a long time.

Kase sat at the end of the table and watched with pride as his wife carried a plate heaped with cookies and Italian delicacies to the table. She offered the plate to Zach, who looked about to salivate over it, then walked around the table to stand at Kase's side.

"I pour you coffee?" she asked.

Kase looked up at her over his shoulder. "I'd love some," he said, knowing full well it didn't matter if he wanted any or not, because she intended to use her new china coffeepot that was covered in delicate pink and red roses. The tea and coffee set had arrived just the week before, a gift Analisa had sent out to Rose from Boston.

She poured him a cup of coffee, paused to admire the pot and shake her head over the beauty of it, then stood beside Zach and went through the ritual again.

After she poured some for herself and accepted a shortbread from Zach, who was loath to relinquish his hold on the plate, she met her husband's eyes across the table. "Speak to Zach of the letter from your father."

Zach managed to stuff a whole, flaky cookie in his mouth before he turned to Kase.

"Caleb wrote to tell us that although he agrees there's nothing he and Mother can do until we find Annika, that Annika's former fiancé, Richard Thexton, wants to come out and join the hunt."

"I told you if you telegraphed them there'd be a flood of relatives crowded in here before you knew it." Zach looked forlorn.

"I had to tell them something," Kase said. "After the Cheyene *Leader* interviewed me and ran that long piece on Annika and her kidnapping I was afraid they would hear about it back home." He glanced at Rose. "I wish I could have been there to tell them in person. I know my mother must be frantic."

Rose tried to imagine her refined, elegantly regal mother-in-law being frantic. "I think she is not so hysterical. I think your mother is maybe the most calm. She is the kind to think first, Kase, to think about what is the best thing to do."

"Maybe"—he shook his head—"but I know she must be thinking of her own experience."

Zach took a long swallow of coffee and tried to set the overly feminine cup down on the saucer without chipping it. "Just 'cause your mom was raped back in the seventies, it don't mean anything of the sort's gonna happen to your sister."

Kase looked pained at the reminder. "If it does, I'll kill Buck Scott."

"Never say that again at this table," Rose warned. "Or in this house. You want for our baby to hear you?"

Zach turned to stare at her stomach. "Hell, he ain't even born yet, Rosie."

She glared over the centerpiece at Kase. "He's got the ears already."

"Does Annika know about what happened to your mother back then?"

Kase shook his head. "Not that I know of. When I found out how I was conceived, Mother and Caleb told me it was up to me to tell her if and when I ever wanted to. We all thought it best she didn't know." Kase quickly changed the subject. "Caleb said Aunt Ruth spends all day casting her star charts and keeps assuring them that everything looks wonderful for Annika." He picked up a spoon, turned it end over end, and set it back down again. "You know, sometimes I forget how old Ruth is. I think she's getting senile."

Zach slouched in the chair. "She was already that way when you were knee high to a grasshopper."

"Grasshopper?" Rose frowned over her coffee.

"I'll explain later," Kase said with a smile. As he watched his wife laughing with Zach he was reminded again how very concerned he had been about her being upset by the news of Annika's kidnapping. Instead, she had taken the news far better than he, even insisting that Annika would be found unharmed. "Who would hurt her?" she had asked. "Your sister is very beautiful," she had assured him, "and a lady. I am sure the man who made such a mistake is now sorry. Wait and see."

"How's the herd?" Zach asked, quickly changing the subject.

"Lost a few head of cattle in that second storm, but the buffalo are all right. They're penned up so close to the place that the hands can drop hay for them when the snow gets too deep." He hoped he didn't lose any of the buffalo over the winter. With only twenty-two in all he couldn't afford to lose even one. The small herd of half-starved stragglers he'd gathered over the past two years had gradually increased their numbers.

Whenever anyone asked why he was keeping the great shaggy beasts alive he would say that he was saving them to show his children. In reality, he knew a great sense of peace whenever he watched the buffalo graze. They were tangible memories of the not so distant past when his own ancestors roamed the great plains and forged a culture built around the life-giving bodies of the giant animals.

"I 'spect you'll be hearin' something about Annika in the next few days," Zach predicted.

Kase looked doubtful. "Not unless the weather clears some. I heard this last storm even stopped the train in its tracks." He looked at Rose. "Remind me to send a letter off to Richard Thexton. There's no need for him to come all this way when there's nothing he can do right now, anyway."

Zach bristled. "That's all we need right now, a damn fool tenderfoot out here tryin' to figure out which end of a gun to point."

"Tenderfood?" Rose said.

Kase sighed. "Tell you later."

Zach pushed away from the table and nodded to Rose. "Well, Rosie, I 'spect I best be headin' on back to town before it gets too cold. Thanks for the grub."

She stood, as did Kase, to walk their guest to the door. "Come again, Signor Zach."

He patted his front shirt pocket, now bulging with stolen cookies. "You can bet on it."

"BUCK?"

Annika's voice was raspy, no louder than a whisper, but the big man resting his head on the table heard her and immediately went to her bedside. He knelt on the floor and took her hand. "How are you?"

Pain thundered in her head and her throat was so sore she could barely swallow. "Not so well." Fear shone in her eyes as memory dawned. "How's Baby?"

"She's got a fever, but she's alive. Before she fell asleep she was asking for the buttons."

Annika realized she was on his bed, turned her head, and saw the child sleeping fitfully beside her. She reached out and touched Baby's forehead. It was hot and dry. She started to sit up, then discovered she was nude beneath the heavy pelts and blankets.

"Where are my clothes?"

Buck colored, and looked away. "You were soaked through. They're by the fire."

She raised up enough to see her clothing strung across the backs of chairs and barrel stools in front of the fire. She tried to keep her aplomb, fought hard to comport herself as her mother would in such a delicate situation.

She tried to ignore the man kneeling at her bedside, who still held her hand in his.

"Might I have my nightgown if it is dry, please?"

She thought she saw him quickly stifle a smile.

"Sure." He let go of her hand, stood, and retrieved her gown. "You need any help?"

With a sidelong glance in his direction, she shook her head and then regretted it when her headache began pounding again. He handed her the nightgown and turned away, occupying himself at the kitchen bench. The bed ropes creaked and fabric rustled as she dressed. Buck stood staring at the cup he was holding tightly in his hands.

This morning he had almost lost them both. During the hours that passed while he tended Baby and waited for Annika to awaken, his mind raced out of control. What if Annika had not saved Baby? What if they had both drowned? How could it have all happened so quickly with him not six feet away? Guilt avalanched over him, pressing him down with its weight until he thought he could not bear any more.

Tears stung his eyes whenever he looked at Baby. Even

now he wasn't sure that he might not lose her; an unchecked fever had a way of draining the life out of a body. Baby reminded him of his younger sister, and Sissy had died of fever. The child's lungs might still contain water, and although he was no stranger to healing he knew of no way to drain them.

He heard Annika clear her throat and immediately crossed to the fireplace where he filled the cup with more tea and carried it to her.

"Thank you." Sitting propped against the back wall, she smiled shyly as she took the cup from him and pressed it to her lips. She grimaced as the tea made its way painfully down her throat.

"Having trouble swallowing?"

She nodded. "My head hurts too."

"You remember anything about what happened out there?"

"I remember Baby falling in the creek and then jumping in after her. I remember trying to get to the cabin, and then I heard you whistle. After that . . ." She shook her head.

"You slipped and hit your head against a rock. I had to stitch it up for you."

She raised a hand to the tender area on the side of her head. "Stitches?"

"I was careful. I don't think they'll scar." He left her again and brought back a cracked mirror in a round frame.

Annika inspected his handiwork. A line of fine, even sutures marched from her temple almost to the corner of her eye. Each stitch was precisely made. "You did this?"

His mistook her meaning. "I'm sorry. I had to."

"It looks so professional. If you hadn't told me you did it yourself I might have thought there was a doctor hiding somewhere nearby."

He couldn't help but feel somewhat proud. The compliments he'd received in his life had been all too few and grudgingly given.

"Finish the tea," he urged. "I'll make a poultice for that sore throat."

Annika drank down the tea and handed him the cup, then leaned back and closed her eyes, thankful that Richard

Thexton could not see her now. For him, her situation would have been intolerable. Richard lived by a strict code of ethics that were very rarely broken. Their long courtship had been dictated by correct social behavior—they were rarely alone, and never had he taken advantage of the situation by giving her more than a chaste kiss whenever they were. As a result, Annika found the fact that Buck Scott had not hesitated to strip her naked extremely shocking, especially when he was unwilling to meet her eyes and seemed so embarrassed by it.

She realized with sudden clarity that she could never share with anyone the intimate details of her life with Buck Scott here in this mountain cabin. When she was back home, she would be forced to keep the memories locked deep inside, certain that her mother, who was always doing what was fitting and proper, would never understand. Nor would her father. Kase might understand, if he didn't let his temper get in the way. She didn't know her sister-in-law well enough yet to know if she could confide in her or not.

He was across the room, opening tins, searching for something. Finally, after a few moments of mixing and puttering, Buck crossed the room carrying a small bowl and a piece of flannel.

He opened one hand to reveal a horehound drop and popped it into her mouth. "This should have you feeling better in no time." Buck held the bowl beneath her nose as he dipped in the rag.

She wrinkled her nose, recognizing the pungent smell as the one she'd sniffed in a jar the day she was searching for tea. "What is it?"

"Bear grease and turpentine. I'm going to rub it on your throat and then wrap it with flannel."

"God, it smells awful."

"If you put it on early enough it works."

"Are you sure?"

He nodded.

"I don't think my throat hurts that badly." Feigning a smile, she swallowed and said, "See?" But she could tell by the determined look on his face there was no escape.

"Tip your head back."

She did and he was presented with the vulnerable white

length of her throat. Dipping three fingers in the rank mixture, he reached out and began to massage in the ointment.

Annika closed her eyes and let his fingers work their magic. Apprehensive at first, she tried to relax, still all too aware of his nearness. She felt the movement of his fingers slow and then cease altogether, but his touch never left her skin. She opened her eyes and found him leaning over her, just inches away. There was something in his sky blue eyes she had not seen before, something wide and questioning as if he were silently appealing to her to understand, to trust him.

Giving in to his silent plea, she did not pull away, but lay pliant beneath the strong, warm fingers across her throat. Mesmerized by the look in his eyes, drawn into the exchange, she waited, as if she were on the brink of some grand discovery. Her lips parted expectantly.

Buck leaned closer.

Annika lowered her lashes to shield herself from the intensity reflected in his eyes. She could feel his warm breath against her face.

He could feel her pulse racing beneath his fingertips.

And then Baby started to cry.

❧ 13 ❧

BABY'S cry was as effective as ice water. Buck and Annika turned toward her in unison and found the little girl tangled in the covers. She cried fitfully as she tried to free herself.

Instinctively, Buck started to reach for her, but since his hands were coated with bear grease he was unable to help. Annika leaned across the bed and soon had Baby unwrapped and comfortable, but the child still fretted with the covers.

"You have to keep the blankets on, Baby." The unfamiliar raspy sound of Annika's voice did little to soothe the child. Crawling toward Buck, Baby fought to escape the bed-clothes again. Annika reached out and pulled her onto her lap.

"Let me just wrap you up, then I'll wash my hands and take her from you," he said.

Annika finally met his eyes. "She's no trouble."

Buck, whose face was aflame for the second time that day, gingerly wrapped the flannel swatch around Annika's throat and then left them to wash his hands.

"She's so hot, Buck."

"I know," he said over his shoulder, trying hard not to let his worry show.

Annika smoothed Baby's hair and tried to cover her again, but the child would have none of it. She began whining, although she seemed content to lay her head on Annika's breast. Annika stroked the feverish brow and cuddled the child close.

"Buttons?" Baby sniffed. "Ankah's buttons?"

169

"You can play with the buttons as soon as you feel better, all right?"

"Buttons?"

Buck came back to the bedside, this time carrying another cup of steaming liquid. "Willow bark tea," he explained to Annika. "We have to get some down her to break the fever."

"You have to let it cool some."

He snapped, "I know that," then set the cup down on an upended crate beside the bed and took Baby from her. The child quieted immediately. His expression suddenly grew serious as he patted the little girl on the back. All the while he stared at Annika.

"When the pass clears . . ." he began.

She waited expectantly as he collected his thoughts.

"When the pass clears and I take you down the mountain, I want you to keep Baby with you."

"Keep her with me? What do you mean?"

She watched the muscles of his face work as he fought to say the words, saw the tic at the side of his jaw and the flash of pain in his eyes. "Keep her. Raise her. She likes you."

Her reply was barely a whisper. "Keep her?"

He could only nod.

"Oh, Buck! I can't do that."

"You don't want her?"

"I couldn't take her from you. She's yours, your blood relation. I know how much you love her."

He tried to deny it with a shake of his head. "She's never been anything but trouble. She'll be better off away from here. I know that now."

Stunned, Annika tried to fathom the reason behind the words that did not fit the sorrow on his face or the defeated slump of his shoulders. He tried to deny his love for the child even as his strong, work-worn hands toyed with the edge of Baby's simple gown.

"You're afraid," she said.

He looked up quickly, as if to deny her words. "I almost lost her today. I'd rather give her up than have something happen to her."

"Buck . . ."

"This is no life for a child and no place to raise one.

Baby'll never have friends or know anyone except hunters like Old Ted, and some of them aren't fit to talk to. She needs a chance."

"What about her mother? Maybe if she knew Baby, if she saw her, it might be just what she needs to bring her around to reality. When was the last time she saw Baby?" Annika wondered how any mother who laid eyes on the angelic face of the child could refuse to claim her.

He shook his head. "Baby was two months old. Patsy was pregnant when her man died. She went insane and stayed that way. I thought when she had Baby it would help her, but it only made her worse. That's why I had to take her away. Ted found the old woman to care for her and I haven't seen her since I left her there."

"But maybe she's all right now. Maybe she's recovered her senses. It might have just been shock."

He looked doubtful. With a shake of his head he said, "I don't think so. Anyway, I can't take that chance and put Baby in danger."

The pain at her temple had worsened. Annika closed her eyes and when she opened them, Buck had already slipped the sleeping child beneath the covers again.

"What about her tea? It looks cool now."

He stepped away from the bed. "Sleep will do her more good. We can try the tea later. What about my question?"

"You don't really want me to agree to your plan. No matter what you say, I know you love that child, Buck Scott. Why, you were willing to marry a perfect stranger just to have someone to care for her."

"But now I know I was wrong," he admitted. "This morning I almost got you both killed. No woman in her right mind deserves this kind of isolated life. Baby deserves better, too." He shoved his hands in his pockets and walked across the room. Standing before the fireplace, he put his fist against the mantel and studied the fire.

"You think about it," he said. "I won't press you. But if you don't keep her, I'll just have to find someone who will."

Two days later, Annika refused to stay in bed any longer. Buck had tended to her sore throat and Baby's fever day and night without thought for his own comfort or health. Finally, when he looked tired enough to drop, Annika took a stand.

"Do you want to make yourself sick in the bargain or can you use some common sense and let me get up and take care of her so that you can rest? Now please, get me the rest of my clothes."

He looked hesitant at first but after a moment's thought, he handed her the chocolate wool traveling suit and did not apologize for the handful of shining round buttons he poured into her hands. She eyed him skeptically, trying not to imagine him ripping her jacket open.

Without a word he brought her the cigar box full of sewing implements and Annika set to work replacing the buttons. Sewing had never been one of her accomplishments, but she thought even she could finish such an easy task until the thread knotted of its own accord and she groaned in frustration.

"If it will get you up and out of there so I can stretch out for a few minutes, I'll finish that for you." Buck stood over her, ready to accept the chore.

"Gladly."

"Your mother never taught you to sew?"

"She tried, but she was a seamstress before she married my father. I was always too slow. She would end up finishing everything for me."

He sat down on the edge of the bed and put the jacket in his lap. Lifting the needle to the light, he carefully wet the thread, then slipped it through the needle's eye. Slowly, patiently, he began to sew on the remaining buttons. He didn't look up when he asked, "Storm's not your real brother, is he?"

Annika wondered where his conversation was leading. "He's my half brother. We have the same mother."

"But he's a half-breed."

She went ominously still.

Buck looked up from his work.

"Then so am I," she said quietly.

"I don't believe it. You don't look it."

"Actually, I'm only a quarter Sioux. My mother is Dutch, my father is half Sioux."

He was quiet again for a time, as if mulling over what she had said.

Annika explained further. "Kase's father was full-blooded Sioux. He died before Kase was born." It was the truth as she knew it, for her mother never spoke to her of Kase's father, except to say that it made her very sad to think of him and those years before she met Caleb. If Kase knew more about his heritage, he had never told her of it, but she often wondered about the reason why he left home so abruptly five years ago and the explosive argument he had with Caleb the day before he disappeared. Both Caleb and Analisa had told her it was something Kase would have to tell her about if he wanted her to know. She respected their decision.

"So you and Storm grew up together?"

"That's right, and as far as I'm concerned, he's my brother. We're very close."

"Except for the fact that he lives outside Cheyenne now and you live in Boston."

"He has a right to his own life."

Buck was silent for a time, then said, "I wish like hell you hadn't been on the train that day."

Annika thought about his statement. "If you're worried about Kase, don't be. As soon as we get to his ranch, I'll simply explain everything to him."

He looked up at the word *we*.

"I will, I promise."

"I'm real sorry all this has happened, Annika. Do you believe me?"

Something warmed inside her at his use of her given name. "I know that." She looked down at her hands before she met his gaze again. "If we're going to start apologizing, I think I need to say that I'm sorry for the shrewish way I've acted up until now."

He put down the jacket and shrugged, a half smile playing at the corners of his mouth. "I guess you acted like any God-fearing woman might who was carried off by such a no-account crazy man."

"Don't speak ill of yourself, Buck."

"Why not, when it's the truth?"

"It's an idea you seemed determined to cling to. Why is that?"

He spread his hands wide. "I told you before, this is all I am. Hunting, trapping, skinning—it's all a part of me and I'm part of it. If I'm not a buffalo hunter, what am I?"

She leaned toward him and said softly, "Whatever you want to be."

He crumpled the jacket in his hands. The sincerity in her eyes made it almost easy to believe her.

Annika reached out and pulled him close. When she pressed a chaste kiss to his lips she was as surprised as he. She almost put her hands over her face, but instead she met his startled expression and raised her chin a notch.

"Don't get any ideas, Buck Scott. That was for your apology, nothing more."

"Maybe I should apologize more often," he said with an easy smile.

She shook her head. "I don't think so."

Buck handed her the jacket and stood up. It was a long time before either of them said another word.

THAT night, Baby took a turn for the worse. The fever that had plagued her for two days rose until the child went into convulsions. Buck wasted no time as he carried her out into the snow and buried her in it to force her temperature down. Baby's lips were blue, her teeth chattering before he brought her in again. She hovered on the edge of consciousness. Her weak cries for Buck, for "Ankah," and demands to see the precious buttons faded until she lay exhausted from her long, two-day battle.

Night had come again but Buck had refused to sleep, even for a few minutes. Annika did the best she could to prepare an elk stew as he watched over Baby and dictated directions to her. By the time the savory concoction was finished, she even felt like having a bowl of it herself, her aversion to meat gone.

"You have to eat," she said, standing behind Buck, ready to take over the task of sponging down the child with tepid water.

He remained hunched over Baby, seated on a barrel stool he'd drawn up beside the bed. "I can't."

"You look like hell," she said.

The comment gained her a look.

Annika nodded. "Well, you do, damn it."

"Cursing now, Miss Storm?"

"Let's keep it 'Annika,' shall we? Now go sit down and eat."

"I'm really not hungry. Not now anyway."

Annika went down on her knees beside him. "Buck, you've done everything you can. You've poured tea down her, made horehound syrup, put a mustard plaster on her chest. A doctor couldn't have done any more. Now all you can do is trust in God."

"That's never worked for me before."

"Try it. And let me help."

He gave up, handed her the wet rag he used to swab the child down, and shuffled to the table to eat the stew and biscuits she had laid out for him.

Baby's eyes were closed, the skin of her eyelids so fragile that every vein showed on them. She was a perfect little girl, a creature unlike anyone he had ever known. Innocent, endearing, no one was ever a stranger to Baby. If he were to lose her now through his own negligence, he didn't know what would become of him.

Buck pushed aside the bowl, folded his arms on the table, pressed his face into the crook of his arm and did something he had not done in years. He prayed.

THE cold light of another Rocky Mountain dawn crept between the cracks in the shutters that barred the windows of the cabin. The air inside was close and heavy, the smell of sickness filled the room. A half-eaten bowl of stew, a layer of grease congealed on the surface, sat on the table near Buck's elbow. At Baby's bedside, Annika dozed, still seated on the uncomfortable barrel stool with her head and shoulders on the bed. The fire had burned itself out sometime during the night, the chill in the air grew rapidly.

Tired of foraging in the snow, one of the mules brayed for its breakfast of oats. The sound woke Annika. She blinked the sleep from her eyes, pushed back the wayward strands of hair that fell across her face, and promptly turned to care for Baby. As she reached out to her, the child was so still, so very peaceful, that Annika expected to find the once healthy, glowing skin cold with the chill of death. *Please, God, no,* she thought. *Let the child live.*

Baby's skin was cool to the touch, but far from cold. Sweat rimmed her hairline, dampening the mass of golden curls. Sometime during the night, the fever had broken. Anxious to tell Buck, Annika stood up and stretched to get the kinks out of her back.

She rubbed her arms against the chill in the room and then drew her cape on over her nightgown. The mule outside was still raising a ruckus, but it was not enough to awaken Buck. Annika stood behind him, tempted to reach out and smooth the tangled curls off his forehead much the way she had Baby's. He had fallen asleep before he could finish his meal, finally giving in to the exhaustion he had long held at bay. She wondered if she should go out and feed the noisy creature herself, then realized he would be as relieved as she was when he learned that the crisis had passed. He needed to know.

She reached out to touch him on the shoulder and thought of the night she had hesitated to do so when he was asleep in the tub. The sight of him hunched over the table, even in sleep, exuded strength. Tentatively, she laid her hand on his shoulder.

He did not stir.

She shook him slightly, aware of the feel of his rough shirt beneath her palm and the warmth of his skin beneath it.

He sat up abruptly, shaking off sleep like a grizzly. He grabbed her hand. "Baby?"

Annika smiled. "She's going to be fine. The fever broke."

Unwilling to believe without seeing, Buck rushed to the bedside and reached over to feel Baby's forehead. As relief overwhelmed him, he knew he had to leave the room or make a fool of himself in front of Annika. He turned away without looking at her, walked to the door, and took his jacket down off the peg.

In a choked voice he managed, "I'll be right back. I gotta see to that blamed mule."

Annika watched the big man leave through her own tears.

VIRGIL Clemmens stared at the reward poster in his hands and knew that this was his lucky day. His grimy, dirt-stained fingers rubbed the edges of the page as if feeling it would reassure him that the poster was real. At the sound of approaching hoofbeats outside the ramshackle clapboard house, he carefully folded the poster along the creases he'd made earlier and tucked it inside his jacket. A little drama would add to the moment.

Boot heels rang hollow on the porch. A quick knock served as his only warning before the door swung inward and Clifton Wiley strode in followed by Denton Matthews. The two of them made the oddest pair that Virge had ever seen. Cliff was as tall and thin as a beanpole, while Denton was as short and round as a cracker barrel. The two had ridden together for years now, or so they'd claimed when Virge joined up with them a month ago, and although he knew he was nothing to look at—not since his ten-year stay in prison—he thought he was a damned sight handsomer than either of the other two, even if his beard had gone gray and he did have only six good teeth left.

"See you're workin' your butt off again, Virge, while we're out lookin' for a way to make a little cash." Cliff folded his lanky form into a chair opposite Virgil's. The lopsided table stood in the middle of the otherwise empty parlor of a deserted house on the outskirts of Cheyenne.

Denton grunted, which was all the comment Denton usually cared to make on almost any subject. Bowlegged, he walked like a man riding a camel across the desert. He rolled his way past the other two and shuffled into the tiny kitchen at the back of the house.

"While you two been out in the cold runnin' your asses around in circles lookin' to make a dime or two, I been studyin' a way of comin' up with some real money," Virge said.

Cliff tilted his chair until the back of it rested against the wall and the two front legs were off the ground. He pulled off his dented hat and tossed it on the table. The sweatband had left an angry mark around his forehead. "And what might this grand plan be?"

Before Virge answered, Denton strolled back in from the kitchen with a handful of crackers. He pulled up his pants and hefted his bulk into the only other chair with four even legs on it and leaned as close to the table as his girth would allow. "You got a plan, Virge?"

"I got a plan, and she's a doozie." With a long pause intended to let their curiosity heighten, Virge opened his denim jacket and reached inside. Slowly withdrawing the poster, he made a great show of unfolding it and then smoothed it out on the table so that it would lie flat.

Cliff lowered his chair until the legs banged against the floor. Denton tried to stretch across the table to read the poster, but failed. He stood up and pulled his chair closer to Virge.

"Neither of us ever landed ourselves in jail," Cliff reminded Virge with a swift look of caution to Denton. "Any plan you got has to be agreed to by both of us."

Virge, who had his hands spread over the poster so the others could only see enough of the print to elicit curiosity, shook his head sadly. "That's the trouble with you two teat suckers. You're scared of your own shadows. What kind of outlaws do you think you make, always this side of scared, doin' the easiest jobs and makin' barely enough to stay alive? I keep tellin' you that you gotta have a plan, a good one, before you set out. That's why I spend so much time thinkin' on one."

Around a mouthful of crackers Denton mumbled, "You had plenty of years in prison to sit and think up plans. Me and Cliff don't plan on passin' the time that way."

"Well, hell, Denton, I jest think a man ought to have more guts than to hold up a grocer for penny candy."

Denton put the remaining crackers on the table and started to reach for his gun.

"Come on, Denton, don't let him get you riled," Cliff warned, eyeing Virge carefully.

Denton relaxed.

Virge held up the poster and turned it so that the other two

could read along as he pointed to the words like a teacher
with a class of two—and a slow-witted class at that.

"This here poster says—"

"I can read," Denton grumbled.

"Well, I cain't. Let 'im read it." Cliff squinted at the
printed page.

Virge started over again. "This here poster says—"

"You already said that," Denton pushed.

"Aw, come on, you two." Cliff shifted in his seat.

Virge cleared his throat. "This here poster says 'Ten thousand dollars reward for the return of Annika M. Storm who
was abducted from the westbound Union Pacific on February 3, just outside of Cheyenne. She is believed to have been
kidnapped by a trapper named Buck Scott, last known to be
living somewhere in the Laramie Range.' Then this here part
tells what she looks like"—he pointed to the description, and
then ended—"Contact the Cheyenne police, Zach Elliot,
Marshal of Busted Heel, or Kase Storm at Buffalo Mountain
Ranch."

Cliff, who had never had much regard for women of any
nature, said, "Ten thousand dollars is a hell of a lot of money
for one woman."

"Ten thousand dollars is a hell of a lot of money, period,"
Virge reminded him, "but I plan on makin' three times that
amount."

Denton wiped crumbs off his lips. They landed on his
shirtfront and the shelf of his stomach. His narrow, piggy
eyes were suspicious. "How?"

Virge smiled an all-knowing smile and let a moment or
two pass. "We find the girl, let the right folks know we got
her, and tell 'em they have to up the ante to ten thousand for
each of us."

"And if they don't?" Cliff's hair was parted in the middle
and greased down. Whenever he was deep in thought, he
took to stroking his oily hair perfectly flat, giving him a
pointy-headed look. He stroked it now as he waited for Virge
to reply.

"They will."

Denton puffed up like a courting dove. "Cliff wants to
know what if they don't—and the man wants an answer."

Virge shook his head, disgusted with the two of them. "I said they will. If they're already giving away a ten-thousand dollar reward, they got more where that came from. We'll just hold the girl until they pay up."

"How we gonna find her?"

"Well, I reckon that's the tough part, and that's what I been plannin'." He leaned close and lowered his voice, although there wasn't another soul around. The cold weather had driven everyone inside for a week and the chances of anyone happening along and finding the once-deserted house occupied were slim to none. Still, Virge spoke in barely a whisper. "I picked this here poster up down at the saloon but I didn't just hightail it out of there. No, I hung around, see, and listened to what's bein' said about this whole thing. Word's out that Scott lives in a valley called Blue Creek. Seems there's a mountain pass into it and that pass is snowed in this time of year."

"So how we gettin' in?" Denton was staring off in the direction of the kitchen again.

"That's the beauty of it. We ain't gettin' in, but we sure as hell ain't sittin' on our asses like the rest of this town waitin' for the first thaw. There's gonna be a stampede through that pass the likes of which you ain't never seen come spring." He smiled, ready to outline their advantage. "No, we go up there now and camp just this side of the pass. Then, as soon as there's enough snow melted to get us through, we go in and get the girl. We can hide out and let her kinfolk know we got her and we want ten thousand each."

Virge handed the poster to Cliff, folded his arms across his chest, and nodded sagely. "How you like them apples?"

"You want us to go up and camp in the snow till the thaw?" Denton's eyes shifted from one man to another. His expression grew more concerned when he realized Cliff was actually considering the plan.

"What's a little cold when there's that much money to be had? 'Sides, what if you'd a been a miner? You'd be willin' to camp in the snow to stake a claim."

"That's exactly why I never went into minin'," Denton grumbled.

Cliff rubbed his jaw and stared hard at the words he couldn't read. "What'da you think, Denton?"

"I think it stinks."

"What do you think, Cliff?" Virge asked the other man.

"Sure seems like a little bit of discomfort for a whole lot o' money."

A smug smile crossed Virgil's face. "So you're in?"

"Come on, Denton, it's worth a try," Cliff told his friend. Denton shook his head. "I don't like it."

"Are you in," Virge asked Cliff again, "or do I go alone?" Denton looked at Cliff and nodded. Cliff turned to Virge. "We're in."

❧ 14 ❧

BABY'S recovery was slow, as slow as the passing of time for the adult occupants of the cabin in Blue Creek Valley. Buck held his cold hands over the low camp fire he'd lit just outside the shed and then bent over the piece he was crafting out of well-tanned buckskin and the finest wolf fur he'd ever cured.

As his niece had slowly gained strength, he had spent more and more time outside, forcing himself to break his bond with the little girl. He drove himself hard, hunting by day and then working over his catch by the weak lamplight in the shed until he was exhausted enough to sleep and not lie awake thinking of Baby, her near drowning, or of Annika Storm.

He hoped that if he left Annika alone with Baby that the woman would come to care enough to take the child down the mountain and keep her, or at least find a good home for her. He left Annika alone for personal reasons, too. Since the crisis with Baby had passed he had more time to think about the moment when he had almost kissed her, and the moment when she had kissed him. Buck attributed the brief exchange to the emotional moment, a combined relief following Baby's rescue that had sparked the sudden intensity between them.

As he carefully stitched the fur to the underside of the hide, he assured himself that he didn't intend to get that close to kissing Annika Storm again. The next time he wouldn't be able to stop himself.

So he spent nearly every waking moment trying to ignore her.

But trying to stop thinking about her was another matter entirely.

During the long, cold hours while he set traps up and down the stream, he continually pondered the reasons she might have had for kissing a man like him. The most he could come up with was curiosity. He wondered if maybe she'd never been kissed at all and just wanted the experience. But the more he thought about her lips that were just ripe for the taking, her deep blue eyes, so exotic against the honeyed tones of her skin, and the thick, waving hair a man could grab by the handfuls and still not hold it all, the more he knew for certain some man had already sampled at least a kiss.

If not, then he guessed there wasn't a man in Boston with any sense.

As far as Buck Scott could figure, Annika Storm had merely been curious, and there was one thing he couldn't forget: she would be leaving as soon as the pass was open, and she'd made it abundantly clear that she hadn't changed her mind on the subject.

Night after night as he worked by a low fire out in the three-sided shed, he convinced himself that no matter what the reason behind her softening toward him, she could never love him. Not a fancy, well-bred lady like Annika Storm.

But she was up to something, and for the life of him, he couldn't figure out what it was. For the past two days she'd been acting jumpy, fluttering around the cabin in a way she never had before, packing and unpacking her satchel, starting with surprise whenever he walked in the door.

She was acting all too much like a woman with a secret. And for the past two days she'd kept him guessing what it might be.

He held up the piece he'd been working on for two weeks now and found it complete. Deeming it his best effort, he carefully folded it and then wrapped it inside a clean burlap bag and set it beneath a pile of pelts. Pausing to look out at the open sky, Buck watched the stars wink against the midnight backdrop of ebony and said a silent prayer of thanks that the Lord had let Baby live. With the sewing finished, he put on his gloves and decided to check on the mules to see that they hadn't wandered off where they might become prey for a hungry wolf or coyote. His stomach growled in protest, but he figured he had some time left before he had to go in and get something together for their supper.

EVERYTHING was ready.

Annika took one last look around the cabin and smiled, proud of herself and her efforts. She had swept the floor clean, stacked Baby's toys in the wooden box, and lined up the chairs and barrels beneath the table. Three places were set for supper and a fresh batch of elk stew bubbled in a cauldron over the fire. She gave the pot a stir and then resettled the lid. The pan of biscuits cooling on the bench looked exactly like the ones Buck usually turned out with such ease. She'd resisted the urge to taste one to be certain.

The surprise meal had been three days in the planning and now that it was about to come off without a hitch, she could hardly wait for Buck to come in.

But there was still one last task to perform.

She turned to the child surrounded by paper dolls seated in the center of the bed. Annika had drawn the figures of a man, woman, and child, on the blank pages in the back of her journal and cut them out. The Sears catalogue had provided the clothes. Baby was still too young to handle the dolls with care that would make them last longer than a few hours, but the respite had provided Annika with the time she needed to fix dinner.

Opening her satchel, she pulled out the gown she had worked over so tediously for the last three days. Black satin *merveilleux* was not a proper fabric for a child's dress, but her water-stained cape was all Annika could spare. The full cut of the fashionable covering provided more than enough material for Baby's new dress.

Annika shook out the little gown, pained with the result of her effort. The hem was crooked, the sleeves uneven, and the neckline collarless, but it was the best she could do under any circumstances. She'd traced the pattern for the dress by using one of Baby's old gowns, much the way she'd seen her mother do so many times before. She was glad Analisa would never see her handiwork, for it fell far below her mother's high standards.

For Baby it was a new dress nonetheless, and one decorated with some of her own precious buttons. Mismatched buttons of every shape and color ran in a line from the center of the neckline all the way to the hem. More buttons edged the cuffs of the long sleeves. Annika considered telling Buck to guard the dress well, for long after Baby outgrew it, he would have a tidy sum of money if he ever found a collector interested in the buttons.

"Come here, Baby," she called, smiling as the toddler backed down off the bed and quickly ran across the room. Annika had not told Baby the dress was to be hers, for then the child would have announced the surprise to Buck. Now it was time to dress Baby and comb her hair before her uncle walked in.

As Annika drew Baby's old faded dress over her head, she couldn't help but worry over the sight of the once plump little body that had lost so much weight during her illness. Both she and Buck had tried to tempt the child with food, force-feeding her at first until he finally decided that when Baby was well she would eat to make up for the loss.

So far, Baby had proven him correct, for now the child ate as if she would never get enough food again.

Each time Annika looked at Baby she thought of the thin thread that anchored a soul to a body and rejoiced over the fact that the little girl was still with them. Never again would she take one day of her own life for granted, nor that of anyone else. For Annika, Baby was living proof that miracles existed and that life was indeed precious.

"Let's put on this new dress," Annika chatted as she pulled the black satin over Baby's head, "and then we'll see about putting on your shoes, too. Would you like that? You haven't had them on for a long time."

Baby took to her suggestions immediately, having become accustomed to spending long hours alone with Annika. At first Annika had worried about Buck's sudden inattention to the child, but then she realized what he was doing. It had become apparent to her the day she had fully recovered that he was purposely stepping out of Baby's life. And, until three days ago, when she conceived the idea of tonight's little surprise, Annika hadn't known how to approach him.

Not that she even had a chance to talk to him before tonight. For two weeks he'd arisen before dawn, set the breakfast out, and was gone before she'd awakened. Ever since her illness he had let her sleep in the big bed with Baby while he remained on the pallet on the floor. He stayed outside until well after dark. Annika thought his lack of proper sleep accounted for his haggard appearance and the dark circles beneath his eyes, but she didn't know how to approach the subject of trading sleeping arrangements.

Baby shook her out of her reverie. "Buttons on my dress?"

"Yes, honey." Annika smiled, turning Baby this way and that. Now that the dress was actually on the little girl it looked much better than it had empty. "Those buttons are for you. Do you like the dress?"

Baby nodded, unable to take her eyes off the new gown. She kept running her hands up and down the smooth satin and touching each and every button. "Mine?"

"Yours." Annika's heart swelled with pride at the sight of Baby in the elegant creation. Buck Scott could no longer ignore the child or deny his feelings.

"Now," Annika said, swooping Baby up into her arms and then settling her on a chair beside the fire, "I'm going to comb your hair and tie it up with this piece of satin. Uncle Buck will think you are the prettiest little girl he's ever seen."

"Me pretty hair," Baby agreed.

"Your very pretty hair." Annika worked quickly, taking care not to pull too hard as she untangled the mass of curls and then tied a wide satin bow atop Baby's head. The black satin against the golden bouncing curls made a delightful contrast.

Annika gave her a few cutouts to play with at the table while she washed her own face and hands and then combed her hair. She left it long, flowing down her back well past her shoulders, and tied up with a satin band like the one she had made for Baby. She wished she had something new to wear

for the occasion, or at least something clean. She'd taken
great care to wash out her blouse and hang it by the fire
while Buck was outside that day, but there was nothing to be
done for her wool suit. She looked in the cracked mirror on
the wall and decided that at least she was somewhat more
presentable.

Wondering what Buck would think, she felt her face flame
with color and turned away from the sight of her face in the
mirror. More than once she had silently thanked him for
staying away from her for the past few days. Whenever he
was around it was hard not to be reminded of the day she had
kissed him so spontaneously and of how much she'd wanted
him to take her into his arms and kiss her back.

Her reaction to Buck was as much a surprise to herself as
it must have been to him, but now that she had faced it,
Annika wanted to see it through, to see if there was a magic
spark between them that had always been missing between
her and Richard. She shook her head as she bent over the
stew again, absently giving it a stir. Buck Scott was the last
man in the world she would have ever thought she would
have been attracted to, but that only served to show that one
should not judge by appearances.

He was rough around the edges, crude, mean if crossed,
and came from a world she barely knew existed before she
had been forced to share it—yet she had come to realize he
could also be responsible, caring, sensitive, and beneath his
rough exterior, undeniably handsome. She wasn't certain
when she had stopped hating this place, but she guessed it
was at the same time she began to care about Buck Scott.

The change had come slowly, one step building on another. She thought of the little things he had done for her
since the day he'd so rudely commandeered her off the
train—the way he'd given her his gloves on the journey, the
way he entrusted Baby to her care, the lessons he'd taught
her so that she might keep herself alive in the event anything
ever happened to him. When she fell ill he had cared for her
with the greatest concern. And even though she still knew
little about his past, she suspected he had opened up to her
more than he had ever done to anyone else in his life.

Annika took a deep breath and tried to still her growing

excitement. What happened between them tonight would be up to him to decide. She would merely set the stage and see how their relationship progressed.

BUCK opened the door and stood speechless on the threshold.

"Well, come in before you let in the cold," Annika called out gaily from where she busied herself before the fire.

The familiar scent of hearty stew filled the air. His mouth watered instantly. Buck avoided looking at Annika as he closed the door, but even with the one quick glance he had spared her, he became aware of the new way she'd combed her hair and the jaunty black bow holding back her shining hair.

He forced himself to think when she began walking toward him, her radiant smile beaming.

"Let me take your coat."

Before he knew it, he'd slipped his arms out of the sleeves and had handed his heavy jacket to her. She stood on tiptoe as she hung it on the peg beside the door. Her own chocolate wool jacket was open revealing the stark white front of her fitted blouse. He was all too aware of the way the crisp fabric hugged her full breasts.

When Buck realized his hands were shaking, he shoved them into his pockets. "Smells good in here," he managed to say.

She turned to him and gave him that smile again. "Thank you." Her eyes sparkled secretively.

Wondering what she was up to, he forced himself to stop staring and took in the room instead. The table was already set for all of them and at one end, Baby sat playing with some bits of paper. He stared, long and hard, at the shining black dress she wore.

"Do you like it?"

He nearly came out of his skin, starting visibly when Annika spoke. She was still standing beside him. He paced around the table until he stood beside Baby. "Where'd she get it?" Buck reached out and gingerly felt the silky material between his rough fingers.

Annika swelled with pride. "I made it."

Knowing how ill at ease she was with a needle, he appreciated her efforts all the more.

"Stand up and show Uncle Buck your new dress," Annika said to Baby.

The child held out her arms to Annika and Buck watched as the woman picked up Baby and stood her on the floor. Baby twirled and preened and then flew to Buck, hugging him about the knees and burying her face against him. He reached down and scooped her up, then held her against him while he admired the satin dress. He touched the row of buttons and looked over at Annika.

"These are yours," he reminded her unnecessarily, wondering at her use of them.

Her sky blue eyes shadowed. "Baby loves them so; I thought she should have a few. If you save them, you can use them for a dowry when she grows up."

He felt a stab of pain at the mention of Baby growing up, swift but cutting, for he knew she would not be around for him to watch her grow. He set the little girl on the floor again.

Annika turned back to the hearth. It was a moment before she said, "I have some stew all made and some biscuits, and you won't believe it, but I even tried to bake some apples. It's not a pie, but . . ." She shrugged.

He watched her as she hovered over the fire, stirring, sniffing, sampling.

"Why?" The word was out before he realized he'd said it.

"Why what?" She turned to face him again. Her cheeks were red, but he wasn't certain if the color was from the fire or embarrassment.

"Why are you doing this?"

She planted her hands at her waist and frowned. "Can't I help out if I want to?"

He pointed to Baby. "But the dress, the dinner. Why all of a sudden?"

She stepped away from the fire and came to stand before him. Buck felt himself becoming increasingly uncomfortable. He took a step back.

Her voice was low, warm as melted butter. It played up and down his spine. "I just wanted to do something for you because you've been working so hard lately, and I thought we should celebrate Baby's recovery. I decided to save the dress for a surprise and I planned this little dinner party."

He knew he was frowning, but he couldn't help it. She was standing so damn close, smelling so clean, so womanly, and looking so pleased that it was all he could do to keep himself from reaching out for her.

Then he heard her whisper, "Please don't ruin it."

Shaking off his dark feelings, Buck tried to smile. "Give me a minute to wash up."

"Go ahead. I'll dish up."

Walking to the basin he was thankful for the reprieve. As he poured water from an earthenware jug into the enamel washbowl, Buck tried to corral his racing thoughts. There was no way he could turn tail and run outside as he had for the past two weeks, not with Annika waiting for him to acknowledge her efforts and join the celebration. He closed his eyes as he splashed water over his face and neck and called on all the strength of will he possessed to see him through the next few hours.

ANNIKA cleared away the last of the dishes and stacked them on the kitchen bench. She left Buck dwelling over a cup of coffee with Baby happily ensconced on his lap as she showed him the paper dolls and the many articles of clothing the pages of Sears and Roebuck had so generously provided them. She had sensed Buck's unease throughout the first few minutes of the meal, but the longer Baby was her endearing self, preening and tossing her curls as she admired her new dress, and the more Annika ignored his discomfort, the sooner he forgot himself and began to relax with them.

He had even complimented her on the meal. The stew, which he had taught her to make step-by-step, had been delicious. The biscuits, although she thought she had done everything she had observed over the past weeks, were as hard as bullets. And the dessert—she poured hot water in the washbasin and then slipped the dishes in one by one—well, the baked apples had only been half baked but edible.

Unwilling to let the mood slide back to what it had been before they sat down to eat, Annika turned away from the soaking dishes, dried her hands on the dish towel, and then joined Buck and Baby at the table.

"Now for the festivities."

He looked at her skeptically, one of his golden brows arched in question. "Festivities?"

She nodded. "At home whenever we have a dinner party we all gather in the parlor after dinner and sing songs, tell stories, and pop popcorn. I thought the least we could do was tell stories."

The life she described sounded idyllic, like a scene out of a storybook. As Buck watched the golden girl sitting across from him speak of home with such a glow in her eyes, the more he became determined to see that Baby would have just such a chance at that kind of life.

"What do you think?" She was watching him closely.

"I don't know any stories."

"Oh, pooh."

He couldn't help but smile. "Pooh? Pretty strong language, Miss Storm."

"You must know one or two stories. Didn't your mother ever tell you any?"

"Not that I can remember. She was a midwife who traveled all over the hills from house to house whenever she was called. When she was home there was the three of us to care for and my father to wait on. She never had time."

Uncertain how to react to his statement, she changed the subject. "Then let's sing."

"I don't know any songs."

"You're lying."

"What if I am?"

"Don't you know how to have fun?"

"What for?"

Frustrated, she put her arms on the table and leaned toward him. "Life isn't all drudgery, Buck Scott."

"You can't prove it by me."

Annika sighed and tried to keep her spirits up. Just when she was about to give up, Buck stood up. He put Baby down on his chair and began to walk away from the table.

Surely he wouldn't just walk out tonight as he had every night for the past two weeks? Annika couldn't believe that even he could be so unfeeling. "Are you going out?"

He heard the disappointment in her voice and shook his head to reassure her. "Just lookin' for something." He stepped up on the hearth and began to shuffle the tins and crocks that lined the mantel. Finally, he took one from the back row and shook it, opened it, and peered inside.

He walked back to Annika and presented the tin to her.

She peered inside and then smiled up at him. "Popcorn!"

"There's not much, but the bugs never found it, so we might as well have it."

"Oh, Buck! This is a wonderful addition to the party."

She held the tin of popcorn to her breast as if he had given her the greatest of treasures.

He was beginning to think that the isolation and the four walls of the cabin were beginning to get to her mind. How else could so humble an offering make anyone so happy?

Annika hurried to pour oil in the Dutch oven and then sprinkled in some popcorn, thankful that Buck was beginning to come around. A moment ago she thought he'd been ready to walk out the door, but now he was holding Baby on his lap again as he talked to the child about each of the cutout figures on the table before them.

He looked up and smiled at her over Baby's head and Annika felt her heart sing with joy.

It was a beginning.

"BABY and I have been talking lately," Annika began, watching Buck intently, "and I think that our celebration tonight is the perfect time for her to choose a real name." She tried to hold back her enthusiasm, but felt it bubbling over as she tried to explain her thoughts of the past few days. "It's as if she's starting her life over again the way she came back to us after the accident, so I think it would be appropriate for her to choose a real name. What do you think?"

Buck offered her the last handful of popcorn in the bowl, but she shook her head. He munched on it noisily as he considered what she'd said. "A name, huh?"

"A real name. I've been telling her about all kinds of names lately and we've even named her dolls, so I think she knows what I've been talking about," Annika said.

"And she gets to choose?"

Annika nodded. Baby was sitting on her lap now, cradled against the crook of her arm, her mouth surrounded by popcorn crumbs and bits of hull. "What do you think, Baby? Remember when we named your dolls and how we talked about you choosing a new name for yourself?"

Buck crossed his arms over his chest, leaned back in the chair, and stretched out his long legs. "What kind of names have you talked about?"

"Girls' names of course, like Mary, Susie, Catherine, Olivia, Elizabeth, Caroline . . . all kinds of names. Do you have any ideas?"

He was staring intently at the child, then his eyes met Annika's. "I guess she'll need a real name."

Suddenly Annika regretted her own interference. Here she was trying to reconcile Buck to the fact that he loved and needed his niece and that to give her up was unthinkable, and now she had made it sound as if Baby were starting a whole new life, a life Buck would have no part in, a life so different that Baby would need a brand-new name to go with it.

"Maybe it's a bad idea," Annika said, wishing she had kept her mouth shut.

"No, I think she should have a real name. Something decent."

Annika sighed. By the resigned look Buck wore on his face she knew things were not going as she had planned. She had no recourse. "What name do you want, Baby? What should we call you?"

The little girl looked up at Annika with trust in her eyes. She smiled across the table at Buck.

"Remember the names we talked about? You said you liked the names Caroline and Susan. Would you like us to call you one of those?"

Baby shook her head emphatically. "Buttons," she said.

Annika shook her head. "We're not playing with the buttons now; it's almost time for you to go to bed."

"Buttons," Baby said again.

Annika looked up at Buck. "On second thought, I think this was a bad idea. Maybe she's too young to choose."

"Buttons," Baby insisted.

"I've confused her," Annika admitted.

"Buttons!" Baby said louder because no one seemed to be paying her any mind.

"I think she's just chosen," Buck said with a smug smile. Annika looked doubtful. "What?"

Baby tugged on Annika's jacket to get her attention. "Buttons. Me name me Buttons now."

Annika groaned. "Not Buttons. That's not a name."

"Me name me Buttons."

"You told her she could choose," he reminded her.

"I wasn't counting on *Buttons*. The point of all this was to give her a real name. Whoever heard of anyone called Buttons?"

"Whoever heard of the name Annika?" he wanted to know. Baby chimed in again. "Me name—"

"I know, I know," Annika groaned. "Why don't you let your uncle put you to bed and we'll talk about it tomorrow?"

"Buck put Buttons to bed." She held out her arms to Buck.

He walked around the table and took the child out of Annika's arms, trying hard to hide a smile.

Annika couldn't help but notice the glimpse of good humor. "Maybe it's not such a bad name at that," she mused softly.

"It's different," he said.

"So is Annika," she said.

"Night, Ankah," Baby called out.

She watched as Buck pulled the satin dress over Baby's head and put the old one on before he tucked her in.

"Night, Buttons," Annika said as she started to wash the dishes.

Baby Buttons was asleep as soon as her head hit the pillow. Annika sensed Buck moving restlessly about the room and hurried through her task, anxious to stop him should he decide to leave her alone as usual. She quickly washed and stacked the wet dishes, gave them a cursory toweling, and nearly threw them on the shelf. When she heard him move toward the door, she spun around and blurted out, "Have some more coffee."

He glanced quickly in her direction, then away, and shook his head. "No, thanks."

Buck put his hand on his jacket, determined to get outside. He needed to be free of the sight of her standing there with her hands clasped at her waist, her eyes searching him for the answers to questions he would rather not have to answer.

"Please don't go outside tonight."

The plea was issued in a tone barely above a whisper. He wished he could oblige her, but he needed to get out into the crisp night air, to breathe in the freedom of the valley, and see the stars. He had to get away from her and try to drive the longing from his soul. Annika Storm made him think thoughts he hadn't the right to think, to want things he had no right dreaming of.

Buck faced her again and drew upon all the courage he possessed. "I think you know why I can't stay here."

She let out a pent-up sigh. It was in the open now, this thing that hung on the air between them like a dark secret. It was now that she must act. "We have to talk, Buck. You can't keep running outside and hiding from the truth."

He shoved his splayed fingers through his hair, turned away from the door, and walked over to the fire. He stared down at the flames for a long while, then finally he spoke again. "Is that what you think I've been doing?"

"I know it is. You stay outside day and night just to keep from being with Baby. You're trying to divorce yourself from that child, but you can't fool me, Buck Scott." Annika crossed the room until she stood not a foot away. She forced him to look at her, not down at the fire. He was tall, taller than any man she'd ever known, but she was no slight maid and could nearly meet him eye to eye. "You love Baby, Buck, love her as if she were your own flesh and blood, and if you intend to give her up, don't try to enlist my help. I won't take her from you, no matter how much I've come to care about her."

"If you really cared about her, you'd take her. You'd make sure she had a good home, a decent home, one where she'd grow up safe and have everything I can't give her."

"You love her too much to let her go." Annika studied him intently, afraid of becoming swallowed up by his burning blue gaze. "I think she's probably the only thing you've ever loved in your life."

She'd come too close to the truth. He watched her speak, his eyes intent on her lips. He lifted his gaze to her hair, noticed the stray wisps that had escaped the satin ribbon to play around her face. He ached to touch her. It would be so easy to reach out and run his fingers down her soft cheek. So easy. But it would be his downfall. And hers.

I think she's the only thing you've ever loved in your life.

Her words echoed in his mind. "You might be surprised," he whispered, thinking aloud.

Then surprise me. She wanted to shout it when she heard his soft reply, but she held her silence. Annika tensed, certain he was going to reach out and pull her into his arms, uncertain of what she would do if he did, but knowing she would welcome the opportunity to find out. The firelight played upon the walls around them, the soft glow of the lamp on the mantel cast the interior of the cabin in a golden light. It was a magic moment, one she knew she would never forget no matter what came to pass in the next few weeks or for the rest of her life, for that matter.

Buck stepped forward, paused as if he were debating his next move, then stepped around her. He grabbed his jacket and slammed out the door.

Annika felt as if her knees were about to give way as she watched his swift departure with fleeting hope coupled with disappointment. Her plan to confront him had failed. Not only had he held fast to his decision to give up Baby, but also he had walked out before he would admit to any feelings he might have for her.

Still, she knew there was no denying the look on his face just before he had stormed out. He had wanted to kiss her as much as she had hoped he would. Armed with that knowledge, she was certain that he couldn't hold out much longer.

If he did she just might have to take matters into her own hands. After all, how else was she to know if kissing Buck Scott would be any different than kissing Richard Thexton? Maybe her response to all men was the same. Maybe there was something wrong with her.

She knew that somehow she had to find out.

❧ 15 ❧

THE evening having ended in failure, Annika decided to change into her nightclothes and make up the pallet she had not slept on for days. It was time to put things back to normal, or at least as normal as they had been before, given the situation. Buck had looked exhausted for far too long and deserved a night in his own bed.

Seated cross-legged on her bed of pelts, Annika pulled her hairbrush out of the satchel and worked her hair to a high-gloss shine. Then she began to weave it into a single, thick braid. She didn't expect him to come back inside until she had turned down the lamps and crawled into bed. Somehow he always knew when that time had come.

When the door swung inward and Buck walked in long before she had finished with her braid, she looked up in surprise. He was carrying a bundle wrapped in burlap. "Was it too cold for you to work outside tonight?" She blessed the frigid mountain night.

He cleared his throat before he said, "I was done."

"Oh."

He walked to the end of the pallet and dropped the burlap in her lap. Whatever lay inside was bulky and heavy. He stood over her, waiting expectantly.

"What is it?"

"Open it."

She frowned, imagining all manner of furry dead animals or their body parts that might be hidden inside the burlap. "Is it dead?"

197

It was slight—only a slight tilt of his lips—but it was still a smile. "Very," he said.

She grimaced.

"It's a gift," he prodded.

Unwilling to appear rude, Annika stood up and carried the makeshift bag to the table. Still wearing his jacket, he followed close behind her.

"What for?" she asked.

Buck shrugged, thinking it was just like a woman to want to ask questions instead of finding out for herself. He'd worked long and hard on the present and was anxious for her to open it. "Look, it's just a gift. A thank-you for what you did for Baby Buttons."

Her hands were shaking. She balled them into fists, then flexed her fingers open. Reaching out, she lifted the burlap and found a softly tanned piece of buckskin inside. It was ivory—nearly white—and folded. As she carefully opened the piece, she realized it had been cut in the shape of a long coat and lined with a fine gray fur—a pelt richer than any she had seen about the place so far.

Annika lifted the coat by the shoulders, then held it in front of her, measuring its length. It was perfectly fitted to her height and hung all the way to her ankles. She gathered the coat in her arms and spun around to face the man waiting silently beside her.

"Oh, Buck! It's the most beautiful coat I've ever owned!"

He reached out and fingered a sleeve, knowing he would not dare to touch it once she had it on. "I doubt that, but it'll keep you warm."

"I want to try it on." She handed the coat to him so that he could hold it while she slipped her arms into the sleeves.

Uneasy, Buck realized he'd never performed the gentlemanly task before and was just wishing she would take her time when it was over all too quickly.

With her back to him, Annika pulled the edges of the coat closed and fastened the carved buttons into the neatly edged buttonholes. "The buttons are wonderful. Where did you get them?" They were big and round and each uniquely different.

"Carved them out of antlers."

She ran her hands along the seams and felt the buttons again. The coat must have taken him hours to fashion.

Buck looked down upon her bent head, admiring the way the light played on the different colors woven into the honey gold strands. Her long braid was richer than any pelt he had ever cured. He knew without touching it that it would slip through his fingers like silken sunshine.

Suddenly, before he could guess what was about to happen, she turned around, threw her arms about his neck, and bussed a kiss against his cheek. "Thank you so much, Buck! It's the best present I've ever received."

He thought of her now-ruined hat, of the gold hat pin, of the can of priceless buttons, of her satin cape and the once-dapper wool suit. They were only a few of her grand possessions and still she found it in her heart to thank him profusely for the buckskin coat.

He reached up and tried to unlock her hands from around his neck.

She wouldn't budge.

"I'd like to thank you properly," she whispered.

Even in the firelight she could see his embarrassment, sense his hesitation.

Slowly, she raised herself on tiptoe, drawing closer. He lowered his lips to hers.

Annika closed her eyes when their lips met. Buck stared down at her, afraid that if he closed his she might disappear. His mouth was soft and warm. Hers was pliant and willing.

She heard him groan before he tightened his embrace until he nearly drove the air from her lungs. Unable to hold back, he ground his lips against hers. She responded by tightening her arms about his neck. His tongue played against the seam of her lips until she gave in to him, opened her mouth and met his searching tongue with her own.

A delicious, heady feeling filled her, swirled up from between her thighs to engulf her with a need so all consuming that she thought she would burst into flames in his arms. Kissing Buck Scott was like nothing she had ever experienced, nothing she could have ever imagined. Was this, then, the same passion that her father and mother had always known? Was this the electric current that held them together and sparked the love that was a near-visible bond between them for over twenty years? She knew the moment Buck kissed her that breaking off her engagement to Richard was the wisest thing she had ever done.

She moaned against his lips and shoved her hands into the mass of wild curly hair that hung about his shoulders as she fought to reach deeper into his mouth with her tongue.

He responded with his own. His hands left her back as he slipped them up toward her hair. His fingers found the satin ribbon. He pulled it loose and threw it aside. He measured the weight and length of her hair with his hands, ran his splayed fingers through it, pulled it out and down until it surrounded her shoulders like a golden cape.

She let go of her death grip on his neck and shoved her hands into the open front of his jacket. Frantic to touch him, to have nothing between them, she grasped the edge of his shirt where it disappeared into his waistband and began to tug it up and out of his pants. She thrust her hands beneath it and then frustrated by his long johns, grasped the knit material by the handful and clung to it.

Without breaking the kiss, Buck let go of her hair and tried to work the new coat off her shoulders and down her arms. When she realized what he was about, she let go of him long enough drop the coat to the floor.

He shrugged out of his own jacket and pushed her back against the table just as the lamp on the mantel ran out of oil and sputtered out.

She unbuttoned the front of his pants.

He lifted her plaid nightshirt and the white lawn gown beneath it. When his fingers skimmed the bare skin of her thighs, sweat broke out on his forehead.

She pulled his pants open, rent the buttons on his underwear, and freed his throbbing manhood. When she followed her instincts and cupped him in her hands, he tore his lips away from hers, rested his forehead against hers, and shuddered.

"I want you, Buck," she whispered. "I want to know what love is."

He heard the words from somewhere far away and tried to

shake them off. It was only his mind playing tricks with him after all of his silent longing.

She didn't mean it.

None of this was real.

This was Annika Storm, the woman he had abducted, the woman who until recently had hated him with a passion.

The woman who was leaving as soon as the pass was clear.

Her hands continued to fondle him. Her fingers closed around his hardened shaft as she began to stroke and pamper him. Did she know what she was doing to him? Could she even guess?

Thankful that Baby was a heavy sleeper, he kicked a chair out of the way, grabbed Annika's hips, and lifted her up to the table. He stepped up into the welcoming haven between her thighs.

His mind worked through the blinding haze of sensation as he spoke against her lips. "This won't work."

"Then let's lie down."

"I mean us, this thing between us, it won't work."

She sealed his lips with another kiss and let go of him long enough to mimic him by placing her hands on his hips to draw him closer. She felt his fully aroused manhood throbbing against her thigh. Throwing all caution and inhibition to the wind, she lay back across the table.

She opened her eyes and watched his thoughts play openly across his face. His expression was as easy to read as a map on which indecision warred with a need as great as her own. Should he turn away now that she had offered herself up to him so blatantly, Annika knew she would die of humiliation.

She reached out, hoping to draw Buck into her arms.

He reached for the hem of her nightgown.

Annika held her breath.

Buck bunched the material in his hand and pushed it up the length of her, slowly exposing her honey-toned skin to his view until she was lying naked in the firelight. He drew the nightclothes over her head and let them fall where they may. Still standing between her thighs, he bent and pressed a kiss to the hollow of her abdomen. He buried his face against her hot skin, nipped and kissed her until she was writhing and whispering his name over and over again.

She felt his hot tongue move over her as he set her flesh on fire. Slowly, sensuously, he worked his way upward until he was lying over the lower half of her body. He cupped her swollen breasts in his hands, measured the weight of them, then teased her nipples with his thumbs until they were open buds begging to be suckled.

Annika gripped his shoulders with her fingers, gouged her fingernails into his flesh as she clung to him in an effort at grounding herself to the earth, but her senses swirled unfettered. If he felt the pain inflicted by her nails he did not flinch. Instead he slowly lowered his head and licked first one throbbing nipple and then the next. He drew one into his mouth, gently tugged on it with his teeth, and then suckled until he extracted a tortured moan from her lips.

She wrapped her legs about his hips and writhed against him.

Buck knew then he could not wait any longer.

He put his hands on either side of her hips and lifted her, probed once at the entrance to her heated womanhood, then slowly, smoothly, began to enter her.

Annika gasped when he slid inside her, stunned by the overwhelming feel of another being delving into that private inner core which until now had been unviolated. She knew that from this moment on she would never again belong solely to herself, but to him. By this merging of their bodies they were no longer two but one, and she would forever think of them as inexorably joined no matter what came to pass.

He filled her slowly, gradually, giving her time to open to him and then swell around his length. He was breathing heavily now, but his every breath matched her own, as did the wild beat of his heart.

When he reached the obstruction that was proof of her innocence, he paused, unwilling to take her. She lifted her hips, urging him on. Softly, she implored, "Please, don't stop now, Buck. Please, give me more."

Before her words could drive him over the edge, he silenced her with his kiss, trying to calm his racing blood before he entered her fully, afraid to let this ever-mounting, exquisite torture end.

Slowly, he started to withdraw, thinking to reenter and thus ease his way, but Annika, misunderstanding, moaned softly and clasped him tighter.

He cried out then—a low, savage growl that came from the depths of his soul—and dove into her. She gasped with the pain but did not cry out. Instead, she buried her face against his neck, tasted his sweat-sheened skin, and began to move with him as he rode her on to greater heights.

The table was hard against her backside but nothing could diminish the mounting pleasure mingled with the slight pain of her lost virginity. As the tension inside her twisted tight as an overcoiled spring, she met Buck's driving thrusts until they drove each other higher and higher toward release.

The table rocked. An enamel mug near the edge clattered to the floor. No longer able to hold back, Buck lunged into Annika until he had buried his shaft to the hilt and she had wrapped her legs around him and began to pump frantically against him.

The world had long since spun out of her control. All she knew was that Buck had filled her completely and she wanted him to ride her until she reached the unfathomable goal she instinctively knew lay within her grasp. She clung to him and cried his name as she rose ever higher, straining to match his passion.

He lunged again, thrusting into her with a harsh, strangled cry. She felt his seed burst forth inside her and then she experienced her own blinding explosion of light. From below its surface, she felt her skin flash hot, turn to ice, then flame again before she shattered into countless fragments.

As their ragged breathing subsided, Buck drew himself up on his elbows but remained encased inside her as he leaned over her. Once more, he rested his forehead against hers and then kissed her slowly, reverently.

She ran her hand over his thick curls, combed them with her fingers, and watched the light shine against them. She wished they could stay this way forever, warm and silent, wrapped in each other's arms with their bodies interlocked in the magic way of a man and woman, sharing the exquisite secret that had finally been revealed to her.

She had never known anyone so in need of loving as Buck Scott. It was nearly inconceivable to her that anyone could exist in a world without love. She had always had a bounty of it from her parents, Kase, Ruth, and Richard. Like a princess born to a wealth of riches, she had taken being loved as for granted as if it were her birthright. She relished this silent, reflective moment, for she couldn't help but wonder how Buck was going to react now that they had let their pent-up passions run away with them.

She did not have to wonder long.

Slowly, he pulled out of her and stood, then drew her up with him until she was on her feet. Still wrapped in the afterglow of their lovemaking, Annika pressed her cheek to his shoulder and put her arms about his waist. She felt his hand smoothing her hair over and over again.

Buck was unwilling to release her, afraid that the moment would signal the beginning of the end. Surely, come the light of day, she would regret her actions and be repulsed by him and what he had done. For now he was content to hold her, to forget about the world outside the cabin door and the fact that her brother would certainly kill him now.

ANNIKA woke with a start to find herself trapped by Buck's well-muscled arm. He was sprawled facedown on the bed, lying between her and Buttons, dead to the world. She raised her head enough to see if Buttons was sleeping as soundly and was relieved to see that she was. Annika slowly, carefully lifted Buck's arm and crept out of bed to start the coffee.

Their clothing littered the cabin floor. She picked it up piece by piece as she crossed the room, shaking and folding along the way. When she found her new coat, she slipped it on over her nightgown and rubbed her cheek against the rich fur lining. She pulled on her socks and shoes and decided to slip outside to the privy while Buck was still asleep. Before she left, she filled the kettle with water, hung it to boil, and stoked the fire.

She slowly opened the door so that it wouldn't creak and

awaken the two sleepers, then slipped out into the chilly dawn. Her breath frosted on the air but she still felt toasty warm from the inside out as she relived every detail of the night before. As her shoes made crunching sounds over the hard-packed snow, Annika wondered what to say to Buck this morning. She could not explain her actions of the night before, nor did she know how something as innocent as a kiss could have turned into such a passionate bout of love-making.

She pressed her hands to her flaming cheeks and paused to look out over Blue Creek Valley, her mind already racing with plans for the future. When the pass cleared, they would all go down the mountain and announce to the world that they intended to marry. Buck would find a job, either at the ranch working for Kase or somewhere in Cheyenne. She couldn't wait to buy new clothes for him and Buttons, to dress them in the latest styles and take them back to Boston to meet Caleb, Analisa, and Auntie Ruth.

A sudden thought struck her. She would have to ask Buck when his birthday was so that she could tell her aunt—not that it would change things in the least. No matter what the stars said, she was determined to love Buck Scott for the rest of her life.

With her arms wrapped about her she twirled around, her eyes locked on the morning sky. The air was crisp and fresh and scented with pine. She wanted nothing more than to drink her fill of it. Never had she felt so alive, so buoyant with happiness. Last night Buck had indelibly changed her by making her a woman, and nothing in her life would ever be the same again.

She was making her way back toward the cabin when Buck rounded the corner dressed in nothing but long johns, a jacket, and moccasins. When he saw her he slowed, ran his hand through his hair, and then stopped a few feet away. He was looking at her as if he had not expected to find her, but now that he had, he didn't know what to say.

"Good morning," she called out cheerfully. "You were sleeping so hard I didn't want to wake you."

Buck slowed his uneven breathing and told himself to stop acting like a fool. When he woke up and Annika was nowhere to be seen he had panicked, certain she had taken off on her own after what had happened last night. Now that they were face-to-face and she seemed happy with him, herself, and the world, he wasn't quite certain what she expected him to say or do.

He waited, silent and watchful, as she crossed the space between them and took his hands.

"Buck?"

He hated the worry that immediately creased her brow, but he refused to make the first move. He stared, mute.

"Buck, are you sorry about last night?"

"Why? Are you?"

Her face lit up like the morning sunshine. "Not at all." She squeezed his hands.

He looked down at her delicate, tapered fingers and rubbed the soft surface of the back of her hand with his thumb. "I never meant for it to happen."

"Nor did I, but it did." She put her hand beneath his chin until he lifted his eyes to meet hers. "It was wonderful."

"You were a virgin," he said quietly.

She frowned. "Didn't you think I would be?"

"Hell, I knew you were the minute I laid eyes on you."

"So?"

"So your brother really will kill me now."

Annika laughed and shook her head. "I don't think so. We'll explain everything to him when we move down the mountain."

Buck pulled his hands away. "What do you mean when *we* move down the mountain?"

She shrugged. "Well, I just thought . . ." Her expression mirrored her confusion and disappointment.

"You were thinking what?"

"I thought that after last night, that naturally . . . you . . . and I . . ." Humiliated and embarrassed, she walked away from him. He followed her to the knoll that overlooked the stream.

Buck laid his hands on Annika's shoulders and turned her around until she was forced to face him. "Listen, what happened last night was just something that got out of control. I'm not saying I didn't enjoy it, but it should never have happened, Annika. You and I are from two different worlds. Hell, you might as well be from China for all I know about a life like the one you've led."

"I love you, Buck." It was hard to see through the tears that swam in her eyes.

"Enough to marry me and live here for the rest of your life?"

His question left her speechless. Of course she would marry him, but to live here for the rest of her life—

"That's what I thought," he said abruptly. He let her go and headed off toward the outhouse.

"Buck, wait!" She ran after him, slipped, nearly fell, then kept going. When she caught up to him she grabbed his sleeve and forced him to stop. Breathing hard, she tried to catch her breath.

He spoke before she could. "Listen, I don't know why you did what you did last night. Maybe it was just something you always wanted to find out about but until now all you had at your disposal was well-bred city boys too afraid to take the chance."

"Stop it!" she cried out, afraid to admit that he was too close to the truth.

"I know you can't take living here forever, I know it as sure as I know pigs don't fly. And I know you'll be hightailing it down the mountain as soon as the thaw comes."

"Buck, listen to me—"

"Why don't we just be honest with each other and look at last night for what it was? I needed it. You wanted it. Just let it go, all right?"

"You bastard." She slapped him. It was a stinging blow that left the imprint of her hand neatly across his cheek.

"I've been called worse."

She couldn't stop the anger that shook her, nor the tears that began to flow. "Do you think I'm that shallow? That I would have done what I did last night with anyone?"

"Then why me?"

Furious at herself for giving in to tears, she wiped her face on her sleeve. "What?"

"Why would you give your virginity to a man like me when you could have anyone you wanted?"

"Because I love you!" She was as shocked as he was by her own admission. She began to reason aloud. "Last night before . . . well, before anything happened, all I wanted was to kiss you, to see if I felt anything at all, any passion—"

"So it was an experiment. What is it like to kiss a buffalo man? Did you need something to tell your society friends about when you get home?"

Good lord but things were in a muddle. She twisted her hands together and tried to put everything she had been thinking, everything that led up to last night's climactic conclusion into words that would make him understand. "I was engaged when I left Boston—"

At that Buck threw his hands in the air and shouted, "Oh, great! Now not only your brother but your fiancé is going to be after my hide."

Annika smiled at the absurd image of Richard Thexton confronting Buck Scott. "I said I *was* engaged. I called off the wedding because I didn't feel I loved Richard passionately enough—and now I know that what I did was right. Never, not in all the time I've known Richard, did I ever feel the way I did when you finally kissed me last night. It was so overwhelming that I guess I just got carried away."

He thought of the way she had nearly ripped his clothes off, remembered her lying across the table bathed in firelight, and shook his head. "You got carried away all right."

Instantly she became indignant. "Well, I didn't do it alone!"

He still didn't have any hope. He knew in his heart she was bound to leave him no matter what he said, so he tried to explain again. "Look, Annika, I'm a hunter and a trapper. It's not what I set out to be, but it's what I am. You, you're a lady, a rich lady from Boston who doesn't belong here, just the way I'll never belong there."

"But, Buck, you could be so much more."

He stiffened. "What's wrong with what I am?"

"You have so much to offer—"

He scratched his head. "Like what? This palace of mine, a kid to raise, possibly insanity?"

"Stop saying that. You're not insane."

"Sometimes I wonder," he mumbled.

"Damn it, Buck."

"There's a hell of a lot you still don't know about me or my past, Annika. A hell of a lot, but I don't intend to stand out here in my drawers freezing my ass off while we argue about it. I'm going to use the privy and then I'm going to have a cup of coffee."

"But nothing's settled."

"Oh, I think it is." He headed for the lopsided outhouse behind the shed.

She followed him. "Well, I think it isn't."

Buck pulled the outhouse door open and turned to Annika. "Want to follow me in here and nag me or can I have a minute's peace?"

"Damn you, Buck Scott!"

Turning his back on her, he stepped inside and banged the door shut in her face.

❧ 16 ❧

B ENT on ignoring him, Annika went about her day much as she always did. She wrote in her journal but could not bring herself to describe any part of what had happened between them last night. He made breakfast. She washed the dishes and waited for him to go hunting. He hung around the cabin instead, drinking coffee, watching Annika closely, playing with Baby.

They spoke to each other in monosyllables.

Baby, who demanded they call her Buttons, insisted she wear her new satin dress.

Buck improvised and called her Baby Buttons. Then, while Annika pretended not to listen, he told his niece that a big girl with a new name deserved her own bed. He went outside and proceeded to build her one. While he was out fitting old pieces of lumber together, Annika took a bath and then bathed Buttons. They were both freshly dressed, drying their hair before the fire when Buck carried in Baby Buttons's new bed.

"Where do you want it?"

Annika looked up, startled to think he was asking her opinion as if she were the lady of the house. Then she realized that he wasn't asking her—he was asking Buttons.

The child marched to the back wall where her toy box stood and pointed.

Buck set the bed down.

Annika watched and wondered if he had moved Baby out of his bed because he thought she would be sleeping with him from now on.

"Think again, Buck Scott," she said aloud.

"What?"

Embarrassed, she turned away, bent over to hang her long hair down, and began brushing it vigorously. "Nothing. I was just thinking aloud."

"About what?"

She continued brushing but didn't look up when she felt him standing behind her. "About how I don't plan to sleep with you now that you have so conveniently moved that child out of your bed."

"Weeks ago, you were the one that suggested she should have her own bed."

"Then why now?" She stood up and flipped her hair back. He was closer than she had expected.

"Why not?"

"Just don't get any ideas, that's all."

"Don't worry, you're the one with the ideas—like me living down with the flatlanders, taking on some job I don't want. You probably already envisioned dressing me up proper, too, didn't you?"

Silent, she couldn't deny it.

"Ha! I knew it." He stalked to the other side of the room and poured himself some coffee. Without another word, he took it to the table, sat down, and continued pinning her with a hard stare.

She tried to ignore him for as long as possible, but she could feel his gaze on her as she put her brush away and then looked for something to use to make up Baby Buttons's bed. By the time she had accomplished the task she couldn't take his silent stare anymore.

"Are you just going to sit and stare at me forever like you hate me?" she wanted to know.

"Is that what I'm doing? I thought I was just sitting here having a cup of coffee. Or is this just one more thing about me you want to change?"

She marched to the table, yanked out a chair, and then sat down across from him. Leaning forward on her elbows she looked him square in the eye and said, "I'm sorry, Buck. I mean it. Forget everything I said about your moving down the mountain, all right? I was wrong to even suggest it."

"Does that mean you're willing to stay here?"

Her eyes flooded with tears. How had it all happened so fast? She wanted to say yes, but what would life be like without the hustle and bustle of the city, without her family nearby? How could she face this endless isolation?

"I don't know," she admitted.

He finished the coffee and slammed the cup down. "At least you're honest. I knew you'd leave the minute the pass cleared."

"But I don't want to go without you." She searched his face for any sign of hope.

"And I don't want to leave, so where does that put us?"

She saw no regret when he said the words, only the stubborn set of his jaw and the way his hands clinched the cup so hard she was certain he would bend the enamel into a shapeless mass.

"I guess that puts us right back where we started the day you took me off the train." Even as she spoke the words, she knew they weren't true. They could never change what had happened between them last night, and she would never forget the way she had felt in his arms. It had all seemed so right at the time, so good between them, that she couldn't bear to think of spending the rest of her life without him.

Buck couldn't take his eyes off her as he watched Annika mull over all he'd said. He knew she was fighting a battle she would never win, for he didn't intend to change his mind, even for her, although it twisted up his insides not to. There would never be another woman in his life like Annika Storm, even a blind man could see that, but not even for her would he suffer going back down the mountain and being ridiculed as ignorant trash and a buffalo hunter. He'd lived with that all the years his father had hauled them from place to place, and he'd be damned if he was going to do it now that he had a choice.

There was one thing he did know—if Annika loved him enough, she'd stay and take him the way he was. It was a woman's place to be with her man, the way it had been since time immemorial. She could damn well be happy with him and a trip into town once or twice a year, but he'd never go back to stay.

Never.

Buck stood up. Her gaze followed him to the door. The disappointment in her sky blue eyes was too much for him to take. "I guess that does put us right back where we were, at least until one of us changes our mind, and I can tell you right now, it won't be me."

He grabbed his coat and without putting it on, left.

Annika put her head down on her arms and sobbed.

"I'M freezin' my balls off." Denton Matthews stomped through the snow until he reached the fire that burned day and night in the camp just below the tree line. "This is the stupidest plan any man ever came up with."

"It's a hell of a sight easier way to make money than any of the harebrained ideas you could dream up even if you had the rest of your life to do it." Virge Clemmens spat a stream of tobacco-colored spit that joined the huge brown patch in the snow a few feet from him.

"Shut up, you two. I'm about to go plumb crazy sittin' up here on the side of this mountain listening to you chip away at each other." Cliff Wiley hated them both, the snow, the cold, and the wind-beaten tent they had slept in every night for the past three weeks.

"How much longer do you think we'll have to be here, Cliff? I can't take it anymore," hefty Denton whined. "Hell, I'm starvin' for a decent meal."

"You wouldn't starve if we tied you to a tree and left you out all winter," Virge mumbled.

"I said cut it out," Cliff warned them.

"Shit." Denton looked despondent. He took a piece of jerky out of his coat pocket and tried to console himself with it.

"Couple more warm days like we just had and the snow'll be down low enough so we can work our way through the pass."

"Maybe we could dig our way through now," Virge suggested.

Denton looked scared. With a mouth full of jerky he mumbled something that sounded like "Avalanche."

Cliff stared up at the mountainside. "Snow's too hard by now. Wind's packed it down like rock."

"What day is it? I lost track," Denton said, taking another chaw of the jerky.

"End of March," Cliff said.

Virge stood up and stared at the pass with his usual anticipation and enthusiasm. "Lookit that rock showin' there on the side of the cliff. You remember seein' that yesterday? I don't. I swear, we're gonna wake up one mornin' soon and just like Moses wadin' through the Red Sea, we're gonna ride through that pass, find us that little gal, and be set for life."

"It's going to be a wonderful picnic, Buttons. Just wait and see."

Wrapping the last of their provisions in a dish towel, Annika tied the bundle at the corners and then made sure she had everything. "Can you think of anything else we need?" she asked the child, not really expecting an answer. She had taken to talking to Buttons rather than Buck, since he wasn't likely to be around anyway. During the long week since their argument, he had taken to disappearing again, distancing himself from both of them.

"I wish I knew how to make some *koekjes* like my mama. Have you ever had a cookie?" Annika paused at her task and looked down at Buttons who stood listening intently beside the table, all bundled up in her coat and ready to go.

"Cookies?" Buttons parroted.

Annika sighed. She was no closer to an answer to her dilemma than she had been before, and nothing took her mind off her problem for long. She wanted Buck, she wanted to see Baby Buttons have all the things a child was entitled to—love, a good home, the advantages she grew up with. But she could not come to terms with living so far from civilization, nor did she feel right about taking Buttons away from Buck to find her a home. Baby belonged with him. He loved her, and he was her family. But as Annika watched the child run across the room to collect her sad wooden doll to take along on their outing, she couldn't help but think of all the things her own family could give the child.

She could just imagine her parents' reaction when she arrived in Boston and announced that she was going to adopt the child of her abductor; Caleb, always the lawyer, would ask questions until he felt comfortable with her decision or had convinced her to give it up. Her mother would think things through silently, keeping her own counsel until she talked it over privately with Caleb, then give Annika her decision. Auntie Ruth would want whatever Annika did, but still she would sequester herself with her star charts and then advise her when and how she felt she should proceed.

"We go now?" Baby tugged on Annika's coat until she bent down and lifted her into her arms.

"Right now. It's too beautiful a day to waste."

She picked up the bundle of food with her free hand. The door opened before she could reach around Baby to grasp the handle.

With his gun over his shoulder and his knife belted to his thigh, Buck stood on the threshold, staring down at them. A brief glance took in their coats and the bundle in Annika's hand. He felt his stomach knot as his hands went clammy.

"Going someplace?"

Annika saw the dark suspicion in his eyes. "On a picnic. It's a beautiful day."

"A picnic, huh?"

She could see he didn't believe her. Did he actually think she would leave him and take the child without so much as a good-bye? Did he think she would steal away like a thief in the night?

"Want to go with us?" She shifted the child on her hip.

Buck reached out and took Baby from her with a quick "She's getting heavy." He looked down at the bundle in Annika's other hand. "Did you ever stop to think you might be in danger having this little picnic alone?"

"It's a beautiful day," she began, then the dark warning in his eyes called to mind Baby's near drowning. "I wasn't going anywhere near the creek," she assured him.

"I wasn't thinking of that. I've seen signs of cat around."

Annika laughed. "Cat?"

"Mountain lion."

She immediately sobered. "Oh."

"Yeah, oh."

Suddenly she saw the excuse she needed to have him join them. "Then I guess you really do need to come along. I have plenty of provisions packed. Actually, I'm waging a one-woman campaign to finish all that elk so that you'll bring home something else to eat."

He ignored her use of the word home. She didn't mean it, after all. "What else is in there?"

"Cornbread."

He stepped aside to let her pass. Before he closed the door, he went in the cabin and called out over his shoulder, "I've got some wine."

"Wine? Where have you been hiding it?" Annika laughed and stuck her head inside as he moved barrels and sacks on the floor. She watched him pull out a tall, amber glass bottle with a cork sticking half out of the top. "If I had known you'd been hiding wine, I would have finished it by now."

"Maybe that's why I kept it hidden. Even I've heard all about how well-bred city ladies like a glass of wine now and again."

She couldn't tell if he was teasing her or not, but she doubted it. "I can't help what I am, Buck."

"That goes the same for me."

It was too fine a day to argue, so Annika did not rebut his remark. Instead, she led the way until they had wandered far enough up a nearby hillside that they could look down on the cabin and the valley beyond.

She pointed to a small meadow, a clearing amid the pines where the snow had melted and patches of pebbled ground showed through. Melting snow ran in rivulets carving glittering ribbons down the mountainside. The wind sang high in the trees, whispered through the upper branches as it carried with it a hint of the fine weather to come. Instead of cheering her, Annika found the warm spring breeze sang a song of parting. She shook off her dark thoughts and spread their picnic out on a large flat boulder, one that was wide enough for them both to sit on and use as a table.

Buck set his rifle down beside them and put the bottle of wine in the center of the cloth.

"I didn't bring glasses," Annika said.

"We can share the bottle, if you don't mind."

Their gazes collided across the picnic. "Of course not."

The bottle would touch his lips and then hers. The thought sent a chill down her spine. It had been a long week, she admitted to herself. Seven whole days. Every night she had been tempted to surrender to the need Buck Scott had awakened in her. When the fire burned low and Baby Buttons was sound asleep in her bed, Annika had been ready to throw caution to the winds and confess to Buck that she needed him, that she wanted to have him make love to her again. But she knew that come the dawn they would only face the same argument again. Would he go down the mountain, or would she stay with him, live here in the wilderness and be his wife and Baby's mother? The answer to being a wife and mother was a simple yes—but no matter how much she loved him, she was not ready to give up the life she had known for one of such isolation.

Buck stretched out on his back on the warm surface of the boulder and watched the clouds play across the vibrant blue sky. For one small fragment of time he wanted not to think, to put aside the pestering thoughts that plagued him, and be happy with the moment. He was alive, the sun was shining, and the woman he loved was at his side.

He tried to take in the scene as a stranger might—the two of them sitting on the rock, their picnic dinner waiting, the bottle of wine catching the sunlight. Annika had spread her thick coat wide and now sat on it. The concentrated sunlight in the meadow made the temperature warm enough for her not to need anything but her wool suit.

Buck snuck a glance in her direction and found she had mimicked his posture. She was lying across the rock on her side facing away from him so that she could watch Baby gather shining pebbles. Her clothing was frayed from constant use, singed around the front of the hem, and wrinkled beyond hope. Even the cuffs of her white blouse beneath the tight-fitting jacket were worn. Her once perfect, very expensive kid boots were beyond salvaging, ruined by mud and water. Her thick, dark blond hair was streaked with sunshine and tied back in a braid.

She would say she never looked worse.

He thought she'd never been more beautiful.

Buck watched as Annika absently fingered the slight scar at her temple. He was proud of his handiwork. As soon as he'd removed the stitches, he had made her rub the angry red mark with bear grease. Now, there were only tiny marks where the stitches had been.

Baby ran around the rock. Annika turned to follow her progress. Their eyes met again.

Annika touched her scar once more. "Did you ever think of becoming a doctor?"

Her words burned like whiskey poured into a raw wound. He steeled himself not to react to her innocent suggestion. "Give up, Annika."

She pulled herself up to a sitting position, then drew her feet up until she could rest her head on her knees. As she spoke, she worked a patch of mud off the toe of her shoe with a ragged fingernail. "No. I'm serious. It just came to me that you would make an excellent doctor and I just wondered if you had ever thought of it."

"No," he lied.

"You have such a gift for healing, though. I mean, look at this scar." She brushed back the few escaped strands of hair that hid her temple.

He didn't have to look at the scar to know it was well healed and barely visible. He'd checked it every day when she wasn't aware he was looking.

"It hardly shows at all anymore. Your stitches were so perfect . . . and when I think of the way you brought Baby through her fever and cured my sore throat. How many other people know so much about which herbs to use for which illness?"

"Plenty of them."

"Ah, but how many of them would also make excellent surgeons?"

Buck drew himself up on an elbow and turned to face her. His heart had already been pounding with her so near, and now with her talk of his becoming a doctor, she was driving him crazy in more ways than one. "What are you talking about?"

Excited by the fact that he was even half willing to listen,

Annika made certain Baby was playing nearby and then turned her attention to him. "Buck, I've never seen anyone as skilled with a knife as you are—"

"I guess not. You never even saw anyone skin a rabbit before I showed you how. That doesn't give you much to compare me with."

She lifted her chin defiantly. "The human body isn't all that different from other animals', not when you consider things like livers and hearts and, well"—she waved her hand in the air—"all that. You already know how to identify those organs in animals. Why, I'll bet you could hold your own in any anatomy class."

"You've been up here too long. This thin air isn't good for you. Let's eat and get back down the hill."

"How did you learn all you know about healing?"

"Pass the cornbread." He drew the cork out of the wine. He didn't know why he loved her. She really was an irritating woman. "Baby, get over here and eat," he called out.

"Not Baby!" came the child's sharp reply.

"Buttons, come eat, then."

"Buck, are you listening to me at all?" Annika persisted.

"I'm trying not to, but you keep yammering."

"Have you ever stitched up anyone before, or was my cut beginner's luck?"

Disgruntled, he took a bite of cornbread and made her wait until he swallowed. "Of course I sewed people up before. There was no one else around to do it."

Excited, she refused the cornbread he offered, but took the wine and without thinking, took a hefty swig. She wiped her mouth with the back of her hand and passed the bottle back to him.

Buck watched in amazement. The woman was on a mission.

"What about when you were buffalo hunting?" she asked.

"What about it?"

"Did you ever stitch anyone up, anyone not in your family?"

He was hesitant to answer, then finally admitted, "Well, yeah."

"Who?"

With a shrug, "I don't know, one or two others. Sometimes a knife would slip and they'd need sewin' up."

"And why didn't anyone else do it?"

"Just because."

"Just because you were the best around, right?"

His pa used to tell everyone that, but there was no way he'd admit as much to Annika.

"Am I right?" She insisted he answer.

"Let it go, Annika."

"How did you learn about herbs and salves and those teas you brew up?"

How could he tell her it seemed he'd always known about healing? He'd picked it up here and there, took to it easily. As a midwife, his ma had always had healing herbs growing around their place because the hill folk had come to her for cures. When his pa took them and left home, he learned more as they traveled across country, always collected whatever herbs and plants he would need and continued to learn different ways with unfamiliar plants. He'd always taken care of them all, Pa, Sissy, Patsy.

And he'd failed with all three.

"It's not impossible, you know," she pushed.

Buck sighed. It was a heavy sigh, long and deep. Would she never cease?

Annika knew she had pushed too far when she heard him sigh and felt him shut her out again. Reminded of her father and his intense questioning, she wished she had never opened her mouth about the possibility of his becoming a doctor. After all, it would take him from months to years of study either at a university or an accredited medical school. He would need money to attend and someone to care for Baby Buttons while he did. And he would have to leave his precious valley.

Buck Scott would never take charity from anyone. Especially her. And she knew well enough he wouldn't give up his life here at Blue Creek.

"You going to eat or talk?" He had pulled Buttons up on his lap and was handing her more cornbread and sliced elk.

"I'm not hungry now." She reached for the wine bottle.

"Go easy on that. I can't carry you both home."

"Don't worry about me," she said, her lips already pleasantly numb, her cheeks tingling.

Buck reached out and took the bottle of plum wine. Maybe after enough of it he could forget the impossible ideas—old ideas he thought had long since died—thoughts that she'd dredged up in his mind. He glanced around the sunny meadow, at the pine boughs bare of snow, at the melting patches that seemed to retreat back to the shadows even as he watched. Buck took another pull on the bottle. Maybe the heady stuff would help him forget that Annika Storm would be leaving soon and that he wouldn't have to put up with her constant nagging anymore.

As the sun slipped behind the mountain the temperature in the meadow dropped quickly. Buck toted Buttons down the hill while Annika followed, carrying the remains of the picnic. By the time they reached the cabin, Buttons was asleep on Buck's shoulder.

"The fire's gone out," Annika told him as they entered the cold, dark room. She rubbed her arms and left her coat on while he put Baby Buttons to bed with her clothes on and then started the fire going again.

The cabin was cold and lifeless. Annika lit the lamps while Buck stoked the fire until it was blazing. Soon the room was growing warm again. Annika hung her coat on the peg beside Buck's.

"Are you hungry?" she asked.

"I had enough this afternoon."

She put the leftover cornbread in a bread box and shook out the towel. There was nothing left to do, no dishes to wipe up, so she took out her journal and ink and sat down at the table to record her thoughts.

Buck pulled out a chair at the opposite end of the table, emptied the remains of the plum wine into a mug, and leaned back, his legs extended toward the fire. He watched Annika as she worked over her journal, and although he couldn't read the words from where he sat, he could still see the fine, even strokes of her pen against the white pages.

Annika looked up and found him watching her intently.

He was sipping at the wine, staring at her over the rim of the cup.

"The pass will be clear in a day or two," he said matter-of-factly.

Without warning, her eyes flooded with tears. She ducked her head and blinked furiously. Teardrops fell and splashed across her neatly penned words and stained the page. Unable to face him, she glanced here and there about the room; at the mantel with the tins and crocks of medicinal cures lined up unevenly on the thick piece of wood, at the dirt floor, at the hearth, and then at the broom made of willow twigs standing in the corner. Annika took in every detail of the room but she couldn't meet his eyes.

He could see she was trying valiantly not to cry even as tears ran unheeded down her cheeks. It gave him little satisfaction to know she was in pain, for he was hurting more than he ever had in his lifetime. Buck drained the cup and set it down harder than he intended.

She jumped at the sound that broke the strained silence and put her pen down on the journal. Batting away tears, Annika sniffed, then finally met his gaze. Her voice broke on every word. She shook her head. "I don't want to leave you."

"Then stay."

"I can't."

They stared at each other for a moment before she said, "Come home with me."

Buck shoved away from the table and stood up. He walked to the mantel, braced his hands on it, and then leaned his forehead against the wood. He thought of what his life would be like if he were forced to live in town again. He'd only felt comfortable in two places—the hills of Kentucky and here in Blue Creek Valley. He didn't need to subject himself to the restrictions and ridicule of civilization. He didn't think he could do it anymore. "I can't," he told her bluntly.

Unable to bear the strain any longer, Annika stood up and crossed the room until she stood directly behind him. He stiffened visibly but did not move. She slipped her arms around his waist and pressed her cheek to his broad back. The flannel shirt was soft and worn, the skin beneath it emanated his warmth. She could feel his every breath, could hear the steady but rapid beat of his heart. The sound marked a beat within her like the steady pulse of a metronome.

Annika began to sway from side to side, slowly, sensuously, listening to the beat of his heart. It had been weeks since she had heard any music. Accustomed to attending a chamber concert or a soiree at least once a week, she was a bit surprised to admit she had not noticed the lack of music in her life. Had Buck ever danced? She would never have the opportunity to dance with him in public. Would he dance with her now?

"Dance with me, Buck," she whispered against his broad back.

He turned away from the fire and slipped his arm around her. She laid her hand in his open palm. They moved to the matching beat inside their hearts, the small space in the cabin restricting them to short, sliding steps which soon slowed to a slow sway as Buck held her in his arms. As if they truly heard an orchestra they soon slowed as if the music had faded away. Annika leaned back in the curve of his arm and let her gaze touch his hair, his eyes, his lips.

"Love me tonight, Buck. Love me once more before I go."

In a move rougher than he intended, Buck covered her mouth with his. His tongue dove between her lips as he ground his lips against hers. Annika moaned and wrapped her arms about his neck. She wanted to inhale him, to enfold and consume him, to absorb him until there was nothing left of either of them but one all-enveloping flame.

Buck held her fast, pressing her up against him with a near-vicious hold, unable to let her go now that he had her in his arms again. She had been his prisoner in the beginning, but now he was hers. She had bound him to her gradually, at first with her beauty, then her presence. He was captured by her radiant smile, her little kindnesses, and then her body. He couldn't bear the thought of letting her go, and yet, he couldn't keep her unless she were willing to stay. He knew enough about taming wild animals to know that sometimes hanging on meant letting go.

Annika clung to him as his lips moved over hers possessively. She ran her hands through his hair and decided she very much liked the unkempt wildness of his curls, his broad shoulders, the corded muscles of his neck and shoulders. She knew as she stood there locked in his embrace that she would never love another man the way she loved Buck Scott. If she were doomed to live out her life an old maid like Auntie Ruth, then she wanted this night to remember and vowed to have it without regrets.

She tore her lips from his long enough to whisper, "Make love to me, Buck," and was relieved to find her request was all the encouragement he needed to lift her into his arms and carry her to the bed.

"We're going to do this right this time," he said against her lips. "No table."

"What about Buttons?"

"She's cursed with the Scott ability to sleep through anything. She didn't wake up last time, did she?"

"But . . ."

Sensing her hesitation, Buck left Annika long enough to carry two chairs to Baby's bedside and then drape a blanket over them so that if she should awaken, she would not be able to see Buck and Annika unless she crawled out of bed.

"Better?"

Annika nodded.

He walked to the bedside and began unbuttoning his pants.

"You're taking off your pants?"

"It's tradition. Get your things off or I'll rip 'em off and you won't be able to leave until you mend them—and that might take years."

She started crying again, her fingers frantic as they moved over the buttons of her jacket. "Don't talk about it, Buck. Please don't talk about it. I can't stay and you won't go."

He pulled his shirt out of his waistband and shrugged it off. His pants fell to the floor. He pulled her into his arms again and reached around to unfasten her skirt. As he lowered his lips to hers again, he whispered, "Shut up, Alice."

❧ 17 ❧

AFRAID he would carry out his threat, Annika undressed faster than she ever had in her life, but she could not bring herself to remove her chemise while he was watching. Stripped down to his long johns, Buck knelt before her and began to unbutton her shoes. The task complete, he set them aside, slipped her ruffled garters down her legs and then rolled down her stockings.

She expected him to stand up and take her in his arms, but he stayed where he was and began to massage the instep of her foot. Annika closed her eyes and leaned back on her elbows, relishing the relaxing warmth that invaded her as he continued to knead the sole of her foot. He released the first and lifted the second, rubbing her ankle, her instep, and then the ball of her foot. She sighed with pleasure and knew that if she could purr she would.

When he let go of her foot he reached out for her hand and pulled her to a sitting position on the side of the bed.

Still kneeling before her he whispered, "You're so beautiful," as he reached up and buried his face against her neck.

She put her arms around his neck again and held him close. The initial explosion of need had quieted now that the strain of holding back had ended. She was happy just to hold him, knowing that he would make love to her this night. Buck felt the same, she could tell simply by the way he was holding her now, as if she were some fragile snow flower that might disappear with the first breeze.

But his hands and lips were not still for long. Soon he was

nuzzling her neck, scattering kisses along her jaw, tracing his tongue around the outer edge of her ear.

Annika moaned and lost herself in the pleasure that invaded her senses.

Buck captured her lips again and kissed her long and hard, his hands roving over her back, along her sides, and then up to cup her breasts. He thumbed her nipples until they were taut and straining against the thin fabric of her chemise. She clung to him, wordlessly begging for more.

He slipped his hands beneath the sheer fabric, careful not to tear the only underclothing she owned, and worked the material up and over her head. He put it aside and then bent to suckle at her nipples, one and then the other, until she was crying out with need.

Smiling, he rose, pulled down the blankets and pelts, and gently laid her back on the bed. He shucked off his underwear and joined her, noticing the way she turned away from the sight of his nudity.

"There's nothing wrong with being naked, Annika."

She buried her face against his shoulder.

"You ever seen a naked man before me?" He had to know, wanted to learn all about her before she left him. He would have the memories to keep.

"No." Her answer was muffled; she shook her head against his shoulder.

"Good. Tell me about this fiancé of yours." He put his lips against her breast again, gently teethed the nipple, and made her moan. "The one that never made you feel this way."

Annika shook her head, barely able to get the words out. "Now? I can't . . . talk about Richard . . . now!"

He traced his tongue from one nipple to the other. "I hope you never talk to him again without thinking of this minute."

She grabbed his face between her palms and forced him to look at her. "No one, do you hear me, no one will ever make me feel the way you do."

He shook his head. "You say that now. You'll get back to Boston and your easy life and someone will come along."

Frightened by his words she pulled him close. His big body was heavy, the bed ropes creaked as he covered her.

"Don't say that, Buck. Don't talk like this. Please, don't talk at all."

He obliged her, kissed her as his hands played over her body, explored the silky length of her. His hand brushed the nest of curls between her legs and she surged upward, pressing herself against his palm. He slipped his fingers into her moist warmth and groaned against her lips. She was ready for him.

His engorged member throbbed against her thigh. Buck knew he couldn't wait to enter her, but knew, too, the bittersweet truth; if he took her to Cheyenne tomorrow, this would be the last time they would make love.

He wanted to pleasure her all night long.

Annika thought she would explode with pleasure when his fingers slipped inside her. She held him tight and tilted her hips to heighten her own pleasure, moving slowly, sensuously against his hand. He stroked her until she could not hold back any longer, until it was all she could do to cling to his shoulders, arch her back, and cry out as wave after wave of ecstasy swept over her.

Buck parted her legs with his thighs and knelt between then. Hot and aching, he rubbed the tip of his swollen staff against her, teasing her, bringing her awareness back, stoking her need once again.

He entered her slowly, easing his way into her inner recesses, pulling back when she threatened to move and drive him to the point of no return. When he slipped his hands beneath her hips and lifted her so that she could accept the full length of him, she whimpered and traced her tongue along his collarbone. Unable to hold back any longer, Buck thrust into her, sheathing himself fully. She clamped her legs about his hips and arched her back to take in more of him.

Buck held still, afraid to move lest he explode and end the sweet torture. Annika sensed his intense concentration, held herself as still as she could, barely breathing as she memorized the wonder of their joining. He was inside her, lying full and heavy against her womb. She contracted her inner muscles and heard him gasp. She did it again and he began to plunge and thrust against her.

Their sweat-glistened bodies glimmered, alive with light

and shadow from the fireplace. The bed creaked and groaned in protest as they writhed together, seeking solace in each other as they tried to stop time and the coming of spring. Buck drove inside her until he knew he could not hold back any longer, then slipped his hand between them and touched the tiny bud that would give her release. He thrust his shaft full-length once more, stroked her until she screamed his name, and then, knowing he had given her the ultimate pleasure, cried out hoarsely and exploded inside her.

IT was still dark outside when Buck awoke and for a while he was content to lie staring at the ceiling with Annika's satin skin pressed against the length of his side. She had fallen asleep with her leg thrown over his, her flesh touching his from shoulder to toe. He brushed aside the stray curls that fell across her cheek and kissed the top of her head.

As they lay locked in the intimate embrace, he knew that he couldn't bear to give her up yet. His mind began to lay plans. If he wasn't there to take her down the mountain, she would be forced to wait until he did, or until her brother came to get her. He wondered if she would try to go on her own. He stroked her arm, knowing she would never leave without telling him good-bye. She had assured him of that yesterday.

If her brother did find them first, Buck hoped that Kase Storm was a reasonable man. He didn't relish the thought of being killed outright.

Time was on his side, and maybe with a little more time and a lot more loving he would be able to convince Annika that she had to stay with him. After last night, he was ready to promise her almost anything.

He thought of his savings buried in the can beneath the table and of the things he would buy to keep her. It wasn't unreasonable to think that he could get a stove up the mountain—surely they came apart. He could haul one in a wagon as far as possible, then lash it onto mules and carry it up in pieces. If she wanted real furniture, she could have that, too. Now that spring was here, he could take advantage of the weather and build another room. Two rooms if he worked fast.

They could take trips to Cheyenne twice a year. He'd buy
clothes for her and Baby, and hell, he'd buy her all the geegaws he could afford.

If she'd only stay.

His mind was running too fast for him to go back to sleep.
If he wanted to keep her here so that he could take time to
convince her not to leave, then he didn't want her to wake up
and ask about going down the mountain. Buck gently
nudged Annika until she rolled away from him and he could
slip out of bed. Carefully, he drew the covers up and tucked
them around her, then pulled on his clothes. Trying to be as
silent as possible, he made coffee and stoked up the fire so
the place would be warm when she and Baby Buttons woke
up. He poured himself a cup and drank it slowly, content to
watch the two of them sleep. With a shake of his head, he
looked at the newly renamed Buttons and couldn't help but
smile. Annika already made a wonderful mother.

Feeling more alive than he had in years, Buck took his gun
down off the pegs over the mantel, set it on the table, and
shrugged into his coat. He pulled up the hood and stepped
outside, anxious to saddle up and ride up the mountain to
hunt. There was a cat out there somewhere and he intended
to bring it down. The pelt would bring a good price. A man
with a family had to provide for them, and that's just what he
intended to do. Her new life might not be what Annika was
accustomed to, but he planned to give her anything it was in
his power to provide.

It scared him to think that she had nearly pushed him into
admitting his old dream. She almost had him talking about
how badly he had wanted to be a doctor when he was growing up. He thought again about her crazy suggestion. Plumb
loco, that's what it was, what with the money it would take
to see him through school and Baby to care for. No, doctoring was out of the question.

The sun was just turning the inky night sky to gray when
he saddled up his horse. Tonight when he got home he'd go
down on one knee and propose properly—no more demands, no more ultimatums. He would promise to give
Annika the best life he could here in the valley, to care for
her and protect her for as long as they both lived.

He could wait until tonight to try to convince her again.
This time he'd use words as well as his body.

ANNIKA hummed as she scrubbed the surface of the table
with a brush she had found in a box beneath the kitchen
bench. Soap suds covered the tabletop, dripped over the
edge, and plopped onto the dirt below. She wondered if she
was not making a bigger mess, but it was a relief to throw
herself to a new task, especially after it had been so frustrat-
ing to wake up and find Buck gone.

Last night had been indescribable, a trip to heaven and
back. But nothing was settled between them, especially after
last night—and now, just like a man, he had snuck out to
avoid another confrontation. His escape had reminded her of
the way Kase had left Boston after an argument with their
parents, and as she ground the brush against the worn surface of the table Annika promised herself she would get her
brother to tell her once and for all the cause of the rift as soon
as she saw him again.

But she wouldn't see Kase until she went to Cheyenne.
The idea of leaving Buck tore her in two.

She tried humming as she worked. Would it be possible to
adapt to life here in the isolated valley where no one ever
came to the door? Would she miss her old life, or would her
love for Buck make up for the other loss?

She thought of the tenderness he expressed as he held her
in his arms last night and saw their lovemaking as a form of
communion, a silent waltz that had carried her to the stars
and beyond. He had told her once that he didn't know any
songs, but she knew better than that. The songs were in his
heart—songs with notes that struck chords upon her own.

Baby Buttons was on her bed noisily shaking the button
tin. Even the incessant clatter didn't bother Annika today.
Nothing bothered her. How could it when she felt light
enough to float? She bent over her work and put aside
thoughts of everything that was missing from her life here at
Blue Creek and focused on all she had. She was independent
now, more so than she had ever been in Boston where her
parents coddled her and society placed well-defined restrictions on unmarried women her age. Up here she had become

an adult and was treated as such, on equal footing with Buck. In the short time she had been with him she had taken on more responsibility and coped with more than she ever had to in all her twenty years. If she did go back to Boston, she was determined to make sure Richard knew there was no hope for a reconciliation, for there was no way she could play the innocent bride.

She straightened and stretched with her hands at the small of her back. It felt good to be useful, especially when there was so much for Buck to see to by himself. She wondered how he had done it all before she arrived. Not only did he hunt and prepare the skins, but also he shoveled snow, carried water, made repairs about the place, cleaned, cooked, and took care of the horses and mules. Not to mention raising Baby Buttons. It gave her satisfaction to know she could help out even a little. Her cooking was nothing to speak of yet, but then, it was more than she'd ever attempted before with a cook in residence at the mansion.

Satisfied with the results of her scrubbing, Annika picked up the bucket and walked through the open door to heave the water out. She paused outside, squinted into the bright sunlight, and then wiped her brow with the back of her arm. Hefting the bucket, she tossed out the soapy water, and then paused long enough to dry her hands on the dish towel she had tied around her waist.

At the sound of a rider approaching, she glanced up the mountainside and smiled. So, she thought, he couldn't stay away all day after all. With quick movements, she smoothed back her hair and felt to see that her braid was still tightly woven. When she noticed the front of her blouse was water stained, she pulled the long queue over her shoulder so that it hung down across her breast, unsuccessfully hiding the wet spot.

"Buck's coming home," she called to Baby Buttons, who soon tumbled out over the doorstep.

She bent over to pick up the child and brush her off when something in the sound of the approaching horse made her wary. The thick trees on the side of the mountain hid the rider from view, and now that the sound had intensified Annika was certain that what she was hearing were the hoofbeats of more than one horse. When three riders came into view, she quickly turned with Baby in her arms and headed for the safety of the cabin.

Too late she remembered there was no lock on the door. Buck obviously never expected any real trouble, but then, he wasn't an unarmed woman. Annika stood just inside, waiting for a glimpse of the riders. She tried to calm her racing heart by telling herself it might be Kase and his men, or perhaps Old Ted had made it through the pass.

Before she knew it, three riders broke through the cover of the pines, their horses eating up the ground beneath them as they closed the distance between the tree line and the cabin. The horses thundered forward, churning up earth and rocks, splashing across the creek bed, and finally pulling up into the yard itself. None of them was Old Ted.

None of them looked reputable.

The oldest man rode in the lead, he was dressed in brown—dingy brown pants and jacket, a brown hat. He smiled down at her when they stopped, and dismounted first as the other two men exchanged glances. The man smiled a near-toothless smile, and tipped his hat in her direction. What little hair he had left was stuck to his head.

The other two, one lean and lanky, and the other rotund and sour looking, stayed on their mounts and kept glancing back the way they had come.

Baby Buttons jammed her thumb into her mouth at the sight of the three strangers. Annika stood firm in the open doorway. She glanced up the hill and then down the valley for some sign of Buck, but there was none.

"Can I help you gentlemen?" She used the term loosely.

The big, gap-toothed man walked toward the door. "I hope so, ma'am. Is this here Buck Scott's place?"

"What do you want with him?"

The man smiled. He had even fewer teeth than she thought. "Well, it ain't exactly him we need. Be you Annika Storm?"

He pronounced her name An-eeka and she smoothly corrected him when she said, "I'm Annika Storm. And that's Aah-neckah." She wondered how he knew her name and how he'd gotten into the valley when Buck contended they couldn't get out.

"Hear that, boys? It's her." With a smug, self-satisfied grin, he turned to the others.

"What do you want with me?"

"You can pack up now, little lady," Toothless said, " 'cause me an' my friends here have come to rescue you."

He was watching her, alternately staring between her and Baby. The child sensed his curiosity and with her thumb still in her mouth, laid her head on Annika's shoulder.

Annika laid a hand protectively on Baby's curly head. "I'm sorry to disappoint you, but you see, I don't need to be rescued. I'm not going anywhere." *Not with you, anyway.*

When he opened his jacket, she took a step back in alarm.

"Hold on, child. This ain't no gun, it's a poster." He held it out to her. "Take a look at that."

She quickly scanned the worn, dirty page. *Annika Storm. Ten thousand dollar reward. Suspected abductor, Buck Scott, notify Kase Storm or the Cheyenne police.*

"This is all a mistake," she said, carefully handing him back the page. "I'm not a captive. As a matter of fact, Buck is taking me to Cheyenne this week. I take it the pass is open?"

"We barely made it through today, and we want to ske-daddle back in case we get a late snow. Hell, Denton's horse almost got swallowed up in a drift." He nodded to the heavy man who looked none too happy about the fact that he had almost been buried alive by snow. "But we're the first here and we ain't leavin' without you so's we can get the reward. Best you pack your things."

"But I can't leave the baby here alone."

He frowned, for the first time carefully studying Baby as he compared her to Annika. "The reward don't say nothing about no kid. Is she yours?"

Thinking they would hesitate to take on hauling her and the child down the hill, Annika nodded. "Yes. She's mine."

The tall thin man who was still astride his horse didn't look about to dismount. He called out, "The poster don't say nothin' about no kid, Virge."

Toothless Virge turned and snapped over his shoulder, "I told her that. Kid's hers though."

The fat man, Denton, whined, "Now what are we gonna do?"

Annika watched as Virge stomped over to the men who sat staring down at him. As they mumbled together, one after the other took turns staring at her. She stepped back over the threshold, moving slowly, hoping to barricade herself in the cabin while they were engaged in their hushed discussion.

Before she was all the way inside, Denton looked her way and pointed, "She's sneakin' inside."

Virge crossed the yard before she could slam the door closed. He shoved it open with a booted foot and pushed his way inside. "We're takin' you and the kid, and we'll take you with the clothes you got on your backs unless you pack up now."

Annika wanted to laugh in his face and tell him that nearly all they had was the clothes on their backs, but instead she set Baby Buttons on the bed and pulled out her satchel, hoping to stall for time. Slowly, meticulously, she began folding her nightgown and Buck's flannel nightshirt. It was part of him that had become hers, she would not leave it behind.

"I have to leave a note," she said, opening her journal as she prepared to rip a blank page out of the back.

Virge stared at the girl, trying to figure out why she didn't want to leave when he thought she'd be damn thankful to be rescued, and then wondered why she'd want to go so far as leave her kidnapper a note. He squinted at her as he tried to reason it out. Denton and Cliff were still talking outside; he could hear them arguing. The two were the biggest mealy-mouthed cowards he could have ever hooked up with and right now he wished he'd never laid eyes on them. He was damned sick and tired of Denton, who'd been riding him since they left Cheyenne. If he had the chance he'd leave them both behind—they were nothing but a nuisance—but they were in on the plan and there was nothing he could do about it.

"No notes," he blurted out. "Let's go."

Annika tried to persuade him. "Are you sure? It won't take long, I promise, I'll just—"

"No note. Hurry up." He didn't want to pull his gun and frighten her; after all, he was supposed to be her rescuer, and if he intended to collect three times the reward money, it wouldn't do to frighten her more than they already had. Still, he fingered his holster just to let her know he wasn't a man she should rile.

Annika packed the journal next, then inkwell and pen, and her comb, and brush. She tried to keep one eye on the man as she packed. She turned to Baby Buttons, wishing she hadn't been so hasty in getting the child dressed for the day. Every minute she could stall would give Buck that much more time to return, if he was planning to come home before dark.

But Buttons was already dressed in her black dress, her shoes and socks on her feet, her hair neatly combed. Annika picked up one of her old gowns and tossed it in the bag. "Get your dolly," she whispered to Baby, who shook her head and would not budge with the stranger in the room.

Annika found the doll and the flannel rag that was its blanket and slipped it in the satchel. *Please find us, Buck. Please find us fast.*

"Let's go," Virge barked, unhappy with the way the girl kept stalling, the way she kept watching the door. "That's all you need."

"What about food? There's plenty in the smokehouse."

Virge started to tell her to mind her own business, then yelled out to Cliff, "Raid the smokehouse. The girl says there's meat to be had." He hoped new provisions would make the ever hungry Denton happy.

"Now, come on," he prodded.

"Buttons!" Baby cried out. The button can lay in the middle of her bed and she pointed to it.

"Shut the kid up," Virge warned.

Annika looked from Baby to the man who was standing so nervously in the doorway. If Baby proved to be too much trouble, perhaps her would-be rescuers would think twice about taking them.

"No buttons," Annika said harshly. She picked up the tin and set it in the center of the table as a silent message for Buck. Surely he would realize she would never intentionally leave the buttons behind, not after the fuss she'd put up to keep them. He would see the tin and know she didn't leave of her own free will.

Baby Buttons whined as Annika made her put on her coat. She slipped on her own, remembered the hours it had taken Buck to fashion it for her, then lifted the child onto her hip. She picked up her satchel and paused long enough to look around the room again. If only there were time to leave Buck some other sign.

Virge grabbed her arm and pulled her outside. Denton was holding a mule, waiting for Virge to help Annika mount up. The three of them argued over who would hold Baby until Annika was settled. Finally they opted to put her on the ground.

Once Annika was on the mule and her satchel was tied on behind her, Virge made Cliff lift the child up to her. Baby howled and clung to Annika, softly sobbing out her fear of the three strange men. It was all Annika could do not to cry herself, but she hadn't fallen apart when Buck abducted her and she didn't intend to now.

She held Baby close and then set the child astride in front of her. Wrapping her arms about Buttons, Annika clung to the mule's mane with all her strength.

"Hold on, Baby," she whispered in the little girl's ear. "Buck will find us as soon as he can."

"Not . . . Baby," the child sobbed. "Buttons."

As the three men prodded the mule up the hill ahead of them, Annika looked for some sign of Buck in the trees, wondering at the twist of fate that caused her to hope that the man who had kidnapped her two months before would come to her rescue now. She turned around, hoping for one last look at the cabin, but the fat man whipped her mule and it lunged forward, forcing her to pay close attention to the steep trail.

❧ 18 ❧

"Fort Sanders is on the other side of Cheyenne Pass. Maybe they can send out a search party from there." Zach Elliot stood shoulder to shoulder with Kase Storm, squinting down at Holt's New Map of Wyoming spread across his desk.

Kase looked at the minute, concentric lines that represented the peaks of the Laramie Mountains. "There are over two hundred miles of mountains up there, Zach. Passes, valleys, and hollows. Annika could be in any one of them." With his hands planted on either side of the map, Kase leaned down, arms spread wide and studied the spiderweb lines and carefully lettered words.

"What else did you hear in Cheyenne?" Abruptly Kase turned his back on the map and Zach and walked to the window of the jail where he stared out at the muddied streets of Busted Heel. One of the first signs of spring was the mud that came with the thaw.

"Talk is, everyone's wantin' to collect the ten thousand you offered. The sheriff there says there's been a run on supplies with this warm weather that's set in. Everyone's bettin' on when the passes'll be clear and who'll be the first in and out to collect the reward."

Kase lifted his tall-crowned hat, smoothed his hair back, and settled his hat back in place. "Damn, but I wish I could ride in and get her myself, but with the baby due at the end of the month, there's no way I can leave Rose." He turned to Zach, "Not after what's happened to her before."

"Hell, I know that, boy, an' I don't blame you. 'Sides, half

237

the state's out beatin' the hills for your sister. She'll be home soon enough."

"I just hate to think what she might be going through in the hands of that man."

"Put yourself in his place." Tired of staring at the map, Zach pulled out the rolling desk chair and sat down, then worked a hunk of chewing tobacco out of a muslin bag he extracted from his pocket. "The man probably just made an honest mistake and is living to regret it right now. What if he brings her back hisself?"

Kase turned on Zach with fury in his eyes. "She tried to tell him she wasn't the woman he was expecting and he took her anyway. Rode off with her at knife point, for God's sake. Besides, there's more you don't know."

"More?"

Miserable with worry, Kase walked to the far wall and leaned against it. He crossed his ankles and stared at the tips of his shining black boots. "Leonard Wilson, the rancher whose land borders mine, read about what happened and came over to tell me he'd heard of this Buck Scott a few years back. It seems his wife is an acquaintance of an old Scotch woman named MacGuire who lives out by Indian Springs near the Nebraska border."

"I know there's a story here someplace." Zach grunted as he worked the chaw in his mouth.

Kase glowered. "About three years ago, Buck Scott looked her up and asked her to take in his sister and care for her. Scott still pays for care and room and board."

"Sounds like a decent sort to me."

"He took his sister to live under Mary MacGuire's care because she'd lost her mind."

"The MacGuire woman?"

Pushing away from the wall, Kase walked to the desk and stared hard at Zach. "Buck Scott's sister is insane. Out of her mind. Crazy."

"That don't mean he is."

"No, it doesn't, but it seems this Mrs. MacGuire claims Scott's sister went crazy when she witnessed her husband's murder."

Zach's face showed true concern for the first time. "You ain't gonna tell me this Buck Scott did it?"

Kase shook his head. "Worse. It seems old man Scott was crazy as a loon, too. They used to keep him tied up, but he got loose one day and killed the girl's husband. Then he tried to skin the man."

"Shee-it!" Zach's eye was as wide as the holes in his underwear. "Always knew a buffalo man was lower 'n a snake."

"I couldn't have put it any better," Kase said. "Buck Scott came home and caught his old man in the process and shot him. I guess his sister was never the same."

"I don't doubt it."

"It seems there was another sister, too. A younger one. My neighbor didn't know much about her, except that she was supposed to be a little, well . . . vacant."

"I'm afraid to ask what happened to her."

Kase shrugged. "They didn't know, but it seems she died sometime back, just after the murder."

Zach aimed to spit into the trash can beside the desk, missed, and shook his head. "And Annika's been up there with Scott for two months now? No tellin' what she's had to put up with." He looked up quickly, concern etched on his face. "Your Rosie don't know all this, does she?"

"No, thank God. I talked to Wilson out in the barn." Kase ran his hand over the lower half of his face and then rubbed his chin. "If I don't hear something soon, I may just go insane myself."

Hitching up his pants, Zach stood and walked around the desk. With a hand on Kase's shoulder, he looked up at the taller man and said, "Don't worry, son. Annemeke's made of strong stuff. Runs in the family. Mark my words, she'll be fine. Has to be, 'cause I got money on it."

THE afternoon sun had slipped behind the mountaintop, casting the hillside in blue gray light. Buck paused and wiped his brow with the back of his sleeve, his bloody hand clutching his skinning knife. A half-dressed deer lay on the ground at his feet, but he ignored it as he paused to take in the sight of the sunset reflected on the mountains on the opposite side of

the valley. The remaining snow was stained with a light ro-
seate glow, the pines stood out vibrant green against it. The
sunset translated itself into reds and pinks across a sky that
stretched from one side of the valley to the other. He wished
Annika was here to see the display.

Anxious to get down the mountain before dark, Buck decided to take the hide and the antlers from the buck and leave
the carcass to the wolves. He wiped his knife off on the
ground and sheathed it, then began folding the scraped hide.
Tomorrow he'd stretch it and begin working it into the fine
piece he knew would bring him good money in Cheyenne.

He heard his horse nicker and paused, immediately alert
to any danger that might be at hand. He left the hide where it
lay and started toward the big bay.

"Easy, boy, what's the matter? You hear something you
don't like?" Buck scanned the woods behind the horse for
any sign of a predator. "Probably just a wolf anxious for us
to leave."

He took two more steps toward the terrified animal that
was pulling at the reins Buck had loosely tied to a tree. With
its eyes rolling in fear, the horse pulled free before Buck
could reach it. He watched the animal bolt down the hillside.

"Damn!" He cursed under his breath. It would be a long
walk back.

He turned back to collect the hide and found himself face-
to-face with two hundred pounds of mountain lion. The big
cat was hunched over the deer carcass, its mighty paws with
claws extended tearing into the deer. Broad nosed, its thick
winter coat still more white than any other color, the feline
let out a warning growl as it ripped off a mouthful of bloody
meat.

Buck eyed the animal's rich pelt and knew he had to have
it, then realized his rifle was propped against a tree not six
feet from the mountain lion. As the wary animal watched,
Buck tried to inch his way sideways toward the gun.

"You're a fool, Buck Scott," he whispered to himself as he
crept toward the gun. But he figured since the animal had
more than enough to eat, he just might not mind a man getting a little closer.

The beast snarled again and Buck stopped. Pretending to

draw back, Buck slipped his knife from his sheath. Darkness crept up the hillside and scattered itself beneath the trees and into the deep gullies. The temperature was dropping. A wolf howled somewhere behind him. Buck looked up at the sky and figured the odds were against him. He'd wait out the lion's meal, collect his gun, and then slip down the mountain before he was forced to spend the night out in the cold.

He hunkered down with his back to a rock to wait, certain that once the big cat ate its fill it would leave. He kept his knife in his hand.

The wolf howl in the forest intensified. The cat snarled, louder this time, the sound piercing the air around Buck. The big animal began to pace back and forth, its tail moving from side to side as it watched the forest for the wolves that menaced its meal.

The heavy animal pawed about in a wider circle. Buck watched the powerful muscles bunch beneath the skin. The lion stopped, sniffed the air, and started to turn back to the deer carcass. Suddenly it paused, as if it remembered the man crouched nearby. The wolf howled again and before Buck could brace himself, the mountain lion marshalled its speed and strength and sprang, flying through the air toward him.

Buck's knife flashed. He stood to try to deflect the assault. Agonizing fire ripped down his thigh as the big cat sank its claws into his left leg. Buck thrust his arm across his face, aiming to hit the animal in the throat.

They went down together, hundreds of pounds of man and animal as the cat pinned Buck to the ground.

It was so close he could feel the animal's hot breath and smell the fetid scent of blood. Its slanted yellow-gold eyes were only inches away from Buck's face.

The cat tried to sink its teeth into Buck's forearm but he kept moving, dragging his flesh out of the animal's grip. Finally, he lashed out in a final effort to save himself and felt a spurt of hot blood across his face as he buried his knife up to the hilt in the lion's neck.

Gasping for breath, he jerked with all his strength, pulling the knife across the mountain lion's throat.

The big cat collapsed on top of him, nearly crushing him with its weight.

Buck tried to drag himself out from beneath the mountain lion but found his strength had suddenly evaporated. His heart was still pounding from the rush of the moment, his breath jagged. A slow, burning ache had settled into his thigh. He felt the damp flow of blood even though his legs were still trapped beneath the heavy cat.

He tried to sit up, heaved with what little strength he had left, and managed to get the lion off him enough to where he could pull himself out from beneath it.

Even in the gathering dusk he could see that his pant leg was stained with his own blood. His sleeves were tattered, but the wounds beneath them didn't seem to be as deep as the one on his leg.

Another howl broke the stillness in the clearing, the only other sound that was louder than his ragged breathing. He pulled himself across the uneven ground until he reached his rifle, then worked his way up to a sitting position against a tree. He looked at the ragged edge of his flesh beneath the torn fabric of his pants and whispered to himself, "Damn you, Buck Scott. Night's comin' on and you're sittin' here in the dark bleedin' like a stuck pig."

The wolves howled in tandem as he shook his head to clear it, then checked to be sure his gun was loaded. Let them come, he thought. Let them try.

He spotted a patch of snow beneath the tree that had escaped the early spring sun and grabbed handfuls to pack along his wound to try to halt the flow of blood that was beginning to pool beneath him. He wondered if the wolves were about to take their revenge.

ANNIKA knew that for as long as she lived she would never forget the trip down the mountain to Cheyenne. The bone-jarring ride on the back of the mule was only exacerbated by the fact that she had to cling to Buttons and worry about the child falling beneath the horses' hooves. They had camped overnight in the woods and were treated to a cold meal—elk again—because Virge wouldn't let the others light a fire.

She knew her so-called rescuers by name and had nicknamed them all—Virge Clemmens, toothless; Cliff Wiley, the beanpole; and Denton Matthews, the barrel—and wondered why they hadn't killed one another by now. The three argued incessantly, so much so that by the time they reached Cheyenne after two days on the trail, she wanted to scream with frustration.

It was dusk when they reached the outskirts of town. She dared to let herself feel hope and relief, knowing that soon they'd be turning her over to the authorities and Kase would be notified. By tonight she would be with her brother and his wife, sleeping in a clean bed, looking forward to Buck's arrival at the ranch. She had hoped he would have found them before they reached Cheyenne and had taken every opportunity to delay the ride out of the mountains. When Baby cried, Annika did nothing to appease her, hoping the men would slow down or at the very least that Buck would hear them if he were searching nearby.

Once, when she had talked the men into letting her go into the woods alone to relieve herself, she managed to loosen one of the cinches as she passed by their mounts.

As it turned out, the loosened saddle had been Denton's, and although the delay was slight, her satisfaction had been great when his saddle shifted and the big man fell off and began rolling down hill. Virge Clemmens had gotten as much of a laugh out of it as Annika, except he did not have to keep his silence. His obvious glee only worsened the animosity between the two men.

By the time they reined in outside a ramshackle house on the outskirts of Cheyenne, Annika knew three things for certain: Denton hated Virgil, Virgil hated Denton, and Cliff was scared.

They dismounted and Virge tied the mule's lead rope to a hitching rail behind the house. He reached up for Baby. Before Annika let go of the child she asked, "What are we doing here? Why aren't you turning us over to the police?"

She watched in dismay as Cliff and Denton ignored her and walked into the shabby house.

Virge took Baby from her. "You don't need to be askin' any questions, little lady. Just get on down from there and do as I say and you'll be all right."

By the time her feet hit the ground, she knew she was shaking from more than exhaustion. What were they up to? What about the reward? Virge handed Baby over to her and stepped aside to follow them across the wooden porch to the back door. The nearest house was two lots away and looked to be in the same condition. When she stepped over the threshold, a musty smell assailed her. The inside of the house was as dismal as the outside with its peeling paint, crooked shutters, and tattered curtains at the windows. Sparsely furnished with the bare necessities, it was cold and dark inside, and it appeared the men were content to keep the place that way.

"Pull down the shades and light a lamp," Virge commanded the beanpole.

Cliff did as he asked while Denton rummaged through the dry sink in the kitchen searching for food.

Even Buttons sensed something was wrong. She started fussing and crying again. Cliff turned away from a window and said, "Keep that brat quiet, you hear? We ain't out in the woods now."

Attempting to make their lives as miserable as possible, Annika brushed aside a lock of hair that had fallen into her eyes and said, "She's cold and tired and hungry, and so am I. I demand to know when you are taking us to the authorities."

Denton turned on her. "You ain't in no position to demand nothin'!"

Without thinking, she snapped back, "Do you think I'll be willing to let you take ten thousand dollars from my family for treating me this way? I didn't even want to be rescued in the first place!"

For a split second she was afraid he was going to hit her, but instead, he turned on Virgil. "Hear that, old man? She's gonna bitch and moan and we're not gonna get a dime."

She wished they would stop arguing long enough for her to sit down, but their words grew more heated. Annika hoped that in their anger they might not see her slip out the back door, so she stayed on her feet clutching Buttons and watching for a chance to escape.

"If you want your share of the thirty thousand, you'll shut up, Denton," Virge warned.

"*Thirty* thousand?" Annika couldn't hide her surprise.

Clifford lit a lamp and held it aloft, the light casting his lean form into a skeletal shadow on the wall. He watched her nervously as he said, "Shut up, Virge."

"This was the *stupidest* plan," Denton railed. He pointed at Annika. "She's gonna waltz into the arms of the law and tell 'em she didn't want to be rescued and then we'll have nothing to show for our trouble but wasted time."

"You're more ignorant than I thought if you think we're just gonna ride up and deliver her to the law. Hell no." Virge slapped his forehead as if Denton were the biggest idiot alive. "We're gonna write a ransom note to say we got her and the kid and then tell the sheriff where we'll leave 'em and where we want the money dropped off."

"I'm a hostage?" Annika nearly laughed in disbelief. "I've been kidnapped again?" Disgusted, she walked out of the kitchen, found a rickety chair, sat down, then began to rock Buttons, who started crying again.

Annika leaned close and whispered in her ear. "You want Buck, don't you?"

The crying turned to a high-pitched wail.

"I want him, too, but the bad men said no," Annika prodded.

The wail turned into high-pitched shrieking. Buttons turned red.

All three men rushed into the room.

"What in the hell . . . ?" Virge grumbled.

Cliff glanced anxiously at the door. "Get her to stop."

"This is the stupidest . . ." Denton looked disgusted.

Virge pulled a gun on Denton. "If you say this is a stupid plan one more time I swear I'm gonna kill you."

Annika clamped her hand over Baby's mouth and tried to shush her.

"Aw, come on you two," Cliff appealed to them both.

Cuddling Buttons close, Annika held her breath as the two men sized each other up. Virge held a gun on Denton as Denton eyed him warily but backed down.

Virge holstered his weapon. Annika breathed an inaudible sigh of relief. Cliff stepped back.

As Virge took command again, he moved toward Annika, turning his back on Denton.

Before anyone could move, Denton pulled his gun and fired.

Annika screamed and Buttons started shrieking again as Virge hit the floor, a bullet in his side.

"Aw, hell, Denton, what'd you go and do that for?" Cliff rushed to the fallen man's side, knelt down, and slipped Virge's gun from its holster before any more damage could be done. "He ain't dead. It's all right, Denton, Virge ain't dead."

Denton took a step toward Virgil, who was moaning and trying to right himself. "Then step outta the way, Cliff, 'cause I'm gonna plug him till he is."

Cliff shielded Virgil Clemmens with his own body and tried to appeal to his partner. "Listen, Denton, you're right, this was a stupid plan. We don't need him. Let's just clear out and leave 'em all. Let him have the ten thousand and the trouble."

"That means we been through all this for nothing. At least step aside and give me the satisfaction of murderin' that dad-blamed idiot!"

Rubbing his temples, Cliff appeared to be trying to think of a plan. Virge clutched his side and groaned very near Annika's feet. Suddenly, Cliff's frown cleared and he said, "I got it! We can tell 'em Virge was holdin' the girl hostage and we saved her and then we'll get the money and he'll be in jail, right back where he belongs. You won't have to do no killin' then, Denton."

With a groan, Virge shook his head. "He'll have to kill me. I'll never go along with it."

Finally, she could stand no more. Clutching Buttons close, shielding the child by pressing her face against her breast, Annika leapt to her feet and began shouting at all three of them. "Stop it! Just stop it right now!" She pinned them one at a time with a furious stare. "I will *not* spend another night with the three of you! As I see it, these are your options: you can take me to the authorities *now* and settle for the ten thousand and I won't say a word about all of this because I just want to get away from your odious presence—"

"Our what?" Cliff said.

Regally straightening to her full height, Annika ignored him. "Or you can stand and argue among yourselves until one or more of you gets killed and winds up facing a murder charge. I hear they often hang murderers from the nearest tree out here in the wild west. Is that still true?"

Denton looked at Cliff. Cliff looked at Virge. Virge groaned.

"Well?" She tapped her foot, feigning impatience, demanding an answer. "I didn't want to be rescued anyway. At least you'll still get over three thousand each. Take it or leave it." It was a terrible waste of Kase's money, but she'd give anything to get away from them.

Denton, who continued to aim the Colt revolver at Virge, shot her an angry glare. "Think you're high and mighty, do you, miss?"

"Not at all," she said, patting the hiccuping child's back. "But I do think I'm the only rational one here." Bone weary and still wearing the heavy coat Buck had made for her, Annika faced them defiantly. She refused to back down now that they no longer represented a united threat.

"Come on, Denton," Cliff urged his partner, "let's get out of here and let Virge settle it between 'em. It'll be jest us, jest like it was before."

The gun wavered before Denton lowered it. "No more partners?"

"Never. I promise," Cliff said, raising his hand.

"Then let's git. I don't give a good goddamn what happens to any of 'em." Denton frowned down at Virge, looking tempted to finish what he'd begun, then holstered his gun and followed Cliff through the kitchen and out the back door.

Annika didn't breathe easy until she heard the sound of their horses' hoofbeats recede into the distance. Weak-kneed, she sank onto the nearest chair and sat staring down at Virge Clemmens, who was slumped against the wall, still moaning and clutching his side, his blood mingling with the layer of dust that coated the floorboards.

Unarmed and wounded, he didn't present much of a problem at all. She didn't relish going out onto the streets of a strange place at night, but she reckoned she wouldn't be any worse off than she had been with the three of them. What she needed now was food, shelter, and peace of mind. The poster still in Virgil's possession proved her abduction was no secret; everyone would be looking for her. Annika pulled herself together one last time.

"If you don't mind, Mr. Clemmens, once I catch my breath I'm going to take your horse and find the local sheriff's office. I wouldn't advise you to try and stop me."

He tried to stand, but fell back against the wall.

Annika took one last look at him and felt no remorse at leaving a wounded man lying helpless in the empty room.

When she walked out the back door, he was protesting so vehemently that she knew he wasn't about to die before she sent someone back to find him.

WITH a full moon shining over them, the pines became hulking black shadows that loomed over Buck in the darkness. The snow helped slow his bleeding and the pain finally ebbed enough for him to slip off his gloves and coat, then his shirt. Wishing he had soot to pack into the open wound to stop the bleeding, he tore the shirt into strips to bind his leg in three places then put on his coat again. He shoved his gloves in his pockets so he wouldn't lose them. The wolves—a pack or just a pair, he wasn't certain—had come no closer, but while they were holding off he wanted to start downhill to see how far he could go before his strength gave out.

Faint from loss of blood and pain, he shook his head and refused to give in to the unconsciousness that threatened to overwhelm him as he pulled himself up, using a tree trunk for support. His rifle proved to be as good a crutch as he could hope for under the circumstances, so he leaned on it gingerly and forced himself to take a step.

Minutes later, he was across the small clearing, hoping the deer and mountain lion carcasses he left behind would be more than enough entertainment for the hungry wolves. Moving slowly and cautiously through the moonlit forest, Buck made his way down the mountain. Sweat poured down his face with his efforts, rivulets of the stuff crept into the collar of his undershirt. Pausing for breath every few feet, he talked himself into going on by thinking of Annika. She would be worried now that darkness had fallen, afraid that something might have happened to him.

If he could have smiled, he would have, knowing how angry she would be when he arrived late. He knew she would fuss and carry on about his wound; it would only add to her argument that he should take Baby and move down into Cheyenne.

He stumbled over a rock in his path, forgot for a second to favor his leg, and growled with the pain that hit him when he put his weight on it. Panting, he leaned heavily on his rifle and wiped the sweat from his eyes.

A doctor. Ha.

She wanted him to be a doctor. Wait until she saw his leg. It would take all his skill to close this wound properly, not to mention all his luck, for infection was sure to set in. He wondered if he could sew up his own leg. He couldn't quite picture Annika pulling the lips of the wound together and then piercing his skin with a needle. But he hoped she wouldn't be so mad at him that she would refuse to sit at his bedside and hold his hand.

He guessed it had taken two hours to reach the valley floor, two hours of stumbling, halting, and cursing. At a shallow point in the stream he lowered himself to the ground and cupped his hands for a drink. He splashed water over his face and neck, noting that his temperature had risen and he'd stopped sweating, even though each step was an effort. Fever would be upon him with a vengeance soon.

Thankful for the full moon, he began to pass the more familiar landmarks that meant the cabin was just around the next bend in the creek. By the time he could make out the shape of the wooden structure, he was shaking from chills. The pain in his leg had receded to a dull throbbing ache that was as much a part of him now as breathing. His left foot was nearly numb.

As he paused for what he hoped was the last time before he reached the cabin, he noticed there was no welcome light streaming from the windows. Annika had already gone to bed.

So much for her worrying long into the night, he thought,

as he started limping forward. He told himself he should be thankful that she had gained enough confidence in him not to worry. How was she to know that the one night she had gone about her business and hadn't waited up for him that he was barely able to make it back?

The cabin reminded him of a tiny matchstick box in the moonlight. He was close enough now to make out the door and the tree stump he used as a chopping block in the yard. Squinting, he searched for the door, then shook his head and wiped his eyes again. They had to be playing tricks on him. From where he stood it looked like a black void in the front wall of the cabin. It would only appear that way if it had been left wide open.

He called Annika's name but there was no response.

Frowning from more than pain, he tried to hurry and cursed the leg that held him back. By the time he reached the well-traveled path that led to the yard, he was huffing and puffing. Hobbling along, he felt his makeshift crutch cut into his side. There was no smoke coming from the chimney. The fire had gone out. *Why?*

"Annika!" He bellowed her name, weaving on his feet.

There was no answer.

His horse ambled around to the front of the house, anxious for a handout. It was still saddled.

"Annika! Baby!" Barely able to stand, he reached the yard and stumbled toward the open door. "Annika, damn it, where are you?" He shouted into the void.

"Annikaaaa!" The hollow sound reverberated off the mountainside and echoed around him.

Arms wide, he grasped both sides of the doorway for support and called her name one last time as pain greater than any physical wound assailed him.

There was no answer.

He was welcomed by nothing more than the cold darkness of the empty cabin.

❧ 19 ❧

THE ride from Busted Heel out to Buffalo Mountain Ranch had not taken as long as she had expected. Annika sat in the buggy with Buttons asleep on her lap. She studied the wide-open landscape and the two-story house that reigned over the empty plains like a grand monarch of all it surveyed. The rolling land around the ranch house and outbuildings was dotted here and there with new spring grass and an occasional tree bent by wind and time. As she watched the grass blow in the wind, she wondered how the tender shoots withstood the onslaught that blew her tangled hair into her face.

Zach Elliot had met her train in Busted Heel. The last time she had seen him she had been seven years old, but even time had not dimmed her memory of him. There was no mistaking the grizzled white hair beneath the floppy-brimmed leather hat, the scar down the side of his face, or the chaw of tobacco under his lip. He'd given her a big hug when she stepped onto the platform in Busted Heel, glanced once or twice at Buttons, but hadn't asked a thing about her kidnapping. She guessed he was leaving the interrogation to Kase.

As they pulled up behind the house, he pointed to the back door and suggested, "Why don't you go on up? I'll ride out to the far corral and fetch your brother. Rosie'll be anxious to see you."

As if on cue, Rose Storm opened the back door and stepped out onto the wide veranda that wrapped around the entire house. As the buggy drew closer to the steps, Rose recognized Annika. She pressed her hands to her cheeks and

251

then waved and was soon off the porch with more speed than Annika thought would have been possible, given the diminutive woman's heavily pregnant state.

Smiling, even as tears slipped down her cheeks, Rose stood beside the buggy while Zach climbed down with Annika's valise in one hand. He reached up for Buttons and held the sleeping child while she climbed down. Rose's questioning gaze briefly touched on the child, but like Zach, she didn't ask about Baby. Instead, she prompted Annika, "Come, we go into the house and wait for Kase. You will get him, no, Zach?"

"No. I mean yes, ma'am." He turned to Annika and said, "Sometimes when she starts talkin' at me in that Eyetalian-English, I get a little mixed up." He turned back to Rose. "Kase out by the far corral, ma'am?"

"*Sí.* Yes. With the buffalo, as always. He will be so happy, so relieved." She shook her head as she put her hand on her sister-in-law's arm. "Come, Annika." Rose ushered her up the steps. "Come, we will sit and you will tell me how you are."

Dead tired, Annika wanted to say. *Worried about Buck.* Wondering when he'll get here and how my hotheaded brother will react. But instead she said nothing as she followed Rose into the kitchen and wearily let her hostess pull out a chair at the table for her. Her sister-in-law made her feel like a mess. Rose was neatly dressed in a navy serge gown with a crisp white apron tied about her expansive waistline. Her hair was wound in a coronet of braids about her head in much the same way Analisa often wore her hair. There was something similar about the two women that Annika had noticed the first time she'd met Rose. Perhaps, she thought, it was the fact that they were both originally from Europe.

Rose clasped her hands over her swollen abdomen. "Sit down, sit down, Annika, and have something to eat."

"Not right now, thank you, Rose. I'm really not hungry." Annika watched the heavily pregnant little brunette open the tin-fronted pie safe and take out a plate of cookies. Coffee was already simmering on the stove, adding to the heady, homey scent of cinnamon, warm bread, and basil. As if she were a stranger in a strange land, Annika stared around the tidy kitchen, took in the eyelet curtains at the windows and the hooked rug on the glossy yellow wood floor. A collection of teapots and rose-patterned cups and saucers lined the open shelves. Everything was in its place, and yet there was an immediate sense of comfortableness, as if anyone was welcome to help himself to anything in the place.

"Do you want to put the *bambina* to bed?" Rose stood in front of Annika, the plate of cookies forgotten as she stared down at the child who had fallen asleep with her head on Annika's shoulder.

Annika shifted the sleeping child on her shoulder. "That's all right—she's not heavy. I'm getting used to holding her." Surprised at her own response, Annika realized she was not just making conversation. It was true. Buttons was no burden.

And as long as she held the child, she felt close to Buck.

Rose was staring hungrily at the little girl. Annika smiled up at the dark-eyed Italian. "Would you like to hold her when she wakes up?"

Rose nodded. *"Che bella chicca."* She reached out to pat Baby's back. "Beautiful little girl. Whose baby is this?"

Annika took a deep breath and tried to smile. "She belongs to the man who took me off the train. Her name is Baby, but she likes to be called Buttons now."

Knowing how much Rose and Kase wanted children, and how many infants they had already lost, Annika knew without a doubt that her sister-in-law would keep Buttons without hesitation. Kase, however, was another matter.

She immediately put the thought out of her mind. After all, Buck would arrive soon, maybe even this afternoon, looking for them. He would come for Baby and he would come for her, and when he did she would have to decide what she was going to do.

Before she could tell Rose any more, the back door swung open. Annika watched Kase walk in, followed by Zach. As she stared up at her beloved older brother, she raised her chin defiantly and met his questioning blue gaze. The sky blue eyes and the height they had inherited from their mother were the only features they shared. Kase was dark, his shoulder-length hair was jet black, his skin a rich bronze that accentuated the lightness of his eyes. Their parents both agreed that they were equally stubborn, although Annika had always thought the term was too mild a description where Kase was concerned. She hoped his marriage had mellowed him, but as he stood just inside the doorway, slowly taking in her tattered clothing and her bedraggled appearance, she saw him stiffen with rage.

He was already thinking the worst had happened to her. And if he thought the worst, then she knew he wouldn't stop until he found Buck and settled the score.

She wanted to clarify the situation before he had worked himself up to a full head of steam. She stood, abruptly handed the sleeping child to Rose, and crossed the room. She wrapped her arms about his neck.

When Kase immediately stiffened, she held her breath, The tense moment passed, and she felt him relax as relief overwhelmed him. Kase pulled her close in a bone-crushing hug that said more than mere words could say. Then, just as suddenly, he held her at arm's length and searched her face.

"Are you all right?"

She nodded and smiled, but was unable to hide the tears that quickly welled in her eyes. He was her brother and she loved him. She wished that she could have spared him his worry and anger. "I'm fine, really," she said softly.

"You look like hell."

"Well, you always said I worried too much about appearances. I guess I'm over that now." She glanced down at her filthy skirt with its scorched hem. "No one gave me time to buy new clothes or to clean up before I got here."

"Exactly how did you get here?"

"Zach brought me." When he gave her his no-nonsense glare, she hastily added, "It's a long story."

He barely glanced at Buttons. "And that child?"

"She's part of it."

Kase pulled her back to the table, sat her down in the chair, bussed his wife on the cheek, and for the first time really looked at Baby Buttons. "I've got time. I think I'd better hear it all. Rose, that child is too heavy for you to stand there holding her like that. Give her back to Annika."

"No."

Annika watched the exchange and bit back a smile. *Good for you, Rose,* she thought. It was good to see that her brother had met his match. Zach sauntered to the stove, took a mug off the shelf nearby, and poured himself a cup of black coffee.

"Anybody else want one?" he offered.

No one answered. Rose ignored Kase, who glared down at the child in her arms. Finally, he reached out and took Buttons himself, held her for the briefest moment, then gently handed her over to Annika. "Sit down, Rose."

His wife didn't budge.

"Please," Kase added.

She sat. Then Kase did, too. Zach pulled up a fourth chair and settled in to listen. Annika hid another smile by pressing her lips to the crown of Buttons's head.

"Start talking," Kase demanded.

"It's good to see you still have your charming demeanor, big brother."

Rose laughed and Kase glowered. "This is no time to be charming. What the hell happened while you were out there and how did you get back?" If the look on his face was any indication, Annika knew she hadn't faced any real interrogation yet.

She sighed and began to relate her experience, carefully editing the way her relationship with Buck had flowered into full bloom. She told them about Virge, Cliff, and Denton, her experience with the men who were little more than bounty hunters, how they made her leave the cabin, how she couldn't leave Buttons there alone, and then about her ride through Cheyenne.

"I got out of the house and took Clemmens's horse. Thank God it was dark." She laughed, trying for a bit of levity as she watched Kase carefully. He was fighting to hold back his rage; his hands clenched and unclenched as he stared across the table at her. If she didn't know better, she could almost believe he was angry at her for being kidnapped. But she knew he was trying not to show any emotion whatsoever. He'd been that way ever since he had gone away to boarding school at thirteen. Since then he had kept his feelings so carefully locked inside that at times it seemed the only emotion he ever allowed to surface was anger.

She watched him carefully as she continued. "I must have looked quite a sight as I rode through town. Oh, and by the way, I'm doing quite well riding astride, I'll have you know, but I must say galloping over hill and dale out here is nothing like riding through the Commons sidesaddle."

"Annika," Kase warned with impatience, "stick to the story."

"The streets of Cheyenne were deserted, but I kept riding toward the taller buildings in the center of town until I came upon the Opera House. The show was just letting out, so I asked some people waiting for a carriage where the police station was and they started asking questions and when they found out who I was, both couples agreed to take me there personally. Just exactly how notorious am I?"

When Kase said nothing, Zach told her, "Been in the paper three times, that and with the reward, well, there ain't too many folks that haven't heard tell of you."

"That's what I was afraid of. What about Mama and Papa?"

Rose reached out and patted her hand. "They want to come as soon as Kase send to them the telegram, but he says that it is no use to sit, to wait."

"I told them not to come out until spring," Kase clarified.

Annika tried to finish her story. "After I reached the police, they wired Zach in Busted Heel and got me a room at the Interocean Hotel for the night. Baby was so upset and tired she was past the point of sleep. We were up most of the night. The sheriff put me on the first train out and Zach was there to meet me."

Zach interjected, "Didn't think I'd need to send a man out with the news since she was comin' in on the six o'clock train. Just brought her on out."

"So, here I am, a little dirty, but none the worse for wear." She hoped she sounded more convincing than she felt at the moment.

Kase didn't move a muscle. He watched her intently. Rose laid her hand on his arm as if to soothe him. He was alternately studying Annika, then the child she held so protectively and the way she kept smoothing the curly blond head so lovingly. He leaned back in the chair, leisurely crossed one booted foot over the opposite knee as if he had all the time in the world, and said, "Now why don't you tell me what really happened?"

He knew as surely as he knew the sun would set that night that his sister was lying. If not outright lying, that she was evading the truth. She'd been alone with the man who had kidnapped her for over two long months, a man with a streak of insanity running rampant in his family. In the telling of it she made the experience sound like nothing more than a stagecoach stop at a way station. Something had definitely happened beyond what she let on. The woman she was now was not the little sister he'd last seen in Boston during the Christmas holiday two years ago.

The old Annika Storm had been preoccupied with her social calendar, her education, her clothes, her books, and little else. This Annika Storm hadn't once apologized for the way she looked, hadn't whined or complained that she needed a bath and a change of clothing, hadn't demanded he avenge her. Nor had she mentioned her fiancé in Boston.

Somehow the outraged, spoiled little sister he had expected to be returned to him had been replaced by another woman—and that was the thought that plagued him most. She seemed more of a woman now than before, and he prayed that literally it wasn't true.

If Buck Scott had raped her and taken her virginity, she wasn't admitting it. Was she trying to hide her shame behind a brave facade? The thought made him sick to his stomach.

"Your sister is tired. I take her up to the room, all right?" Rose stood up, as if asking his opinion was just a formality.

He reached out for his wife's hand and pulled her down onto the chair beside his again. "You sure Scott will come after the girl?" Kase asked Annika.

"Of course." She nodded, but his question caused a niggling doubt to creep into her thoughts. What if Buck didn't come after them? What if he came to his original conclusion that what Baby needed was a real home and decided not to come after them at all? Annika had no idea how to find the cabin, even if she could convince Kase to take them there.

"And you say she's his sister's kid? Not his?"

"That's right. She's Patsy's."

Kase leaned forward, elbows on the table. "What do you know about this Patsy?"

Annika colored. "I know she's . . . well . . . she's not quite right."

"That's putting it mildly," he said softly.

Instantly, she was alert. "What do you know about Buck's sister? And how?"

He didn't like the way she said the man's name or the fact that a defensive tone had crept into her voice. "This country's not that big. I know she's crazy as a loon. Thinks she's Cleopatra."

Annika laughed outright. "Cleopatra? Really, Kase if you can believe that—"

"It's true. My neighbor knows the woman who's caring for her. Furthermore, Scott's whole family was insane."

She opened her mouth to protest, but knew she didn't know enough about Buck's family to defend her argument. Instead of falling willingly into a trap, she closed her mouth again.

"Would you mind if Rose did show me to my room? I'm exhausted and I think I'd like to get some sleep before Buttons wakes up."

"Buttons?" He looked at her with an I-told-you-so expression on his face.

"I'll explain the name later."

"Your trunks are unpacked upstairs. Rose never doubted your safe return." He hoped to see relief overwhelm her. Instead, all she did was nod, then said quietly, "That's good."

Kase frowned. It wasn't the response he expected from a woman who used to change dresses up to four times a day.

Something was definitely up, and he intended to find out what it was.

"GET up, Buck. Papa wants you."

Buck pulled himself up to a sitting position on the bed and wondered what Sissy was doing there. "Sissy?" He forced his lips to move again. "Sissy?"

His little sister moved closer, just out of reach, and

swayed toward him. He thought he felt her hand brush his cheek, but wasn't sure. Her touch was cold. It sent a chill through him. She stood over him for a moment more, smiling her vacant smile, watching him with eyes that showed no spark of inner life.

"I never wanted to do bad, Buck."

"I know you didn't, Sissy. I know you didn't."

"They wanted to give me things, pretty things. That's why I always let 'em touch me."

Buck shook his head, trying to convince her he didn't blame her for what the buffalo men always managed to do to her when he wasn't around to keep an eye on her. She'd done whatever they had asked—done it for trinkets, cheap jewelry, a hair ribbon, a shiny new mirror. Hell, she'd lie with them for a smile. He never blamed her—Sissy didn't know any better—but he blamed the men who should have seen that she had the mind of a child.

He tried to sit up, to see her clearly, but he couldn't move his limbs. His body wouldn't obey. He wondered why he'd built up the fire so high. He was burning up.

"Sissy?"

Where had she gone? He squinted and tried to bring her back into focus, but the vision left him and he fell back against the pillow.

"Here, Buck, here's some rabbit. I fixed it just the way you like."

It was Annika's voice, he'd know it anywhere, for it dripped smooth and sweet as honey from a honeycomb. He wanted to ask her why she'd left him, but he already knew it was because he had been a buffalo man. Now he was nothing but a trapper and she was city born and bred. But she even took Baby with her. Had he asked her to near the end? He couldn't remember.

He rolled his head toward the sound of her voice and saw Annika standing there with a pair of bloody rabbits hanging from a piece of rope. "Isn't this the way you like them?" She lifted her hand and the rabbits dangled near his face.

"Don't go again." The words sounded like a plea, even to his own ears, and he was ashamed—but even his shame couldn't keep him from calling out to her once more. "Don't leave me again, Annika. Stay with me." He closed his eyes against the pain. When he opened them, she was gone.

The throbbing pain in his leg brought him out of himself. He looked down and tried to focus on the dried blood caked on his torn pant leg. He wondered who had tied his leg up with pieces of his shirt. Had Annika? Had she cared for him before she left?

A new voice startled him from his thoughts.

"Let her not say 'tis I that keep you here."

"Patsy?" He put his arm out to shield his face from her. He couldn't be certain what Patsy would do. Even in his fever and delirium, he could not forget the danger she represented to him, to Baby. She was crazy, like Pa had been at the last. Crazy enough to take her own child up to the roof where, like Abraham, she had said, she intended to sacrifice her.

She held her hand up in warning, her fingers splayed, clawlike. "Pray you stand farther from me." Though she faced him, her eyes were focused on another place and time. Her words were the distorted words of a queen as put down by a sixteenth-century bard. Her face was just as distorted, but her regal bearing left no doubt who she thought she was. "See where he is, who is with him, what he does."

Buck knew he was at her mercy. "Patsy, forgive me. I had to do it. I had to take you away."

Still quoting Shakespeare, she said, "Then turn aside and weep. . . . Then bid adieu to me, and say the tears belong to Egypt. Good now, play one scene of excellent dissembling, and let it look like perfect honor."

Her gown was of diaphanous silk, swirling about her body, clinging to her. Upon her head she wore a disk of gold that shone like the sun, so bright it nearly blinded him. An eagle with wings outspread adorned the luminous disk. Buck started shaking as he stared up at her, unable to control the chills that racked his body. He had no strength to fight her off, no will left to force the vision of his mad sister to leave him in peace.

She came close to the bed and drew the edge of her silken sleeve across his face. His shivering intensified. Leaning over him, he could feel her chilly breath upon his cheek.

Once more the words she uttered were those of the Egyptian queen. "We'll bury him; and then, what's brave, what's noble, Let's do it after the high Roman fashion and make death proud to take us."

In that moment, Buck knew he was about to die.

LATE afternoon sunlight streamed through the curtains, creating a delicate pattern upon the octagonal tile floor of the bathroom. Annika leaned back in the tall, ornate tub and tried to soak the stiffness out of her aching joints. As soon as Rose left her with Buttons in the guest room, Annika had taken her cue from the child and napped for the rest of the afternoon. Now, after she'd bathed Buttons and turned her over to Rose, it was Annika's turn to pamper herself. She relished every precious moment, pausing to inhale the heady fragrance of the rose bath crystals that scented the water, lathering the soft soap into a thick foam, spreading it over her limbs.

She scrubbed and scrubbed her hair until she felt as if she had washed away the trying experience of the last two days with the dirt. Finally, when the water had cooled and she began to feel guilty for leaving Rose at the mercy of Baby Buttons for so long, Annika stood up slowly so she wouldn't slosh the water over the sides of the tub. She reached for the thick Turkish towel Rose had left folded over a towel bar for her.

As she patted herself dry, she thought back to two nights before when she had lain in Buck's arms and enjoyed his touch. Frowning, she wondered exactly when he would arrive, for she wanted to be certain she was with Kase when the two men met for the first time. The expression she'd seen in her brother's eyes warned her that nothing good would come of their first exchange if she was not there to temper it. Kase would be too furious to listen to reason—Buck too tight-lipped to explain.

She toweled her hair until it was no longer dripping, then hung up the towel. From the hat tree in the corner of the tiled room she took down her own violet silk robe that Rose had so thoughtfully left there. Rose had been certain she would be rescued.

Annika wanted to protest that she hadn't, in the end,
needed rescuing, but she didn't yet trust her sister-in-law to
keep such news from Kase. She needed to talk to Rose, to
speak honestly and share her experiences with another
woman, but she didn't know her brother's wife well enough
to know whether or not to open up to her. Wondering if she
might eventually share her secrets with Rose, she padded
down the hall barefooted to the guest room.

Compared to the cabin in Blue Creek Valley, the small
room was a palace. The high four-poster was covered with
a buttercup spread. Ruffled pillows were mounded high
against the headboard, and matching curtains hung at the
windows. Her clothes hung in the tall oak armoire; the per-
fumes and ribbons she'd packed were all lined up and ready
for her on the chest of drawers.

She walked over and reached out to touch the fine silks
and satins hanging side by side in rainbow hues. They had
been purchased by a girl with nothing more to worry about
than what she should wear, not a woman whose heart was
torn by indecision and longing. Two months had passed
since she'd had her grand possessions with her and in that
time she realized she didn't really need any of them. The
coat Buck had labored over hung amid the gowns, the contrast one that only called to mind the differences between
Buck and her. As she let her hand fall away from the striped
gown she was fingering, she knew she would give all of it
away if she could only see him again.

As she stood before the mirror and pulled up the lace-
edged collar of her silk robe, she wondered what Buck
would say if he could see her now. He would probably shake
his head and tell her that he knew he was right, that she
needed a life of comfort more than she needed him. She ran
her fingers through her hair to untangle it, then absentmind-
edly picked up her ivory comb and began to work it through
the wet strands.

She studied herself in the mirror. Did the change in her
show? Could anyone tell she had given her virginity to the
man who had carried her away? Would they understand if
she told them that she was no longer the sheltered girl who
thought she knew all there was to know of the world and of

her place in it? That she had been given a glimpse of a life she might have never even imagined, nor would she have wanted to, but that now she was considering embracing that life and the man who went with it?

The sound of Buttons's laughter drifted up the stairs. Annika smiled when she heard it. She wondered what Buck would say when he saw the child dressed in the finery Rose ordered for her. Zach had returned to Busted Heel with a list of things to have sent out for Buttons to wear and Rose had made him promise to bring them back by tomorrow. For now Rose had chosen one of her own soft blouses and had cut it down into a long, nightshirt affair tied with a wide pink ribbon sash. Buttons agreed to wear it while her satin dress and the one ragged one Annika packed were drying.

Annika's old chocolate wool suit lay in a heap by the door. There was nothing to salvage of it, and so she planned to throw it away. Still, when she looked at the suit, she couldn't help but be reminded of all that had passed in the last two months. Despite the hardship, the confusion, and doubt, her days at Blue Creek had been some of the best of her life.

She walked over to the window to watch the sun slip behind the mountains and wondered if Buck was out there somewhere watching the sunset, too. Hopefully, darkness would spur him on.

❦ 20 ❦

I T was his worst hallucination yet.

The thing stood on Buck's chest. The size of a rat, it had moist, bulging eyes that shifted nervously from behind a short snout of a nose that emitted snorting noises. Uneven black whiskers sprouted out on either side of the snout. Spindly matchstick legs looked about to collapse under the half-bald, bedraggled fur body that shook with unceasing tremors. The creature opened its mouth, emitting the horrid scent of dog breath and licked him across the lips.

Buck grimaced and turned his face away, trying to escape the slimy wet tongue. "Get off me, Mouse." He tried to bat the Chihuahua away, but barely had the strength to raise his arm.

He heard a shuffling sound and turned his head in time to see Old Ted approach the bed. The man reached down, scooped up the little dog, and shoved it inside his jacket. " 'Bout time you woke up."

"I'm not dead?"

"Not unless the dead started talkin' and I ain't heard about it, you ain't. You look like you been to hell and back, though."

There was coffee boiling, the scent mingling with one he couldn't quite place. He tried to raise his head, but fell back against the pillow. "I can't seem to move."

"Fever drained you of your strength. I got some vittles ready, if you feel like eatin'. Can ya sit up, or do I have to pull you up?"

Buck tried, then admitted defeat. "I need help."

Grudgingly, Old Ted bent over him, grunting and groan-

264

ing until he'd dragged Buck's big body into a sitting position. He straightened the pillow and then stepped back. "What'da ya want?"

"What have you got?"

"Smoked elk, biscuits, gravy, coffee."

"A biscuit and coffee."

Old Ted shuffled back to the table and picked up a plate. He put a biscuit on it, poured a cup of coffee, and set it alongside the bread, and then carried it to Buck. "You're lucky I came along."

From the mess scattered around the room, Buck knew Ted had been there more than just a few hours. "How long have I been out?"

"I been here a week. I figure you'd been out a good day or two before I came along. One of your mules had wandered in here lookin' for a meal."

"That explains the smell."

"I tried to clean it up," Ted admitted.

Buck bit into the biscuit and then slowly took a sip of his coffee. His leg was still throbbing. He didn't know whether to take it as a good sign or not. At least it hadn't gone numb, but he was afraid to pull aside the blanket and find it gone black with gangrene.

"What happened?" Ted wanted to know.

"Cat. Mountain lion. I downed a deer and the cat wanted a piece. I was in the way."

Ted cleared his throat and looked everywhere but at Buck. "So where's the kid?"

It hadn't hurt because he refused to call her to mind, but now the pain of losing both Baby and Annika ripped through him harder than the mountain lion's claws. "Gone. The woman took her down the mountain."

"You let her?"

"I told her to go," Buck said. Ted didn't need to know that Annika had left him, crawled away after taking his heart and crushing it as easily as a man crushed a gnat in summer.

"You did?" Ted leaned forward, his ruddy cheeks bobbing. He smoothed his hair flat across his forehead, which was wrinkled in thought.

"More coffee." Buck held out his cup, hoping to shut the

man up. When Ted left to fill it, Buck tried to change the subject. "Fever, huh?"

"You had it bad. Were out of your head when I walked in." He handed Buck the cup again. "I cleaned out your leg as best as I could and packed it with bread, but it's still seepin' under the bandage."

"Infected?" Buck realized with all-too-certain clarity that he really didn't care if his leg were infected or not. He didn't really care about anything at all.

Old Ted shook his head. "I been keepin' it clean, but it needs sewin'."

"Why didn't you do it?"

Ted shrugged. "Hands ain't steady as they used to be."

Buck set the plate and cup down on the crate beside the bed and then lifted the cover back. He was still in his filthy underwear, but Ted had cut the left leg of the long johns off and had bound the wound with strips of cloth.

"Take it off."

Ted slowly removed the bandage and the packing.

All things considered, Buck thought, it didn't look too bad. The lips of the wound were jagged and raw. The middle of the deep slash seeped a watery red but there was no yellow infection present. As he leaned over the wound, Buck felt his head spin. He sat up and shook his head, then closed his eyes. "Get me the cigar box in the chest at the foot of the bed. I'll sew it up."

Ted got the box and set it in Buck's lap. Then he went over to the table and picked up his whiskey crock. He poured a liberal amount in Buck's coffee cup and held it out to him.

"I'm not drinking that until I'm done sewing," Buck said shortly.

Ted downed the whiskey himself. "Well, I'm not watchin' without a drink."

Buck threaded the needle with the same black thread he'd used on Annika's face. *Don't think about her.* He bent over his own leg and before he could stop to think of the pain he was about to inflict upon himself, he pushed the needle through his flesh.

Ted walked to the other side of the room and sat down.

Sweat beaded across Buck's forehead and upper lip as he

slowly, steadily sewed up his wound. By the time his thigh
was pieced back together, he was as near to fainting as a man
can get without actually keeling over. He cut the last stitch
with the scissors and then, hands shaking, set the box aside.

"I'll take that whiskey now." His voice was weak.

"Here." Ted already had one poured for him. He pulled up
a chair and sat down. He began rubbing the ears of the little
dog that peered nervously at Buck from inside his master's
jacket. "You want to talk about it?"

"About what?" Buck hoped his forbidding expression
would shut Ted up. But it didn't.

" 'Bout the woman leaving. Takin' the kid."

"Nothing to tell."

"I saw a lot of tracks outside the cabin when I got here.
Hard to hide anything in tore-up muddy ground."

"I said—"

"You said she went down the mountain. I asked how."

"Her being here was a mistake. She left when the thaw
came, that's all. I was out hunting."

"Hmmm."

"What do you mean by that?"

"Nothin'. Just hmmm." Ted swilled more whiskey. "She
didn't leave alone."

Buck stared at him, the cup arrested halfway to his lips.
"What are you gettin' at, old man?"

"You sure she wanted to leave?"

"You saw her that first day. She sure as hell didn't want to
stay, did she?"

"That was then. This is now. You mean to tell me nothin'
happened to change her mind while she was here? You ain't
exactly the unpersuasive type."

"Nothing happened," Buck grunted. He ran his hand over
the lower half of his face and felt a week's worth of beard.
Good. He would never shave again. Not for her. Not for anyone. He'd let his beard grow long as Ted's, let it go until it
hung down to—

"Who you suppose took her back?"

"I don't know. Most likely her brother."

"She really had a brother then? I should have taken her up
on her offer to take her back that first day."

"Her brother's Kase Storm. Ever heard of him?"

Old Ted scratched his nose and then he scratched the Mouse behind the ears. "He ain't that marshal that wiped out most of the Dawsons, is he?"

"The same."

"Hell, good thing you were out huntin' when he got here."

"Yeah." Buck tried not to imagine Annika's joy when her brother rode up to the cabin. Had she flung herself in his arms and poured out the story of her misery? Had she told him how she had duped the big fool who kidnapped her into thinking she loved him? Had she shrugged off Baby as a burden she only had to bear until they could drop her off somewhere in Cheyenne?

He closed his eyes and leaned back against the wall.

"More?"

Buck opened one eye and peered at Ted, who was holding out the whiskey crock. "Why not?" He held out his cup.

He was too weak to walk. What would it hurt if he got stinking pie-eyed? The worst that might happen would be that he would fall out of bed.

The best thing that would happen would be that he wouldn't wake up at all.

"I'll be goin' down into Cheyenne as soon as you're up and around. Want me to take your winter haul down and sell it for you?" Ted offered.

If he let the old man go down and conduct his business for him, then Buck wouldn't have to chance hearing about Annika. Her rescue was still bound to be all the talk in the saloons. If he waited long enough before he went back to Cheyenne, the story would die down.

"Sure. Why not? You plan on comin' back through this way?"

"If I take your load down I will. I'll bring back your money and word of the girl."

Buck turned on Ted, his hand clamped around the cup, his jaw working furiously. "I don't want to hear about her. I don't want to know what happened to her or Baby. Never."

"Never's a long time."

"Shut up, old man."

Setting the whiskey crock on the crate beside Buck, Ted stroked his beard and shook his head. But he said nothing. He turned away from the sight of Buck sprawled in the bed in his underwear, one leg hanging out exposed, the jagged black stitches running from just above his knee to well up his thigh.

"Where you going?" Buck frowned as the old man walked toward the door.

"For a walk. I'll be back when you're not in such a piss-poor mood."

THE expansive corral held twenty-two buffalo all marked with the Buffalo Mountain brand. Dressed in a simple shirt-waist and navy skirt that flared prettily about the ankles of her matching blue boots, Annika stood on the lowest rail of the fence with her arms hooked around the highest and watched the massive animals amble about. Most of them seemed content to stand staring at the ground or lie on their sides contemplating the flies that buzzed around them. She tried to imagine them roaming free, the way Kase had told her they once had, moving in wave after wave, a shaggy brown mass rolling across the prairie, cutting down everything in its path. He told her how the earth used to shake when the herds ran free.

The two bulls in the corral scared her just to look at them. Their horns were sharp, curved upward above huge, woolly black heads. Behind the head was a sloped hump of faded brown. Their hides were shedding, huge patches of fur had fallen out or had been rubbed out as they wallowed in the mud holes on the ground.

"There's something mysterious about them, isn't there? Can you feel it, or are you just biding your time out here until Buttons wakes up?"

She started when she heard her brother's voice so near her elbow. Kase always had moved lithely for so large a man. When they were younger, she was always accusing him of sneaking up on her. Brushing her windblown hair back off her face, she smiled as he leaned against the fence beside her.

"They make me feel peaceful somehow. I can't imagine why, unless it's because of the way they just stand there. It almost seems as if they're just waiting for something to happen."

When he spoke, Kase's voice was sad. "They are waiting

for things to be the way they used to. They're waiting to run free across the plains with their brothers who will never return. They're waiting to be hunted by the Sioux who will never ride to the hunt again."

"How do you know?"

"I feel it. Don't you?"

She shook her head. "I'm not sure."

"Someday maybe you will. Do you realize the plains people lived on nothing but the buffalo? They were independent of the white men as long as the buffalo roamed the land. Tipis and robes came from the hide, glue from the hooves, thread from the sinews, knives from the ribs. The paunch provided water bags."

Annika watched a cow move across the corral. "Where did you find them?"

"It wasn't easy. We rounded them up one at a time, sometimes two. They were wandering strays, barely existing. It took two years to find nineteen. The young-looking ones were born here."

"What will you do with them?"

Kase looked off toward the mountains. "Keep them. Feed them and care for them so that my children will know what a buffalo is, so that their children's children will know." He turned to her, stared down into her eyes as if he could see into her soul, and said, "Men like the one that took you captive nearly wiped them off the face of the earth."

She swallowed. "Maybe they didn't know. Maybe they thought there would always be enough."

Kase shook his head. "They knew. The men that paid them knew. When the buffalo were gone, the Indian would be gone as well. It was a grand scheme."

"Surely not," she protested.

He looked at his sister, at her fair hair and features so like their mother's. It was not her fault. She didn't know, couldn't feel what he felt. He had always known he was Indian, in his blood and his heart. Annika was more white than Indian. Perhaps she would never feel the things he felt. He thanked God she had never faced the prejudice he had known but had slowly learned to live with, just as Caleb Storm had.

"How long will you keep the child here?" He changed the

subject abruptly to catch her off guard. His ploy worked. He watched her face blanch, saw pain behind her eyes before she looked away.

Annika fingered the wooden rail and then gnawed on her thumbnail. She shrugged. "A month ago, I thought Buck would be coming after her. Now I'm not so sure."

"Buck? You say his name so reverently."

She turned to him again. "No I don't."

He ignored her protest. "I'm worried about you, Annika. You don't eat, you spend all day working in the house for Rose."

"Aren't you glad? She can barely move now that the baby's almost here. I'm trying to do as much as I can for her, Kase."

"That's what worries me. It's just not like you."

"Thank you so much, brother."

He pulled his hat down low over his eyes until they were shadowed. "The little sister I left in Boston was only concerned with her social affairs and wearing the latest styles. You would never have so much as boiled water for your own tea at home—"

"That's not fair, Kase. I never had to work at home. Here, it's different, and now I'm doing it to help out Rose."

He turned on her then, scowling down at her to hide his deep concern. "No, you're different. That man hurt you more than you'll admit, but I can wait to find out just how much, Annika. I have to wait until Rose has the baby, and I have to wait until you're ready to tell me all about it, but I'm a patient man now. More than I ever was before. I'll wait."

She watched him walk across the dusty ground toward the barn that stood between the house and the buffalo pen. When he disappeared inside, she turned back to the fence, tempted to lay her head on her arms and cry. Instead, she straightened her shoulders, took a deep breath, and tried to think things through.

Why hadn't Buck come? She needed to see him, wanted desperately to tell him she was ready to live anywhere he wanted. Anything was better than this separation. She had thought of asking Kase to take her back into the mountains to search for him and Blue Creek, but they couldn't go until Rose had her baby and had safely recovered. Besides, given the way he felt about Buck Scott, she knew it would be ridiculous to even ask. If she told him the truth, she was afraid he really would want to have Zach lock Buck up and throw away the key.

She tried to put herself in Buck's place. Would he believe she could never leave him so abruptly on her own, or would he see it as an escape? He had suspected her of trying to escape the day she had packed the picnic, but after the tender way he had made love to her that night, after the way she had responded so openly, she didn't know how he could doubt her feelings.

Now that she had been forced to be without him for a month, she realized it didn't matter where he wanted to live. She needed him more than she needed anyone else in her life. The thought of returning to Boston without him brought tears to her eyes. Even the idea of staying on here in Wyoming was no consolation without Buck in her life.

The wind had picked up. It blew constantly, so much so that she was growing used to it, but now, as dust swirled across the corral, she decided she'd had enough. Head down in thought, she crossed the barnyard. Her skirt swirled around her ankles, the hem swaying evenly, barely dusting the ground.

She looked up at the gaily painted house with its creamy yellow exterior the color of rich, fresh butter. The trim was a brilliant white enamel, every spool, every spoke, carefully painted. For a moment she envied her brother and his wife. Like her parents', theirs was a love that was so apparent, so alive, that the two seemed as one whenever they were in a room together.

It was hard to imagine she and Buck working together as man and wife. They had such a strange beginning, their worlds were so opposite, that she wondered if she were insane to even pursue a reunion.

Reunion? She chided herself. He didn't even care enough to come and take her back. Maybe, she thought, just maybe he'd gotten what he wanted. He had used her in bed, found a convenient way to see Baby Buttons safely out of his life, and was now free to live exactly as he wanted—alone and free. He had told her himself he didn't really want a wife, that he had only written to Alice Soams so that he might have a nursemaid for Baby. Why should he have changed his mind just because she had fallen so willingly into his arms?

As she stepped up on the back veranda and opened the door, she wanted to cover her face in shame. Dear God, to think that she had almost attacked him that first time—and had made love on the table, no less.

"There you are," Rose called out, startling Annika so that she almost jumped.

Annika's eyes were riveted on the kitchen table for a moment, then, with her face flaming at the memories of another table and another time, she guiltily eyed her sister-in-law. "I was out looking at the buffalo."

Rose smiled. "Like your brother. The buffalo have something for you and not for me. I see them and I see only the dirt and the flies. But"—she shrugged—"Kase gets joy from them and so I do not care."

Stepping up beside the woman who was at least a head shorter, Annika watched as Rose rolled out a perfect slab of pie dough. "Where's Buttons? Has she been bothering you?"

"Never. She is the perfect *bambina*. For now, she naps."

Annika shook her head, but smiled nonetheless. "She can be quite a little imp. You didn't carry her upstairs, did you?"

Rose shook her head and lifted the dough. Carefully, she laid it in the pie pan, pressed it down, and then picked up another ball of dough. Every movement seemed instinctive. Rose talked as she worked while Annika marveled at her skill. An earthenware bowl full of peaches tossed in sugar—and from the mouth-watering scent, they'd also been mixed with cinnamon—sat ready to go into the pie shell. Annika couldn't help but sneak a peach slice.

"Again, like your brother. I tell him not to steal the fruit before the pie she is finished."

Rose looked at Annika over her shoulder, studying her intently, her hands still for the first time. Annika leaned against the kitchen cabinet and waited. She had come to love and trust her sister-in-law. Perhaps if she told her all that lay so heavily on her mind she would come to some conclusions. Finally, since Rose seemed to be waiting for her to speak, Annika asked, "What is it?"

"I am just thinking that perhaps there is something you want to tell to me. You are worried, no?"

Sighing, Annika looked down at the dusty toe of her shoe. "I need to talk to someone."

"But you cannot talk to your brother?"

With a shake of her head, Annika admitted quietly, "Not about this."

"It is the man, yes? The one that took you away?"

Annika nodded.

"Ah. I know so. Tell me."

"You won't tell Kase?"

"If you say no, I don't tell."

"Please don't then. I'm afraid I'll eventually have to tell him, but I can't yet. He's still too angry, and you know how he is when he gets angry."

Rose rolled her eyes and began spooning peaches into the bottom crust. "Oh, I think he is not so bad as he is when I first come to Busted Heel. He is not so angry all the time as before."

Annika knew her brother had come to terms with his heritage, most of which was unknown to her. With her own problems and his anger at Buck, she had hesitated to ask him about the rift with their parents that had forced him to move to Wyoming five years ago.

"I couldn't tell Kase everything—I couldn't tell anyone—but now I don't know what to do and it's driving me crazy, Rose."

"Start from the front."

"Well, at first I hated Buck Scott, mostly because I was so afraid, and then I think it might have been because no one had ever treated me unkindly before. He wouldn't listen to reason when he carried me off like that, just kept insisting I was the woman he'd sent for and then, by the time he knew he'd made a mistake, we were snowed in."

"This much of the story I know. Tell me what you have in your heart for him."

Annika looked up, startled. "My heart?"

"I can see your heart is in the eyes when you are thinking of him. I can see that you wait, always watching, always listening. When a horse or wagon comes to the house, you jump and run to the door. Your brother thinks you are afraid for man has come back, but I think you are waiting for him."

As if a great weight had been lifted from her shoulders, Annika turned to face Rose. Her sister-in-law wiped her hands on her apron, left the pie forgotten on the cabinet, and with her hand on Annika's elbow, drew her over to the table. "Sit. It is better to talk if you sit down." Rose kept hold of her hand and Annika wondered why until she realized tears were plopping on the front of her white shirtwaist.

"Oh, God, Rose, I didn't mean to cry like this, but I've had to keep this inside for a month now and . . ."

"Is all right. Talk." Rose glanced at the door.

Annika wiped her eyes, afraid for her brother to see her like this. He would force her to explain.

"Buck wasn't what I thought in the beginning. Oh, he was rough, he's poor, but in a sense he's richer than some people will ever be. He lives in the mountains where the sky is so close you can almost reach out and touch it. The air is clear and always scented with a hint of pine. He's far from uncivilized; I guess you'd say he has his own code of ethics. He would never have touched me if . . . if I hadn't wanted it."

Rose was visibly relieved. "Kase, he thinks the man rapes you. He worries that this is why you are so afraid, and that you don't eat. He can only think of what happened before—" As if she had said too much, Rose was suddenly silent.

Annika had heard her last words and frowned. "Before? What happened before?"

"Just as you ask that I do not say what you tell me to Kase, I cannot tell his story to you."

"But, Rose, rape? Dear God, Kase didn't rape anyone, did he? I never knew why he left Boston so suddenly, but . . ."

Her face darkened instantly with anger. "Never would your brother do such a thing. Never forget this."

"I know, I know. I'm sorry I even said it, but—"

"That is for him to tell you about. Now, this man, this Scott—"

Annika balled her hands in her lap and said softly, "I fell in love with him."

"And then the men who wanted the money took you away," Rose concluded.

"That's right. And I thought Buck would come after Buttons and me as soon as he found us gone, but he hasn't, and now I'm afraid he didn't really love me. He just wanted someone to take Buttons for him." She looked up at Rose again and felt another tear slide down her cheek. "I'm afraid he used me."

"So you have been with him, as a woman is with a man?"

Annika nodded. "We made love. Now I'm so ashamed. I initiated it. I'm the one that broke through his reserve."

"This is not so bad. No one will know if you do not tell them," Rose reminded her.

Annika leaned forward and put her head in her hands. "That's not the worst of it, Rose. I'm afraid I might be carrying his child."

Rose was silent for so long, Annika was forced to meet her gaze. The other woman had leaned back in her chair, one hand lying upon her abdomen. "What will you do?"

Annika wanted to laugh. She had hoped Rose would give her advice. So she shrugged and said honestly, "I have no idea. My mother will never forgive me. She always had such plans for me, for my future in Boston. Ever since I was a little girl, she has told me how my wedding would be, how I would wear a white gown and walk down the staircase on Caleb's arm and marry a kind man, a wonderful man like Caleb and live in a fine home in Boston. It was all she ever wanted for me, to be happy just the way she is with my father. You would think it would have been easy enough to do that much, to live up to her dreams for me. Now I'm so ashamed."

"Ashamed of this Buck you love?"

"Never. Never ashamed of him. I'm ashamed of what I've done, especially now, when it's clear he didn't really want me."

"You must try to find him, then. To let him know when you are certain, if it is true that you will have a child. Kase will take you. He will help."

Annika grabbed Rose's hand. "Oh, please, don't tell him, Rose. Please don't say anything."

They both started when they heard a soft footfall from the front hallway. Annika's worst nightmare stood in the kitchen doorway in the form of her six-foot-four brother.

"Tell me what?" he said.

❧ 21 ❧

THERE was no doubt that Kase was beginning to simmer. "Tell me what?" he demanded as he stood in the doorway between the kitchen and the hall, alternately watching Annika and then Rose.

While Annika debated whether to give in to her cowardice and run out the back door or have everything out in the open once and for all, Rose stood up to confront him. Annika watched in amazement as the petite woman stared up at Kase with her hands on her hips and actually began to bully him.

"Your sister, she needs to talk but I say no if you say you will yell."

Kase glared down at his wife. "She'll tell me the truth whether she wants to or not."

Rose folded her arms beneath her breasts where they rested atop the mound that was his child. Annika saw her brother soften immediately.

"You must listen and not yell," Rose warned him.

"Can you hear yourself, Rose? You're yelling right now."

Rose reached out and poked him in the chest as she said, "Be nice to your sister."

Kase looked down at Annika without promising anything. "Let's go in the parlor."

She stood up, feeling like a prisoner with a noose around her neck sitting on a nervous horse. Kase took hold of her upper arm and dragged her along the hall to the parlor. Rose was trailing behind them, but as they entered the room, Kase closed the door and left his wife out in the hall.

"I don't need both of your pestering me," he told Annika. "Now, talk."

He reminded her of Caleb as he leaned against the fireplace, waiting for an explanation. His clothes were perfectly tailored to fit his large frame; his hair, though longer than was fashionable, was brushed to a high shine and tied at his nape with a beaded ornament. His shirt was made of the finest linen and was black, like his pants. The open vest he wore was made of expensive calfskin. If fate hadn't made him her brother, Annika knew she might have fallen in love with him. How then, she wondered, had she ever fallen for Buck Scott? True, he was as tall as Kase, if not taller, but where Kase was dark, Buck was light. Kase was polished, stylish, well educated. Buck was rough edged and unkempt, knowledgeable about his surroundings, a diamond in the rough. Buck was—

"I said start talking."

She nearly jumped at the sound of his voice. Annika wished she had braided her hair; blown by the wind, it hung tangled and unmanageable. She shoved it back over her shoulders, but it refused to stay and kept falling into her eyes. She pushed it back one last time before she began to pace the room. "You said you thought there was more to my abduction and there is."

"I knew it!" He sounded so pompous, so smug, that he was almost gloating.

"But it's not what you think."

"What is it you think I think?"

He stood firm, his arms crossed over his chest. Annika couldn't stand still. She passed in front of the crushed velvet settee, passed the pedestal table, spun, and walked back. "You think that Buck raped me," she said.

"Didn't he?"

She paused and looked him straight in the eye so there'd be no mistaking her words. "He didn't have to."

She'd never seen a man get the wind kicked out of him before, but she had seen sails on a sailboat when the wind suddenly died. Kase had that same deflated look about him. She paused, standing not a foot away from him. His face mirrored his disbelief.

His voice was low. His words slow but audible. "Exactly what are you saying?"

"I let him make love to me," she whispered.

Kase burst out, "*Make love?* Ha! I doubt if a buffalo skinner knows how to make *love*! You're sure you *let* him, Annika? Or is there some perverse reason you feel you have to protect him—because if he raped you, so help me God, I'll—"

She grabbed his arm and shook it, hoping to stop his tirade. In an even, measured tone she said, "I *begged* him for it."

He slapped her without warning.

Annika sank to the wing chair drawn up before the fireplace as Rose came sailing through the door, her dark eyes blazing. "*Basta!* Kase, stop!"

With a look of shock, Kase immediately sank to his knee beside her chair. He tried to take Annika's hand, but she pulled it away. She refused to touch him or the stinging red mark across her cheek.

"Oh, hell, I'm so sorry, Annemeke," he said humbly.

"Maybe I deserve it," she whispered, suddenly more forlorn than she had ever been in her life. Her brother hated her now, her parents would never speak to her again, and for what? She had lost Buck anyway.

Kase put his arm around her. Rose quietly left them alone again when Annika laid her head on his shoulder and sobbed.

"I shouldn't have slapped you," he said, apologizing again. "I just can't believe this is happening."

Sniffing, she wiped her eyes on the back of her hand. "It's all true."

Kase sighed. Now that she had calmed somewhat, he released her. "Now what?"

With a catch in her breath she said, "I don't know."

"You love him?"

"Yes. I thought he loved me, too, but he hasn't come for me."

"What about Buttons?"

Briefly she explained how Buck had wanted her to stay with him, how she had wanted to marry him but had refused to live up in the mountains, and how he had tried to persuade her to find Buttons a home. "I thought I could eventually convince him to move into town. He would make a wonderful doctor. . . ." When Kase looked skeptical, she said, "He would. But then those other men came and so very kindly *rescued* me. Now I don't know if Buck ever loved me or not. Why hasn't he come to get me? How can I go back to Mama and Papa now?"

"Rose and I can keep Buttons," he said without hesitation. "You can go back and no one ever needs to know what happened."

"It's not that simple." She took a deep breath and steeled herself for another onslaught of his temper. "I think I may be pregnant, Kase."

He stood up, walked to the mantel again, and picked up an ebony vase detailed in gold. For a minute she was afraid he was going to throw it against the fireplace, but then he surprised her by gently setting it down. With his eyes averted he asked, "Would you marry him?"

"Yes."

He walked back and hunkered down in front of her chair. Kase squeezed her limp hand. Like a father promising his child a gumdrop, he said, "Then we'll just have to find Mr. Scott, give him the happy news, and help him settle down."

A warning went off inside her. "You can't force him, Kase. That's not what I want." She waved a hand toward the window. "Buck's like your buffalo out there—he doesn't belong in a pen. He's the last of his breed and he values his freedom. Besides, if he doesn't come to the conclusion that he wants to marry me all by himself, well . . . I won't force him." She quickly added, "And neither will you."

Kase took a deep breath as if the issue were settled. He stood up and said, "Why don't we make sure you really are pregnant before we jump into this, all right?"

She stood up and smiled through tears. "Thank you, Kase."

He reached out and with his forefinger beneath her chin tilted her face until she was forced to meet him eye to eye. He examined the fading mark on her cheek. "I'm sorry I hit you. I've never hit a woman before."

Suddenly, she was reminded of what Rose had said earlier. Then, before she could ask Kase what her sister-in-law had alluded to when she had mentioned rape, Rose came through the door, her eyes dancing, her face alight with a glowing smile.

"Annika! At the back door, there is a man coming to the house. He is tall and he—"

Annika picked up her skirt, shoved past her brother, and rushed by Rose. With her heart in her throat, she tried to smooth down her hair as she ran out of the parlor. With wings on her feet she rushed through the dining room and down the hall toward the kitchen. The swinging door rocked behind her as she crossed the painted kitchen floor.

Through the thick lace curtain over the oval window in the back door she saw the silhouette of a tall man slowly walking up the steps. Sunlight glinted off his hair. His heels rang out on the veranda.

She took a deep breath and jerked the door open. Her heart plummeted to her toes.

"Annika! Thank God!" The well-dressed man on the doorstep gathered her into his arms.

Fighting the urge to burst into unwanted tears again, she managed to choke out, "Richard? What are you doing here?"

IT was a flawless day, one worthy of the first week of May. The sun shone down on the clearing in the meadow, on the emerald pines that whispered in the breeze, on the shirtless man chopping wood inside the new split-rail fence around the cabin. The muscles across his sweat-sheened back flexed and relaxed with every motion. His hands moved up and down the ax handle that had been worn smooth as he swung it over his head and then brought it down with a vengeance on the splintering pieces of pine. Even though the summer would soon be in full bloom, he still needed firewood. Spring and summer nights in the mountain valley were often cold.

Buck rested the ax on its head and wiped his arm across his sweating brow. Reaching to his back pocket, he pulled out a faded bandanna and wrapped it around his brow to keep his hair from falling forward and keep the sweat out of his eyes. In a glance he quickly surveyed the valley. His surroundings were the same as they had always been, but now he saw them through different eyes. Before, he heard music in the whispering pines. Now, he heard none. Before, he saw the sun sparkling on the water of the creek. Now, he saw none. Before, he heard the laughter of a child and took it for granted. Now, all he heard was the silence of his soul and the lonesome beat of his heart.

Before Annika, his life had been different.

Now, there was nothing but work to mark the empty days.

From his vantage point he spotted Old Ted working his way along the stream. Something of the old Buck wanted to rush out to meet him, to walk back along the creek with Ted just to savor the sound of another human voice, but he knew if he did that Ted would sense the weakness in him. He couldn't let anyone know that he ached with a loneliness so deep it was incurable.

So he waited, marking Ted's progress with the growing pile of firewood. Buck hefted the ax and didn't stop chopping until the old man led his horse into the yard and dismounted.

"How goes it, Bucko?" Ted hitched up his pants and led his horse and mule past Buck to the shed where he fed and watered them, then ambled back.

Buck followed along slowly. "Goin' fine, Ted. Just fine. Never better."

What a liar you are, Buck Scott.

"How'd you make out with my pelts?" Buck asked.

Ted took off a thick pouch tied around his expansive middle and smiled. He held the money pouch up so that Buck could watch it swing heavily. "You're all set for a winter or two. Got you the supplies you wanted."

"Good. I'll help you unload them later. Right now I need to get off this leg." Buck picked up his plaid flannel shirt and shrugged it on but left it hanging unbuttoned. He led Ted into the cabin. The door was wide open, so were the shutters. Light streamed in every window.

"How is your leg? When I left you could barely hobble."

"Not bad. Still can't take all my weight, but I keep rubbing bear grease into it and working it every day. It'll come around."

Ted pulled out a chair and took the Mouse out of his shirt. He set the animal on the floor where it tiptoed around, sniffed, started shaking, and then stood beside Ted's chair, begging to be lifted up again.

"Still got that dog?"

"The Mouse is man's best friend."

"You make me glad I don't have a best friend," Buck mumbled, unwilling to watch Ted kiss the dog on the lips. They made quite a sight, the white-bearded old trapper and the tiny, balding dog. Buck dished up some beans without asking Ted if he wanted any and set them down in front of his friend. He placed a slab of cornbread alongside. After he poured them both a cup of steaming hot coffee, Buck pulled up a barrel chair, stretched his bad leg out beside him, and waited for Ted to straighten up from where he slouched over his plate, elbows spread wide.

"Cheyenne about the same?" Buck wanted to cut out his tongue for having to ask but at the rate Ted was going it would be hours before he got around to it.

"'Bout." Ted shoveled beans into his mouth. Cornbread crumbs littered his beard like chicks in a haystack.

Buck tapped his thumbs against the tabletop. He stared up at the soot stain on the ceiling near the fireplace. He cleared his throat. "So, no news then? You bring a paper?"

From between the wingspan he had formed over his plate, Ted looked up at Buck. "I made sure I didn't bring any Boston papers this time."

"Good."

Finished at last, Ted shoved his plate aside and drew the coffee toward him. "Didn't just go to Cheyenne, though."

"That what took you?"

"Yep." Ted nodded sagely. And remained silent.

Buck shifted on the barrel. He ran his finger over his lips and then felt his half-inch beard. He was damn proud of it, this sign of his freedom and independence. It was blond and curly, bleached nearly white by the sun, as was his hair, which hung well past his shoulders. He liked to shake his head to make it stand out all over. It gave him a wild feeling that helped fill the void. Whenever he looked in the scrap of broken mirror near the door, he knew who he was and why he was all alone.

"So where you been?" Buck tried to sound casually uninterested.

"Got any whiskey for this coffee?" Ted asked.

Buck stretched out, reached behind him for the two-toned crock on the bench, and shoved it toward Ted. The Mouse whimpered, reminding them of its presence, and Ted kissed it on the head. "Just a minute, little Mouse," he said in the falsetto he reserved for especially tender moments with the dog. "You wanta little bitty bitsa beansies?" He set the dog on the table and let it lick the nearly empty plate, which was twice the size of the Chihuahua.

Buck eyed the Mouse suspiciously. "That dog gonna fart?"

"Mouse would never do that. Why, Mouse is a good dog. She's a perfect little dog." Ted's voice rose again. "Ain't you, Mouser? Ain't you jest about the best little—"

Buck thought he would come out of his skin. He almost reached across the table to grab Ted by the throat. *"So where you been?"*

Ted allowed a very small smile to appear at the corners of his mouth. It was nearly hidden beneath his beard. Buck hated him for it, hated having to beg for information. Hated wanting to know.

"Busted Heel."

"Busted Heel? What in the hell were you doing there?" Buck felt the air go out of him. Here he thought Ted had been to Cheyenne to see where Annika left Baby Buttons and he'd gone off on some lark.

"Busted Heel, need I remind you, is the town where Kase Storm was marshal," Ted said smugly. "He owns a ranch outside of town."

A cold sweat broke out on Buck's forehead and clammed his palms.

"And," Ted continued, patting the little dog who was only halfway across the plate, "that's where your intended missus, or I should say, your mistakenly intended missus, ended up."

Damn. Buck had to wipe his brow. He hoped Ted didn't see how his hand trembled when he pulled off the bandanna and swiped it over his face. If the old man mentioned the show of weakness, Buck swore to himself that he'd strangle him.

But Ted swiftly put him out of his misery, or attempted to when he said, "I heard all about it in Cheyenne. Then I went out to Busted Heel to see for myself. You ready for this?"

"For what?"

"It weren't her brother that came up here an' got her. It were three men lookin' to collect the reward."

"Reward?"

"Her brother put up ten thousand dollars to get her back. Hell, when I heard that, I knew I should have taken her myself that first day." He picked up the little dog and began chirping again. "You done, little Mouser?" He set the dog on the dirt floor and proudly watched it hip-hop away. "When I heard she didn't leave of her own accord—"

"You heard *what*?"

"Well, I guess these three men took her down to Cheyenne and tried to hold her for more money, but somehow she got away, her and Baby, and no money changed hands. She's stayin' on her brother's ranch. So's Baby."

Barely hearing the last words, Buck tried to comprehend it all. Annika hadn't left him. She had been taken from him, maybe even against her will—if he let himself believe she really had loved him.

Ted was talking to the Mouse again, but Buck's mind was running away with the possibilities of what the old man's news meant. Why hadn't Annika come back? Maybe her brother wouldn't hear of it. Maybe she didn't know how to get back. Maybe she thought he would go after her, and then when he hadn't shown up—

Ted had taken up the story of his visit to Busted Heel again. ". . . then, I was lucky enough to be in Busted Heel the very day they came into town for supplies."

Buck nearly leapt across the table. "What? Go back."

"I said, there was no way I was showin' my face at the ranch, not with her brother's reputation with a gun and me bein' your friend. I didn't know which way the wind was blowin', so just before I left Busted Heel thinking I wouldn't see her, there they were, the woman and Baby, ridin' as smart as you please in a new black buggy with a skinny fella that looked like he'd been spit shined and pressed in a Chinese laundry."

"Her brother?"

"The 'breed? Not likely. I saw this one was a real dude, collar stiff enough to poke his eyes out, looked like he had a corncob stuck up his—"

"Who the hell was he?" Buck growled, tired of the rambling commentary.

"I'm gettin' to it now, jest listen. I slink around, belly up to the bar an' wait. Pretty soon, the marshal comes in. He's an old codger, one eyed. Starts tellin' the barkeep all about this Storm woman an' the dude. The marshal tried to place a bet on whether she'll go back to Boston or not." He paused long enough to take a final swig of coffee and then backhand his mouth. Finally noticing the yellow crumbs in his beard, he brushed them down onto his plaid shirt and then to the floor.

Buck waited on tenterhooks, afraid to hear the rest, afraid not to.

Ted belched. "It was her fai-on-cee. From Boston."

"Shit."

"Exactly what I said to myself. Went back out on the street and hung around, watched 'em from a ways off. Baby looked good dressed like a little china doll, ruffles and bows, button shoes and socks. A real pert little thing now that she's all cleaned up and rigged out. The slicker seemed to take to her, too. Carried her around for the woman."

Buck's blood ran cold in his veins. He shoved away from the table. Pain shot through his leg when he forgot to favor it. He caught himself and limped out the door. Thankfully, Ted left him in peace.

At the knoll overlooking the stream he paused, his arms crossed over his bare chest. So, she had given up on him. It was what he wanted, wasn't it? Baby was safely out of harm's way. She'd have a family, a home, the best of everything if Annika and her city slicker kept her. At least he knew that the child was still with her, and that she cared enough to have taken care of Baby this long. Everything had worked out for the best. He was free, Baby was well cared for, and Annika could pick up the pieces of her old life in Boston.

He shoved his hands into his pockets and balled them into fists. Glancing over his shoulder he studied the cabin. Not much to show for a man of his years. There was enough money in his savings can for him to move, to strike out again and put it all behind him. But what was the use of moving when wherever he went, he would still be without Annika and without Baby Buttons.

Buttons.

When he'd first stumbled into the cabin the night he'd been wounded, and again when he finally recovered, the sight of the button tin had sent him into a rage. He'd seen it as her way of appeasing him when she walked out. She had told him more than once that the precious collection was worth a lot of money. From the minute he saw the button tin on the table it stood for her betrayal.

If, indeed, she had betrayed him.

Surely she hadn't been waiting for him to come to her?

He ran his hand through his hair, more confused than he had ever been in his life. The breeze lifted his shirttails and flapped them against his hips as he stood staring at Blue Creek.

It isn't that far to Busted Heel.

If he had any guts at all, he would ride down and see for himself if Baby was truly happy. He'd find out if Annika had really forgotten all about him.

And if she still wanted him?

He hurried as fast as his leg would allow. There was only one way to find out, and the fact that her fiancé had come to Wyoming worried him. What if he was too late? What if his abandonment had forced Annika back into the other man's arms?

By the time he reached the cabin door, he was almost running. It was the fastest he'd moved in weeks. He almost stepped on the Mouse when he ran in. The little dog yapped and snapped at his moccasins. Buck feigned a kick in the dog's direction and earned a curse from Ted.

"Count out the money you owe me," he barked at Ted. Shoving the table aside, he grabbed a heavy spoon, knelt down with a groan, and began digging up his money can. "You can stay for as long as you like, but I have someplace to go."

Ted leaned back in his chair. He stroked his beard as he chuckled, chortled, wheezed, and patted his belly. "Now, how did I know you were gonna say that?"

BUCK SCOTT'S skinning knife couldn't have cut the tension that was building between the occupants of the ranch house.

Richard Thexton had been there for nearly a week, and for all that time Annika had managed to avoid being alone with him. Now, as they sat together in the parlor like two strangers making polite small talk, she wished that Rose would come to her rescue as she had all week. Even Kase had somehow sensed her need to keep the man at a distance, so he occupied Richard's time whenever he could. But today her brother had ridden into Busted Heel to try and talk the doctor into coming out to the ranch to stay until Rose—a week overdue—had her baby.

Annika stared down at her folded hands that rested so primly in her lap and winced. The tableau was all too reminiscent of her old life in Boston. Richard was seated the appropriate distance beside her on the settee, while she primly sat on the edge, her back as straight as a broom handle. An overwhelming sadness pervaded her when she realized that everything about her life with Buck was slipping further and further away until she was afraid the entire experience would soon become irretrievable, even in her memory.

Ignoring the man beside her, she traced the heavy embroidered swirls that embellished the skirt of her velvet gown. The bright heliotrope decorated with yellow stripes had been the latest in fashionable colors when she left home. The dress itself was seamless, another Worth creation, and the tightness of the fitted waistline only gave her cause for more worry.

With Richard's arrival immediately on the heels of her conversation with Kase and Rose, there had been no opportunity for her to visit the doctor in Busted Heel and find out

for certain if she was carrying Buck's child. In a hurried conversation by the barn the night of Richard's arrival, Kase had
suggested that she should consider marrying Richard and
going back to Boston.

"And pawn off someone else's child on him?" She had
been appalled at the thought.

Kase had countered, "You still don't know if you're really
pregnant or not. Maybe your monthly is just late."

At the time, as they stood huddled in the long shadows of
the barn, she couldn't believe she was having such an intimate conversation with her big brother. But she found it less
difficult than she would have imagined.

"It's never late," she had insisted in a hushed whisper.

"Then you had better tell him the engagement is definitely
over so he'll leave. He's bent on taking you back to Boston
and marrying you to put an end to any gossip the news articles might have spawned."

"I'll talk to him," she had promised Kase that night, "as
soon as the time is right."

But until now the time had never been right. Either Kase
or Rose or Buttons had been with her whenever Richard was
around. She had recently suggested he drive her into Busted
Heel to pick up some baking soda for Rose, and although she
hoped the hour alone on the isolated road would give her
time to explain, Annika couldn't find the words—or the
courage—to tell him she would not be going back to Boston
with him. Nor had she the nerve to make up an excuse to
visit the doctor.

Outside, gray clouds threatened to deliver spring rain. The
ornate silver clock resting on the mantel prodded her with
every tick to tell him she could not marry him and have done
with it. She looked over at Richard, who was contentedly
scanning the front page of the Cheyenne *Leader.* Long and
lean, he seemed slight in comparison to Buck. His fingers
were slim and tapered; they belonged to the hands of a man
who worked with papers and ledgers. His celluloid collar
was stiff, fitted to his neck like a shackle. His dark blond hair
was neatly combed to one side, the part as perfect as the center fold of the page he held in his hands. She realized she had
never seen him with his collar off. She had never, for that

matter, seen him with his shirt unbuttoned, nor had she seen his neck, his throat, his collarbone.

Curious, she leaned closer. Of course, she'd never seen his chest, either. Was it covered with a thatch of golden hair like Buck's? Were the muscles of his chest as sharply defined as an armor breastplate, like Buck's? Her cheeks aflame, she let her gaze drop to the crotch of his pants. Was there anything about Richard that was like Buck Scott?

As she sat there mentally undressing him, she knew he would be aghast at her blatant perusal and speculation over his anatomy. She nearly leapt off the settee when he glanced up from the paper and met her curious stare.

He smiled. His teeth were white and even, his skin smooth and freshly shaved. She wondered if he shaved twice a day to keep it that way. Buck would surely have to.

Buck again.

And again and again.

Buck Scott might be lost to her, but he was never out of her mind. It wasn't fair to Richard to let him dangle on the end of a long rope.

She had to end this travesty and end it now.

But before she could speak, he said, "Is Rose making tea?"

Annika cleared her throat. "Yes. Yes, she is. I should go see if I can help."

Coward. Coward.

He folded the paper shut with a snap, set it on the pedestal table beside him, and took her hand. "I'd prefer it if you stay. I haven't had you to myself for a moment since I arrived."

Tongue-tied, she looked down at their joined hands.

Unfortunately, so did he. "You aren't wearing my ring."

Annika pulled her hands away from his and smoothed her skirt for the hundredth time. She cleared her throat. "No. I left it in my mother's keeping. I'm certainly glad that I did, under the circumstances. Richard, I—"

"Annika, I want you to know that I'm still willing to marry you despite what's happened."

"I'm glad you've finally brought it up because, you see, I—" Just when she had gathered courage for her revelation, he cut her off again.

"I hope you don't think your abduction matters to me. Oh, I know you were forced to spend two months in close proximity with that barbarian who carried you off, but the mere fact that you survived and were able to keep your wits about you only goes to prove what strong stuff you're made of. That's the kind of woman I need beside me. I've always been intrigued with your exotic nature. With you beside me I can conquer the world, or at least my little part of it."

She tried to imagine Buck uttering such romantic phrases, but the idea seemed ludicrous enough to make her smile. Richard had to be the most understanding man in the world, the most forgiving. Anyone who had read the account of her abduction in the papers knew that she had spent two months in intimate contact with a stranger—and now Richard was willing to overlook such scandal when most men would not.

She felt terribly guilty turning him down again. He was exactly the man her parents wanted her to marry. He was the epitome of Back Bay Boston. His hands were soft and his skin hardly ever saw the sun, but that was no reason to cast him aside for a man who didn't even care enough to find out if she were dead or alive.

With a glance toward the parlor door, Richard leaned closer.

He's going to kiss me now. Then I'll know. I'll know for certain.

But he did not kiss her. Her merely squeezed her hand and said, "I love you so much that I'm willing to overlook your abduction just as I have everything else."

Taken aback, Annika frowned. "What *else* is there?"

He shook his head as if she were the simplest creature alive. "Well, you know, the Indian blood and all."

✖ 22 ✖

"*T*HE *Indian blood?* What *exactly* do you mean by that?"
Annika jerked her hand away from his and stood up,
her throat tightening.

He got to his feet and put a hand on her shoulder. "I had no
idea it was such a sensitive subject or I would never have
brought it up."

"It's not a sensitive subject. It's just not a subject at all."

He looked so condescending she wanted to slap him and
slap him hard. "I suppose it's best you handle it that way."

"That's not what I meant. I just never think about it one
way or another. It's part of me, just as it's part of Kase and
my father."

"I'm sorry. I can see I've upset you, darling."

"Please, tell me what you meant by *overlooking* my Indian blood."

He reached out, fingered the matched pearls at her throat.
She stepped back, unwilling to let him touch her.

"Surely you must understand. I just wanted you to know it
doesn't matter to me in the least."

"Meaning that it does to some people?"

"You can't tell me you don't realize your family has never
been fully accepted in Boston? Good heavens, everyone
knows the stories about your half brother and his savage
temper."

"Don't use that word in reference to my brother!"

For the first time ever she saw a flicker of anger cross
Richard's face. "Which word," he said, "temper or savage?
It's a well-known fact that your brother lost his job at the law

292

firm because he nearly strangled a man in the office with his bare hands."

She remembered Kase's abrupt departure from Boston. "I'm sure there's a reasonable explanation."

"And the fact that your mother has been involved with not one but two Indian men?"

"*Involved?* You make it sound as if she's been having an affair all these years! Caleb is her husband. And my father, too, so don't ever forget it."

He was sweating now. A thin line of moisture beaded his upper lip. "The only reason they have a foot inside the door in Boston society is because of Caleb Storm's father's family background and his connections in the capital."

"Why, Richard, I thought perhaps you had forgotten he's a lawyer, not just a *savage*. His connections in Washington go back twenty years."

"Annika, let's not fight over this, please. As I said, it means nothing to me."

"Stop saying that! If it meant nothing to you, you wouldn't have brought it up." Unable to settle her rattled nerves in his presence, she turned away and walked to the parlor door. She strained to hear Rose in the kitchen, but the house was silent. Determined to end it, she swung around and met his stare.

"I can't marry you, Richard."

"Look, I've apologized," he said.

"It's not only because of what you said today. I just don't love you enough. I don't think I ever did."

"But—"

"I was infatuated. I think perhaps what I loved most was the idea of being married. I wanted it all—the wedding, a home of my own. I wanted independence, not marriage." She turned away from him and walked to the back of the settee. Grasping the walnut trim that outlined the velvet upholstery, she squeezed until her knuckles whitened. "My parents, bless them, have always made my world safe and secure. Obviously a little too sheltered. Because I don't look Indian I've escaped the slurs my father and brother have faced, but I've never turned my back on my heritage. They kept me from the truth, obviously to spare me this sort of pain." She thought of Buck and the vast differences between them, of her initial reaction to him and his way of life, and then of the change that had come over her when she opened herself up to love.

"I see now that my mother and father should have at least given me a glimpse of real life, complete with its poverty, its prejudice, its pain, and its promise. I've had a taste of a new life since I left Boston and it agrees with me, Richard. I want to know more. I want to have the pleasure and the pain. I want to live. I want to face up to what I am and what I want, whether it's good for me or not."

Richard's face slowly colored from the neck up. The only other visible sign of his tightly controlled anger was the way he held his fists balled at his sides. "You're making a big mistake, Annika."

With a slight half smile, she shook her head, denying his words. "I don't think so."

"Ankah! Ankah!" Unaware of the strain between the two adults, Buttons ran into the room. She grabbed Annika about the knees, bunching the many yards of velvet in a great hug.

Annika swept Buttons up into her arms and held her, burying her nose in the little girl's thick, bouncing curls, and breathed in the fresh smell of soap and talcum. Hugging her tight, Annika used the child to comfort her own aching heart. She was further comforted when Buttons hugged her back. Richard stood immobile, staring at the two of them.

"I don't understand how you can keep that child with you. Surely she can only remind you of that man," he complained.

"Apparently there is a lot you don't understand."

"Rose says come now." Baby was tugging on the strand of pearls around Annika's neck.

"Rose says come? Is she in the kitchen?" Annika asked.

"Upstays."

Annika shifted Buttons from one hip to the other and held her away so she could understand what the child was trying to tell her.

"Rose needs me upstairs?"

Buttons put the strand of pearls in her mouth, sucked on them a minute, then let them drop onto the bodice of

Annika's gown. She nodded yes over and over. "Go get a baby."

"Oh, my God!" Annika thrust Buttons at Richard with a curt "Please watch her," gathered her skirts, and ran up the stairs. At the top of the landing she raced down the hall, nearly tripped over a wrinkle in the carpet runner, skidded to a stop, and then as calmly as she could she opened the door to the master bedroom.

Rose was slowly pacing the room, her hands at the small of her back, her forehead shining with perspiration.

"Oh, God, Rose. Is it the baby?"

"*Sí.*" Rose stopped, panting for breath, and then kept walking.

"What can I do?"

"Nothing. I think I do it all."

"This is no time to joke, Rose."

"Kase is back?" The usually headstrong woman looked panicked without her husband at her side.

Annika shook her head, trying to stem her own mounting nerves. "He's still in town." She stared at Rose's abdomen. "Oh, God."

Rose paused long enough to grab both of Annika's hands. "*Basta,* Annika. Stop. Oh, God, oh, God. Maybe Richard will find Kase. And the doctor. Maybe there is time. I think though, it is better Kase is not here." Her dark eyes swam with tears. "It is too hard for him when the babies die."

Shaking, Annika held Rose's hands tightly and tried to calm her. "Don't say that, Rose." Then, pulling herself together, she tried to smile. Someone had to take charge. "We'll do just fine. Now"—with the efficiency of a seasoned nurse, she led Rose to the bed, folded back the coverlet and sheets, and plumped the pillows—"you just relax. I'll take care of everything. We can do this, Rose, just you and I, if need be."

Rose sat on the edge of the bed but refused to lie down.

"I'm going to send Richard to town after Kase and the doctor, then I'm going to come back and I won't leave you again."

"Buttons?"

"Don't worry. I'll get Richard to send in one of the hands

before he leaves. They all love to play with her." She frowned, hoping there was a plate of cookies she could use as a bribe to entice one of her brother's cowhands into baby-sitting.

She raced back downstairs, wishing she hadn't donned the heavy gown. It was a stupid thing to wear on a ranch, but she had felt guilty wasting all of the beautiful clothes she'd brought along with her. Back in the parlor, she found Richard seated on a chair, leaning forward with elbows on his knees, as he watched Buttons turn a somersault. Her three ruffled petticoats and full skirt completely covered her head and shoulders. Her plump round bottom swathed in frilly pantalettes stuck up in the air.

"You have to go to town to get Kase," she ordered smoothly. "There should be a horse already saddled—he's had one ready every day for three weeks. Send Tom in before you leave. When you get Kase, bring the doctor and come straight back. Rose is having the baby."

She expected him to refuse after the way she had just treated him, but ever the gentleman, his refined background wouldn't let him do anything so dishonorable. "Of course." He stood and coolly bowed. "I'm on my way."

She felt her shoulders sag with relief. "Thank you, Richard."

He paused in the doorway. "Annika, I'm going to forget our conversation of this afternoon and I hope you do the same. I'm willing to take you back once you've come to your senses."

Before she could reply, he turned on his heel and walked out of the room.

"I have come to my senses," she said aloud. "For the first time in my life."

"ANOTHER one, marshal?"

No matter how many times he told them not to call him marshal anymore, the citizens of Busted Heel ignored Kase Storm's request. He nodded to Paddie O'Hallohan, the barkeep, and tapped the rim of his glass. The bald Irishman with a fringe of white hair above his ears liberally sloshed whiskey into his glass.

Kase looked past Paddie and stared at himself in the mirror over the bar as he tossed back the drink. He never drank this early, hardly ever imbibed at all. Liquor didn't agree with him. But when he'd scoured the town looking for the only doctor available for miles and found him missing, he had needed a stiff one to calm his nerves. It was too early for any of the cowhands to be in. It was too early for him, too, but he needed it. The place was deserted except for him and Paddie.

The last few weeks had been hell. He was scared to death for Rose, terrified she'd lose this baby. He wouldn't even let himself think about losing Rose. Before he left the ranch today he'd forced himself to climb the slight knoll behind the house, to walk into the fenced area beneath a wind-twisted tree, and stare down at the tiny graves of his babies. He went down on his knees and called upon all the gods and prophets he could think of: Wakantankan, the god of his Sioux ancestors, Jehovah, Jesus, Allah, Buddha, Mohammed. He then opened his heart to the universe and swore that this child, this spark of hope, would live. His prayer was not a plea but an affirmation of hope. His child would live and Rose would live. He thanked the gods as if it were already true.

The plan to house the doctor at the ranch had been his own. The long wait and building fear that Rose would have to deliver without an expert at her bedside worried him nearly to death. The first baby had come long before expected. It arrived in a rush of blood and was far too small to survive. He had delivered it himself and swore he'd never do it again.

The others had been premature, too, one stillborn, the next lived less than three hours. She had perfect little hands and feet and features just like his. He had hidden his pain. It had seemed easier for Rose. She claimed God was testing her as she cut roses for the graves and visited the tiny mounds on the hill. She dealt with her grief openly and then lived life to the fullest.

He couldn't do the same. He was terrified. The doctor had arrived in time for the last two births, but barely. Now, with Rose already a week late, Kase was sick of getting up every morning and saddling a horse so that he could send a man off at a moment's notice. This morning he had asked himself, why not have the doctor at their beck and call? He was ready to pay the man a year's wages to get him to agree to stay on at the ranch until the baby came, but his trek into town had been futile.

Before he started back, Kase had decided a drink was in order. A drink or two. He deserved it. Living with two temperamental women under his roof was getting him down. Annika was a bundle of nerves. And Richard Thexton? He wondered what his sister had ever seen in the man. He was everything Kase had left Boston to avoid. Straitlaced, dictated to by society's rules, Thexton hadn't so much as held his sister's hand in front of him.

Kase stared down at the empty glass and waved Paddie away when he started to pour another. It wouldn't do to go home drunk. Rose would have his head.

Hell, he thought. No wonder poor Annika had fallen for Buck Scott—if Richard was any indication of what she'd been exposed to, Scott was probably the first real man she'd ever met. Still, Kase didn't know what he would do if he ever met Scott face-to-face. Not after what the man had done to his sister.

Annika. Kase shook his head. Now there was a pickle.

"Need something, marshal?"

"Just thinking, Paddie."

If Annika was pregnant, he'd help her by doing everything he could to soften the blow for his mother and Caleb. God, but fate could be unkind—and they said lightning never struck twice.

He picked up his hat off the bar and centered it on his head. He ran his fingers around the brim, pulled it low, and pushed away from the bar. "Thanks, Paddie. See you next time." He flipped the man two bits.

Paddie caught it in the air.

BUSTED Heel wasn't any different from any other small town Buck had drifted through in his youth. The false-fronted stores and saloons, the Chinese laundry, the livery, and the blacksmith were like all the rest. And like all the rest, Busted Heel was no doubt full of small-minded people set in their ways. That's how it was with towns. Strangers were rarely welcome.

He reined in the powerful bay and dismounted outside the saloon and pulled his rifle out of its holster. Standing in the dirt in the street, he pushed back the brim of his hat and stared up at the sign across the building: RUFFLED GARTER SALOON. With a quick twist, he wrapped the reins around the hitching post and stepped up onto the boardwalk. It was dark inside the saloon, but the doors were open. As he crossed the walk, his moccasined feet soundless against the wood planks, he hoped he wouldn't have to be in town long. All he'd come for were directions to the Storm ranch. Hopefully the first man he asked would know.

KASE turned in time to see a hulking form fill the doorway. Silhouetted from the outside, the man was impossible to identify. The sun backlit his stark blond hair until it looked like a wild nimbus around his head. A momentary flash of thought made Kase think of Thor, the Viking god of Thunder.

"Anybody know how to find the Storm ranch?" Buck stepped inside and squinted, waiting for his vision to adjust to the dim light. The saloon smelled like stale cigar smoke, whiskey, and sweaty men—just like all the others he'd ever been in.

Fingering the Colt he wore when away from the ranch, Kase said quietly, "Who wants to know?" He hoped he didn't have to face down another young tough trying to prove himself by drawing on the man who'd brought down the Dawson gang.

Buck heard the warning in the low voice and braced himself. He waited a split second longer, recognized the big half-breed with long hair. It was the man he'd seen at the station in Cheyenne the day he'd taken Annika. It was Kase Storm.

He saw the man's hand hovering above his holster and knew he was a dead man. There was no way he could throw his knife or lift his rifle before Storm drew on him. Convinced he was about to die, Buck almost welcomed the release. *Might as well get it over with,* he thought. "I'm Buck Scott."

He expected to feel a bullet hit him between the eyes. When Kase Storm launched himself across the room and tackled him to the floor, Buck was felled more by surprise than the other man's strength. When Kase hit him in the mouth, Buck felt his lip split and instinct took over.

Buck started swinging without thought. Chairs crashed to the floor as they rolled across the room. Both men's hats went flying. Kase wound up on top and pinned him to the floor. He straddled Buck across the chest and planted his fist against Buck's jaw.

Buck countered with a right to Kase's cheek just below the eye.

Kase dodged and Buck unseated him. They rolled beneath a table, knocking three more chairs to the floor. The barkeep was yelling something Buck couldn't discern. The man's footsteps sounded on the floorboards near his ear and faded away.

Buck held Kase down by the neck and rammed his fist into the man's nose. Blood spurted out. When he pulled back for another blow, Kase reached up behind him, grabbed his hair, and bent his head back.

Buck roared with pain and rolled to his side to get away.

Kase wouldn't release his hair, so Buck grabbed his adversary's long black queue. Locked in battle like two bull elks, they rolled out beneath the swinging door and onto the boardwalk.

When Kase clinched his fingers around Buck's ears and pulled, Buck let go and grabbed Kase around the neck with both hands. Kase's eyes widened, but Buck didn't see fear behind them. As they stared at each other, both of them were panting heavily. Sweat ran down their brows and dust coated them from head to toe. Buck wondered how in the hell he could get out of this predicament without killing Annika's brother.

She'd never forgive him if he did.

But he might die if he didn't.

Kase Storm stared up at the giant from whose lip blood was dripping down onto his clean shirt. Rose was going to give him hell for that. The man's meaty hands held his throat in an iron grip. Kase wondered how he could extricate himself without killing Annika's lover.

She'd never forgive him if he did.

Kase's face was growing redder as Buck's grip tightened. Buck wished Storm would let go of his ears.

Suddenly, a shot rang out, deafening them both. Buck closed his eyes and waited for the pain of a bullet to hit him. Kase held his breath. Neither felt a thing.

Another shot went off. Someone stepped up and kicked them both in the ribs. "God dammit, you varmints, let go of each other 'fore I plug you both! Let go! Break it up!"

Kase recognized Zach's voice and slowly let go of Buck Scott.

Buck waited a split second longer, frowned down at Kase, then rolled off him. He managed to get to his knees and wiped his bleeding lip on his torn shirt sleeve.

Kase sat up and pressed his hand to his nose. "Hell, I think you broke it," he grumbled.

Buck didn't say anything. He found himself staring down the barrel of an old six-shooter held by a time-worn old man who was squinting down at him with one eye. The old codger spit a stream of tobacco and waved the gun in his face.

"Hand me that buffalo knife, son, then tell me who you be and what's goin' on?"

"Buck Scott. I was just askin' directions." He unsheathed his knife and handed it to Zach handle first.

"Well"—Zach eyed him warily—"you get 'em?"

"Yeah, but I'm not following them." Buck pinned Kase with a hard, swollen-eyed stare. "I'm looking for the Storm ranch and I'll whip every man in this town if I have to until I find out how to get there."

"Stay away from my sister." Kase finally got to his knees. "You'll have to kill me."

With more speed than either man would have credited him with, Zach reached out and relieved Kase of his gun. With a weapon in each hand, he aimed them at the men on the walk.

"First thing you gotta learn, young man, is not to say that unless you mean it if you don't know who you're talkin' to."

"I know who I'm talking to." Buck spit blood on the walk.
"And I know who you are," Kase growled.
Zach rocked back on his heels. "Now that we're all ac-
quainted, how about both of you gettin' up and walkin' over
to the jail with me?"
For the first time, Kase took his eyes off Buck and looked
up at Zach. "Aw, Zach, come on."
"Get up. I'm marshal, not you, and I'm haulin' you two in
to cool off."
Resigned to his fate, Buck stood up and brushed himself
off. Paddie hovered near the doorway, both men's hats and
Buck's rifle in his hands. He handed one hat to Buck and
backed away. "Here, marshal." He dusted the black hat off
before he handed it to Kase.
"I'm marshal here," Zach reminded him. "Somethin' this
one here must of forgot." He nodded at Kase. "Now, both of
you get movin', no argument." He took the rifle from
Paddie.
Kase tried to stall. "I gotta get home, Zach."
Zach prodded him with the barrel of his own gun. "You
shoulda thought of that a'fore you jumped this man."
The sidewalk was crowded with Busted Heel's more
colorful residents. Flossie Gibbs, the madam who ran the
Hospitality Parlor next door to the saloon, along with two
of her girls, stood sleepy eyed, staring at both of the
men.
"Kase Storm, is that you? I would a thought you knew
better," Floss called out. "What's Rosie gonna have to say
about this?"
Head down, rubbing his jaw with one hand while he
cupped his bleeding nose with the other, Kase ignored the
laughter and led the way to the jail.
Raindrops the size of silver dollars began to fall. Buck followed in his wake, determined never to ride into a civilized
place again. "What about my horse, old man?" His bay was
loaded down with his bedroll and other belongings.
Zach stopped and unhitched the horse, then handed the
reins to Buck. Arms full of weapons, Zach continued to prod
the men across the street. When they reached the jail house,
he dumped the guns and knife on the desk and searched for

the key to the only cell in the building while his prisoners ignored each other. Finally, Zach waved his gun toward the cell and said, "Cain't find the key. Just go on in and sit down a piece and I'll keep lookin'."

Kase led the way. The sooner he went in and sat out his stay, which he hoped would be brief, the sooner Zach would let him go home to Rose. He didn't bother to see whether Buck Scott followed him or not. He didn't much care. The bed in the cell was built into the wall like a shelf. Kase sat down on the hard surface that usually served as Zach's bed and waited to see how long the old man would make him stay.

When Buck Scott walked into the cramped cell, he took a seat at the opposite end of the bed. The old marshal slammed the door shut behind him, but didn't lock it. Instead, he grumbled something about having lost the key. It seemed they were on their honor not to escape. Annika's half brother was still bleeding from the punch in the nose he'd given him, but he didn't much care. His own lip was still bloody, the side of his mouth swollen. Fine sight he would make if and when he saw Annika. He thought of her fancy fiancé from Boston and almost decided to head back home.

He stared at the floor, then the wood door with its small barred window, then the ceiling. He refused to acknowledge the man sitting not three feet away. Kase Storm could rot for all he cared.

"What do you want with my sister?" Storm growled.

Buck briefly glanced at his cell mate. "Nothing."

"Nothing? Why didn't you come see her before now?"

Buck looked down at his bloodstained plaid flannel shirt. One sleeve had torn away from the shoulder. The three top buttons were gone. The material gaped open to show his chest. "Until two days ago I thought she'd left me of her own free will." He felt Kase's eyes on him, so he finally turned to meet the other man's gaze. The eyes that looked back at him were hauntingly familiar. They were just like Annika's, a brilliant blue that was almost iridescent.

"She didn't." Kase informed him coolly.

"Well, she didn't come back, either."

"How was she supposed to get there?"

"I don't suppose you would have volunteered to take her," Buck grumbled.

"Damned right." Kase didn't bother adding that he might have taken her back into the Laramies if Annika had begged him.

They stared at the door across from them in silence, Kase trying to imagine his refined, beautiful sister in Buck Scott's bed. No matter how hard he tried, he couldn't conjure up the sight. The man was a giant. As tall as Kase himself but a good thirty pounds heavier and all of it muscle. Scott's hair was nearly as long as his own, and he looked to have a good month's growth of beard. The man's blue eyes shone with intensity, but he was clearly lucid, and that much Kase was thankful for, given what he knew of Buck's family history. While his eye nearly swelled shut, Kase gave up trying to decide what Annika saw in Buck Scott. Hell, he thought, people probably couldn't figure out why Rose had married him, either.

Shifting uncomfortably, Kase let go of his nose. The bleeding had subsided. He wiped his hand on his leg and leaned back against the wall. "I can't remember the last time I really let go and brawled."

Startled, Buck turned to Kase and saw a half smile playing on the man's lips. He nodded in agreement. "Me either. Most times I have to talk myself out of it. There aren't a lot of men my size around. I'd hate to kill someone I only meant to maim."

Understanding completely, Kase laughed, then winced. "Me too."

A commotion outside the door drew their attention. Kase started to rise, then stepped back when the door swung open and nearly hit him in his already battered face. Richard Thexton stepped inside the cell, stared from Kase to Buck and back to Kase again.

Buck felt the acid churn in his stomach. The man standing in the doorway could be none other than Annika's Boston fiancé. Exactly as Old Ted described—tall, lean, and so clean he looked like a polished apple. He wore a tweed coat that matched his pants. Even though it was raining out, his half boots shone brightly beneath a layer of dust, his collar was still starched and impeccably clean. A bowler hat clenched in his hands, he ignored Buck and concentrated on Kase. When his initial shock at the sight of the damage wore off, he said to Kase, "Come on, Storm. While you've been here tearing up the town, your wife has been having a baby."

"Already?"

"Not yet. Annika sent me as soon as we knew it had started. Did you get the doctor?" Richard glanced at Buck and then away, dismissing him.

"He's gone to Cheyenne."

"What now?"

With his expression nearly as dark as his hat, Kase Storm pushed past Richard and left the cell. Buck followed him out. He watched as Storm holstered his gun and glared at the one-eyed marshal, daring him without words to stop him.

"You fellas cooled off any?" Zach laughed.

"Rose is having the baby, Zach. I'm leaving."

" 'Course, you are. Kiss Rosie for me."

The city slicker walked out the door with Kase on his heels, but before he could leave the jail, Buck laid his hands on Kase's arm to stop him.

Kase swung around as if he wanted to hit Buck again for causing the delay. "Get your hand off me, Scott. It's finished."

It took every ounce of courage Buck ever possessed to ask, "Is she gonna marry that man?" He nodded toward Richard Thexton.

Toe to toe, Kase looked Buck square in the eye. "No."

"Then I'm coming with you."

❧ 23 ❧

R AIN had been falling steadily for nearly an hour. Annika
wiped the sweat from Rose's brow, smoothed back her
hair, and then glanced over at the water-streaked windows
that lined the front of the second-story room. The gray pall
that darkened her spirits stained the sky outside. Richard
should have been back with Kase and the doctor over thirty
minutes ago.

Although it was only late morning, she had lit the lamps in
the master bedroom to dispel the gloom. The fire in the fireplace in the corner was stoked and roaring to keep the place
toasty. Everything was ready for the baby's imminent arrival. Everything but her.

Under Rose's direction, Annika had gathered together
clean towels and sheets. Tom, the hired hand she commandeered into watching Baby, had water boiling downstairs.
When Rose could no longer walk, Annika helped her change
into her nightgown and climb into bed. Following instructions had been the easy part; calming her own frayed nerves
was impossible. Each time Rose suffered through another
contraction, Annika let the woman clutch her hands until she
was afraid her own fingers would break. Rose panted between surges of pain, stoically silent, visibly scared. Annika
sensed Rose was holding back as she alternately panted,
writhed, and then prayed that Kase and the doctor would arrive in time.

Annika didn't know who was praying harder, she or Rose.
If there was one thing she was certain of, it was that she did
not relish the thought of delivering the baby alone—not after

306

Rose had already endured so many losses. Annika knew that if she unwittingly harmed the child or Rose through her ignorance, she could never forgive herself.

"Annika?" Rose gasped and clung to her hand again as if she were a lifeline. "I cannot . . . I cannot . . ."

"Yes you can! You are going to do fine. You *are* doing just fine." She hoped Rose didn't notice that her own hands were shaking.

"I want Kase," Rose moaned.

I do, too. "He'll be here any minute."

"Something is wrong. Where is he?"

"On the way, I'm sure of it." Annika looked over at the windows again. "It's been raining out. I'm sure that's what's slowed them down."

Rose gritted her teeth and fought against the pain before she sank back against the pillows. She glanced toward the windows and then away. "Rain is bad luck," she mumbled.

"Absolutely not." Annika shook her head, hoping to reassure Rose. "It will bring spring flowers. Just think, all your rose bushes will bud soon. Rain is part of spring; it's a sign of growth and rebirth."

Rose closed her eyes. "Rain is sometimes bad luck. Evil. You must do something for me."

"What?"

"Cross the keys."

Convinced Rose had slipped into delirium, Annika didn't even ask what she meant.

But Rose persisted. "Cross the keys. They are hanging by the door in the kitchen. Go down and lay them on the table. Cross them, like this." She held up her hands and positioned her index fingers in an *X*. "It will keep evil from coming into the house with the rain. They are my *Zia* Rina's keys, her gift to me when I come to America."

Annika's couldn't conceal her skepticism. "Really, Rose—"

"Please . . ." Rose gasped, tightened her grip on Annika's hand again, as she lunged to a sitting position. She wrapped her hands around her distended abdomen, cradling the child within as if to hold back the inevitable. When the pain subsided, she lay back against the mound of pillows and pressed her sweating palms against the bed. "Go and go quickly."

"I'm not leaving you."

Rose shook her head. "The baby is not coming. I know."

"But couldn't it be any minute now?"

Stubborn to the last, Rose shook her head again. "No. Something is wrong. You must go cross the keys."

Annika stood up beside the bed, hesitant with uncertainty. She dared not leave Rose alone, but the woman insisted she go down and cross the iron keys that hung on a nail beside the back door. The pains were coming closer now, one after the other. She walked to the end of the bed and lifted the sheet that modestly covered the lower half of Rose's body, hoping to see some sign besides the blood-tinged fluids that stained the towels beneath her, but there was no sign of the baby's head emerging yet.

Brushing back the wisps of hair that had escaped her up-swept hairstyle, Annika wiped her brow with the back of her hand. Before she could argue anymore, she heard the sound of heavy footsteps racing up the stairs and ran for the door. At first she fought with the handle, then flung the door open.

"Kase! Thank God!" Her brother brushed past, but not fast enough to hide the livid purple bruises and cuts on his face. He hurried to Rose's bedside, threw his hat on the floor, and knelt beside the bed. His hair had come unbound and there was a wildness about him Annika had never recognized before. Seeing him in this state made her realize that her brother was a man to be reckoned with, definitely not one to be crossed.

Annika hovered behind him and then caught her breath when she got a good look at his face. It had been battered far worse than she realized. She watched Rose reach out and tenderly touch the gash across his cheek and then the purple crescents beneath each eye.

"What happened?" Rose whispered. Tears spilled over her lower lashes.

Kase merely shrugged and cupped his hand against her cheek. "You should see the other guy."

Annika could wait for an explanation about his face. What she demanded to know was, "Where's the doctor, Kase?"

She paced to the door and watched the empty staircase expectantly, furious to think that while she had been agonizing over his arrival, her brother had been brawling in town. She stalked back across the room, her temper overriding her fear. "Well? Where is he?"

Kase's shoulders slumped visibly. With the addition of his bruises, his wet clothing, and the bloodstains streaking his shirt, his dark countenance only heightened the dismal feeling that had entered the room with him. "He's in Cheyenne."

Annika watched the frightened couple. Kase held Rose's hand. Rose looked confused and alarmed. No matter how foreboding Kase might appear, he had obviously lost his nerve completely where childbirth was concerned. Someone had to do something and she was the only someone left. The blind leading the terrified. Annika took a deep breath and said with as much authority in her tone as she could muster, "Kase, go wash up, you'll scare that child to death when it sees you. There's fresh water in the pitcher on the washstand."

Like a condemned man, Kase slowly rose to his feet. At the same time, another pain gripped Rose and she cried out. Kase sank to the bed beside her and grabbed her shoulders. "Damn it, Rose, this is it. This is the last time. I won't lose you!"

A floorboard creaked behind her and Annika turned toward the open doorway, expecting to see Richard hovering on the threshold. The bottom fell out of her stomach when her gaze collided with Buck Scott's. His face was in no better shape than her brother's. Suddenly it was all too clear from the blood streaked down the front of his soaking wet jacket and the rip in his shirt that the two men had already met in town. Met and fought.

And from the look of it, they had nearly killed each other.

Buck filled the doorway with Buttons in his arms, looking much the same as Annika had last seen him except for the shadows beneath his eyes, the beard, and a new thinness to his face. Against the collar of his buckskin jacket, his hair was longer than she remembered. He'd lost the rawhide tie that usually held it in place and the rain had rejuvenated the curl until he sported a halo of ringlets much like that of the child in his arms. She'd never seen a more beautiful sight.

"Ankah! Buck! Look it, Buck!" Buttons squeezed her arms tightly about his neck and pressed her cheek to his.

Annika couldn't keep from staring at Buck—at his hair, his eyes, his battered lips. She wanted to hug him as tightly as Baby Buttons and never wanted to let him go again. Only the drama unfolding behind her kept her from going to his arms.

Buck felt much the same after the initial shock of seeing Annika subsided, but the sight of her in her fine purple gown, the intricate hairstyle so different from anything he was used to on her, her familiar regal bearing adorned by the strand of pearls and the pearl and diamond earrings glittering against her honeyed skin—all of it instantly convinced him he had been very wrong in coming to see her.

One quick glance around the well-appointed room, the memory of the furnishings he'd seen on his way from the kitchen, the man Richard, who claimed her as his—this was all part of the world she belonged to. This was what Annika Storm deserved, the life she was entitled to. Thinking he might woo her away from such riches was the second greatest mistake of his life. Falling in love with her had been the first.

And he knew it all in a glance.

Then, the small, dark-haired woman nearly lost amid the bedclothes of the high four-poster behind Annika drew his complete attention. He could tell from the frequency of her pains that the child fighting to be born had to come soon or it would be lost. Wordlessly, he handed Buttons to Annika and walked to the end of the bed. The heat in the room was stifling. He wiped his brow.

Rose glanced at him and away as she cried out again and clung to Kase.

"Shh. Shh. It's all right, Rose. It'll pass." Kase swabbed her face with a wet cloth as he murmured low and tried to calm her.

"Let her yell." Buck cleared his throat. "Is the head showing yet?"

Annika moved up behind him. "Not yet," she whispered.

Kase swung around and glared at Buck. Annika hovered beside him holding a squirming Baby Buttons.

"Get him out of here." Kase uttered the words in a low growl and turned away from the sight of the buffalo man standing so close to his sister.

Annika watched Buck watch Rose and suddenly knew an overwhelming relief. If anyone could save Rose and the baby, it was Buck Scott. "Let him help, Kase."

Kase came to his feet in an instant. He threw the wet rag in the bowl on the bedside table and with clenched fists said, "Get him out before I kill him."

"Kase!" When Rose cried out in pain, Kase turned away from Buck.

Annika stepped up to her brother and frantically whispered, "He can do it, Kase."

"I don't want that man's hands on my wife."

"Please, Kase. He knows what to do." She glanced at Buck for affirmation and was relieved when Buck nodded.

Buck added, "That's right, Storm. My mother was a midwife. I've seen more babies delivered than I can count."

Kase didn't even turn around to face him. Rose was crying now, writhing in almost constant pain, arching almost off the mattress.

"I delivered Buttons," Buck added.

"Let him help, Kase, please. At least talk to him," Annika pleaded.

Buck folded his arms across his chest. "From the looks of it, there's not much time left, Storm."

Kase watched Rose, who was fighting to hold back her pain, fighting the contractions. He glanced up at his sister's hopeful face, then at Buck Scott. The big, crudely dressed man looked as out of place in the elegant bedroom with its walls covered in cabbage rose paper as the proverbial bull in a china shop. But Scott was right. There was not much time left.

"What can you do?" Kase whispered.

"I can handle this without falling apart, for one thing. Your wife is terrified and you're scared to death yourself. Do everyone a favor and get out of here. Go downstairs and get drunk." Dismissing Kase, Buck shrugged out of his coat,

threw it over a chaise in the corner, and rolled up the sleeves
of his torn flannel shirt. "Annika, take Buttons downstairs. I
have some herbs in my saddlebags. See if there's some skull-
cap and brew it into tea. Bring up a pot of it as fast as you
can, along with some wine if there's any around."

Annika hesitated, willing but uncertain. "I don't know
what it looks like."

Buck bent over and washed his hands in the basin on the
washstand.

Kase stood by the doorway watching the scene unfold. Finally he offered grudgingly, "I can find it."

Arrested by the sight of Buck standing there, still barely
able to believe he had finally come for her, Annika didn't
move when Kase left the room.

Buck straightened. He stared at her briefly, then said, "Get
going, but before you do, open a window. What were you
trying to do? Boil the baby when it got here?"

"I didn't want it to catch cold," she snapped at him.

He almost smiled, then turned away. "Open a window and
then get the tea." He walked over to Rose and laid his hand
on her forehead. In a low, even tone he asked her, "Can you
hear the rain, Mrs. Storm?"

"Sí, I hear."

"Do you like rain?"

"Is bad sometimes, but I like."

"Me too," Buck said. He looked into her eyes, studied the
color of her skin, measured her temperature with the touch
of his hand on her brow. "Don't fight the pain. Lean into it.
Push." He put his hand on her abdomen and felt the child
moving inside. "We'll have that baby out of there in no time
if you cooperate, Mrs. Storm."

Through her pain, Rose looked up into his blue eyes and
listened to the confident voice of Buck Scott. "My name is
Rosa."

When Annika returned with the tea a few minutes later,
she set the tray down and poured a shallow cup. Buck was
still standing beside Rose, elevating her head and softly en-
couraging her to push when the pain came. Rose seemed
calmer, more confident with each passing second. Annika
held the tea, silently watching Buck deal with his patient.

He turned to her and said quietly, "See if you can see the crown of the baby's head yet."

Annika set down the cup, did as he asked, and shook her head. "Nothing."

"Something is wrong." Rose's voice grew weak.

"Not at all, Rosa. You're almost through." Gently, he laid Rose back against the pillows. He encouraged her to sip some tea, then a little more. That done, he uncorked the wine.

"Will the tea relieve her pain?" Annika asked, hoping he would say yes.

Buck shook his head. "No, but it will calm her nerves."

"When do you give her the wine?"

"The wine's for me." He pulled out the cork with his teeth and took a deep swig of the burgundy and handed the bottle to Annika. Closing her eyes, she mimicked him and drank down a hearty draught and felt the warm liquid work its way to her toes.

"Sometimes fear is the worst problem," Buck was saying. "Your brother was scared enough to pass his fear on to Rosa. Her holding back only made things worse."

"I wasn't much help, either," Annika whispered. She met his stare. "We all thank you, Buck."

"Don't thank me yet." He turned away without a word and encouraged Rose through another pain. As Annika looked on, he slowly, calmly handled her, breathed with her, smiled, and assured Rose that everything was progressing normally. He pressed her to take another sip of the calming brew.

"Look again," he said aside to Annika after another fierce contraction had passed.

Annika lifted the sheet. Unable to hide her excitement, she cried out, "I see it! I see the baby's head."

"A lot of it?"

"Just a peek."

"Push again," Buck encouraged Rose.

She pushed.

"Scream if you want to," he encouraged.

She shook her head and bit her lip.

"Do it," he commanded. "You'll feel better."

Rose screamed and Kase burst into the room.

"Get out," Buck said calmly over his shoulder. "We're almost through." Kase looked at Annika; she nodded and smiled. He backed out of the room and closed the door.

"I see more now!" Annika cried out. "The head and one shoulder. Oh, Buck," she said, smiling up at him through tears, "it has dark hair just like Kase."

Buck moved to the end of the bed. He knew that if the cord which was the child's lifeline was wrapped too tightly around its neck the baby would die before it was fully birthed. One look told him that this would be the case with Rose Storm's infant if he didn't act and act fast. He tried to slip his finger between the tight cord and the child's neck but couldn't. "Push, Rose," he said, trying to keep the panic from his voice.

The command in his tone brooked no argument. Rose pushed as Annika took Buck's place and helped her lean into the pain. Buck slipped his hands beneath the infant's sleek wet body and patiently waited for it to slide from the birth canal. Rose cried out as the baby tore its way into the world.

Annika held her breath as the child slid into Buck's hands, stunned by the miracle she had witnessed, forgetting for the moment all that had passed between them. Buck was magnificent. She knew that if she lived to be a hundred she would never forget the sight of the huge outdoorsman holding the tiny, pulsing scrap of life that he had ushered into the world.

"It's a boy," Buck told them, looking first at Annika, then Rose. With the baby cradled in his big hands, he quickly unwrapped the cord from around its neck. Buck then picked up the little boy by his heels. He gave the buttocks a slap and then another before Kase and Rose's son lustily announced his arrival. "Put a towel on her stomach," he directed Annika, and after she had, he laid the child on Rose. The afterbirth came on a last wave of pain.

Exhausted, Rose fell back against the pillows and stroked the baby's shining black hair. *"Mio bambino . . . mio bambino."* Through her tears of joy, she repeated the words like a litany as Buck tied off the cord and severed it with the sharp scissors she had made certain were clean and ready. He then wrapped the baby in another towel and told Rose, "You can hold him for a minute more before I clean him up." Just as he lay the baby in Rose's arms, the door opened and Kase walked in.

"Is everything all right?" Unashamed of the tears that flowed unchecked down his cheeks or of his red-rimmed eyes, Kase looked to Buck for reassurance.

Buck toweled his hands and arms up to the elbows. "She's fine and so's your son, but I'd feel better if I could stitch her up a bit."

Kase glanced at Rose, who nodded without hesitation before he sank to the side of the bed, certain his legs would not hold him any longer. Annika moved to his side and put her hand on her brother's shoulders. "Isn't he beautiful? He looks just like both of you."

The baby's cries had subsided to whimpers as Rose cradled him in her arms. Almost afraid to touch the squirming bundle in his wife's arms, Kase simply stared down at the baby for a moment before he looked up at Buck. "Is he all right? Can you tell?"

Buck paused, wondering how Kase Storm could look at such a robust, healthy infant and even ask the question. He glanced at Annika, who was also waiting expectantly for his answer. "He's fit as a fiddle, far as I can tell. By the time he's grown his punch will probably pack the same wallop his daddy's does."

Buck carried away the afterbirth in a china washbowl. He had quickly draped a towel over it when he saw Annika blanch at the sight. All he needed now was to have her passed out on the floor.

The Storms inspected their son while Buck waited patiently. Finally, he interrupted. "Annika, why don't you and your brother go downstairs for a few minutes and leave Rose in peace? When we're through here, I'll call you."

Annika couldn't hide her pride when Buck issued the smooth command. His bedside manner was as practiced as any doctor she'd ever seen, city or country. She volunteered to act as nurse, but Buck shook his head. "You look exhausted. Just close the window and then get me some silk thread, a needle, and more hot water. I can manage." To reassure Kase he said, "It will just take a few minutes."

"I can't understand why your brother allowed that man in this house."

"Richard, I'm really too drained to answer now." Seated at the kitchen table, Annika pressed her hands to her burning eyelids and tried to focus. Buck had yet to come down from Rose's room, although Kase had been granted entrance. She had too much to think about now that the crisis with Rose had passed to want to deal with Richard Thexton.

But he wouldn't let her rest. "Obviously, *your brother* isn't thinking clearly—"

"His name is Kase."

"Well, I still contend he's not thinking clearly, Annika, or he wouldn't abide that man's presence."

"Buck just saved their child. I imagine Kase will give him anything he wants."

Richard stopped pacing across the kitchen floor and glared at her. "Including you?"

"That was uncalled for."

"Was it? I think you're glad to see him, as crude and uncouth as he is. That's why you are barely able to sit there on the edge of your chair, why you jump at every sound—you can't wait for him to come down. I think you've been waiting for him to come back ever since you were rescued. Am I right?"

Tension mounted upon tension forced her to snap. She slapped her hands down on the surface of the table and pushed off her chair. Annika paced across the room until she stood before Richard Thexton, refusing to back down. "You're right," she said in a menacing tone. "In fact, you're right about everything you've said today. I am waiting to see Buck Scott again. And if he'll have me, I intend to go wherever he wants me to."

He looked as shocked as if she had slapped him.

She wished she had. "I guess it's just my wild Indian blood, Richard. The blood you were so very graciously offering to overlook a few hours ago."

He reached out and grabbed her by the shoulders. This untamed fury was a side of the usually unruffled man that Annika had never seen or even suspected he possessed.

"You little bitch." He spoke from between clenched teeth. "You think you're so high and mighty. If you hadn't been tucked away in school or under your parents' wings all your life, you'd have had your eyes opened and know where you stand."

"Say what you have to say and get it over with, Richard."

"Your brother slunk out of town after he attacked a client in his law office. Your mother was forced to marry that half-breed Caleb Storm because she'd already been some Indian's Dutch whore. Where do you actually think that precious 'brother' of yours sprang from?"

She tried to twist away. "Let me go."

He gave her a vicious shake instead. "Have you ever asked them, Annika?"

"I said let me go!"

"Have you asked?"

She tried to blot out the sight of him leering down at her by closing her eyes. *Yes*, she wanted to scream. Yes, she'd asked them, but the answer was always the same. Kase was her half brother. Her mother had been married before Caleb, but the past was too sad for her to talk about. The subject had always been so swiftly and effortlessly changed that afterward she hardly remembered she had asked. As she grew older, she grew afraid to hurt her mother, and even more afraid to find out that Kase was not her half brother at all, but perhaps was some foundling that Analisa and Caleb had raised. So she stopped asking. Kase was simply Kase. Her idol. Her big brother. It didn't matter who had fathered him—but now this man she had almost married was accusing her mother of whoring, even suggesting Analisa was not good enough to marry anyone but Caleb Storm, a half-breed.

"I guess blood will tell," he said in a tone just above a whisper. "My mother tried to tell me that. Thank God this wild streak in you came out before we married."

His fingers pressed into her forearms, bruising her. The sound of the rain beat a heavy staccato on the roof of the veranda, ran in streams off the lip of the porch overhang, and splashed into puddles that surrounded the house.

Annika tried to wriggle free, twisting against his punishing fingers. "For the last time, let me go!"

Buck Scott stepped into the kitchen. "Let her go, Thexton." He didn't know what was going on, but he had heard Annika demand release and intended to see that Thexton carried through.

"Gladly," Richard sneered. He shoved Annika aside so hard she hit her hip against the table and nearly stumbled over a chair.

Buck flew across the room, tackled Richard, and shoved him backward until both of them crashed into the back door. The hinges gave way and the door fell with them on it, scarring the white enamel paint on the veranda. With a stranglehold around Thexton's throat, Buck drew back his fist, ready to plunge it into the man's startled face. Somewhere behind him, he heard Annika pleading with him to stop. He had hated this man on sight, and when he saw Richard Thexton shaking Annika, when he heard her demanding release, it triggered an immediate reaction. All of his bottled-up anger and frustration erupted. Thexton would be lucky if he didn't kill him outright.

As he took aim at Thexton's face, a grip with the strength to match his own arrested Buck's downward swing. He tried to shake off the hand that held his wrist but couldn't, so he turned to glare at the offender.

"Don't do it," Kase warned. "I don't really have the energy to fight you again, but I will if you push me."

Annika stood beside Kase, clutching her brother's arm, but her eyes were for Buck alone. She silently appealed to him to stop.

Buck took another look at Thexton and then at the splintered door frame and shattered glass of the oval window.

He had made a mess of things again.

Buck unstraddled Richard and stood up. There was no apology in his tone when he said, "I guess I'll be leaving."

"Leaving?" Annika couldn't believe what she'd just heard. She turned on her brother. "Richard insulted me. Buck only did what you would have done if you had heard him, Kase. You can't let him leave."

"You're not going anywhere," Kase ordered Buck. "Not

until I've had a word with you." He extended a hand to his sister's former suitor and jerked Thexton to his feet. Kase then said bluntly, "You, on the other hand, Thexton, *are* leaving. If you hurry, you can catch the last train headed east from Busted Heel." As Richard brushed past him to pack his bags, Kase lifted the oak door and leaned it against the house and then walked to the edge of the veranda. Over the sound of the rain, he whistled loud and long until a man appeared at the bunkhouse door. He shouted to the cowhand across the yard, "Will two of you come and get this door put back up, Tom? Can't have the house get cold, not with my new boy in here."

The man in the doorway waved back and shouted, "Right away, boss."

Beaming despite two purpled eyes and a swollen nose, Kase Storm walked back inside and poured himself a cup of strong black coffee. His expression sobered as he pointed to two empty chairs at the table, took in Buck and Annika with a glance, and said bluntly, "You two sit down. We need to talk."

Annika held her breath, certain that Buck would bristle at her brother's authoritative tone. She didn't think she could watch the two of them come to blows. Instead, when Buck immediately pulled out a chair for her and waited for her to sit down, she simply stood and gaped at him.

ॐ 24 ॐ

"**A** NNIKA?"

She glanced up at Kase, read the impatience in his eyes, and plopped down onto the chair Buck was still holding for her. Buck chose a chair opposite her brother's. He leaned back, hooked an arm over the back of it, and appeared resigned to listen to whatever Kase had to say.

"Coffee?" Kase asked.

Buck shook his head. Annika declined, glancing from Buck to Kase and back. They reminded her of two titans ready to do battle. Everyone in Busted Heel must still be talking about their fight.

"I know what went on between you and my sister, Scott," Kase said without preamble.

Annika felt her cheeks flame and knew without looking over at him that Buck's eyes were on her. "Kase—"

"Because of what you've done for Rose, and for me, I don't intend to force you into anything." Kase waited until Buck looked at him again. "But under the circumstances, I won't have you under the same roof with my sister tonight. You'll sleep in the bunkhouse."

Because he knew the man was right, because he would have handled the situation in exactly the same way, Buck listened to Kase Storm without uttering a word. He refused to glance over at Annika again but he knew by the riot of color that had stained her cheeks, she was completely embarrassed by her brother's frankness.

There was nothing Buck could say to Kase Storm, no excuse he could give for what had happened at Blue Creek.

320

Staring down at his torn and filthy shirt, the blood stiffened on the front of the plaid fabric, at his scarred, work-worn hands, Buck wondered how he'd ever dared to touch her in the first place.

Even now she looked like a ray of sunshine in the afternoon gloaming. Despite all she'd been through that day, her colorful striped gown was still nearly spotless. Perched as she was on the edge of her chair—all prim and proper like—he could not even believe that she had ever made love with him on his own table. It didn't matter that his memory told him different. Nor could he imagine this new, elegant Annika Storm ever living in his cabin again.

"What did Richard say to upset you?" Kase demanded of Annika.

Buck looked up and watched Kase interrogate his sister. He, too, wanted to know what Thexton had said to upset her so.

Annika, to her credit, drew a deep breath, locked stares with her brother, and told him, "That's something I want to discuss with you later. Right now, since you've insulted both of us, I think Buck and I are entitled to at least one conversation alone. That is, if you are finished upbraiding us like two disobedient schoolchildren."

Buck bit the inside of his lip to keep from smiling. He had to hand it to her: there weren't many women who would have faced up to a man as forbidding as Kase Storm. He watched Storm drain his coffee mug, then surprisingly enough set it down, turn, and walk to the kitchen doorway. "I'm going up to see that Richard leaves immediately, then I'll visit Rose and Joseph. I'll expect to speak to you in the library when your conversation with Mr. Scott is over, Annika."

When he left the room, Annika sighed. Buck could not relax as he stared at her openly for the first time. She remained on edge, perched as if the first loud noise would send her flying. She traced a knothole in the wood on the table. "I'm sorry about my brother's rudeness, especially after all you've done for him today," she said.

"Yeah. I beat him up, broke his door, hit your fiancé. I'd

tally that as a good day's work, all right." His words hinted at humor, but he failed to smile.

Boot heels louder than the rain sounded on the veranda outside as two of the hired hands came across the porch to fix the door. They set their tools down with a clatter and then stared curiously at Buck and Annika as they fit the door in the opening.

"Do they know all about us, too?" Buck asked softly as he watched the men.

"Of course not, and I'm sorry now that I even confided in Kase."

"If he knew what went on, I'm surprised he didn't kill me this morning when he had the chance."

She shrugged. "It looks like you got in one or two good punches yourself. He's really not as bad as he seems."

"You could have fooled me." He licked his cracked lower lip.

While the men on the porch cast suspicious glances their way, Annika stood up and twined her fingers together in front of her striped skirt. "If you come upstairs while I check on Buttons, I'll help you get cleaned up."

He almost declined and denied himself the pleasure of being completely alone with her, but as always where she was concerned, his will gave out and he followed the delicious sway of her skirt as she led the way up the stairs.

She didn't need to warn him to be quiet; he'd heard Buttons protesting her bedtime all the way down the hall when he'd been finishing up with Rose. When they reached the room that Annika shared with Buttons, she opened the door and stood aside so that he could enter first. The child was sleeping on a featherbed amid a mound of bleached and starched embroidered pillows. He tried to read the saying across the closest and wondered if the sewing was her handiwork. As if she guessed what he'd been thinking, she said, "Rose bought them from a woman in town. She can't sew very well either."

"Oh." The frilly atmosphere was so foreign to him, he felt lost. It made Buck want to run for cover.

He stood uncomfortably in the center of the room, afraid to move and wake up Buttons, unwilling to even perch on the edge of the bed or the chaise near the window and smear dirt on the clean upholstery or eyelet bedding. He wanted to touch Buttons, smooth back the riot of curls that kissed her pink cheeks and feel the satin ribbon that adorned the neck of her stark white nightgown, but she was sleeping so blissfully with her old wooden doll clutched in her arms that he dared not.

Instead, he looked away and took in the abundance of toys scattered about the hooked rug on the floor. A well-dressed doll with bisque head and arms was seated on a child-sized rocker in the corner surrounded by small wooden animals around a toy Noah's ark. He reached down and picked up a book that lay on the table beside the bed. *The Brownies, Their Book*, he read before he flipped it open and stared down at the peanut-shaped little men that adorned the pages.

"She loves those stories," Annika said, startling him. He snapped the book closed and carefully set it down. While he waited, she poured water from a pitcher into a washbowl and then dipped a clean towel into the tepid water.

"Sit down." She indicated the chaise.

"I don't think—" His response was a whisper accompanied by a shake of his head.

"Please. Let me help you."

He did as she asked, hoping she would touch him. As she moved close to stand beside him, his senses ran riot. The rustle of her silk petticoat jangled his nerves. She smelled like rose water while the warmth of a spring day emanated from her like captive sunshine. He held his breath as she reached out and pressed the wet towel to his battered face, touching it here and there as lightly as the wings of a dove might brush against the sky.

He felt her hesitate before she pressed the cloth against his lips, and when she did, he closed his eyes and imagined that the soothing moisture was from her kiss.

When he opened his eyes, he discovered hers were but inches from his own. Blue on blue, they were gazing back at him as if she were seeking out the secrets hidden in the very depths of his soul. He longed to hold her, but found her as untouchable as a priceless museum piece. An unbearable ache made him long to get away.

When he pulled away from her touch, she immediately stepped back.

Annika wadded up the towel in her hands to hide their trembling. She had nearly kissed him while his eyes were closed. What would he have done if she had? Buck still had not explained the reason behind his sudden appearance. Had he come for her? She could see him poised and ready to get away. Annika didn't think she could bear the thought of seeing him walk out the door.

"Did you find the buttons I left?" The moment the words were out, his face darkened, the expression behind his eyes shuttered until it grew cold and hard. It was the wrong thing to ask.

"I did. But I don't need your charity."

"What are you talking about?"

"I thought you left them behind as payment."

She wrinkled her brow. Her trembling had subsided, but she still didn't trust herself to free her hands. She twisted the towel and then began to fold it. "Payment? For what? I left them so you'd know I didn't leave of my own free will. Clemmens and his men didn't give me time to write a note. They made me pack up Baby and our things and go. I thought when you saw the button tin that you'd know I would never willingly leave it behind."

"I thought you left on your own," he admitted.

Annika was stunned. "How could I?"

He shrugged. "I wasn't in much shape to ask myself that question."

At first she took his statement to mean that he was upset about her leaving. "What do you mean, not in any shape?"

"Nothing."

"Buck . . ."

"I didn't get home until late that night. I met up with that mountain lion I had told you about."

She twisted the carefully folded cloth again. "Were you hurt? How badly?" He didn't seem scarred in any way that she could see, aside from the cuts and bruises he'd sustained in the fisticuffs with Kase.

"Got me in the leg. I took fever and probably would have died if Old Ted hadn't come along."

It was true she hadn't really studied his walk, for he'd followed her up the stairs. Earlier, in Rose's room, her mind had been elsewhere. Speechless, she slowly lowered herself to the chaise beside him. The minute she sat, he stood up.

"You could have died and I would never have known." Her voice was so soft it was barely audible above the sound of the rain.

He limped across the room and stood with his back to the window. Even the soft glow from the lamp on the side table couldn't dispel the evening gloom. "Would you have cared?"

Realizing that he could be wounded frightened her more than she would have guessed. He was mortal, after all. Annika was on her feet in an instant. "Buck Scott, what are you talking about?" Thankful Buttons was not a light sleeper, she lowered her voice again anyway. "I told you the last time I saw you that I loved you. My feelings haven't changed." Taking a deep breath, she steeled herself and delivered the questions that had plagued her since she'd laid eyes on him. "Have yours?"

He couldn't lie. But he couldn't tell her the truth, either. It would complicate things, so he said, "No. I still want what's best for you and Buttons. I came to see her. To see if she was happy."

Annika weighed his words. "So you didn't come for me?" Framed by the weak light from outdoors, his blond hair shone where the lamplight caught the highlights. His eyes narrowed in thought as he stared back at her. She was desperately afraid of what he would say next.

"Look around you, Annika. Wake up to the way life really is. I can't give you half of what you already have. You and I are from two different worlds and any idea I might have had to the contrary was a damn crazy one." He ran his hand through his hair and then shook the long blond curls against his shoulders. Placing his hands wide apart on the windowsill, he leaned back and rested his hips against it. "Coming here has only reconfirmed what I've known from the beginning. Seeing the proof for myself, I know you'd never adjust to living with me in the mountains. But now I do know that

Buttons can adjust to another way of life. She'll have everything she deserves."

"Buck, it looks like that now, but she cried herself to sleep asking for you for the first two weeks we were here."

"But she's forgotten that now." He paused, as if afraid to say what he thought, then added, "I'd rather she not live with you and Thexton, though."

"That's over now. Besides, how can you think I'd even consider marrying him?"

"He'd be a fool not to want you."

She crossed the room and stood directly in front of him. "Tell me you don't love me."

"Don't do this, Annika. Let it go."

She was tempted to tell him about the baby now that she was almost certain she was pregnant. For a moment she was tempted—it would be a way to keep him by her side—but she didn't want Buck that way, not trapped like one of the animals he hunted. He had to want to come to her of his own free will, had to want her without the flimsy excuse that he wasn't good enough, that their worlds were too far apart to bridge even by love.

Turning aside before he could see her tears, she walked to the washbasin and set the towel down beside it. "I think you had better go before I make a fool of myself."

"Annika . . ."

She heard his footsteps, could feel him standing behind her, hovering there, waiting for her to turn around. She gripped the towel rack on the washstand so hard she thought it might snap.

He said, "I'll spend the night in the bunkhouse."

Barely able to choke out a reply, she straightened, but did not turn around. "Will you say good-bye to Buttons tomorrow?" *Will you say good-bye to me?*

He paused in the doorway and glanced once at the child asleep on the bed. "I can't."

Annika watched his reflection in the window, saw him lean down and kiss Baby Buttons tenderly on the cheek. She closed her eyes against the sight and the intense pain that accompanied it.

* * *

ANNIKA met Kase in the library after she had given the hired hands a supper of cold chicken and fried potatoes. The meal was nothing compared to the ones Rose usually prepared, but it was edible and no one went hungry. Buck hadn't appeared with the others, although casual questioning revealed he had indeed taken a bed for the night in the bunkhouse. Terrified that he would leave before she could talk to him again, Annika thought about taking him a covered dish later in the evening. When Kase came in and told her he wanted to see her in his library immediately, Jim volunteered to take Buck his dinner and Annika could think of no plausible reason to refuse to let him.

She followed her brother down the hall and stepped into the cool dark room. While he lit the lamp, Annika looked around. Kase's library was reminiscent of her father's with its wall-to-wall bookshelves, massive burl wood desk, and stuffed chairs. The shelves were not all lined with books, not yet, but there were family photographs of the Storms beside Rosa's family in Italy. Annika picked up a small silver frame and stared down at a photograph of Kase and her that had been taken when she was six, the year before he went off to school. The picture reflected their personalities—she sat posed on a small wooden wagon, her head tipped to her shoulder, smiling gaily into the camera, while Kase stood beside her protective, proud, and unsmiling. They were holding hands.

Her anxiety fled as she set the picture down. Kase had always loved her. He would see her through her dilemma. Annika turned to face him, and found him seated on the corner of his desk, one leg up across his knee. He was waiting for her to begin.

"How's the baby?"

"Fine. Rose fed him for the first time. He's doing well."

"Have you definitely decided on the name Joseph?" She was stalling. She knew it. He knew it.

He obliged her. "Joseph Caleb Storm, after Rose's father and mine."

It was the opening she needed. "Will you tell me the truth if I ask you some very personal questions?" He tensed; she saw it in the way he shifted and straightened his shoulders.

"Why don't we start with the reason we're here?" he countered. "I want to know what Richard Thexton said to you that made Buck Scott tear into him like that. Or is it just Scott's habit to hit first and ask questions later?"

She ignored his last comment. "Richard said that blood will tell. That he was glad he found out I had such a wild streak before we married."

Kase stood up but didn't move away from the desk. Stone faced, he waited for her to go on.

"He said people in Boston have gossiped about our mother for years"—she took a deep breath and forced herself to repeat Thexton's cruel words—"that everyone speculated over whether she had whored for Indians or not. They think that's the reason she married a half-breed. He said everyone wonders where you really came from. No one's ever told me, either. I just want to know the truth."

His face took on a terrible darkness she had never seen before. With his hands clenched into fists at his side, Kase stared down at her, his exotic features at odds with the stateliness of the library. "Sit down."

The two words shattered her more than anything he might have said, because she assumed by his tone that it was all true. Just as stubborn as he, she remained standing. "Tell me."

Kase took a deep breath. "Our mother was raped by reservation renegades when she was sixteen. Most of her family was killed. Her younger sister and brother were taken captive and eventually chose the Sioux way of life. She found herself pregnant, but she refused to give me up despite the rejection she faced at the hands of her own Dutch kinsmen. The rest you know. Caleb met her when she was living in a sod house outside Pella, Iowa. They were married a short time later and he adopted me. I was five. You were born the next year."

Annika tried to picture her mother at sixteen, facing the loss of her family, enduring rape and the birth of a child conceived during the vicious attack. "To think that all these years I've thought of the story of her house on the prairie and Papa's meeting her as a fairy tale. My God. Poor mother." Then she looked up at her brother, her lifelong protector and friend. Needing a tangible connection between them, she reached out and took his hand. "At least you really are my half brother, Kase. When Mama and Papa would never tell me the truth, I quit asking because I was afraid to find out that they had adopted you."

He pulled her close and hugged her. "When I learned the truth, I didn't want them to tell you. We all thought it would upset you too much, because after all, you were only fourteen then. Mother, understandably, can't and won't talk about the rape. In fact, they would never even have told me if I hadn't forced it out of Caleb."

When she spoke, her words were muffled by his shirt. "That's why you left home so abruptly?"

He nodded. "Suddenly I didn't know who or what I was. My anger had always been hard to control, I couldn't stand the intolerance I faced in Boston, so I learned to fight it with my fists. Then, when I heard the truth, I was afraid I was becoming exactly like the man that fathered me."

She pulled back to look up at him. There was no doubt in her heart or mind when she said, "That's impossible. I can't believe how I could have walked so blithely through life ignoring what was going on all around me."

"It's easy to understand. Mother and Caleb made certain you were insulated. You were always with the two of them or with Ruth. Then there were all the years of schooling. Richard is your first close contact with Boston society, and in a way, I'm glad Thexton's brought it all out into the open."

"I'm just thankful I didn't marry him."

Kase smiled for the first time. "So am I. I think you know now why I was so certain Mother would understand your . . . predicament. Even if you are pregnant, Annemeke, she and Caleb will stand by you. So will I, and if you want us to, Rose and I will raise your child, and Buttons, too, for that matter."

Annika stepped away from Kase and walked around to the back of his desk before she turned to face him. "Is it already that apparent to you that Buck won't marry me?"

"What did he say when you talked to him alone?"

Tears threatened, but she fought them back. "He said he

only came here to see about Buttons, to see if she was happy."

"He's lying."

Annika grasped at the thin straw of hope his words offered. "Do you think so?"

"I know so. After the beating I gave him, anyone who didn't really love you would have hightailed it out of here. When we were in jail in Busted Heel he asked me if you had married Richard."

"In jail?"

Kase smiled and shrugged. "You know how cantankerous Zach can be. It was his idea of a joke to lock us up together. Anyway, I think Buck came here intending to keep you from marrying Richard, which leads me to believe he wants to marry you himself."

Annika folded her arms. "He told me he didn't want Baby Buttons to live with us if I did marry Richard."

"Didn't you tell him the engagement is off?"

"Yes, and I told him I still love him." She took a deep breath and met her brother's eyes. "But it didn't matter. He thinks we're from two different worlds and that it would come between us."

"He may be right."

"What about you and Rose? You are both as different as night and day, but your marriage has worked." She rubbed her arms to ward off the night chill that had crept into the unheated room. "I know Buck doesn't appear to be much more than a trapper, but he has a gentle, loving heart, and as you saw today, he has a gift for healing. With a year or two of training Buck would make a wonderful doctor. He's a stubborn man, Kase, as stubborn as you, but I love him."

"It doesn't matter to me what he is, even if he used to be a buffalo hunter. The thing is, he put us through hell when he took you off that train, Annika." He ran his hand through his hair and then shook the raven strands back over his shoulder. "Did you tell him you think you might be pregnant?"

Unwilling to admit that she was more certain than ever that she was, Annika shook her head and said, "No. I don't want him if I have to get him that way." She walked back to his side and stood next to him. "I'm afraid I'll lose him before I change his mind. He said he's leaving in the morning."

Kase put his arm around her shoulder and walked her across the room. "You know I'll do anything I can to help." Before he opened the door he paused and frowned for a moment. Then he added, "If you need more time, I think I can arrange to keep Mr. Scott here a while longer."

STRETCHED out on his bunk with his hands behind his head, Buck lay wide awake after a sleepless night and stared at the ceiling. Beneath the covers he was still dressed and ready to leave before the first light of day slipped above the horizon. The uneven racket of the men snoring in the beds lined up against the bunkhouse wall had not kept him awake as much as thoughts of Annika and Buttons had. Every time he shut his eyes he imagined Annika dressed in her finery, smiling at him with love shining in her eyes, or he saw Buttons playing on the floor of her new room surrounded by her toys.

He swung his legs over the side of the bed. Impatience brought him to his feet. He straightened the bedcovers, fluffed his pillow, and then pulled his saddlebags out from under the bed. Planning to creep into the barn and saddle his horse before anyone else was about, he knelt on one knee and drew his rifle from beneath the bed and cradled it in his arm. A sudden draft whirled through the bunkhouse. Buck turned toward the door.

Kase Storm stepped inside and looked straight at him.

Buck swallowed.

"I need your help," Kase said.

It was the last thing in the world Buck had expected the man to say. He thought Storm had come to throw him off the ranch before Annika was awake, then he thought of Rose. "Is your wife all right? The baby?"

"They're fine."

The men in the room began to rouse themselves from sleep. A young man with a drooping handlebar moustache that covered his entire upper lip sat up bleary eyed. "What's up, boss?"

"Someone left the buffalo corral open and about half the

herd is missing. Wake the rest and be ready to ride in five minutes."

The young hand quickly pulled on his trousers and began to rouse the others as Kase continued to watch Buck. "Can you ride with us? I'll need all the help I can get and I don't think four men will do it."

Buck weighed the consequences. If he stayed, he'd be forced to come back in broad daylight and risk the chance of seeing Annika again. He would have to say good-bye to Buttons. Tempted to tell the man no and let Kase Storm round up his own buffalo, Buck lifted his saddlebags to his shoulder.

"Well?" Storm tried to block his exit.

Buck met him eye to eye. If he stayed he would spend hours in the saddle debating the same questions he thought he had settled last night.

If he stayed he might change his mind.

"I need an answer," Storm said as the other men fumbled into their clothes, pulled on their boots, grabbed coats and hats, and then began to file out the door.

If he stayed he'd have one more day with her.

"What the hell," Buck grumbled under his breath. "I'll go with you."

❧ 25 ❧

W IPING her hands on a gingham apron that covered her
tartan wool gown, Annika blew a strand of hair out of
her eyes and then reached for the apple pie on the kitchen
cabinet. Step after careful step in yellow kid boots, she
crossed the room, set the pie on top of the stove, and opened
the oven door. Then, taking great care not to spill its contents, she slid the pie plate into the oven and closed the door.
A glance at the clock told her it was one-thirty.

Rose told her that morning that Kase had taken the men
out to round up missing buffalo and that he had intended to
ask Buck Scott to join him. The men were still gone, so
whether or not he had succeeded she didn't know. Her
nerves were near the breaking point.

Household chores had kept her hands occupied even
though her mind was constantly on Buck. She had carried a
breakfast tray up to Rose early that morning and again at
midday. When Rose grew tired of wrestling with a fussy
baby, Annika had rocked Joseph in her arms and walked the
floor with him. The task gave her an excuse to go from window to window and watch for the men. Then, there was Buttons to bathe and chicken to fry, biscuits to bake and gravy to
stir up for the men's dinner. She was proud of her efforts, for
the chicken was as golden brown and tender as any Rose had
ever made.

The apple pie had been her own idea, and throughout detailed instructions issued from Rose's bedside, Annika took
notes and then hurried downstairs to carry them out. Now

333

the pie was in the oven and she had a few moments to herself while both little ones and Rose were napping.

Annika took off her apron, hurried up to her room, and sat down at the oak secretary with the drop-leaf front. She set out her inkwell and journal and began a new entry.

> *May 2, 1882*
> *I can't help but feel that today will be a momentous day in my life, for one way or the other, my future with Buck Scott will be decided. If only Auntie Ruth were here, I would have her chart the stars and tell me what she sees. Perhaps I'm waiting for Buck to return with Kase, only to learn he left here this morning without so much as a good-bye.*
> *Until I lost my heart to him I never fully understood the pain behind the words of Mrs. Browning's lines,*
> *Go from me. Yet I feel that I shall stand*
> *Henceforward in thy shadow. Nevermore*
> *Alone upon the threshold of my door*
> *Of individual life, I shall command*
> *The uses of my soul, nor lift my hand*
> *Serenely in the sunshine as before . . .*
> *Now I do know the pain of parting, just as I've learned I will survive, but I fear my broken heart will never mend if indeed he has left me.*

The sound of horses' hooves in the stable yard drew her attention. She lay down her pen, ran to the window, and pushed aside the flounced curtain. The afternoon sun shone on muddy ground churned up by half a dozen horses. She held her breath as she searched the group and suddenly felt her heart begin to pound. Buck's broad shoulders and height were unmistakable. He dismounted at the barn, stood with his reins in his hand, and glanced up toward the house. Kase stood beside him. Even though she couldn't hear what he was saying to Buck, it appeared her brother was trying to talk the other man out of leaving. Finally, she saw Buck nod, and then, when he followed Kase into the barn, Annika turned and hurried out of the room.

She raced downstairs to the kitchen, checked on the pie

that bubbled and filled the air with a heady cinnamon-apple scent. She pinched her cheeks to bring color to them, smoothed down her skirt, and tied on her apron. When boot heels sounded on the veranda, she nearly dropped the stack of dishes she was carrying to the long trestle table in the middle of the room.

Her brother walked in first. She glanced nervously at him and smiled, then looked down at the table, intent on her task while the men hung their coats and hats on the wall pegs near the door. Buck walked in behind them.

"We're starved," Kase said, his voice overloud and far too jovial.

She paused long enough to look at him but not at Buck. "Did you get all the buffalo?"

"Every last escapee."

"How did they get out?"

He looked like he wanted to choke her. "I don't know, Annika. They just did."

Too late, she remembered his promise and knew her brother had let his precious buffalo loose so that he might keep Buck there a while longer. For her.

She smiled at Kase and then set down the last plate. "I'm glad you got them all."

"Me too. Believe me." He grabbed a whole apple from a bowl of fruit on the counter and headed toward the door. "I'm going to run up and see Rose and the baby."

"I'll fix a tray for you both so you can eat with her."

"Thanks." Kase smiled, taking her newfound ease in the kitchen for granted. He spoke to the youngest of the group, a lanky youth of seventeen. "Dickie, don't dawdle over your meal. When you're through, come upstairs. I've got a little errand I want you to go on."

Buck watched Annika in silence, and followed the men's lead as they pulled out the long benches and chairs around the table and took their seats. They talked jovially among themselves, laughing at the ups and downs they'd encountered during the buffalo roundup. There had been times during the day when he'd wondered how Kase Storm had succeeded as a rancher for the last five years. The man did more to spook the buffalo than gather them, and for a mo-

ment or two on the range Buck wondered if Kase had been
trying to delay his departure.

While the others sat talking and laughing, waiting for
Annika to serve them, Buck fidgeted in his chair, then stood
up. She was ignoring him, that much was evident, and he
didn't like the chill he felt whenever she turned a cold shoulder to him. He felt the other men's eyes on him as he crossed
the room and stood behind Annika who was piling fried
chicken on a platter. He ignored the men and tried to keep his
eyes on her instead. It was an easy task he'd set for himself.

"Can I help you?" he asked softly.

"No, thank you."

"What's wrong?" he whispered.

"I thought you had left without a word." Turning away
from him, she carried the chicken to the table and handed it
to Dickie who began to pile some on his plate. Annika ladled
boiled potatoes and carrots out of a Dutch oven.

"I was going to," he admitted.

"What stopped you?"

"Your brother needed help."

As soon as his words were out, she turned her ice blue
eyes on him. "At least you're honest," she snapped.

Again he was treated to the sight of her back as she carried
the vegetables to the table. When she returned to the cabinet
she said curtly, "You'd better sit down or you'll miss getting
anything to eat."

"Did you cook all this yourself?"

"I did." When her pride mingled with defiance, she
couldn't help but lift her chin a little. Just wait until he saw
the pie—

With a startled cry, Annika ran to the stove, grabbed the
holders from a hook on the wall, and jerked open the oven
door. The pie was a darker gold, the crust a bit crisper than
she would have liked, but the dessert was more of a success
than she had hoped. When she set it on top of the stove and
closed the oven door, Dickie called out, "That pie sure looks
fine, Miss Annika. Is it apple?"

She couldn't help but glance at Buck to watch his expression when she said, "Yes. And I made it myself."

"Looks every bit as good as Mrs. Storm's," Tom assured her.

"Thank you." She beamed at him.

Buck wanted to wipe the grin right off the other man's face. He paced back to the table. A loud thump on the floor of the room overhead caused all of them to look up. The sound was followed by crying and a call for "Ankah" to come up. Her hands full, Annika turned to Buck. "Could you go up and bring Buttons down?"

Buck could feel the men's eyes on him as he left the room and was glad to get away from their scrutiny. They'd been watching him all day, probably speculating among themselves as to what was going on between him and the boss's sister. Kase had kept him by his side all day, encouraged him to "at least stay for dinner." Now he was trapped in a net of his own weaving. He could hear Buttons crying. He immediately walked down the hall and opened her door. "Hello, Baby. What's the matter?"

When Buttons saw it was Buck, she dropped her new doll and ran across the room. She squealed when he lifted her high over his head.

"Go home now, all right?" Buttons, wearing a navy dress with a middy collar adorned with red stars, nodded rapidly in answer to her own question.

His smile faded. "Nope. Time to eat. You hungry?"

"Me go home. And Ankah, too."

"Let's go eat instead," he said, knowing how Buttons could be once she got on a subject and wouldn't let it go. As he shifted her to his hip, he tried to ignore the familiar weight in his arms.

When he stepped into the hallway, he met Kase coming up the back staircase carrying a tray laden with food. Kase Storm paused, nodded at Buck, smiled at Buttons, and disappeared into the master bedroom. Buck headed downstairs.

SHE noticed his limp again the minute he walked back into the kitchen and realized his wound must have been far worse than he had let on.

Annika watched with concern as Buck pulled out a chair.

He sat down with Buttons on his lap and pulled his plate toward him.

"We saved you some," Dickie volunteered, shoving the platter of fried chicken toward Buck.

Buck nodded at the same time he wondered why Annika was staring at him so intently. He let Buttons pick out the piece of chicken they would share, heaped his plate with vegetables, broke open biscuits and smothered them in chicken gravy, and then settled down to eat.

She pulled out a chair and sat across from him. "Want me to hold Buttons so you can eat?"

"No!" Buttons yelled.

Annika almost smiled. It wouldn't be as easy for him to get away from the child as he might have thought. Now, if only she could find time to convince him that they belonged together, that with her beside him he could become anything he wanted.

The other men downed their meals in silence, intent on the food as they shoveled it down as if they were starving. She picked at a plate of vegetables, toyed with a chicken wing, and somehow got through the meal without staring at Buck Scott. When the others were finished, Annika cleared the table, served up the pie and coffee, and then waited as one by one the men complimented her as they left the table and went back to their chores. Finally, when she was alone with Buck and Buttons, Annika poured herself a cup of coffee and tried to think of something, anything, she could say to ease the tension between them.

"Go home?" Buttons asked again.

Annika felt her heartstrings tighten. She longed to ask, Yes, can we? but she refused to invite herself.

"Want some more pie?" Buck tried to divert Buttons's attention. She shook her head no so hard she set her curls bobbing.

"You were limping," Annika said.

He looked at her. Finally. "When I get tired my leg hurts. All that riding around in circles today didn't do it much good." He took a sip of coffee. "If I didn't know better, I'd think your brother didn't know what he was doing out there today."

"He's new at this."

"Yeah. Right."

"I'm glad you stayed to help."

"This won't work, Annika. No matter how many buffalo get loose, chickens you fry, or apple pies you bake."

"You won't even give it a chance?"

"Not at your expense."

"Why don't you let me worry about me?"

He rubbed his hand over his beard and then through his tousled curls. Buttons squirmed on his lap. He set her on her feet. She walked over to Annika and tugged on her apron until Annika lifted her onto her lap.

"We go home?"

"No." Annika shook her head. "Buck says we have to stay here."

"No!" Buttons began kicking the edge of the table.

With a helpless glance at Buck, Annika let Buttons climb down again. She ran off toward the parlor.

"Will she be all right?" His gaze followed the child.

"There are some toys and books in there for her. She'll play alone for a while; she's good at that." She fingered the hem of the tablecloth, folding and refolding it, pressing it with her fingernail. "I'm not going back to Boston."

He shook his head. "You'll change your mind."

A half smile curved her lips. She'd never go back, not now. She'd changed too much. She belonged here, if not with him, then near him. His child belonged here. She shook her head. "I don't think so."

"What will you do?"

"What do you care?" she said softly, purposely trying to push him to anger. Anything was better than his silence.

When he slammed his palms against the table, she jumped. Dishes rattled; a water glass fell over, spilling the remains of its contents. "I care, dammit. I care too much or I'd already have left here by now." He was glaring at her, his eyes blue shards of ice as they bore into hers. "My life was just fine before you came along. I had my cabin, my work, I knew who I was and what I had to do."

"You seem to have conveniently forgotten that you went

looking for a wife and mother for Buttons and now that you've found one, you don't want her," she snapped back.

"I can't afford her!"

Furious, Annika stood up and pushed back her chair. She leaned on the table, so close to his face that he was forced to meet her eyes. "I didn't want to tell you this, because I know how you'll react, but I have enough money to last me for the rest of my life. What you need to do is swallow your stubborn pride and face the truth. I can support us while you go to school and become a doctor if that's what you want to do. If not, I'll give every penny to my brother if that's what it takes to make you happy."

He slammed his palms down again and pushed himself to his feet until they were nose to nose. "Do you think *that* solves the problem? You want me to be a kept man?"

"No, I do not."

"You do, too! You're dangling medical school in front of me so you can buy me as easily as you do a new dress or hat or pair of shoes."

She slapped him. Hard.

He grabbed her shoulders, but the table between them prevented him from doing more than shaking her slightly.

"Well, this is a delightful scene."

They both turned in unison and found Kase standing in the doorway.

Buck let go of Annika.

She faced her brother just as defiantly as she had Buck. "Can't we have even a *minute* of privacy here?"

"With all the yelling I didn't think this discussion was secret."

Buck strode to the back door and paused while he took down his hat and coat.

"I wouldn't go anyplace if I were you," Kase warned.

"Am I a prisoner?" Buck dared Kase to stop him.

"No, but there's a buggy pulling up out front and I think the folks in it probably came to see you."

Buck frowned.

"Who is it?" Annika demanded irritably. Wouldn't they ever have more than a few moments alone?

When a loud knock sounded at the front door, Kase started

off to answer it. "Better come with me, Scott," he called out over his shoulder.

Buck cursed beneath his breath, shoved his hat and coat back onto the rack, and stomped after him.

Annika pressed her hands to her burning cheeks and sighed.

Then she followed the men to the front hall.

BUCK stood behind Kase Storm as he opened the front door. "Hello, Leonard," Kase called out. "What brings you over this way?"

Buck knew what had brought Storm's neighbor to his doorstep. Seated in the buggy beside the well-dressed rancher who swung down off the high seat was Mary MacGuire, the old woman he paid to care for Patsy and beside her sat Patsy herself. Although he hadn't seen his sister for nearly three years now, there was no mistaking her. Thick blond hair that fell to her hips in waves was partially covered by a poke bonnet that tied beneath her chin. Patsy was thinner than he remembered, her long arms and legs concealed by the sleeves and skirt of her dress, but her swanlike neck and hollow cheekbones bespoke that thinness. She was dressed in faded calico, a dress he didn't recognize, and a wool capelet.

Buck felt Annika's presence when she moved to stand beside him and almost forgot himself as he started to slip his arm about her waist. He caught himself before he did, thankful that she did not seem to notice.

Annika paid him no mind, for she was curiously watching the occupants of the carriage as they alighted one by one. "Who are they?" she asked her brother.

"That's Leonard Wilson," Kase explained. "His ranch borders mine. I've never met the women."

"I have," Buck said.

Annika turned to Buck and noticed his blanched coloring and the intent way he was watching the emaciated blond woman with the regal air following the other two up the stairs. She immediately knew without asking that it was his sister—there was only one woman in the world who could look so much like both Buck and Buttons.

"That's Patsy, isn't it?" she whispered.

He merely nodded, never taking his eyes off his sister.

Hearing the commotion in the hallway, Buttons ran in from the parlor and tugged on Buck's pant leg. When he didn't respond immediately, she turned to Annika, who quickly lifted her up.

Kase and Wilson exchanged pleasantries. Mary MacGuire was introduced to Kase and then Annika, who studied the older woman for a long silent moment. She had never seen such a character before. The woman's face was burned as dark as a berry by the sun and as lined as dry ground in late summer. Her hair was so thin that it was nothing more than gray wisps sticking straight out around her head. She clenched a thin cigarillo tightly between her teeth and squinted through the smoke. Even more amazing, Mary MacGuire was wearing a pair of trousers and a man's leather vest and overcoat.

Buck had hired Mary to care for Patsy, but as Annika compared the two, she thought Mary looked far crazier than her charge. But then, appearances had proved to be all too deceiving of late. Patsy stood without looking at any of them as she studied the ceiling of the veranda. Neatly gowned and wearing a poke bonnet and short wool cape, she paid none of the others any mind until finally it was time to introduce Patsy Scott. Mary MacGuire placed her hand on Patsy's elbow. Patsy scowled down at Mary and shrugged free, then resumed her regal stance, this time staring Buck right in the eye. " 'Pray you stand farther from me,' " Patsy ordered him.

Annika watched the exchange. Patsy's odd tone sent chills down her spine. Buck held his breath and placed himself between Annika and Patsy. From what he could tell, Patsy wasn't any more sane than the last time he'd seen her; she still thought she was the Egyptian queen, was still quoting from Shakespeare's *Antony and Cleopatra*.

Ever the host, Kase calmly said, "Shall we all go in?"

The strange party made its way into the front hall. Annika remained firmly planted beside Buck with Buttons held tightly in her arms. Kase looked from Buck to Annika to Patsy. He cleared his throat and suggested Mary and Leonard accompany him to the kitchen for a cup of coffee. "What do you think, Mrs. MacGuire?" he asked the older woman.

Mary gave Patsy a look of warning. "Behave yourself now, your highness, you hear?"

Patsy ignored her as she stared at a point over Annika's shoulder.

Uncertain what his sister would do, or what she was capable of, Buck braced himself for a scene. "Maybe you should take Buttons to the kitchen," he said aside to Annika.

"Buttons is her child, Buck. She should have the chance to see her," Annika whispered back. Then she spoke directly to Patsy. "Shall we all go in the parlor?"

Patsy stared at Buck as if she had not heard a word Annika had said. She raised her head and in a clear, loud voice said to him, "O, never was there queen so mightily betrayed! Yet at the first I saw the treasons planted."

Buck's voice was filled with sadness. "I had to do it, Patsy. I had to see that you were safe for your own good and the baby's."

"Thou art turned the greatest lair," Patsy said bitterly.

Annika watched the strange exchange, saw the faraway look in Patsy Scott's eyes, and hugged Buttons closer. The child was arrested by the sight of the woman who looked so like her uncle and spoke in a way that commanded such attention.

Buck glanced up the stairs to the second story where Rose and Joseph slept, then toward the kitchen where he heard Kase talking to Wilson and Mrs. MacGuire. "Let's get out of this hallway and into the parlor."

Annika led the way. Buck waited until he was certain Patsy had followed her. He closed the door behind them. Determined to try to call her attention to Buttons, Annika said, "Patsy, this is Buttons. She's your little girl."

Patsy raised her brow, looked down upon Buttons with disdain, and then coolly said, "The child cannot be mine. Behold! The child born of Egypt was laid in a reed basket and cast upon the waters of the Nile. It is said she dwells now amid the great pyramids."

Buck folded his arms across his chest, determined to show Annika the futility of her efforts. "This is the baby you tried to throw off the roof, Patsy, and if I hadn't stopped you, she'd be dead now."

Stunned by the revelation, Annika stared at Patsy, unable to believe the stiffly composed woman had ever been insane enough to try to kill her own child.

Patsy stared at Buttons and her eyes widened. "All strange and terrible events are welcome, but comforts we despise. Our size of sorrow, proportioned to our cause, must be as great as that which makes it."

"What does that mean?" Annika whispered to Buck.

"She's quoting Cleopatra again."

"I was told to sacrifice the child, for as He called to Abraham, and bid him sacrifice Isaac, I being Egypt could do no less." Patsy's gaze began to shift rapidly back and forth between Annika and Buttons.

Buck turned to Annika. The sadness in his eyes was almost her undoing. "She mixes up stories in the Bible with *Antony and Cleopatra*. Those were the only two books we owned besides the medical almanac."

As if the visit were ended, Patsy abruptly turned toward the door. "Our lamp is spent, it's out!"

Buck turned to Annika, his expression grim. He looked down at his hands, then at her. "I guess you see now why I never told you everything about Patsy or the rest of my glorious family."

"Oh, Buck. It doesn't matter."

"It does to me," he said.

Annika guessed Patsy's sudden arrival had been her brother's doing, one more of his attempts to keep Buck at the ranch. She wished none of it had happened as she saw the deep sorrow on Buck's face.

Patsy stood in front of the parlor door, unwilling to open it herself. "Your honor calls you hence," she said to Buck.

He turned away from Annika and crossed the room to open the door for his sister. "Come on, Patsy. We'll find Mary and you can go home now."

As if he were no more than a servant, Patsy walked past him without acknowledgment.

Annika's knees were shaking when she sank to the settee and laid her cheek against the top of Buttons's head. She tried to blot out the recurring image of Patsy standing on the roof of Buck's cabin threatening to throw the infant off. "I love you, Buttons," Annika whispered as she picked up one of Buttons's books, an alphabet primer.

Buttons smiled up at her. "Me love Ankah."

They read for a few moments, Annika straining to hear the noise from the front hall that would signal the departure of Wilson and the others. She was just about to take Buttons up to visit Rose and Joseph when the rustle of material in the doorway gave her pause. Her heart jumped to her throat when she glanced up expecting to see Buck and found Patsy standing there alone instead.

As casually as possible, Annika stood up holding Buttons and slowly put the settee between herself and Buttons and the other woman.

"Hast thou affection for him?"

Patsy's blunt question startled her, but Annika managed to nod.

"And the child?"

"Yes. I hope you don't mind, Patsy." She wondered whether Patsy answered to her own name or to "Cleopatra."

Patsy glanced back toward the door. Seemingly alive with an energy of its own, her waving blond hair swayed around her shoulders as she moved. She took a step forward until she was close enough to reach out and touch Annika. Only the settee separated them. Patsy looked left and right, her eyes wide like a creature who was being stalked by hounds. What ghosts haunted her mind? And why?

"Give me the child," Patsy said.

Buttons understood the tone of the command and hid her face against Annika's neck. Annika tried to protest. "I don't think—" *Where was Buck. How could Patsy have gotten away from him?* Annika stepped back again.

"*Give her to me!*" Patsy's voice lowered menacingly as she took a step forward. Her fingers curved as she extended her hands toward Buttons.

Footsteps pounded against the floor in the room overhead. Frantic now, Annika glanced at the wall behind her. There was no escaping through the parlor door but there was a window behind her. She prayed it wasn't locked. If she could just get close enough to open it and set Buttons outside, the child could then run around the veranda to the kitchen and alert the others.

Just as Annika backed into the corner and began to turn toward the window, Patsy dropped her hands to her sides and began to speak again. Oddly enough, her eyes held the clarity of sanity as she shook her head and softly said, "You would never understand. You don't know what I saw. I could not live with it forever, and so it is far easier for me to be Egypt than who I was."

As Annika tried to understand, she watched the blue eyes so identical to Buck's glaze over again as Patsy appeared to be looking past Annika into a world of her own.

Buck rushed in the door. He pushed past Patsy and took Annika's hand as he glanced between her and Buttons. "Are you all right?"

"Yes. We're fine."

"One minute she was right beside me and the next she was gone. I heard a noise upstairs and ran to see if she had found Rose and the baby. I should have watched her more closely. If she had hurt you . . ."

Annika heard Wilson and Kase in the hallway. Relieved that Patsy would soon be gone and Buttons would be safe, Annika told him, "Go and tell her good-bye, Buck. We'll go upstairs with Rose."

IT was the longest climb of his life. Buck mounted the stairs slowly, still favoring his injured leg. He found Annika and Buttons in Rose Storm's room, Annika seated on a rocking chair drawn up beside the bed as she talked softly with her sister-in-law. He paused for a moment to stand unnoticed in the open doorway so that he could watch her for what would be the last time. She smiled as she reached down to pat the new baby on its well-padded, blanketed behind.

"Are you feeling all right, Rose?"

"Sí. Thanks to your friend Buck, I am good. So is Joseph. I still think about what might happen to me if he did not come here. I am grateful to him and to you."

Buck saw Annika hesitate, hated the sadness that crept

across her face and darkened her radiant smile. "Yes, I'm
glad he was here to help, too."

Before she could say anything else, Buck cleared his
throat and both women looked in his direction. "I came to
see how you're doing, Mrs. Storm, but it looks like you're
doing fine."

Rose smiled up at him. Her color was good, her eyes clear.
She even looked rested. Rose had twisted her long hair into a
single braid that hung over one shoulder as she lay propped
up against a barrage of pillows. The simple hairstyle reminded him of the way Annika had plaited hers at Blue
Creek before she went to bed at night. It was a far cry from
the upswept hairdo she had assumed now that she had returned to civilization.

"You just tell your own doctor about those stitches,
ma'am, and he'll see to them and take them out when the
time comes."

Rose colored bright red at the mention of such a delicate
matter, but nodded all the same. "*Sí,* I will do this, Mr.
Scott."

He forced himself to cross the highly polished floor, to
tread the thick Persian carpet in the center of the room with
his weathered moccasins to stand close to Annika. He
looked at Joseph and smiled. The little boy was one thing he
could be proud of.

"Will you hold him?" Rose asked.

He heard a soft, choking sound from Annika, but dared
not look at her again. He shook his head and thrust his hands
in his pockets. "No, that's fine. I wouldn't want to upset the
little fellow. Is he eating all right?"

"Like his papa," Rose said with a laugh. "Hungry all the
time."

"From the looks of him, he'll be a tall one." Buck felt out
of his element standing in the cozy atmosphere of the bedroom while he made small talk with another man's wife. He
found himself wanting to turn and walk out the door and out
of the house without a word to Annika Storm, but he knew
he couldn't give in to his cowardice and simply disappear.
He turned to her, found her staring up at him with round blue
eyes filled with hope and love that he knew he didn't de-

serve. Not now. Especially not now, when he knew full well
he was going to leave her.

"Will you walk me out to the barn?" he asked Annika.

The rocker stopped but she continued to stare up at him as
if she were memorizing every bit of him, his unruly hair and
every black-and-blue corner of his face. She didn't answer
him, merely nodded, then stood up and began to walk out of
the room. Annika paused in the doorway and spoke softly to
Buttons. "Stay here with Rose, will you, Buttons, and be
very quiet, because Joseph is asleep."

"Me go, too, Buck?" Buttons looked up from where she
was piling wooden spools into a lopsided triangle.

He turned to Annika for help, but she quickly looked
away. "No, you stay here. Annika will be right back," he
promised the child.

When he turned back to face her, Annika had already disappeared down the hall. He heard her muffled footsteps on
the stairs.

SHE had promised herself she would not cry.

But promises are made to be broken, she decided, as tear
tracks stained her cheeks. The wind blew across the open
land, and because she had forgotten her coat, Annika
wrapped her arms about her and rubbed her hands up and
down to warm herself. She walked ahead of Buck like a condemned man as they approached the barn. Late afternoon
shadows filled the interior of the huge, open building that
smelled of hay, horses, and dust. The men were still working; one could be seen across the stable yard repairing the
broken corral gate. The barn was deserted when Annika
walked inside and moved far enough away from the entrance
so that they would be hidden by shadows.

She refused to say anything more to try to change his
mind. She had already all but begged, and begging was
something she was not about to do. Strength came to her as
she thought of her mother, knowing Analisa would do the
same under the circumstances. Recalling her mother's stand
against the ridicule of her neighbors would keep her own
spine stiff and her hands from reaching out to Buck. He
would remember her for her strength and stubbornness if

nothing else—she was determined of that as she stood waiting in the deepening shadows.

He walked over to the stall where his big-rumped bay was stabled. She waited while he slipped on the bridle and then saddled the horse. It gave her time to wipe her tears and straighten the wisps of hair that had escaped the upswept style. Her fingers touched a dangling hairpin and she shoved it back into place. Glancing down, she noticed her bright yellow button shoes were muddy.

"Annika?" He was standing before her, turning his big hat over and over in his tanned hands.

"Well," she said, drawing in a deep breath, standing straight and tall, "I suppose this is good-bye."

He looked taken aback for a moment, as if he had actually expected her to weep and wail and cling to him. Then he said, "I guess it is."

She held out her hand. "Then I wish you well, Buck Scott. It has been quite an adventure for me. I hope it wasn't all bad for you."

"Annika, I—"

"And there's no need to worry about Buttons." Before he could say or do anything to shake her false courage, she interrupted him. "Rose and Kase have asked to have her, and I'm sure you can see she will have the best home any little girl could want." *As if I could give her up now.* She heard herself speaking in a clear, steady voice and wondered how it could be so when she felt as if she were breaking into millions of tiny cells that would soon dry up and blow away on the Wyoming wind.

It gave her satisfaction to see him fidget with the reins he held loosely between his fingers. She was thankful for the weak light—it helped to hide the tears that still threatened.

"I'm so sorry, Annika. I wish it could be another way."

"No you don't," she said. "If you did, you would believe me when I say I'm willing to try to live wherever you want, instead of telling me you know what's right for me."

He put on his hat. It covered his shining curls and cloaked his face in shadow. He took down his heavy jacket from where he had thrown it over his saddle and shrugged into it.

She raised her hand to touch the curls that fell over the back of his collar but drew it back before he noticed.

He wanted to kiss her good-bye. She knew it by the tension in his stance, his hesitation about leaving.

She wanted his kiss more than life itself at the moment, but she knew it would hurt forever if she let him touch her. This way she stood a chance of forgetting.

Annika stepped back, a silent signal for him to go.

Buck hesitated for a moment more, then walked his horse out of the barn.

She watched him mount up, stood ramrod straight with her arms clutched about her as he rode out of the yard without a backward glance. She could still see the top of his hat and his broad shoulders silhouetted against the sunset as he made his way past the bunkhouse and then the buffalo corral. It was a portrait of times past and present, the buffalo hunter outlined against the setting sun with the last few milling buffalo appearing as dark, nearly undefinable shadows in the foregound.

Annika waited until he was nearly out of sight before she dropped her arms and let her shoulders slump. Then, she picked up her skirt and started running.

Her yellow boots were not made to travel over lumps of last year's dried buffalo grass and mud, but still she ran. Nearly falling facedown in the muddy earth, she let go of her skirt, stepped on the hem, then caught herself. Sobbing openly now, she raced on, away from the setting sun, away from the sight of Buck Scott's silhouette growing smaller and smaller on the horizon, running until she reached the small knoll with the twisted cottonwoods where her brother's babies had been buried.

There, heartbroken, Annika sank to the earth and buried her face in her skirt. She cried for Buttons, who would never see her uncle again, for Patsy with her demented mind, for Buck who had forced himself to give up his niece so that she would have the best life had to offer.

But most of all she cried for herself because Buck Scott had not believed in the power of their love.

26

BUCK kicked his horse and rode toward the blazing orange and gold sky, forced himself to look directly into the sunset, and tried, unsuccessfully, to tell himself that was the reason his eyes burned with unshed tears. The mountain peaks to the northwest—hulking gray shadows against the intense sun—stood hunched together like the humped backs of Kase Storm's buffalo.

Just as she had done since the moment he'd first laid eyes on her, Annika Storm had just surprised him. He had expected her to argue with him one more time, to lay out all the reasons why he should stay and change his ways, take up her foolish notion that he could be educated and pronounced a doctor without a lick of trouble; it would be easier to change a leopard's spots. But she hadn't argued, nor had she asked him to take her with him, and that surprised him, too. She hadn't insisted he say good-bye to Buttons, either.

Hell, come to think of it, she'd practically waved him on his way like a distant relative who had overstayed his visit.

Buck took a swipe at the irritating moisture in his eyes and pulled his collar up against the wind. It might be May, but the nights could get downright cold once the sun set, so he planned to be in Busted Heel by dark. He also planned to be downright drunk within an hour of his arrival.

One thing about getting down-and-out drunk—waking up the next day was a little like being reborn. Everything that had gone on the night before always seemed a little groggier, a little more distant. It was that distance that he craved.

While he had not been paying it any mind the sky had

transformed itself from hues of yellow, gold, and orange to soft reds and pinks with streaks of violet. The underbellies of the high, scattered clouds were tinted red. Movement a mile down the narrow road drew his attention, and as he galloped toward it, the outline of a black buggy took shape against the weakening light. As the buggy drew nearer he slowed his pace, curious who might be heading toward the Storm ranch this time of day.

His initial thought was that it might be Richard Thexton returning to apologize to Annika and try to win his way back into her favor. Buck frowned at the thought. He had relinquished all claim to her when he left, but the thought of pasty-faced, buttoned-up Richard Thexton ever taking his anger and spite out on Annika again would make him turn around in an instant. Even if he couldn't claim Annika for his own, he wasn't about to let Richard take advantage of her.

Buck all but stopped in his tracks as the buggy neared and he was able to make out the shape of a man in a tweed suit trying to negotiate the vehicle over the badly rutted road. When the buggy was but a few yards distant, Buck saw that the man driving was not Thexton. He waited, nearly blocking the road, with one hand resting on his rifle in the fringed scabbard hanging from his saddle. He nudged his horse off the road to make room for the buggy and the driver slowed to a halt. The covered buggy looked weathered and well used.

"Been out to the Storm ranch, by any chance?" The man in the rumpled tweed suit stared up at Buck from behind round spectacles. His curly brown hair stuck out from beneath a bowler hat that had been pulled too far down on his forehead. As he waited for Buck to answer, he grabbed a top coat off the floorboards and set it on the cracked leather seat beside him. Even in the receding light, Buck recognized the black instrument bag that the coat had hidden from view.

"You the doctor?" Buck asked.

"That I am. Doctor Richard Earhart. On my way to see Mrs. Storm. You been out to the ranch looking for work?"

Buck could tell by the quick once-over the man gave him that the good doctor doubted someone like Buck might have been visiting the Storms. "Yeah. I been there. Mrs. Storm had her baby yesterday."

Earhart's face fell immediately. "Everything all right? Did it live?"

Buck nodded. "It's a boy—healthy as a horse. You might want to take a look at Mrs. Storm's stitches." He would have given anything just then for a photograph of the doctor's face at that moment.

"Who delivered her?"

"I did."

"And she's fine?"

"Believe it or not."

An unmistakable look of relief washed over the doctor's face. He put his thumb under the brim of his hat and pushed it back off his forehead. "Well, that's great news. Great news! Congratulations in succeeding where I've failed before, young man." He slapped his thighs. "When I rode into Busted Heel and found out Kase had come for me I felt terrible. Nothing to be done for it, though, I had to go clear into Cheyenne for supplies and stop off at three ranches on the way back. Not another doctor around between here and the Montana border. Spend most of my time driving over hill and dale only to do too little too late." He picked up the reins and threaded them through his fingers.

With no reason to linger, Buck kneed his horse away from the buggy.

"What'd you say your name was?" Dr. Earhart called out.

"I didn't, but it's Buck Scott."

"Well, Buck Scott, I could use a good assistant, if for nothing else but delivering babies. It'd free my hands for emergencies."

A chill ran down Buck's spine. If he didn't know better he would have suspected Annika was behind the man's sudden appearance. He looked at the emptiness surrounding them. The sun was completely gone, the land and sky turned gray. "I'm not a doctor," Buck said. "I'm a buffalo man."

Earhart barked out a laugh again. "Since when did that stop anyone west of the Mississippi from doctoring if they had half a mind to? Shoot, I've seen a veterinarian take out an appendix and I knew a seamstress who shoved a man's intestines back in and sewed him up clean as a whistle." He flicked the reins and his horse lurched forward. His coat slid to the floorboards again. As he pulled away from Buck he called out over his shoulder, "It'd beat chasing after buffalo that aren't around anymore, son."

Riding as if all the hounds of hell were after him, Buck kicked his horse again and bent low over his neck, pushing the big bay toward Busted Heel. But even the familiar cadence of hoofbeats and the creaking leather saddle couldn't drown out the doctor's parting words.

"Buy me a drink, mister?"

Buck straightened up, pushed away from bar, and wiped his mouth with the back of his hand. A blond—young in years but wise behind her eyes—stood as close to him as possible and leaned one elbow against the bar. One feathered strap of her frilly lavender chemise dropped low off her shoulder. He didn't say a word, just stared.

"D'you hear me, mister?"

"I heard you," he grumbled. He'd had more than his share of whiskey already, but he was still lucid, still aching. Now, as luck would have it, he was confronted by a half-naked blonde near enough in age and looks to be Annika if he squinted and the light fell across her face just right.

The hair was too different, though. Where Annika's was tawny gold shot with honey-colored strands, this girl's was brassy yellow, frizzled and frowsy, nearly standing on end around her head. It looked like somebody had been chewing on it, and since she looked the type that would let a man pay for anything, someone might have been doing just that.

Buck turned a cold shoulder to her and splayed his elbows on the bar again. He stared down into his whiskey but didn't find any relief floating in the amber liquid. He threw back the drink and looked up, studying the occupants of the barroom in the mirror behind the long bar. He watched the girl's reflection as she shrugged and walked away.

Two of the men near the door looked like drifters. They had an unshaved, unwashed look about them that bespoke homeless wandering. The rest were cowhands, their Levi's worn in the seat and baggy at the knees. One, a tall, lanky man with red hair to his shoulders and a moustache that drooped to his chin, sat on a chair tilted back against the wall, laughing with a group of four others.

No one had paid Buck any mind. To a man they studiously ignored him. He guessed they had heard of or recognized him from his fight with Kase Storm.

Although he had carefully avoided his own reflection, it finally caught his eye as he tipped back the drink. Buck lowered his glass and studied himself. His buckskin jacket and pants marked him as a trapper. His lip was still cut and bruised, but the swelling was gone. A short slash running vertically down his lower lip marked the place where Kase Storm's fist had connected with his mouth. His month-old beard had filled in during his time alone in the mountains. He wondered how long it would take him to grow it as long as Ted's. Years? How many?

How many long and lonely years would it take?

Stop it. You made your choice. It was best for everyone.

He pulled his hat lower to shield the blue loneliness he saw reflected in the eyes that looked back at him from the mirror, but he couldn't hide as easily from the thoughts that plagued him nor the memory of Annika's face when he'd left her.

How does it feel to be the biggest coward alive?

His mood was so foul that if any man in the room had called him out, he would have beat him beyond recognition. But how could he rid himself of his own conscience?

She said she loved you. That she was willing to go anywhere with you.

Back to a run-down cabin at Blue Creek that couldn't hold a candle to what she's used to? Back to doing without and living with nothing?

She said she had money, enough to last her for the rest of her life.

Not enough to carry civilization up the mountain. Not enough to keep her from harm or the isolation that can drive a soul mad. Not enough to buy me.

What's the difference when you'd buy her if you had the money.

He slammed his empty glass down. The stout barkeep

jumped, then hurried over to him. From the nervous glances
he threw Buck's way, Buck knew the man hadn't forgotten
the brawl.

"Another one, mister?"

Buck shook his head. "I'm leaving."

He'd pushed off the bar and turned to go when he noticed
the one-eyed marshal ambling toward him with a bowlegged
gait. He noticed that the man was wearing a pair of moccasins not unlike his own. The marshal made a beeline toward
Buck and leaned on the bar right beside him.

"Rose Storm have her baby?"

Buck nodded. "She did." *She had it because I was there to
save her, because I caught it in my hands and started it
breathing. She's alive because I saved her life and the
child's.*

"Boy or girl?" the old man asked.

"Boy. They call him Joseph."

The marshal summoned the barkeep with a wave. The
man walked over to them. "You owe me four bits, Paddie.
Rosie had a boy."

Buck stepped away from the bar.

"Scott . . ."

He halted at the sound of the marshal's voice and turned
around. "How did you remember my name, old man?"

Zach Elliot stepped up to Buck and kept his voice low because every man in the place was eyeing them. "You're a
hard one to forget. Not a man within a hundred miles of here
don't know you, not after the kidnapping stories in the paper,
not after you showed up and tried to take a piece outta Kase
Storm—"

"He jumped me first."

"That's just details. What I want to know is, what's to become of Annika?"

Glancing over Zach's shoulder, Buck could see the bar-
tender straining to overhear. "You got a bet riding on it?"

Zach rubbed a hand across the lower half of his face and
shrugged. "Not yet."

"Then don't waste your money bettin' on me," Buck said.
He turned his back and left the one-eyed marshal staring after him.

If he rode long and hard, he would reach the base of the Laramies before sunup.

"ZACH brought out a telegram. Mother and Caleb are coming out at the end of the month."

Annika started at the sound of her brother's voice. "Oh, no."

"Oh, yes." Kase couldn't help but notice her red-rimmed, swollen eyes. He was sorry he'd let Buck Scott off with so light a beating. Leaning against the kitchen cabinet, he folded his arms across his shirt front and watched as his sister cut biscuits out of rolled-out dough. "What are you going to do?"

She drew herself up, pushed a strand of hair off her face with the back of her hand, and smeared flour near the faded scar at her temple. "I'm going to tell them what happened and ask them to stand by me. I want to raise Buttons and I'd like to live near you"—she glanced up at him and tried to smile—"if that's all right with you."

"You know it is. You can live with us if you want."

She shook her head. "You and Rose have a family now. And if Rose has her way, there'll be more *bambinos* in this house. I want to do this on my own."

"Like our mother did."

"Like mother."

"Annika, are you hoping Prince Charming will ride up and pass out at your front door the way Caleb did mother's? That's a fairy tale that doesn't happen every day."

She thought of the last vision she'd had of Buck, of his silhouette against the crimson sky. Annika shook her head. "No," she said softly, "no, I'm not hoping that at all." She couldn't tell him that her prince, the one she'd melodramatically compared to Victor Hugo's Quasimodo, had ridden off into the sunset without her. There was no one to wait for now.

The biscuits were cut. She carefully lifted them onto a baking pan and then rolled the scraps of dough into a ball. She sprinkled the cabinet with flour, patted the dough ball flat, and cut out two more biscuits. Brushing her hands off, she lifted the pan and carried it over to the oven, opened the door, and expertly slid the flat pan onto the rack.

As she closed the door, she straightened and walked back to Kase. "Don't feel sorry for me," she told him.

"I just wish it could have been different. I want you to be happy."

Annika shrugged and untied her apron to reveal a creamy yellow silk gown of simple lines. She wore it nearly every day, for it was one of the few near suited for work about the house. "We always want those we love to be happy, don't we? But some things are out of our hands."

"But if only you could have been spared all of this—"

"That would mean I would never have met Buck Scott, never known another side of life or the love we shared for a time. If he hadn't come to town to find me he wouldn't have been here to deliver Joseph." She walked over to the trestle table and looked down at it without seeing the even row of plates that lined both sides or the cutlery laid out for the men's breakfasts. "I can't help but think that this was all meant to be, Kase, no matter how it worked out. Our paths had to cross, Buck's and mine, and now I have to let him go. Maybe he didn't love me enough to stay. Maybe he didn't trust me enough to believe I meant it when I said I would give everything up for him. I know he loved Buttons with all his heart, yet he gave her up so she would be safe and have a chance for a better life. I can always hope he loved me at least half that much.

"In a few months, if God is willing, I'll have his baby, and just like our mother did when she kept you, I will keep Buck's child and cherish it and hope he'll grow up as strong and as proud as his father." The tears she thought had ended began to flow again. "And like you."

HE'D been back at Blue Creek for three days now, awake for two long nights staring at the ceiling, wandering the forest by day, ignoring tracks as he glanced up at snatches of sky between the dark pines. Signs of summer had come. Wildflowers blanketed the meadows; yellow balsam root, monkey flower, and arnica. The pale blues wove a carpet of bluebells, blue gentian, and flax. Reeds and cattails grew along the creek again. Green rushes lined the bank. Great blue herons fished where trout as long as a man's arm skimmed over the rocks and tempted Buck to try to net them in the pools, but when he looked down into the rushing water, he was reminded of Buttons and the day she'd almost drowned.

The song that once hung on the breeze was gone. The meadowlarks had gone mute, or at least he didn't notice their singing anymore. His loneliness was far worse now because he didn't have to guess anymore what Annika's life was like—he'd seen it for himself—seen her smiling at her sister-in-law, watched her in easy conversation with the ranch hands. He knew firsthand the bond between her and her brother, knew how she dressed and saw the wealth she took for granted.

There was no longer any need to imagine. Everything about her was branded on his brain.

One lone lamp lit the room. He stood up, tired of the quiet, and threw the door open to let in the night sounds—the whine of the crickets, the cry of a lone wolf, bullfrogs singing at the moon.

Hands on hips, he stood on the threshold and stared up at the stars that winked back as if they knew what a joke life had played on him. Turning his back on them, he left the door open and paused in front of the mantel. The tins and jars that held his herbs and curative powders lined the heavy timber. He shifted the cans around, arranged them by size. The nearest living soul who might need his help was miles away.

I could use a good assistant, if for nothing else, for delivering babies.

I've seen a veterinarian take out an appendix.

I knew a seamstress once . . .

Buck balled his fist against the mantel and leaned his forehead against it. Was it too late to go back? Was there too much that stood between them?

Money was only one obstacle.

Insanity ran in his family. His pa and Sissy were gone, but Patsy was living proof.

It doesn't matter, Annika had said.

Words and pictures played over and over in his mind: Annika wary of him on the train; Annika dancing with him before the fire; the sight of her as she dragged Buttons out of the stream; her blood running crimson against the snow after she hit her head; most of all he remembered the thrill that swept through him when she gave herself to him in the firelight.

Annika was everywhere he looked. Her memory would haunt him forever.

KASE poured himself a cup of black coffee and out of habit walked to the back door to look out the window at the stable yard. Too late, he remembered there was no longer a window in the door thanks to Buck Scott, and while one was on order from Cheyenne, he found himself staring at a board nailed over the oval opening.

The house was still dark and quiet. The gray light before dawn was his favorite time; he savored seeing those moments when the world stood on the brink of a brand-new day. Greeting the sun was a time for him to give thanks and he was a man with much to be thankful for these days. He was eager to give thanks for Rose, for Joseph, for the abundance in his life. He took a sip of steaming coffee. A good strong cup of the heady brew made greeting the dawn that much easier.

He opened the door, careful not to make a sound that might disturb the sleeping women upstairs. If Annika knew he was up and about she would insist on rushing down to get breakfast started. As much as she tried to hide it, he could see she tired more easily these days and the shadows beneath her eyes only confirmed it.

A sound across the veranda alerted him to a man's presence even before he saw him sitting there in the shadows. Kase braced himself, every muscle ready for an attack. When none came, he looked closely at the silent figure seated in the wicker rocker. The big figure dwarfed the white chair and looked absurdly out of place against the floral patterned cushions. The man held the rocker perfectly still; his hat rested on his knees.

Kase spoke just above a whisper, "What are you doing here, Scott?"

"I came to see Annika."

"To cause her more pain? I'll kill you before I let you do that again."

Buck uncurled to his full height and walked across the distance that separated them. "I came to see if she'll still have me."

"For good?"

"For good or for bad, but I mean to keep her."

Kase didn't say a word as he sized the man up.

"I know you hate me, Storm," Buck said.

"That's beside the point. The problem is, my sister's in love with you."

"Can I see her?"

"She's not up," Kase informed him coolly.

Buck thought of Annika nestled in the deep featherbed, the clean white sheets with their frills and embroidery, remembered her thick blond braid and how it would be neatly draped across one shoulder as she slept—

"Can I go up?" His own words shocked him once they were out. He knew it was an improper request, knew what Storm would say.

Kase surprised him when he nodded.

Buck had to be certain he understood. "I can?"

"I don't see why not. It's too late to worry about you stealing her virginity. You've already done that."

Buck curled his hands into fists but knew it wouldn't do him much good to push Kase Storm any further.

"What if I had told you no, you can't see her?" Kase asked.

"I'd have gone in anyway."

"That's what I was afraid of." Kase took a sip of coffee. "That's why I said yes. So if you're going in, you'd better get before I change my mind."

Buck brushed past Kase and stalked across the veranda. As he disappeared through the open doorway, Kase looked directly at the rising sun and smiled.

BUCK started up the stairs, his feet silent on the carpet runner. When he heard a gasp he stopped dead still and looked up. Annika stood at the landing at the top of the stairs, her bare feet peeking out from beneath her white nightgown. She looked just the way he knew she would, tall and graceful, rumpled from sleep. Her hair was in a braid.

He smiled.

She rubbed her eyes and stared down at him as if he were a ghost.

"Buck?" She whispered his name, glanced over her shoulder toward the master bedroom, and stepped down two steps.

He stepped up one and held his hand out to her. "I had to come back."

Wary now, she whispered, "Why?"

He took her hands in his and looked up at her. "For you. For Buttons."

"But—"

"Is there someplace we can talk?" He glanced back down the stairs, knowing Kase could hear every word they uttered in the stairwell.

"How did you get in?"

"Your brother is on the porch," he told her. "He let me in."

He stood aside and let her pass him on the narrow stairs, tempted to reach out and take her in his arms. He waited. There would be time. All the time in the world, he hoped.

Annika turned away from the kitchen and led him into an alcove beneath the stairs. A hall tree stood on the wall opposite them, the stairway formed the angled ceiling in the small, dark space.

"Talk," she said.

"You look tired," he told her.

She smiled. Had she really expected love words from Buck Scott? "That's not exactly what I've been dying to hear."

"I can't live without you, Annika. I've tried and I can't. I'm willing to be anything you want me to be."

His open sincerity and the power it gave her frightened her. She let go of his hands and crossed her arms beneath her breasts. "I don't want you to be anything but what you are, Buck."

He hung his hat on the hall tree and turned back to her.

"I've been thinking about what you said about me becoming a doctor, you've been pushing me from the beginning—"

"And I'm sorry for that, Buck. I love you. I'll take you just the way you are."

He looked up at the ceiling before he met her gaze. "Let me finish. I always wanted to be a doctor, Annika. It was a dream of mine long before you mentioned it. I grew up watching my ma heal the neighbors and bring their babies into the world. Then, when my pa brought us out West, I had to wake up and let go of my dreams. Sissy and Patsy had to be cared for—Pa insisted I become a skinner as soon as I was old enough to help bring in more money.

"Over time, I forgot about doctoring, but I never forgot what I'd learned. I came by it naturally, helped whenever anyone asked, but as for becoming a real doctor, well . . . my chances ended when Ma left and we headed west."

"And now?" she whispered, daring to hope he might dream again.

"Helping Rose, holding that little boy in my hands, it was a miracle that I helped make happen. When I think about how many others I might help with some real training—"

She grabbed his hands, turned them palms up, and kissed them. "I tried to tell you that you have a special gift, one that time can never steal from you. You are a natural healer, Buck. Just think of what you can do when you're a doctor."

"It'll take a long time, but I have money of my own saved up." When she looked about to protest he cut her off. "I won't take charity."

"Then how about a loan?" She threw her arms around his neck and smiled.

He laid his hand against the small of her back and molded her hips against him. "A loan might be all right. But we'll need official loan papers."

He kissed her then, long and hard, and when she looked up she said, "As many official papers as you want. My father and brother are both lawyers. If there's one thing my family knows it's official papers."

"We'll have to get married." He kissed her slowly, carefully, holding her as if she were made of the finest porcelain.

When his lips left hers, she smiled a secret smile. "We'll very definitely have to get married. Now, tell me why."

"Why what?" he teased.

Annika began to unbutton his shirt. "I want to hear you say the words, Buck."

The teasing smile left his face as he studied her intently. He took her face between his hands and forced her to stop and look him in the eyes. "I love you, Annika. The sun doesn't shine for me without you."

She pulled him close. "I love you, too, and I don't intend to let you get away again," she whispered against his ear. In the next moment her fingers slipped inside the waistband of his trousers. And found what they were looking for. She cupped him gently.

"I might go crazy in my old age," he warned her with a groan against her lips.

"Ah, but what if you don't, and we live to be a hundred years old together? Who knows what will happen to any of us, Buck? My mother always taught us that happiness comes when you look for the good and let go of the bad." With light, teasing kisses, she covered his cheek, his lower lip, his chin, stroking him all the while. "After all, you stole me by mistake and it turned out to be the best thing that ever happened to us."

He lifted the hem of her nightgown and found her deliciously naked beneath. "Your brother didn't seem to think so."

Annika held her breath as he ran his hands up her thighs. Then she managed to whisper, "He was only worried about me, after all."

"I can see why. Do you greet all your morning callers this way?" He slipped a finger into her moist recesses, thrilled to find her ready for him.

She clutched his shoulders and leaned into him as he backed her into the wall. "Only . . . only the ones that arrive unexpectedly."

They both froze when they heard Kase's footsteps on the stairs above them and held their breath until the even tread retreated down the long second-story hallway. Finally, when they heard the door to the master bedroom close, Annika relaxed against Buck.

"Buttons will be awake soon," she whispered against his lips as she unfastened the last button on his pants and began to shove the waistband past his hips.

"Then we'd better not waste any more time." Buck cupped her buttocks in his hands and lifted her until he could sheathe himself inside her. The alcove was shadowed and private, filled with the comingled scents of the beeswax Rose used to polish the hall tree and coffee. The house was quiet as morning crept in beneath the window shades, the silence broken only by the sound of their stolen kisses and heavy sighs. The wall behind Annika was smooth and cool, Buck's hands on her flesh were searing hot. She wrapped her legs around him, locked him inside her, and welcomed him home, meeting his every thrust with a soft moan. She lay her head on his shoulder and kissed his neck, closed her eyes and let his movements drive her until she met him thrust for thrust and finally stiffened to hold back. Ready to climax, aching for release, she grabbed his hair and pulled his mouth to hers. She kissed him long and hard, let his tongue imitate the movement of his swollen shaft and then ended the kiss so that she could free her lips and beg him to take her over the brink and spill his seed inside her.

Buck needed no such urging to comply. He lifted her higher, shoved her against the wall. Burying himself to the hilt inside her, he joined Annika as she shattered and lost control. She cried out. The sound filled him with satisfaction and pride and at that moment he didn't care if the whole world heard them.

Heartbeats combined, their breathing slowed second by second. Buck cradled Annika in his arms, unwilling to separate himself from her. He kissed her again, smiled down into her eyes, and shook his head. "I think you're getting the hang of this, Miss Storm."

"Thanks to you, Mr. Scott."

Heavy footsteps pounded overhead again. They could hear Kase poised on the landing above them. Annika slipped her hand over Buck's mouth and shook her head, her eyes wide, but she didn't attempt to leave his arms.

"Annika?" Kase called out.

She kept her hand over Buck's mouth as she answered back, "Yes, Kase?"

"Annika, are you getting married to that man, or do I have to come down there and shoot him?"'

Buck tried to shake off her hand.

She shushed him and yelled back, "Yes, Kase, I am."

There was a long, silent pause above them, then the sound of retreating footsteps again. Annika sighed and relaxed, dropping her head to Buck's shoulder.

"Is that it?" he whispered.

"That's it," she said.

"He's not coming down to kill me?"

"No. Besides, he's not going to kill the father of my child no matter how much he'd like to."

Buck gently backed away and lowered Annika to the ground. She smiled at him as he adjusted his pants and buttoned them up again. When he cleared his throat, she knew he was ready to make a pronouncement.

"Annika, I think it'll be a while before we can have a baby. I mean, there's already Buttons, and with my schooling—"

"You aren't going to make a very good doctor if you don't realize how long it takes for a woman to carry a baby. The way I see it, it will be about seven more months before you have to deliver ours."

"Ours?"

"Ours. Yours and mine." She beamed up at him and hoped he took the news better than he looked like he was going to.

"But how?"

"You need medical school more than I thought. Don't you remember the nights at Blue Creek when—"

"You've been pregnant since then?" His words echoed around the alcove.

She nodded, quite proud of herself and her announcement.

"And you let me ride out of here two weeks ago?"

Her smile faded when she saw the storm clouds darkening his eyes. "I had to, Buck. I didn't want you if I had to use our child to win you."

While he studied her carefully, Annika held her breath.

When he finally relaxed his stance and reached for her again, she sighed with relief. With her face buried against his bare chest she asked, "Are you mad at me?"

"What good would it do?" he wanted to know.

"None at all, Mr. Scott. You're stuck with me now."

He kissed her brow, her lashes, her lips. "I guess I am, but with a baby on the way I'll have to borrow a little more money."

"Of course." She laughed. "I'd like nothing better than to have you in my debt for years and years."

"It'll mean more papers." He sighed.

"Kase will be happy to draw them up, or we could wait for my father. My parents are coming out in two weeks."

Buck shook his head and began to button up the front of his shirt. "I'm certainly getting a lot more family than I bargained for when I wrote to Alice Soams."

She helped him with the last two buttons. "We could hire someone to find her if you're still partial to the idea."

He crossed his arms over his chest and pretended to contemplate the idea for a minute or two before he shook his head. "I guess I'd better keep you."

"Why?"

Even in the shadowed alcove he could see her bright blue eyes shining with happiness. "Because I love you, Annika Storm. You were the best mistake I ever made."

Epilogue

"T HEY'RE here."

Buck turned at the sound of her voice and saw Annika framed in the light streaming through the bedroom window. Sunshine outlined her silhouette like a halo and set her golden curls ablaze with light. She was dressed in a creation of plaid silk taffeta, a dress that whispered all too seductively whenever she moved. Toting Buttons high on his arm, Buck crossed the room and joined his wife as she stared down into the yard below. As he moved, the floorboards of Kase Storm's guest room creaked exactly where they always creaked. The sunlight filtered through the lace tie backs as was usual every afternoon. Everything was so normal that he almost had to remind himself that this was not just any ordinary afternoon.

Today he would meet his in-laws, and sooner than later if the approaching buggy was any indication.

As he joined her before the window, Buck slipped his free arm about Annika's shoulder and she immediately leaned back to rest against him.

"Are you scared?" he asked.

She shook her head against his shoulder. "Are you?"

"No. If your parents are like you and your brother, they'll be fair."

"If you'll recall," she said with a smile in her tone, "I wasn't exactly enamored of you at first meeting," she reminded him. "Neither was Kase."

He smiled to himself and adjusted Buttons, who had begun squirming. "Look at the big horse." He pointed, trying to divert the child's attention to the scene outside the window.

Buttons was dressed in starched white eyelet from the huge bow on her head to the hem of her pinafore-covered gown. Only her suede, high-button shoes were black. Her curls were freshly washed and combed, her cheeks shiny clean. She was so clean, in fact, that Buck was afraid to put her down before she met Caleb and Analisa Storm.

He watched the carriage, which was accompanied by Zach Elliot on horseback, as it drew near enough for him to clearly see its occupants. The driver appeared quite tall, even though seated. The man's features were clearly Indian, although more finely cut than Kase Storm's. As he commanded the reins, he leaned down to better hear what the elegant blond woman beside him had to say.

Buck's attention shifted to Annika's mother. As she gently laid her hand on her husband's forearm as if to make a point, Caleb Storm bent near. Buck could read love and respect in that warm touch and understood it well, for whenever Annika did the same she held his own heart in her hand.

He kissed her temple as he studied her mother, Analisa Storm. The woman's golden loveliness had definitely been passed on to her daughter.

"I never thought about having in-laws," he admitted, reassuring Annika as he gave her shoulder a squeeze.

"Not even when you wrote to Alice Soams?"

Aware of her nervousness, he was glad she could still tease. "Especially then," he said.

Kase appeared in the yard below. Buck watched him wave to his mother and stepfather, witnessed his parents' joyous response as they waved and called out to him in return.

The carriage was in the main yard now, the horse drawn up close to the house. Kase stepped forward and took his mother's hand to help her down. She held her skirts aside and began to climb down, but just then her son put his hands about her waist, lifted her out, and whirled her around before he set her on her feet in the dusty yard. They laughed together for a moment while Analisa looked up at the darkly handsome man who towered over her. In a loving, motherly motion, she reached up to brush a wayward lock of raven hair off his forehead.

Caleb waved to someone near the house, and Buck assumed it was Rose. She had dressed and undressed little Joseph four times since morning, afraid he would not look perfect enough to meet his grandparents.

As the group in the yard disappeared beneath the roof of the veranda, Zach Elliot led the horse and buggy as well as his own mount toward the barn. Annika stiffened in Buck's embrace and he cleared his throat. He suggested, "Why don't you go down and greet them before we join you?"

She turned to him, eyes shining with love, all trace of worry gone, and said, "How do you always know what I need when I need it?" She reached up to straighten his collar.

He glanced down at the front of his starched shirt and the itchy wool suit he had donned to meet her parents. Annika had insisted she wanted him to be comfortable and to wear his own clothes, assured him he didn't have to put on any airs, but he dismissed her arguments and not only had a suit tailored, but his hair trimmed as well. It was tied back in a queue at his collar. Now he wished he'd taken her advice and worn his own clothes. His discomfort and self-consciousness only added to his nervousness.

"I make it my business to know what you need, Annika, and as long as I'm alive, I'll see that you have it."

She stood on tiptoe, her hands resting on his arms that held Buttons close, and kissed him promisingly. "Don't leave me down there alone too long," she warned.

"Good luck." He watched her walk out the door and close it silently behind her.

ANNIKA stood on the landing above the entry hall and listened to the voices of her parents, Kase, Rose, and Zach as they filtered out from the parlor. Her heart was beating like a flag in the wind as she pressed the palms of her hands to the plaid taffeta of her wide skirt. Adjusting the collar of her dress, she reached out for the security of the bannister and let the smooth oak slide beneath her fingertips as she descended the stairs. The thought of Buck waiting upstairs with the impatient child to strain his already taut nerves made her hasten her steps.

"He's just about the best little boy I ever seen," Zach said.

"What do you mean, 'just about'?" Kase wanted to know.

Waiting outside the parlor door, Annika recognized

Zach's drawl and imagined the scene inside. Joseph Caleb Storm deserved to be admired and cooed over without her diverting the attention from her nephew. She waited another long moment or two, took a deep breath, and tried to smile as she walked into the parlor.

Everyone turned to greet her, but it was her mother's eyes she met across the room.

Annika tried to ignore the ache that tugged at her heart when she saw Analisa's eyes fill with tears. Unable to bear the visible sign of heartache her abduction had caused her mother, she quickly let herself be enveloped in her father's strong embrace.

He hugged her silently for a long time, rocking slowly, smoothing her hair as he had done since she was a child. "Are you all right, Annemeke?" he whispered against her hair.

"Yes, Papa," she whispered, wondering how she would ever find the courage to tell them that she and Buck had not waited for their arrival, but had been married two weeks ago in a civil ceremony in Cheyenne. How could she tell them why?

"Let me see." Caleb drew back and tilted her chin up with his thumb. His piercing blue eyes studied her closely.

"You see, Papa? I'm fine." She thought of Buck, of all they had been through since that bleak February day he abducted her from the train, remembered how very much he loved her, and smiled. "And I'm more than fine. I'm married."

She heard her mother's swift intake of breath and finally found the courage to face her again without becoming teary eyed herself.

Annika turned away from Caleb and hugged her mother tight. "Yes, Mama. I'm married. We didn't wait for you, and I'm sorry if that is upsetting, but when Buck comes down, we'll explain."

Caleb ran a hand through his hair. The impression the sweatband had made across his forehead was still visible. "Do you realize what your mother's been through worrying about you? I thought you were going to wait until we got here. Until we could meet this man." He sounded formidable, but Annika knew his sharp tone came more from relief at seeing her safe than from anger.

She held her mother's hand as she turned to him again. "I

know what you've been through, but I'm the one who was kidnapped, Papa."

"Don't get cheeky, Annika."

"No, sir," she promised, holding her temper for Buck's sake. She didn't want him to walk into a room full of hostility.

"I think I'd better go outside and check on somethin'." Zach put his worn hat on the back of his head as he made his way to the door.

Kase was right behind him. "I think I'll check on it with you." He glanced at Rose, who was blissfully unconcerned as she stared down at the child in her arms. "Rose, don't you think Joseph needs a nap?"

"Nap?" She met Kase's gaze squarely and shook her head. "No need. Not long ago he woke up."

Kase nodded toward the trio standing awkwardly in the center of the room and then indicated the door with another nod in the opposite direction.

Comprehension suddenly dawned on Rose's face. "Ah! Sí. Now I remember. I think after all that Joseph is maybe sleepy."

As Kase ushered his wife and infant out the door, Caleb called out, "Thanks, son," before he slipped an arm around each of the women left in the room.

Annika led them to the settee and with a wave of her hand encouraged them to sit down. She pulled a footstool covered in a needlepoint of cabbage roses in front of them, smoothed her skirts, and sat down.

"I guess you're waiting for an explanation." She folded the material of her skirt into a small pleat and smoothed it with her thumbnail.

"No. We just want to know if you love this man you married. Don't we, Anja?" Caleb said.

Annika glanced at her mother, who nodded. "And we want to know why, Annika. Why did you marry this man who kidnapped you?"

Annika straightened her skirt, squared her shoulders, and met their worried stares. "I married Buck because I love him. And he didn't do anything but love me back."

"But . . ." Analisa shook her head. Her bright yellow hair

was bound into an upswept knot that had been mussed by the removal of her hat.

She was dressed fashionably in a tailored traveling suit, and except for the fact that it was royal blue, it was much like the jaunty chocolate wool Annika had worn for weeks at Blue Creek. The sight of it brought back so many memories that Annika smiled a faraway smile and then forced herself to listen to what her mother was saying.

". . . to marry him was not necessary. Surely you know that no matter what has happened, Annemeke, we can face it together."

Annika put her hands together in her lap and stared down at them for a moment before she looked up at her mother. She reached out and took Analisa's hands in her own. "I know, Mama. I know now that you would understand, my abduction was never like what you suffered. Buck never . . . I mean, he didn't . . ."

"You don't have to go on," her father said, shifting forward, stopping her before she could say more. He braced his forearms on his knees and laced his fingers together.

"So. Kase told you about what happened to me so long ago?" Analisa's words were little more than a whisper.

Annika squeezed her mother's fingers. "He told me he was conceived when you were raped at sixteen. But he did so only because I was certain you would be disappointed in me. I thought you would never understand what I had done, and I was so ashamed, so scared to face you . . ."

"Exactly what *did* happen?" Caleb straightened, his features suddenly dark and threatening.

"What did you do?" Analisa echoed Annika's own admission.

Annika felt her face flame with color. "I—"

"She didn't do it alone."

The Storms turned at the sound of a low, gravelly voice in the doorway. Annika smiled in relief when she saw Buck bending to let Buttons down. The little girl ran to Annika's side, leaned against her, and stared at the newcomers.

"Hi," the confident little girl said to Caleb and Analisa.

Analisa smiled down at the child. Caleb tried to hide a smile.

"This is Buttons," Annika said as she tugged on a vibrant blond ringlet and let it bounce. "She's Buck's niece. We've adopted her." With a glance over her shoulder, she silently asked Buck to join her.

"And I'm Buck Scott," he said as he approached the settee. Buck paused behind Annika and put his hands on her shoulders.

Caleb finally found his manners and stood up. He didn't offer Buck his hand, merely stared at the huge man who was now his only daughter's husband.

In a show of solidarity, Annika stood up and linked an arm through Buck's.

Analisa cast a worried glance at Caleb and put a warning hand on his coat sleeve. "Caleb—"

Trusting her father to show the patience he was known for when he worked for the Bureau of Indian Affairs, Annika said quickly, "Buck loves me, Papa. And I love him. I explained almost everything in my letters to you. He abducted me by mistake and once we were snowed in, there was nothing he could do to bring me back. As time went on, we fell in love." She shrugged and smiled. "It's as simple as that."

When Buck added, "Well, not quite that simple," Annika wanted to kick him.

"Not *quite*?" Caleb turned an icy stare on Annika.

Buck ran a finger between his throat and his shirt collar and blurted out, "She's pregnant, Mr. Storm."

Annika did kick him then, but Buck pretended not to notice.

"A baby?" Analisa whispered, her hand at her throat. She looked from Buck to Annika and back.

Buttons began jumping up and down around their knees. "Me gettin' me a baby!"

"Buttons! Settle down," Buck commanded sharply.

Annika scooped the little girl up and handed her to Buck without a word.

"Put me down! Put me down!" the child yowled.

With his nerves near a breaking point, sweat caused the accursed wool suit to itch even more. Buck shrugged inside his jacket and growled sharply, "Buttons, I swear—"

Dismayed, Annika glanced at her mother. "He's usually very good with her." *Dear Lord, can this get any worse?*

Suddenly, faced with a situation she knew she could handle, Analisa Storm took complete command. She reached out for Buttons and as Buck gladly released the whining child, she cooed, *"Ach liefja."* Buttons quieted immediately. Holding the child close, Analisa then turned to her husband. "Caleb, I think it is best if you take Mr. Scott—"

"It's Buck, ma'am."

"Buck—outside and talk to him there. Annika and I will meet you on the veranda in a few moments. Go, *echtgenoot.* Do this for me, and keep your temper, *ja?*"

Caleb looked as if he couldn't wait to get Buck out on the veranda alone. Annika gave her father a warning as Buck led the way toward the parlor door. "Don't hurt him, Papa."

Caleb sized up the back of his new son-in-law who had already ripped the shoulder seam of his coat when he picked up Buttons and shook his head at his daughter. "I don't think you have to worry about me hurting him, honey. Do you think I'm safe?"

For the first time since the encounter began, Annika was able to smile a genuine smile. "Of course, Papa."

"Then we'll see you two in a few minutes."

Annika turned to Analisa who had let Buttons down. The child was pulling toys out of a basket and showing them to her one at a time. Pushing aside a doll, a Brownie book, and a toy carpet sweeper, Annika sat down beside her mother on the settee.

"Mama, I hope you can forgive me."

Analisa looked surprised. "There is nothing to forgive."

"No?" Annika shook her head. "I didn't mean to hurt you and Papa, and I know how much you wanted me to have a big wedding, but we thought with the baby coming and all, that it would be best to be married as soon as possible."

"I understand." Analisa took a carved wooden horse from Buttons, admired it with a smile and a nod, and handed it back.

"Mama . . ." Annika paused, trying to frame her words precisely, "all these years, I thought of your life as a fairy tale, and you as the princess in the story, but until I spent those weeks in Buck's cabin, living much the way you must have lived in the soddie in Iowa, I never knew, Mama, I never could have imagined how hard it was for you. I'm so sorry."

She shook her head and watched a tear splash on the back of her hand. "I'm so sorry about what happened to you."

Buttons watched the two women in silence as Analisa enfolded her daughter in her arms and held her close. "Never feel sorry for me, Annemeke, because I *am* like the princess in your story. I have your father and Kase and you. I have Rose and Joseph, and now this beautiful child, and the one to come. I even have this Buck Scott that you love so much. I am blessed with all I will ever need or want." Analisa rested her chin on her daughter's head and smiled to herself. "You may think you understand now that you have been in such a place, but I will tell you a secret. Sometimes I look back on those years in the sod house, and as hard as the life was, the memories are still beautiful to me, for I had Kase to love. When there is nothing else, love is all the more precious, is it not?"

Annika pulled away. "*Ja*, Mama," she said, reverting to the Dutch she learned as a child, "love is very precious. I learned something else at Blue Creek, Mama, and again when Kase told me about what happened and how he was conceived. Sometimes good comes hand in hand with bad. When things look bleakest, we have to remember to wait and see what seeds have been sown for the future."

"You will be a very wise mother." Analisa smiled as she wiped a stray tear from her cheek.

"Thank goodness I'll still have you to go give me advice." Annika shook her head and laughed as Buttons turned the toy basket over and plopped it on her head.

The deep sound of the men's laughter drew their attention to the veranda.

"I think your father has let go of his temper," Analisa said.

"It's very hard to stay mad at Buck," Annika admitted. "Why don't we join them now that the smoke has cleared?"

"THEY like you," Annika told Buck as he slipped out of his shirt and tossed it over a chair in the corner of the darkened room.

"The feeling is mutual, although I wish your father would quit staring at me when he thinks I'm not looking."

She wriggled further down beneath the sheet and smoothed Buck's pillow. "I didn't notice."

"He did it all through dinner."

"He'll get used to you."

"I think he'll never get used to the fact that we're sleeping together." He pulled back the sheet and slipped into the bed.

"Maybe fathers don't ever want to admit that their daughters actually sleep with anyone." She shrugged. "He is thrilled that you'll be studying medicine. Mama is, too."

"They took the news that we won't be moving to Boston better than I expected." Buck put his arm around her and pulled her close. He bent over her and pressed a kiss on her lips. Annika kissed him back until he slipped his tongue between her lips, then she stiffened.

He pulled back. "What's wrong?"

"My *parents* are in the next room."

"So?"

"So I can't do this," she whispered.

He kissed her neck. "Do what?"

"This!" She squirmed as he lowered the shoulder of her gown and kissed her above her breast.

"You're joking, right?"

"No, I'm not. I can't do this. What if they're listening?" As he nuzzled the peak of her breast she tried to push him away. Finally she grasped his hair and tugged until he raised his head.

He paused for a moment, his head cocked to one side listening for the slightest sound from the guest room next to theirs. "I don't hear anything."

"Exactly. Because they're listening."

"I don't think so." He dipped his head to kiss her deeply.

Against her will, Annika felt herself begin to relax as his heated kiss made her go liquid inside.

Buck lowered his mouth to her breast again. She slipped her arms around his neck.

"Feeling better?" he mumbled.

His mouth sent shivers through her from her neck to her toes. "You'll be quiet, won't you?"

"I'll try," he promised. "Just close your eyes and I'll take your mind off whether or not they might be listening."

Annika closed her eyes and Buck made good on his promise.